A VR ACADEMY NOVEL

KIARA KOLE

AND THE
KEY OF TRUTH

1

KIARA KOLE AND THE KEY OF TRUTH

Published by Drezhn Publishing LLC
PO BOX 67458
Albuquerque, NM 87193-7458

Print Edition - April 2024
Third Edition

Cover illustration by Jonathan Myers
Cover design by Drezhn Publishing LLC

Hardback ISBN 978-1-947328-51-8
Paperback ISBN 978-1-947328-49-5

A VR ACADEMY NOVEL

KIARA KOLE

AND THE KEY OF TRUTH

DANIEL LUKE KUHNLEY * MARSHA KUHNLEY

CHAPTER ONE

AT WORLD'S END

BEADS OF SWEAT SATURATE every square inch of my skin as I lean against the trunk of my favorite oak tree with my legs sprawled out in front of me. The shade offered up by Old Hank—that's the name I gave the tree, given its gray, wrinkled bark—provides little refuge on a July afternoon like this one. Thinking back on it, this summer's been hotter than any other I remember.

Dust cakes and clings to my sweaty legs through the network of holes in my denim jeans. The holes remind me of swiss cheese. Mom's always looking to throw these jeans out at every wash, but I've finally got them broken in just the way I like. She just doesn't get it, but Grams does. Grams, my dad's mom, is just about the only person in the world who truly understands me. Well, her and my best friend, Robin.

Plumes of radiation rise from the ground and radiate off Betsy, Dad's old '78 Chevy pickup. From the looks of it, I bet I could fry an egg on Betsy's hood in under a minute. The challenge tempts me, but it's not worth getting in trouble over.

Sparkles, my pet pig, lies next to me, her potbelly exposed to the world. Nothing I do keeps her yellow sun dress from rolling up into her little armpits, but she doesn't seem to care. Mom insists that pigs don't need clothing, but she doesn't know Sparkles the way I do. No one does. I'd swear in front of a judge that Sparkles smiles every time she sees herself in the floor-length mirror attached to the back of my bedroom door. It's proof enough for me that she's a princess.

"My princess." Her coarse, black hair sticks to my damp fingertips when I rub her, and she fires off several low grunts. It's her way of saying she loves me. "Maybe I should've named you Miss Piggy."

Sparkles looks up at me, cocks her head, and lets loose a stream of grunts interspersed with some squeals. These are the moments I'd give anything to be like Dr. Dolittle, even if it was only to understand Sparkles.

I rub her ear between two fingers. "It's okay. I don't need to be a doctor to know what you're saying."

A glass of lemonade sits to my right, its last remnants of ice melted long ago. Only a swallow remains. I down the last swig and choke on its hot, acidic taste, sending me into a coughing fit. Sparkles jumps to her feet, eyes wide and alert as she stares up at me.

Half coughing, half laughing, I stroke her back to calm her. "I'm okay. Promise." She leans into my hand and then flops onto her side, belly beckoning. "A belly rub it is."

The hinges on the kitchen screen door creak and moan behind me, shortly followed by the thwack of the door as it finds its way back home. Shoes crunch on the small patch of gravel. Must be Greta coming out to check on me.

Greta serves as my babysitter on Mondays and Wednesdays, and Grams watches me on Tuesdays and Thursdays. Apparently, it's against the law to leave an eleven-year-old home alone, even in Podunk, Texas, population 3,418. Wait, that was before the tragic Carmichael accident two weeks ago. We're at 3,414 now. Anyway, if not for Buford Labs, the place where Mom and Dad both work, the population would plummet to about 34. Even that's being generous.

"It's as hot as a billy goat in a pepper patch out here, Kay-Kay."

"Grams!" Kay-Kay's her special name for me, and she's the only one allowed to use it. To everyone else, I'm Kiara.

"Why don't you come inside and sit a spell," says Grams.

The weariness of the day evaporates in an instant. Moments later, I'm hanging from Grams's neck like one of the many strands of pearls she loves to wear. A bear hug and three kisses on the cheek later, we let go of each other.

Grams bends down and scoops up Sparkles. Knowing she loves Sparkles almost as much as I do puts a smile right on my face. Lifting Sparkles up to her face, Grams kisses Sparkles on the top of her nose. "You been taking good care of my precious girl, Miss Sparkles?"

"She always does," I say.

Sparkles grunts with pleasure and nuzzles Grams's hand when she pulls her back down and holds her under her arm like a football. It's Sparkles's favorite way to be held. Living in Texas, everyone's required to be a fan of the pigskin, and Sparkles is no exception. Perhaps she wouldn't be if she knew what they made the ball from, but I'll never tell her.

My mind flips back to Grams. "Greta didn't mention you were coming over today."

She takes my hand and wraps it behind her back as we walk back toward the house. "Well, I hadn't planned on doing so until about twenty minutes ago. Tommy called and asked if I'd come over as soon as possible."

It makes me giggle every time Grams calls Dad Tommy, and this time is no exception. But my glee evaporates as I ponder the reason for him calling us together. No rational explanation comes to mind.

"Why would Dad do that?" I ask. "He never calls anyone when he's at work."

Grams pulls the screen door open and sidles me through. "Honestly, I'm not too sure." She sets Sparkles down, and Sparkles heads straight for her food bowl next to the fridge. "Tommy mentioned something about a big announcement but didn't have time to discuss it. Said he and your mother would both be home shortly."

"Where's Greta?" I ask, realizing the sound of her afternoon soaps isn't blaring from the living room.

"Oh, I sent her home as soon as I got here. At Tommy's request, of course." Grams's lips curl into a smile. "I haven't heard your father so excited in years. No matter what the news is, I'm excited for him. For all of you, really."

My stomach gurgles as Grams and I sit down at the small kitchen table. What could possibly make Dad so excited? A thousand thoughts fly through my mind, leaving me a bit dizzy.

Did he win the lottery? No, he'd have to play to win, and Dad's no gambler. Neither is Mom. So, what then? Did they discover something at work? Maybe something that might save the world?

Save the world. Those three words are one of my triggers. A constant reminder of the state of the world. That alone wouldn't set me off, but it's what their meaning implies that pulls me down into the depths of despair. Without fail, they place me firmly at world's end.

Last night's fear slinks back into my mind, bringing with it nightmares of open graves and bottomless pits. Death. The table's edge bites into my palms as I clamp my hands around it to keep from falling into the abyss.

So many nights I lie awake in bed thinking about death and its finality.

When I do, it paralyzes me. Drives fear deep into my bones. I love my life in Podunk, and I don't want to die. After all, death is the end. Nothing remains but icy darkness and an emptiness that can never be filled.

The veins in my neck leap beneath my skin. Ratchets my fear up another level. Chest tight, breathing labored. It's all ridiculous. I know it. But I can't stop it.

White-knuckled fingers, drained of every drop of blood, cling to the table as though my life depends on it. Maybe it does, but I don't have the time to think about it. Traitorous tears form in the corners of my eyes. Burn with fire. The last thing I want right now is a lecture from Grams about her God that created the universe, so I blink them back before Grams detects them.

I'm smart enough to see through the lies of a promised eternity, but Grams holds fast to her beliefs. Mom and Dad straddle the fence on the God theory, both agnostic at best. If I were to press them, I think they'd lean toward atheism. It's the reason they both work so hard to find a cure for death. Believe me, I'm rooting for them every day.

As I sit here in this rickety old chair with a cushion way past its expiration date, a thought crosses my mind. Something I've never contemplated.

Maybe Grams believes in God because she's afraid of death, too. The revelation leaves me mind blown.

Grams is sixty-three and approaches that fateful cliff of death with breakneck speed. The thought of losing her forever catches the breath in my throat. A lump the size of a Texas apple. More tears replace the ones I fought off moments ago.

Grams's right hand slides across the table toward me.

She knows.

Her fingers, wrinkled with age yet still beautiful, touch the back of my hand. My gaze focuses on her slender fingers and the perfect, ruby-red nail polish brushed over long nails. It's all I can do to maintain control. One look into her eyes, and the dam will break. I can feel it.

"Are you alright, Kay-Kay?" Grams's voice, a pure, melodic soprano, bores into my heart. Plucks and severs all the strings I painstakingly placed around it. "Your face is gaunt."

I nod, unable to form words without breaking down. The front door groans on its hinges, drawing Grams's attention. She rises from the table.

"Tommy, is that you?" Grams asks.

"It's Evelyn, Rose. Thomas is still outside on the phone. He'll be in shortly."

Grams heads out of the kitchen and into the dining room. I quickly wipe my eyes and follow her. Mom meets us under the archway leading into the living room. She and Grams kiss each other's cheek.

I settle on a simple wave. "Hey, Mom."

Mom's brow furrows, and she tilt's her head to the side when she looks at me. "Everything alright, Kiara?"

I nod and force a smile as my fingernails dig into my palms. No one needs to know how I'm feeling except for me. "I'm good. Just a bit weary from the heat."

Mom approaches and places the back of her hand against my forehead. "Still a little warm." Her all-knowing gaze strips me bare. "You were out by the tree, weren't you?" She doesn't even need to raise her voice.

"Yeah, but only for a little while," I say. "I promise."

Disappointment burns in her eyes. "You complain about the freckles on your cheeks but refuse to protect your fair skin."

Heat rises in my neck and creeps up the sides of my face, settling in my cheeks. "I was in the shade."

Grams places her hand on Mom's shoulder. "Let it go, Evelyn. She's just a girl."

Tension hangs in the room, and I start to cringe thinking about what Mom's response is going to be, but then Dad bursts through the front door. A grin the size of Jupiter stretches across his face, oblivious as to what was about to go down. Mom and Grams turn toward him.

"Pizza's on the way," he says. A quick wink in my direction settles my nerves. His hands ball into fists in front of him. "Oh, I can't wait to tell you both the news!"

Mom shakes her head. "Seriously, Thomas. You're more childish than Kiara at times."

"You could learn a thing or two from him," Grams mutters. The jab sneaks just under Mom's radar.

Dad holds out his arms and beckons me to him. "Get in here before I die of loneliness."

His bear hugs are almost as good as Grams's. Almost. Admittedly, his aftershave takes the win over Grams's perfume. I bury my nose in his neck and breathe deep. Everything in the world falls back into place.

"Love you, Little Bear," he says in my ear.

Chills envelop me. "Love you back, Daddy Bear."

Only in these intimate moments do we exchange such words, and at a volume no one else can hear. It's our little secret, and I cherish it more than just about anything else on earth. Except maybe Grams and Sparkles. They reside on another level altogether.

Grams settles down on the couch. "So, what's this big news?"

Pulling back, I say, "Yeah, what's got you so excited?"

Dad winks at me and then glances over at Mom. "You want to tell them, or should I?"

Mom crosses her arms. "You're the one all worked up over everything. Wouldn't want to spoil your excitement."

Just once in my life I'd like to see Mom act happy. Nothing ever turns the corners of her mouth up. At least nothing I've ever seen.

Dad rubs his hands together. If he holds his excitement in a moment longer, he might burst. "We're going to New Eden!"

Excitement builds in my chest and deep within the pit of my stomach as my mind churns on his words. *New Eden.* I've heard the name before. Seen ads for all the fancy hotels that line its streets. From what I remember, they call them "Experience Hotels," each boasting a different interactive theme. "Get washed away in Hotel Titanic" one ad claims. A bit macabre if you ask me, but I'm kinda into that despite my fear of death.

"We're going on vacation?" I manage, my voice squeaking out three octaves higher than usual.

"I'll do you one better than that," says Dad. "Your mom and I both got jobs at GIST."

"Gist?" The name holds no meaning, and the room darkens beyond my scrunched eyes.

Grams shoots to her feet. I've never seen her move so fast. "You're moving to New Mexico?" Her cheeks flare with a rose-red hue.

Pulse quickens. Palms dampen. Chest constricts. Fear slithers its way into my ear canal and burrows deep within my mind. "Wait, what?"

"It'll be good for you, Kiara," Mom says. "New school. New friends."

Suddenly, I find myself standing next to Grams, fists balled at my sides and fingernails on the verge of piercing my skin. "I don't want to go to a new school or make new friends." Stomping my foot, I jab my finger toward the floor. "I like it right here."

Dad's glee falters. "Sit down." His glare turns on Grams. "*Both* of you." We comply, but neither of us is happy about it, Grams's shaking leg evidence of her fury.

Mom takes a seat in the chair opposite the couch, facing us. "This is a once-in-a-lifetime opportunity for your dad and me, Kiara. You must understand what this means for us." She looks at Grams. "*All* of us. GIST leads the world in the fight to save humanity."

"Save humanity?" Grams says. "Psht. That's a ripe pile of horse manure if I've ever smelled one."

"No need to be crude, Mother." Dad paces. A caged lion. He always does when he's disappointed with something or someone.

Me…

Guilt tightens my throat, but it doesn't change the way I feel. There's no possible way I could leave Podunk behind. Everything I have, no, everything I am is wrapped up in this place. Grams and Robin live here.

"I don't want to leave," I say. "It's not—"

"This isn't a debate, young lady." Mom's gaze drills into the center of my forehead and stills my tongue from lashing out. "Look, it's obvious the way humanity's heading. We're running out of natural resources, the climate is out of control, and our world is reaching the point of overpopulation. We can't sit back and do nothing."

Grams shakes her head. "Where's your faith, Evelyn? And yours, Tommy?"

"Don't you dare bring faith into this." Mom's cold green eyes rip the warmth from the room. "As you well know, God left us here to take care of the planet. What better way to do so than to join GIST at the forefront of the battle?"

Dad stops pacing and kneels in front of Grams. He takes her hands in his and kisses her knuckles before releasing them. "Look, Mother. I believe these new jobs will help us fulfill God's plan, not hinder it."

Grams folds her arms across her chest and snorts. "The answer is God, not technology."

He turns to me, his smile back. "Speaking of technology, bet you didn't know every house in New Eden comes with a robot."

I mimic Grams and cross my arms over my chest, and then I stare into my lap, frowning so hard it hurts. "I don't need a stupid robot. I've got Sparkles."

He smooths back my hair. "Don't worry, Sparkles will come with us, too."

No. No, no, no.

My world crashes down around me, and I'm helpless to stop it.

Unless…

Latching onto Grams's arm, I pull myself as close to her as I can. "Please let me live with you. I promise I'll behave and do whatever you ask of me. Anything."

Grams frees her arm from my grasp and slips it around me. "You know I love you more than words, Kay-Kay, but I'd never place myself between you and your parents."

World crashing. Harder.

Tears bubble in my eyes and spill onto my cheeks. "But I'll die without you."

"Nonsense." She kisses the top of my head. "I'll always be just a phone call away. And we can do that video chat thing. It'll be like I'm right there with you."

"Video chat—" Another thought pops into my head. Brings a shred of hope back into my bleak world. "Come with us to New Eden. You must!" I pull away from Grams and lunge for Dad's neck. "Tell her she can live with us. Please, Daddy. Don't make me go it alone."

His hands wrap around me. Pull me tight against him. "Actually, the thought did cross my mind. Turns out that the place next door is available. We could really use you there, Mother. What do you think?"

I rip myself away from Dad's grasp and turn back to Grams. Excitement bounces me from one foot to the other. Dropping to my knees in front of the couch, I clasp my hands together in front of my face. "Please, Grams, say yes!"

"It would be quite convenient for you to be close, Rose," Mom says.

Grams slowly shakes her head. "New Eden is of the devil, not God. I'm sorry, but no. I could never live in such a place."

Grams, the room, and the world blur as I gaze upon the end of my life through tear-filled eyes. "I... I thought you all loved me."

Springing to my feet, I turn and head toward my room, but something grabs my arm and twists me back around. Arms wrap around me. Squeeze me. Bury my head in soft fabric laced with the scent of Old Spice.

Daddy. My protector. My hero.

Sobs wrack me. Jerk me with violent convulsions. He holds me tighter, but it only deepens my sorrow.

My skin prickles. Heart aches. Darkness so deep and fear so heavy, my legs give out. I slip from Dad's grasp and crumple to the floor at his feet.

How could he betray me? How could he make such a decision without consulting me or thinking about my wellbeing? I thought I was his Little Bear.

"You're being ridiculous," says Mom. Her tone stings and drives me farther into despair. Sometimes, I wonder if she knows what goes on with me at school.

Bullies…

Admittedly, I'm tall for my age. Like six inches taller than any of the other girls. And, being rail-thin with green eyes, they naturally call me Green Bean. It wouldn't be so bad if they didn't flick green beans at me during lunch every time it's on the menu. One or two always manage to find their way inside my shirt. It's gross, especially when they've been chewed a little first. On more than one occasion, I faked being sick on a day green beans were being served. I'm certain no one would blame me if they knew. Well, except maybe Mom.

Why doesn't she understand me?

Sometimes I wonder if it's her or me that's from another planet. All bets are on me if I'm being honest. I'm awkward around most people and find it near impossible to make friends. If not for Robin literally crashing into my life on the playground in second grade, I'd be alone. Some might say the two of us being chased by different bullies and running into each other was fate. I say we just hit it off.

What will I do without you, Robin?

While wallowing in a muddied pit of sorrow, my mind reminds me about another fact I gleaned from an ad about New Eden. Being a high-tech city and a model for future living, they have virtual school. If I could attend without physically going, it'd at least save me from being bullied by a whole new set of mean kids.

Thin as it is, virtual school is the only thread of hope I have left to cling to. With a glimmer of renewed hope, I scrub my face with my shirt, pick myself up off the floor, and then broach the subject. "If I have no choice but to move to New Eden with you, can I at least be granted one small request?"

"Depends on what it is," says Mom.

I was talking to Dad!

Fingernails bite into my palms just as I'm about to fire back, saving me from crashing and burning before I get my request made. Fear of denial chases me through my mind, but the alternative of not asking would seal my fate, so I blurt it out before I find myself unable. "I saw on TV that New Eden has a virtual school option. Can I do that? I won't complain about the move anymore if you let me. I promise."

At least not out loud.

"Yes," Dad says, just as Mom says, "We'll have to see." The two of them share a long glance.

The doorbell rings. Based on all our reactions, I'm certain no one remembered the pizza.

"We're in the right district," Dad says. He smiles at me and winks before heading toward the front door. "In fact, there's no way around it."

The bleak darkness and fear surrounding me recedes. Just a little. Then, a spark of hope ignites within me. It's not much, but it's more than I could've hoped for while standing at world's end.

CHAPTER TWO

NEW EDEN SKYRISE

HOW DOES ONE GO about telling their best and only friend goodbye? For the record, I'm still not sure, but that's what I had to do this morning. To complicate the matter, we had to do it over the phone because Robin and her folks are visiting relatives in New Hampshire. Then, to top it all off, I had to say goodbye to Grams. It might not be for forever, but it sure feels that way.

The human heart is strong; far stronger than I imagined. Aching like nothing I've ever felt before and shattered to bits in my chest, it continues to do its job. And my eyes. Swollen. Bloodshot. Still on fire. How many tears can a person cry before they run dry? As far as I can tell, the supply is limitless. I've not stopped crying since we left, and now the lights of New Eden loom on the dark horizon ahead.

To put things into perspective, we've been on the road for the better part of ten hours. It's the longest I've ever been in a vehicle and by a large margin. According to Google Maps, Podunk lies on the northeastern edge of the Texas Panhandle and New Eden nestles the eastern slopes of the San Andreas Mountains in New Mexico, just north of White Sands National Park.

500 miles of tears.

Twenty minutes later, we pull up in front of one of the tallest buildings I've ever seen. Well, at least in person. The tallest buildings in Podunk belong to Buford Labs, and none of them rise more than three stories. The town's water tower dwarfs everything. Some kids like to climb to the top of the tower, but I never had the nerve. Me and heights have never been on friendly terms, and that's putting it lightly.

Dad unhooks his seatbelt and turns in his seat to face me. "So, what's your first impression of New Eden?"

Glancing around, a thought occurs to me: we're sitting in the only vehicle on the street. Given the sheer number of roads we traveled and buildings we passed driving through the city, I don't understand how it's possible. "Where are all the other cars?"

"Interesting, huh," Dad says, a smirk on his face. "A million people live here, yet you'll rarely see vehicles. At least not ones like ours."

I scratch my head as I look around again. "But how do people get places?"

Mom touches Dad's arm. The "signal" as I call it. "It's late, Thomas."

I knew it.

Her gaze meets mine through the rear-view mirror. If I didn't know better, I'd say she's been crying, too, her mascara runny and smeared underneath baggy eyelids. "How about we save all the questions for tomorrow." She says it with finality.

"Right." Dad gives me a wink and then moves to get out of the vehicle.

"Wait a minute," I say, my pulse rising. He turns back toward me. "I don't understand. Where are we?"

"Home." Mom gets out of the vehicle and shuts the door.

Home?

Remnants of the burger and fries I ate for dinner come alive in the pit of my stomach. A churning maelstrom of doom. "But where are all the houses?"

Dad stretches back over the middle console, pulls my head to his chest, and kisses the top of my head. "Relax, Little Bear. Everything will make sense. I promise."

"But how can it? You've ripped me away from everything I've ever known and loved."

Dad pulls back and gently takes my chin in his palm, forcing me to look him in the eye. "Everything? That's a bit harsh, don't you think?"

Conjuring the deepest scowl manageable, I say, "You know what I mean."

He kisses my forehead one last time and then retreats to the front seat. "Grab Sparkles and come with me. What you're about to see will knock your socks off. I guarantee it!"

Looking at my bare feet, I manage a small chuckle. "No socks to knock off here."

Dad opens my door and waits as I gather up my things and shove them into my backpack. Then, reaching into the pet carrier on the seat next to me, I gently pull Sparkles out using her favorite fuzzy pink-and-purple blanket. She's sound asleep and doesn't stir as I scoop her into my arms. For some reason, she loves to sleep in the car. Perhaps it's the road noise or maybe the rhythm of the tires on the asphalt. Who knows?

With a grunt, I hand Sparkles over to Dad and climb out onto the wide sidewalk. When I say wide, I really mean wide. Like ten or twelve feet. Seems as wide as the streets in Podunk.

Looking around, I notice one thing missing. "Where's Mom?"

"Heh, she's already gone up. She and driving don't mix well."

I cock my head. "In what way?"

"Motion sickness. Gets her every time." He frowns at me. "You don't remember us pulling over on the way here? Twice?"

Thinking back on it, most of the trip was a blur. Likely from all my crying. "Nope."

Dad shrugs and then leads us over to a set of mirrored glass doors at the front of the building. A black box hangs about mid-waist to the right side of the doors. When he places his right hand on it, a blue light flashes for several seconds. Then, a bolt or something magnetic disengages and the doors swing open into the building.

"Welcome home, Mr. Kole," says a male voice, but there's no one around.

My eyes widen. "It… knows you?"

Dad turns and faces me, his eyes full of mischief. "As you'll soon see, we're far from Podunk."

I stare at the black box. "So that thing read your palm or something?"

"Sure did." Dad smiles. "Neat, huh?"

I nod as the doors close and lock. "Yeah, I guess."

He looks around and then leans close. "You want to give it a go, Little Bear?"

My pulse races. "Does it hurt?"

Dad examines his hand for several moments. "Pinches a little."

"Auh!" I retreat a step.

Dad laughs. "I'm teasing. You won't feel a thing."

"Okay." I step up to the box and take a deep breath. An outline of a large hand is just visible on its top surface.

It's just a light. It's just a light.

Another deep breath, and then I place my hand on the box inside the outline. Blue light radiates around my hand for a few seconds, just like it did Dad's, but then the box vibrates, and the light turns red. I jerk my hand back and almost swear.

The male voice returns. "You are unauthorized to enter this building. If you are visiting a residence in this building, please advise them of your arrival and remind them to add you to the visitor log. If you find this message to be an error, say 'help' now and I will assist you. Thank you, and have a pleasant evening."

Dad scratches the back of his neck. "Yes, right. I forgot we haven't added you to the residents list yet. We'll do that first thing in the morning."

After Dad opens the doors again, we step into the building lobby and onto black marble floors with swirls of gray. But the floors aren't what catches my eye. Nothing Dad could've said would have prepared me for what lies beyond them.

My eye sockets fail to hold my eyes inside my head. "Whoa!"

A luscious park with benches, gravel paths, and streetlights stretches out before us. Green grass, palm trees, evergreens, bushes of many varieties, and flowers across the color spectrum fill the place. Overhead, the moon shines and the stars twinkle. I've never seen a place so beautiful.

"Pretty spectacular, isn't it?" Dad says.

All I can do is nod, my mind lost in its beauty. Then, a thought occurs to me. A devious, devilish thought.

You can't like this place. It isn't Podunk.

Guilt builds in my chest even as my mouth hangs agape.

"It'll be a nice place to get away from everything, but not tonight." He takes my arm and pulls me around to my left. "Come on, there's a lot more to see."

Ahead of us, six white plates roughly three feet in diameter lie in a single row, each embedded in the marble floor. About three feet separates each plate, both from each other and from the far wall. We stop a few feet from them. Each is marked with a number, 1 through 6, from left to right. It takes a few moments before I notice the faint columns of green light that encircle each plate and stretch from floor to ceiling. The ceiling also houses six white plates, each perfectly centered over its counterpart on the floor. The six numbers, ghostly white, also float within the columns at eye level. The word "LOBBY" glows in a neon-blue hue on the wall behind the columns.

"What are—" The second plate from the left, number 2, turns red, both on the ceiling and the floor, and the column of light between the two plates transitions from its faint green to a bright red. A caution sign with the words "PTB Active" curves around the column of light and flashes. An ethereal male voice says, "Personal Transport Beam two active." It's the same voice as the one from the palm scanner outside the building.

Is he a real man?

My thought evaporates in an instant as the red column—empty a split-second before—now contains a black woman dressed in a loosely cinched bathrobe and slippers. My breath catches as she steps through the light and into the lobby. Smoke pours from my ears, the circuits in my brain completely overloaded and fried. At least that's what I imagine happens.

I gawk, not at the woman herself but at the way she appeared. My mind still can't wrap itself around what my eyes just witnessed.

The woman looks up from the device she's holding and gasps. "Oh, my. I'm so sorry."

Dad averts his eyes, his neck and cheeks several shades redder than normal. "It's okay. Truly."

"Lobby's usually quiet this time of night." The woman taps her breastbone three times but doesn't cough or belch.

Why did she tap her chest?

The answer becomes clear seconds later when her beige, fuzzy bathrobe morphs into a pink T-shirt and jean shorts. By clear, I mean like hunting for a quarter at the bottom of a muddy lake. The answer stares me straight in the face, and yet I can't comprehend it. Somehow, I've stepped beyond the boundaries of reality and into a world straight out of some science fiction movie.

"Whoa…"

The woman smiles at me. "You must be new to New Eden." My slow nod urges her on. "Yes, of course you are." She extends her arm toward Dad. "Pamela Daltrey. Fifth floor."

"Penthouse? Very nice." Dad shakes Pamela's hand. "I'm Thomas Kole. You can find us on the fourth floor." He gestures toward me with his head. "This is my daughter, Kiara."

"A pleasure." Pamela eyes the bundle cradled in Dad's arm. "Is that a pig?"

"Sparkles," I say, much louder than intended. "She's a princess."

"Oh!" Pamela tips her head down and curtsies. "I'm honored to be in the presence of royalty."

"Well, she's not really a princess," I say, "but don't let her know that. She understands more than you might think and can be quite sensitive at times."

"Understood. It'll be our little secret, right?" Pamela pretends to zip her lips.

"Yep." The thought of Pamela's quick attire change fights its way back into the front of my mind. As an avid sewer of pig clothes, I must know her secret. "How did you make your clothes change?"

"Magic," she says with a twinkle in her eye. "You've read Harry Potter, yes?"

My nose wrinkles. "Of course, but everyone knows that magic isn't real."

"Sure, it is," Dad says. "But magic doesn't have to be supernatural."

"Your dad's correct. For instance, the love you share with him is a special kind of magic. It's the same as the love I share with my two boys."

I chew on my lower lip as I consider her words. "Like Harry and his mother."

Pamela nods. "Precisely. Now, as far as my clothing goes, the magic that makes it all work is something called nanotechnology. More specifically, nanites."

Nanites?

The strange word might as well be Japanese. "And how does this—"

"It's time we head up, Kiara." The inflection in Dad's voice is subtle, but I know it well. It's his way of signaling the end of a discussion. "Besides, I'm sure Ms. Daltrey has better things to do than answer your questions all night. Not only that, but Mom's probably wondering what happened to us."

I totally forgot Mom isn't with us. "Yes, sir."

"Good." He moves Sparkles to his other arm. "Miss Sparkles is getting heavier by the minute, too." He dips his head toward Pamela. "Good evening, Ms. Daltrey."

"For the record, it's Mrs. Daltrey, but please call me Pamela." The left side of Pamela's mouth curls upward. "I insist."

"Fair enough," Dad says. "And you shall call me Thomas."

Pamela sweeps her jet-black hair away from her face with a flick of her wrist. "It's been a pleasure talking with both of you, and I'm certain we'll run into each other again soon."

"Likewise," Dad says.

"Bye," I say.

I turn and watch Pamela head across the lobby with her transparent device held out in front of her. She turns and disappears into the park.

"What now," I say, dreading what I'm certain will be Dad's answer.

Dad tousles my hair. "We teleport!"

My pulse hammers in my ears. A dirge. "But that's only possible in the movies."

His grin morphs into a frown. "You just saw Pamela do it, right?"

Did I?

My mind still isn't quite ready to accept what my eyes witnessed. "Honestly, I'm not sure what I saw."

"It's okay to be scared." He kisses the top of my head. "This is something quite new for you."

Tremors race head-to-toe, and my stomach gurgles as we turn and face the six columns once again. "Does it hurt? Being torn apart, I mean."

Dad laughs aloud. "Tingles a bit, but you'll get used to it." He steps onto the number 3 plate and the green column of light turns red.

"Personal Transport Beam three active," the male voice says. "Please state your floor destination."

Dad turns around and faces me. "Just follow my lead, alright?"

"Um… okay I guess." But it's not okay. Not even a little bit. Every muscle in my body tenses up, and I can't remember how to make myself move.

"Relax, Little Bear." The tone of Dad's voice and his special name for me sends a wave of warmth right up through the bottoms of my feet.

I stuff my hands in my armpits. "What do I do?"

"Go ahead and step onto plate number four."

"Please state your floor destination," the voice repeats.

It's only light. It's only light.

Eyes wide, I step forward and through the green light. The plate depresses, but just so. Otherwise, I feel nothing.

"Personal Transport Beam four active," the male voice says. "Please state your floor destination."

Dad and I turn and face each other, both of us bathed in red light. He smiles. "Ready?" I nod as my stomach crawls up into my throat.

"Floor four." In a blink, Dad and Sparkles are gone.

Suddenly, I can't breathe. My mind begs me to step off the plate and out of the light.

"Please state your floor destination."

Terrible, horrible thoughts fill my head.

What if I can't be put back together? What if I get stuck somewhere between here and there and can't breathe? Will I suffocate?

My throat tightens as I suck in air so thick it swallows like jelly. Then, another string of thoughts twists my stomach in knots.

What if I get up there and Dad and Sparkles are a puddle of mush? Can it distinguish the atoms that make each of them up? What if Dad comes out with a pig snout and Sparkles has his nose?

Even worse thoughts and images fill my head. Bombard me from every direction. Monsters from every book I've ever read conjure in my mind. Each awaits me on the fourth floor, lurking in the shadows and ready to pounce on me as soon as I arrive.

"Please state your floor destination."

The lobby blurs through tear-filled vision.

Grams, I need you.

With a final deep breath, I close my eyes and clench my fists at my sides. The air expels from my lungs as I say, "Fourth floor."

CHAPTER THREE

NO PLACE LIKE HOME

EVERY INCH OF MY skin comes alive. Tingles. Tickles. But the sensations last no more than a heartbeat.

Now, I'm afraid to open my eyes.

Afraid of what I'll find waiting.

But I'm still alive.

"Thought I'd lost you."

Dad's voice.

My heart leaps in my chest as my eyes spring open and take in the surroundings. Everything's blurry, so I wipe my eyes with the sleeves of my shirt. Dad stands a few feet in front of me, a warm smile on his face. He says nothing of my tears, and I'm grateful for that. He's the best dad on the planet, even if I don't get to spend as much time with him as I'd like.

Plates on the floor and ceiling flank me. Three in total, including the one I'm standing on. Just like the ones in the lobby but without numbers. We seem to be standing in a small room. Maybe ten feet wide and six feet deep. A tinge of red coats every surface. That's when I remember I'm still standing within the column of red light.

"I'm here." My voice sounds hoarse, like I've been screaming and nearly lost it.

Stepping off the plate and through the column of light, the room brightens tenfold. The floors, walls, and ceiling are stark white. The only two things in the room that aren't white are the massive silver door looming behind Dad and the black pad that accompanies it.

Dad scans his palm, but the silver door doesn't swing into the room behind it, nor does it slide to the side or upwards. Instead, it disintegrates.

I blink several times, but the door's still gone. "Did you see that?"

Dad shakes his head and snickers. "I told you it'd knock your socks off, and you haven't even seen the best of it."

"I haven't?" The idea is incomprehensible.

He walks through the giant opening and into our new home. I follow him inside and linger at the opening, determined to figure out how the door works. Twenty seconds later, the door materializes, but I'm no closer to understanding how it functions.

I shake my finger at the door. "You win this round, but I'll be back."

"And where are you headed at this late hour?"

The strange British accent spins me around on my heels and brings me face to face with some sort of humanoid robot. I take a step back and find myself pressed against the front door. But then the door isn't there, and I'm tumbling backward to the floor. My backpack prevents me from smacking my head against the marble floor but landing on it doesn't feel good and knocks the wind out of me.

The robot glides over to my side, hovering an inch off the floor. "I've scanned you for injuries and detect none. However, your pulse is elevated, and you are dehydrated." One of its metallic arms extends toward me as it offers me a beige, silicone-wrapped hand. "Allow me to help you to your feet."

Feeling like a turtle on its back, I take the robot's hand. It pulls me up without effort and with a gentleness I never would've expected.

"Thank you," I say. "I'm Kiara."

"I am Artie," it replies. "Pleased to meet you, Kiara."

Artie. What a strange name for a robot.

"Sorry if I frightened you," Artie says.

"It's okay. I just wasn't expecting something like… you."

"And what was it you did expect?"

"I'm not sure."

"Very well. Shall we go back inside, or are you still headed out?"

I giggle. "It was just an expression. I'm not going anywhere."

"Good. May I offer you a bottle of water? Or perhaps a soda?"

Now that I think about it, my throat is quite dry. "Water would be good."

"Coming right up." Artie's chest opens, and he pulls out a bottle of water and hands it to me. It's ice-cold.

"That's amazing! How did you do that?"

His chest seals back up. "Teleportal. The house account has been charged."

"What else can you do?" I ask.

"I am equipped to function as a house maid, an EMT, a gardener, a companion, a servant, a protector, and much, much more."

"Does it hurt when your chest opens like that?"

"I am not equipped to feel pain. I have pressure sensors on my fingertips, fingers, and palms to prevent using excessive force when handling objects."

"Do you eat or go to the bathroom?" I say with a snort.

"I consume electricity and excrete excess heat through hidden exhaust fans, so, in a sense, yes."

"You're funny!"

"I try. Really, I do."

"Do you always speak with a British accent?"

"I can speak any known language and mimic any voice as long as there is a sample available on EdeNet."

"EdeNet?" I scrunch my face. "What's that?"

"EdeNet is a private network accessible only within the city of New Eden. It is like what the world calls the internet or world wide web, but it is much faster and more reliable. Everything you will ever need is accessible through it."

"Everything?" I blurt out the first thing that comes into my head. "Can you talk like Wreck-It Ralph?"

"Turns out I don't need a medal to tell me I'm a good guy." Artie's voice sounds exactly like Ralph.

"That's amazing!"

"Would you like me to make this my default voice?" he asks, still with Ralph's voice.

"No," Mom says.

Where did she come from?

"Very good, Mrs. Kole," says Artie. His British accent is back.

"Kiara, it's late. Get Sparkles settled in and go to bed. We have a full day planned tomorrow."

Mom has a way of sucking the joy right out of the room. It makes me wonder what happened in her life that made her the way she is. I also wonder what attracted Dad to her in the first place, besides her subtle beauty. Guilt crashes down on me, and the weight of the day piles on top of it.

Don't think like that.

I know she loves me in her own strange way, and it's good enough for me. "Yes, ma'am."

"Show her the way, Artie."

"Very good." Artie turns and beckons me to follow. "Right this way."

The entryway quickly opens into a sprawling living room furnished with gray and brown leather chairs and couches, several floor lamps made to look like palm trees, and a fireplace that stretches across the far wall. Lavish, faux fur rugs separate several sitting areas, each a different color and all of them inviting me to sprawl out on them. What I don't see is a television. Or windows. In fact, the home lacks a kitchen as well. But there are two bathrooms and a large dining room with a table that could probably seat twenty.

Step by step, my enthusiasm of this New Eden skyrise wanes. I cross my arms and stuff my hands into my armpits. "Where are the bedrooms? Where is the yard? Where will Sparkles live and play?"

"I sense a level of anxiety in your voice," Artie says.

"You think?"

"Only as far as my programming allows. I am adept at self-learning as well."

I roll my eyes. "Whatever. Where's Sparkles?"

And Dad.

Artie touches the wall in front of us. Like the front door, the entire wall disintegrates, revealing an outdoor space far larger than I would've thought possible. Stepping out onto the concrete patio, my gaze locks onto the row of trees that line the back perimeter of the yard. Fruit hangs from their branches. From where I stand, it looks like there are apples, oranges, lemons, pears, peaches, and cherries. Some kind of nut tree as well. Surrounding and in front of the row of trees is an area of luscious green grass. No brown or yellow spots exist, and it's perfectly manicured.

Closer still, my gaze settles on the swimming pool. It's not huge but surpasses the water trough I often use in Podunk. A terraced garden runs along the perimeter to the left, all the way from the edge of the patio to the row of trees. On the opposite side runs a wide area of dirt and mud, cordoned off by a three-foot-high slatted fence.

The pool beckons me, but guilt and the night hold me back from indulging myself. Sparkles squeals with delight as she comes running out of the fenced area and straight toward me. Bending down, she races right into my arms. I hug her tight and stroke the top of her head. "Well, what do you think of our new digs?"

She grunts and then wiggles her way out of my grasp. With a snort, she turns and heads back beyond the fence and into the dark. It's then that I notice the mud clinging to my shirt.

"Ugh! Thanks a lot, Sparkles."

"It's only mud. You'll be fine." Turning around, I spot Dad stretched out on a lounger on the patio, his gaze skyward.

I follow his gaze toward the heavens. The stars are magnificent. Just like what we would've seen from Podunk. In fact, the view is somehow better. Almost perfect.

"Looks so real, doesn't it?" Wonder fills his voice.

"It's not?" I squint to see what he means, but the universe above doesn't fade or change.

Dad sits up. "Well, yes and no."

"What you see is a live feed of the sky above you," Artie says.

Maybe it's the long, miserable day affecting my brain or me being dehydrated from crying so much. Whatever the case, I don't understand. "A live feed?"

"Yes." Artie moves closer. "Watch the sky and I will demonstrate for you." In a blink, the night sky disappears and gray concrete and steel beams a good forty feet above us replaces it. "What you see now is reality. The underside of your neighbor's yard above you."

"Whoa… The entire ceiling is a big monitor?"

"In a sense, yes," Dad says. "Like so many other things in New Eden, the ceiling is made up of nanites."

There's that word again: *Nanites*…

Artie continues, "Precisely, Mr. Kole. Nanites are tiny little robots—also called nanobots—that can be programmed to do almost any task needed, including creating complex objects such as myself."

I twirl my finger in my ear, certain I didn't hear Artie right. "You're not saying that you're made up of hundreds of tiny robots, right Artie?"

Artie shakes his head. "Of course not. My skeleton and skin alone are made up of billions of nanites. That doesn't take into consideration my propulsion, cognitive, speech, sight, touch, and hearing system, to name a few."

"The wall and front door, too?" I ask.

Artie says, "Now you understand."

But I don't really. At least not beyond the understanding that these things called nanites are used everywhere. Comprehending what they really are—what they look and feel like and how they function—is beyond my grasp.

Dad must see the truth of it on my face. "Take the wall for example. Did it really disappear, or did it simply turn transparent? If it did disappear, where did it go? Can electrons cease to exist? If not, then you must've walked right through the wall, right?"

My mind spins out of control. "I… I walked *through* the wall?"

"Yes." He chuckles. "Had you known it was still there, would you have been able to do so, or would your mind have stopped you?"

"But… but…" My circuits are fried once again. Had I felt anything when I walked outside or when I came through the front door? No matter how hard I think about it, I can't remember.

Dad rises from the lounger, puts his arm around me, and leads me over to the transparent wall. "Watch," he says, and then proceeds to thrust his hand through the opening and then withdraws it. "Did you see it?"

"See what?" I hadn't even blinked.

"Don't watch my hand but the area around my hand as it goes through the opening."

Isn't that what I did?

"Okay." I lean forward, my nose nearly touching Dad's hand. "I'm ready."

Dad moves his hand through the opening again.

"Auh!" My heart gallops in my chest. "It rippled!"

"Exactly. The nanites compensate and adjust their position as my hand pushes its way through them."

"That's amazing."

"Yes, it is. Inventions such as this will help save humanity. This is why we've come here to work for GIST. Does it make more sense now?"

On the one hand, it makes perfect sense. The world will not survive humanity for much longer unless we make changes. On the other hand, why can't Mom and Dad help save the world while living in Podunk?

I shrug. "Kinda, I guess."

"I know you're already homesick for Podunk, but I promise you'll grow to love New Eden before you know it."

Will I?

As cool as New Eden seems, there's something missing. Grams and Robin for certain, but something more. I can't place my finger on what it is, but it's something important. I just know it.

"I just wish Grams were here."

"So do I. Maybe she'll come around one of these days and decide to move here after all."

"I hope so."

Even if she does, this will never be Podunk.

Dad points at the opening again. "How about you give it a try. Concentrate on feeling the slight resistance the nanites provide before moving out of the way."

Three tries later, it happens. A resistance so minuscule that it's almost undetectable. But it's there. Undeniable.

"So, I can just walk right through the door and wall without stopping, even when it's not translucent?"

"The word is transparent, and no. Try that, and you'll wind up with a broken nose or something worse. When activated as a wall or a door, these nanites are soundproof, cold and heat resistant, and can stop a bullet."

I stare at the wall that isn't there. "Really?" I look up at him and search his eyes but see no hint of deceit. "You're not just pulling my leg?"

"Never," he says with a wink. Then, he hauls me up onto his back and carries me inside. "It's way past both of our bedtimes."

"I'm still not tired," I say through a long yawn.

Dad pats my leg. "Oh, I believe you."

In a single blink, Dad's setting me down on a gray tile floor with white flowers. My weak legs struggle to keep me upright. Dad keeps me balanced as I shake the sleepiness from my head.

Dad chuckles. "I'd hate to see you if you were tired."

I shoot him my best glare through the mirror above the sink. "Not funny."

"Too soon?" He chuckles again. "Everything you need to get cleaned up and ready for bed should be on the counter." He walks over to the bathroom doorway and then turns back. "Mom and I are the first door to the left and on the left. Your room is to the right and on the right. Come find us when you're ready." I nod, and he exits the bathroom. The door materializes behind him.

Guess every door disintegrates.

Twenty minutes later, after washing up and finding my way into a pair of Tinker Bell pajamas—my favorite ones, for the record—, I'm ready for bed.

Trouble is, I'm not sure how to get myself out of the bathroom. Touching the door does nothing. Neither does banging on it. My pulse rises. I yell for Dad and wait a good minute, but he doesn't come to my rescue. Now, my palms are sweaty, and I can't seem to catch my breath.

Am I running out of oxygen?

Heartbeats thunder in my ears.

I bang on the door again with my fist, but the result is the same.

Hands tremble. Can't stop them.

Each new breath takes more effort than the last.

Tears fill my eyes. Spill onto my cheeks. Drip off my chin and puddle on the floor.

I don't want to die.

Sliding to the floor, I cry into my arms as massive waves of despair crash against the shores of my mind once again.

Why did we leave Podunk? Why did we have to leave you, Grams?

Like Dorothy in *The Wizard of Oz*, I'm far from home, New Eden my Emerald City. There's no place like home, and this will never be my home.

"Artie," I say through a sob. "Please help me."

"How may I be of assistance?" His voice echoes through the small room.

My heart flutters. "I'm trapped inside the bathroom."

"Trapped is an interesting choice of word."

"How do I open the door?"

"Touch the yellow square on the wall next to the door."

I pull myself up off the floor, wipe my eyes on my shirt, and then touch the yellow square. The door immediately disintegrates, and I gasp for air. Artie hovers right in front of me.

"Your levels are elevated. Your pupils are dilated. Your face is paler than usual. Are you in need of medical assistance?"

"No, Artie. I'm fine now."

"All indications say you are not."

He's nothing but a machine, but he's not wrong. I'd give anything right now to hop in the car and go back home.

"Kiara?" Mom's voice floats down the hallway.

"I'm coming."

After saying goodnight to Mom and Dad, I go to my room and crawl underneath the crisp pink sheets of my new bed. The plush mattress cradles me as I settle in. Admittedly, it's far more comfortable than the one I left behind in Podunk.

As I lie here, the sounds of the night begin to fill the room. Chirping crickets, croaking frogs, and the hum of cicadas. Stars sparkle above me. A vast sea of light teeming with life. It's as beautiful as anything I've ever seen, and I want it to help me forget Podunk. But it's just not the same. Nothing is.

Nothing will ever be.

CHAPTER FOUR

THE GIST OF THINGS

THE SUCCULENT AROMA OF bacon draws me from my slumber. By the time I throw on some clothes, my stomach's quaking with hunger. Downstairs, Mom and Dad sit at the dining room table, each lost in their cup of coffee. A plate of eggs, bacon, and waffles, all drenched in maple syrup, beckons me. Wasting no time, I wolf them down in three minutes flat.

After waging war with my parents about leaving Sparkles at home alone and failing miserably, the three of us teleport down to the main lobby. To be honest, it's a pretty cool experience now that I know what to expect. Beats taking the stairs any day. Although, the staircases inside our house or apartment or flat or whatever it's called are not to be dismissed. The two of them spiral around each other like two intertwined serpents. One goes up and the other goes down, sort of like escalators but much, much cooler.

Back outside, I notice our vehicle is no longer parked at the curb. "Where's the car?"

"Took it over to storage earlier this morning," Dad says.

"Storage? How are we supposed to get around town?"

"No multi-person personal vehicles are allowed in New Eden, especially ones that run on fossil fuels." Mom eyes me. "You know the emissions will eventually kill us all."

Looking around, I see no solution to our dilemma. "Yeah, but now what?"

"New Eden was designed from the ground up." Dad chuckles. "Literally. We have an underground subway system that can get us to certain sections of the city within minutes. They are magnetic propulsion trains to be precise. It's like riding on the inside of a bullet. Then, there are the MagBuses for shorter distance, inner-city travel. Besides those two options, you can purchase or lease a hover bike. Think of those like the Star Wars speeder bikes from *Return of The Jedi*."

My mouth salivates. "I want one of those."

"No can do, buckaroo. You have to be sixteen to operate one."

"Not even then," Mom says. "You'd wind up hurting or killing yourself or someone else."

Far down the road, I see a shiny black vehicle approaching. Seconds later, it pulls up next to the curb in front of us. Windows, black as obsidian, line the side of the long vehicle. My estimates put it at a gazillion feet long, and I'm positive I'm not far off. The vehicle has no wheels and floats about a foot above the concrete road.

Silver lettering stretches across a good portion of the vehicle's side. Four capital letters, about two feet tall and separated with periods, spell out "G.I.S.T." A solid silver line runs parallel beneath the four letters, separating them from another set of silver letters that reads "Global Institute of Science and Technology." The lower lettering is sized to span the width of the top four letters.

Mom and Dad's new employer.

Two doors ease out from the side of the vehicle about four inches and then slide apart, creating an opening about six feet wide. A single stair the width of the opening lowers from underneath the vehicle and extends out toward us.

Dad nudges me toward the vehicle. "This is our ride. Go ahead and climb on in."

The inside of the vehicle doesn't reflect what I'd imagined when it first pulled up. For starters, the space is one of what I imagine to be many compartments. About seven feet wide and maybe ten feet from end to end. The interior is stark white, from its rubber mat floors to its plush white paneling to its white leather captain's chairs. A polar opposite to the outside of the vehicle. The eight chairs sit in four rows of two each, all of them empty, and every two rows face each other.

I climb in and take the farthest seat to my left. Dad sits next to me, and Mom sits opposite Dad. Harnesses automatically strap us in, crisscrossed on our chests. I'm about to ask why we need them when the vehicle lunges backward and throws me against the restraints as we pick up speed and rocket through the city. It takes a good five seconds before I can finally sit back in the seat again. Every turn sends my stomach higher in my throat. Thankfully, there are no windows to watch the buildings fly by. If there were, the seat in front of me would be covered with bits of egg, bacon, and waffle.

A few minutes later, the vehicle begins to slow. "Short trip," I say.

"Twelve miles in four minutes," Dad says.

Mom looks at me. "How fast is that?"

Math isn't my favorite subject, and Mom knows it. She does this kind of thing to me all the time. Calls it "learning through life." I call it torture.

"Well… twelve divided by four is three. Multiply that by sixty… Whoa! One hundred and eighty miles an hour."

"Good, Kiara," Dad says.

Mom scowls at me. "You need to work harder on your solving speed if you expect to get a good job in one of the sciences."

Just as I'm about to say something smart and dig myself a hole, the vehicle comes to a stop in front of a massive building on my side. I crane my neck next to the window to get a better view of its height as I count the number of floors. *Twelve stories.* It's by far the tallest building I've ever seen.

The vehicle doors slide open on my side, revealing the elegance of the building's smoke-red glass face. The building is beautiful yet foreboding. Its top dons the same branding and style of lettering as this vehicle, but the giant letters are more like a dozen feet tall and white instead of silver.

A black man stands just beyond the doors. He wears a navy, single-button suit, a white shirt, and a red tie, and his short-cropped hair parts on the right. His eyes bulge behind thick glasses.

"Good morning, Kole family! My name is Dr. Terence Oxford. On behalf of the Global Institute of Science and Technology, I'd like to be the first to welcome you." Terence's pearly-white teeth shine from his parted lips like a beacon.

Dad steps out of the vehicle first and shakes Terence's proffered hand. "Dr. Oxford. It's good to finally put a face to the name, so to speak."

"Likewise, sir," Terence says. "Likewise."

Mom exits the vehicle and greets Terence with a slight nod—her usual. Terence obliges with a nod of his own. I straddle the middle of the road and go with a nod and greeting. "Hi, Terence. My name's Kiara."

"Of course it is!" His bubbly mood is infectious and puts a smile on my face. He bends down toward me. "What do you think of New Eden so far?"

I shrug. "Not sure yet. It's certainly different from Podunk."

"Worlds apart." He straightens, claps his hands together, and turns his attention back to Mom and Dad. "How about we get the tour started?"

Mom, always full of tact, cuts right to the chase. "No offense, Dr. Oxford, but where's Dr. Prince? He said he'd personally give us a tour."

"Please, call me Terence." He glances toward the building and scratches the back of his neck. "You know how it can be. Running a company the size of GIST can change one's schedule drastically every minute. Dr. Prince will join us later, if his schedule allows it."

"I see." Mom sighs loud enough for the entire city to hear it. "Very well. Carry on, Terry."

"Terence, ma'am." He turns and heads up the seven deep steps toward the building. "Follow me. We've got a lot of ground to cover."

Twenty minutes into the tour, and I'm looking forward to leaving. Sure, the facility is impressive, but it's nothing like what I'd imagined. No dark labs and mad scientists experimenting on mice, rats, or other animals. No aliens. No spaceships. No rovers set for Mars. No rockets. The only things I've witnessed are normal people working on theoretical quantum mechanics and a slew of labs dedicated to herbology.

Why did we leave Podunk for this?

As we step through the ten thousandth set of galvanized steel doors, I'm looking for an exit. From the looks of my parents' faces, I think they are as well.

"Can we—"

"Greetings, Dr. Kole." The four of us turn toward the source of the baritone voice behind us. It belongs to a tall man dressed in black slacks and an ice-blue dress shirt. He approaches quickly, his stride long. A canary-yellow tie swings from his thick neck and brings out the yellow flecks in his otherwise brown eyes.

Mom's gaze locks onto his. "Dr. Prince. I… We've been looking forward to meeting you."

"And I, you." He takes Mom's hand, lifts it to his lips, and kisses her knuckles. "A pleasure."

A tinge of red colors Mom's cheeks, and a smile she seldom wears graces her face. The exchange between them leaves my stomach feeling queasy, but Dad seems oblivious to it. He proffers his hand toward Dr. Prince.

Dr. Prince takes Dad's hand, but his gaze lingers on Mom for several moments before he finally meets Dad's stare. "Dr. Kole, welcome to GIST."

"We are thrilled to be here," Dad says.

Not all of us.

Dr. Prince takes notice of me. I wish he hadn't. "And you are?"

"Kiara." Unwilling or perhaps unable to meet his gaze, I stare at the strange cufflinks he wears. Golden triangles with swords inside them.

"Yes, of course. Didn't expect so much country. But never fear, this place has a way of bringing out the best in all of us. You'll fit right in soon enough." There's a smugness to his voice, and the dig hits a nerve, but I manage to keep my mouth shut.

I don't want to fit in.

After dismissing Terence, Dr. Prince gives us the real tour of GIST: a network of underground lab facilities. Each lab brings with it hope for the future of mankind, from gene therapy for disease to human hybridization and everything in between. Skin applications that can withstand bullets. Mice that can communicate via telepathy. Chips implanted in the brain that help control robots. Chips in the brain that promote accelerated learning. Plants and animals capable of not just surviving but thriving on Mars. Personal space rockets capable of reaching Mars in days. Autonomous robots and drones capable of building entire cities in just a few weeks. Tractor beams. Light-wave travel. Organs and food printed by organic 3D printers, both healthier than what nature provides. Prosthetics indistinguishable from flesh and blood with ten times the strength.

Two hours later, my mind refuses to intake further information. The frontier toward a better future and the path to escape death are clearer than ever before, but it all seems superficial. Especially Dr. Prince. He's the face of New Eden. The spokesperson. He jokes about being the Prince of New Eden, but I'm certain he's not laughing.

Dr. Prince stops in the middle of a long corridor. "There are a few more areas to tour, but I'm afraid Kiara isn't authorized to access them. We'll drop her off with my daughter, Gemma Ray."

Gemma Ray. The play on words isn't lost on me, but who would do that to their daughter?

After a shuttle, several hallways and corridors, and two elevator rides later, we step into a hallway with cultured marble floors. Swirls of silver and red on a white backdrop. The hallway contains a single door. Steel. No seams. Etched into its surface are letters that read: Dr. Gregory Prince, CEO.

The door disintegrates without a touch. "Head on in," Dr. Prince says. "We won't be more than thirty minutes." I glance back at Dad, and he gives me a nod.

Guess I have no choice.

The first thing I notice when I walk through the doorway is the overwhelming scent of lavender and lilac. When I look back, the hallway is empty. A moment later, the door materializes. I swallow hard and take a deep breath. Not the best option, given the air quality.

Three steps into the room, I spot the source of the perfume and halt. A young girl about my age leans back in a brown leather chair with her feet propped up on the desk in front of her. A pair of purple-and-pink sneakers, the likes of which I've never seen. Strange yet cool.

Probably made with nanites.

She holds a tablet in her hands, her gaze fixed on it. Blond hair, straight and bobbed just above the shoulders, frames her tanned skin. Perfect complexion. No freckles or blemishes of any kind as far as I can see.

"Hello?" The word squeaks from my lips.

The girl looks over at me. Her yellowish-brown eyes narrow. Nose turns up. Nostrils flare. "You lost?" Her cold tone matches her gaze.

Retreat! That's my first instinct, but there's nowhere for me to go. "Um… I'm Kiara. Dr. Prince told me to wait in here."

"Ugh." The girl rolls her eyes and then drops her feet off the desk's edge. She sets her tablet on the desk. "Don't just stand there looking stupid. Come closer so I can get a better look at what I'm dealing with."

I walk toward the glass-and-chrome desk and stop a few feet away, next to one of two straight-backed leather chairs. "You must be Gemma?"

"Duh. Who else would I be?" She stands up and walks around the side of the desk. Even with thick rubber soles, she's a few inches shorter than me. It makes no difference though. Her hard stare shrinks me down as she sizes me up. Gold and silver bracelets clank together on her wrists when she crosses her arms. There must be a dozen on each arm.

Perspiration dampens my palms as the seconds tick by. As casually as possible, I press my hands against my jeans and pray she doesn't notice. But my prayer isn't answered.

Gemma's nose wrinkles. "Gross."

"Sorry," I say. "My palms always sweat when I'm nervous."

"Ew!" She steps back and eyes my hands, her entire face scrunched together like some sort of smashed-face dog. "I was talking about your wretched clothes."

I peer down at myself. A pink shirt underneath denim overall shorts and tan sandals. "What's wrong with what I'm wearing?"

"As if you didn't know. You just stepped off the farm, didn't you?" Gemma sniffs the air between us and recoils, plugging her nose with her hand. "Ugh. You must've. What *is* that disgusting smell? Eau de Barnyard?" She snorts.

Welcome to New Eden, Kiara.

"Funny." I turn to leave, but Gemma grabs my arm and twists me around.

"Ease up, farm girl. I'm just yanking your chain."

I jerk my arm away and rub it. "Who do you think you are?"

Gemma heads back around the desk and sits down. "I'm the CEO's daughter, but you already know that." She gestures toward one of the chairs in front of the desk. "Take a seat."

The last thing I want to do is sit down and face this girl, but what other option do I have?

None.

The chair whines when I plop down on it, but Gemma doesn't seem to notice. "What do you want?"

Gemma leans over the desk and props her head on her palms. "Why are you here?"

"Because my parents want to help save the world."

She laughs. "You're afraid of the end of the world and of dying."

"Aren't you?" I ask without thinking about it.

"Nope. My future is already secured."

"Really? How so?"

Gemma sits back up. "My dad already has a plan for me. He says I'm gonna live forever. They've already stored my DNA, and I've got a first-class ticket to Mars as soon as it's safe to live there." She tilts her head in her hands. "I feel sorry for people who can't afford to live forever."

She didn't say "like you," but the implication couldn't have been clearer. "And how will any of that help you live forever?"

"Don't be so dense. It's only part of the plan. I'm first in line to have my brain mapped." She leans back, a smug smile on her face.

Shouldn't take long with such a small brain. Oh, I want to say it out loud so bad. Instead, I say, "For what purpose?"

Gemma thrusts her arms in the air. "Seriously? What rock did you crawl out from under?"

I stare at my hands. If it wasn't already obvious that I don't belong here, it is now. "My parents are the scientists, not me."

"Still." She shakes her head. "What grade are you in?"

"Sixth," I say.

"Really? Guess they grow the beanpoles big wherever you come from."

First day in New Eden. Do I have a sign on my forehead or something? Please insult me and call me names.

"Where *did* you come from?" Gemma asks.

According to my watch, it's only been five minutes. Dr. Prince said he needed thirty with my parents. How will I endure twenty-five more minutes with this mean girl?

"Texas."

"Ah, figures. Everything's bigger there, right?" She snickers. I'm not sure why.

"I wouldn't know. This is the first time I've ever left town."

"I'm in sixth as well, but I'm smart enough to be in eighth. The only reason I didn't skip grades is because of the CEVR program. My father helped create it just for me. What school are you going to? New Eden Secondary?"

"I don't know what it's called, but it's the virtual one."

"*You're* going to CEVR Academy?" Gemma huffs. "I thought the standards were higher. Father's going to hear about this." She glares at me. "Stay out of my way at school, or I'll make your life miserable."

You already have.

I pull my knees up to my chest and hug my legs. "You won't even know I'm there."

"Wish I didn't, now." She takes a deep breath and fake cringes. "Ugh. At least I won't be able to smell you through the video feed." She picks her tablet up off the desk and spins her chair around until her back's facing me.

The reprieve from her insults and smugness lasts all of thirty seconds. She spins back around. "Lucky for you, I'm feeling charitable today."

"Lucky me." I don't bother looking up at her.

"For the record, once my brain is mapped, I'll be able to live forever."

"Forever where?"

"Inside an android body. Or maybe within a virtual world so real that you wouldn't know it's computer generated. Bet you haven't seen anything like that before."

"And you'd be right."

"My father showed me Virtual Haven. It's amazeballs."

"What is it?"

"Oh, just the most beautiful place ever created by GIST." She gazes at the ceiling as though viewing the world now. "Only the elite will have access to it. At least at first. One day, the entire universe might live there. No crime. No death. No hate."

"Then you won't be there," I say.

She springs out of her chair and leans over the desk, her palms supporting her weight. "What did you say?"

"I said it sounds wonderful."

Dr. Prince walks into the room, followed by Mom and Dad. "I'm guessing you two girls had a lot to talk about," he says.

Gemma picks up her tablet and straightens the chair behind the desk. "Yes, Father."

By Gemma's tone, I sense her relationship with her father is far less affectionate than she lets on. Given the unease produced by Dr. Prince's presence, I almost feel sorry for her. Almost.

"You ready to head out?" Dad asks.

I stand up and nod. "Yeah, I'm ready to go back home."

Back to Podunk.

CHAPTER FIVE

BRAWL IN THE MALL

WITH SPARKLES HELD TIGHT to my chest, I stare up at the ceiling in my bedroom. Only there's no ceiling to be found. Artie calls what we're experiencing "story mode." Everything I describe comes to life and plays out above me. It's one feature of New Eden I'd love to take back to Podunk.

"Dark skies brood overhead. Lightning flashes, setting the sky aflame with each new bolt. A rare thunderstorm within the domed city of New Eden." I shudder at the realism, and Sparkles chimes in with several squeals.

I hug Sparkles tighter and continue, "Far below, synthetic streets made to mimic asphalt glisten with each flash, an ominous sign for the treacherous day that lies ahead. Strong winds turn trees sideways, morphing pine needles into deadly darts."

From the corner of my eye, I glimpse Dad in the doorway, his attention drawn to the ceiling. My nerves settle with his presence. A hero behind wire-rimmed glasses.

I continue, "Red eyes burn within the shadows—advanced machines designed without caution and birthed through human innovation. Stalking the streets like packs of hyenas, they threaten life as we know it."

"It would be far more accurate and believable if the packs were coyotes or wolves and not hyenas," Artie interjects, "given the population of coyotes and wolves in the state of New Mexico."

"Next time." Dad perches on the edge of the bed and tousles my hair. "For now, it's time you get ready for the day. You and Mom have some shopping to do."

Me and Mom?

My world teeters on a cliff's edge, threatening to plunge itself into the abyss without a moment's notice. "What about you?"

He shrugs. "First day of work, I'm afraid. Wish I had a little more time to spend with you, but you know how saving the world is. The end waits for no one."

Tumbling end over end, the abyss draws ever closer. "Can't shopping wait until the weekend?"

"Absolutely not. You've got to get your school supplies and uniform."

"Uniform?" I'm certain I just regurgitated several chunks of last night's meatballs. The acrid taste burns the back of my throat and lingers even after swallowing several times.

"Don't worry," Dad says, "you'll get used to wearing a dress."

Every time I think New Eden can't get worse, it proves me wrong. I relinquish my hold on Sparkles and latch onto Dad's arm with both hands. "Please, Dad, don't make me do it. Send me back to Podunk." Tears blur my vision.

After several seconds, Dad's eyes are the first thing to betray him, sparkling with mischief. Then, his upper lip begins to quiver. The corners of his mouth rise toward his nose, and he laughs aloud.

A ruse, and I'm not amused. I pull my arms back and brood. "It's not funny."

Dad grins. "Kinda is."

I wipe my eyes with my shirt sleeves. "You know I hate dresses."

"My girl, the tomboy."

"But there's still a uniform?"

"It's virtual school, remember?" Dad stands. "Your avatar will wear a school uniform, but you can wear whatever you want—except pajamas. As you know, pajamas are forbidden to wear at school on all planets."

"Fine. No pajamas and no dress," I say.

"Kiara, let's go." Mom's voice echoes throughout the house.

I stare at the ceiling that now looks like a normal plastered ceiling. "How did she do that?"

"Special parental privilege." Dad winks. "Now, let's go before she comes up here."

Two hours later, Mom and I find ourselves near the back of a long line of kids and their parents. Apparently, there's only one store in the entire district that sells school supplies for virtual school. Not only that, but I must also register for a virtual library membership and get a small chip inserted into my right palm.

"Why do I have to get the chip? Can't I just get a normal library card and be done with it?" I say as we get closer to the front of the line.

Mom shows me her right palm and the small red mark at its center. "We all must have a chip to live in New Eden. The chip has dual functionality. Not only will it grant you access to the library, it will also allow you to attend school, make purchases, open doors, and perform various other tasks around town."

I'm excited about the library but not looking forward to the injection. I stare at my palm and its creases. "Does it hurt?"

Suddenly, we're at the front of the line. "No, so suck it up."

A short, older woman with silver hair stands on the other side of a narrow table. "Papers."

Mom hands the woman my birth certificate and a copy of the lease to our new home in the skyrise. "Her name is Kiara Kole."

The woman examines the documents. "Yes, I can see that." She blinks twice and then hands the papers back to Mom.

A gray box with a quarter-inch hole in its top sits on the table between me and the woman. She looks at me and points to it. "Ready when you are." When I don't move, she says, "Place your right hand on the box and keep your mouth shut tight. We don't want to lose another tongue today."

"Auh!" I recoil.

The woman snorts. "I'm only teasing. Now, hurry it up before I'm old and gray." A moment passes, then she says, "Ah, too late. Look what you've done to me."

No amount of humor could keep my stomach from bunching up in knots as I reach toward the box with a trembling hand. I can't keep it still no matter how hard I concentrate. With catlike reflexes, the woman smashes my hand against the box with her palm. She's much stronger than her frail frame indicates.

Sweat beads on my brow.

The woman starts counting down. "Three… Two…"

Ca-thunk!

Blistering pain erupts in my palm and shoots liquid fire through my hand and into the veins in my arm, all the way up to my shoulder. "Ouch!" I jerk my hand out from under the woman's hand and rub it.

"All done," the woman says.

I stare at the puncture wound on my palm. "How does it know who I am?"

"Scanned your documents and uploaded them to the chip." The woman cocks her head and stares at me like I've got three noses. "How else would it work?"

Understanding clicks in my brain. "The blinking, right?"

"You're new here, aren't you?" she says. "Of course it's the blinking. Bionic eyes." She chuckles.

I lean forward and squint at her grayish-black eyes. "Whoa. I've never met anyone with bionic eyes before."

Mom shakes her head. "You still haven't." She takes hold of my arm and leads me away from the table. "That wasn't so bad now, was it?"

My palm and arm still ache, calling her bluff. "You lied to me."

She pulls me to a stop and faces me. "I told you what you needed to hear."

I jerk my arm from her grasp. "All I needed was the truth."

"Admit it. The truth would've sent you running."

I hate it when she's right, but I'll never admit it to her. "Not true."

Mom frowns and stares at the floor for a solid minute. Then, she says, "I'm sorry."

"What for?" I ask, my mind spinning. Given no context for the apology, it could pertain to just about any interaction or conversation we've had over the last several weeks.

Mom walks over to a metal bench and plops down on it. I join her and wait for her to say more. After several moments of silence, she says, "Everything."

I take her hand in mine. It's the most intimacy we've shared in months. "I don't understand."

"It may not seem like it at times, but I love you, Kiara. I hope you know that."

My throat tightens. "I love you, too."

"This new job means more than you can imagine, and not in terms of my career. I've seen firsthand what lies on the horizon, and it scares me to death. Not just for myself, but for you. For everyone." She pauses and takes a deep breath. By the haunted look on her face, she's seen more than I know or can imagine.

Mom continues, "The stress of our plight brings me to my knees at night. It fills my heart with fear and my eyes with tears. Please just know that I love you unconditionally, no matter how things may seem or how I might act at times."

"I know you love me, and I forgive you."

She squeezes my hand and then kisses the top of my head. "Thank you."

Rising from the bench, she says, "How about we get some lunch and then do some clothes shopping. Sound good?"

I hop to my feet and push away all thoughts of the stressful morning. "Can we get Panda Express?"

"Yes, and you can pay for it with your new chip. It'll be a good test of it and the parental controls I've placed on it."

Parental controls?

Joy seeps from my pores and puddles on the floor. "What does that mean?"

"What it means is that you're allowed to make food and transportation purchases—with limits of course. Any other types of purchases must be approved by me or your father. Comprendes?"

"Yes."

After wolfing down a bowl of chow mein noodles and orange chicken, Mom and I head over to a kiosk for a virtual store called Hi-Tech Clothing. A holographic face appears in front of us. An Asian man with black hair and bleached-blond tips. He looks like someone straight from a South Korean K-Pop band.

"Welcome to Hi-Tech Clothing… Kiara and Evelyn!" the man says.

The sound of my name triggers my sweat glands, turning my nape and pits into swampland. Eyes wide, I stagger backward a few steps. It's the chips in our palms that broadcast our identities. I know that, but it doesn't ease the tension building in my chest and throat.

The man continues, "We have the largest selection of programs in New Eden—more than ten million and counting—and we get new ones every minute."

I look up at Mom. "Programs?"

"Nanite clothing, and don't scrunch up your face like that."

"Like what?" I say, knowing full well what she means.

Mom shakes her head. "Keep it up, and your face will eventually get stuck that way." She got that from Dad.

"Ugh. Fine." My attention returns to the kiosk. "So, this *is* a clothing store and not a store that sells software?"

"It's both. Nanites require programming in order to function. Without that programming, they'd just be a pile of metallic dust."

"Step inside the orange circle, and we'll get you fitted in no time," the man says.

Mom places her hand on the small of my back and applies pressure, but not enough to physically move me. "Go ahead, Kiara."

Hands balled at my sides and lower lip squeezed between my teeth, I take three steps forward until I'm just inside the circle. Mom moves into the circle, too. Orange light shoots up from the circle on the floor, all the way to the ceiling. The mall beyond the cylinder of light fades as the orange light solidifies and becomes opaque.

"Please remove all articles of clothing and step onto the pod," says the man.

Heat rises in my cheeks. "What?"

The man repeats himself, but I was talking to Mom.

Mom gives me a stern look. "Really, Kiara? For heaven's sake, I gave birth to you."

My gaze locks on the floating head. "It's not you I'm worried about." But it is the first time today that I've been glad Dad isn't with us.

"There's nothing to worry about. All these systems are run by AI. No humans are involved."

"I know the system uses artificial intelligence, but what if it records me? Naked."

Mom's arm shoots up, and I cower against the wall, eyes squeezed tight. It's a strange reaction I don't even understand. She's never laid a hand on me except to spank my bare bottom, and only when I did something really bad. In all honesty, I can't remember the last time she did spank me. Several years at least.

When the smack doesn't come, I open my eyes. Mom's already stripped down to her underwear and bra, and those don't last long, either. She smiles and pushes a strand of hair behind my ear. "Figured it might help if I went first." I nod, and she steps onto the pod.

"Welcome, Evelyn," says the man. "This might tickle a little, so be sure to hold still."

The man's face fades along with the light, casting us in total darkness. Then, a spotlight above the pod Mom stands on turns blue, and the sound of beads flowing through a rain stick fills the circular space. I look all around but can't determine the source of the sound.

"Look at my feet," Mom says.

A silver substance, fine as silt, flows up from the pod like water and begins covering Mom's feet. Upon closer inspection, I realize that the substance isn't flowing at all but crawling. An army of nanites. It only takes twenty or so seconds for the nanites to completely cover her from toes to fingertips to neck. A suit of quicksilver.

"Measurements are complete," says the man, his head reappearing. The orange walls turn white, and then a carousel of clothing surrounds us. "Please make a selection."

As Mom swipes the air, the carousel spins, presenting us with a never-ending selection to choose from. I'm not one for clothes or fashion, but the cool factor of this store has my heart pumping. By the time Mom finishes selecting several dozen "programs" for herself, I'm antsy to give the machine a try.

I strip with abandon and step onto the pod moments after Mom vacates it. Everything happens just as it did with Mom: head fades, space goes dark, blue spotlight shines down, and the rain stick rattles. My gaze locks onto my feet as the first of the nanites crawl onto my toes and over my arches. I expected to feel something spindly like spider legs, but the sensation is like nothing I've ever felt. It's as if the nanites can't decide on what they are. Cold, then hot. Rigid, then silky-smooth. Heavy, then light. Wet, yet dry. Flowing and staggering. Undulating as they ascend my bare legs.

Then, a thought enters my mind. One I hadn't contemplated. It turns my body rigid. "They won't go where they shouldn't, will they?" My voice squeaks.

Mom laughs. It's the first time in eons that she has. "Of course not."

It's not that I didn't believe her, but relief washes over me when the nanites rise above my waist without incident. Once encased, the man returns and brings up a carousel of clothing, just like he did for Mom. However, the clothes presented to me are brighter and aimed at my age rather than hers.

Rather than surfing through the endless carousel, I specify what I'm looking for. "Denim jeans."

A thousand pairs, styles, and colors present themselves. I'm usually one to go traditional, but a pair of pink trousers with tapered legs catches my eye. After touching the image, the nanites on the lower half of my body begin to vibrate ever so slightly. I watch as they morph from silver to pink and begin taking on the characteristics of denim. It blows my mind when I touch them. Soft yet grainy, and stretchy. If I hadn't seen the transformation with my own eyes, I would've thought they were real denim jeans.

An hour later, I'm exhausted from searching through so many programs.

In that time, I've selected five pairs of jeans, four pairs of shorts, three pairs of pajamas, a dozen pairs of socks in various colors, four pairs of shoes, two jackets (one light and one heavy), and fourteen T-shirts. One of the T-shirts has an animated unicorn that peeks its head out from behind a grove of trees and then walks into a meadow of golden grass and a myriad of flowers in pinks, yellows, blues, greens, purples, reds, and oranges. It's already become my favorite shirt ever.

"We're finished," Mom says.

"Thank you, Evelyn. Your account has been charged," the man says. "Thank you for shopping at Hi-Tech Clothing. We look forward to serving you again soon!"

The walls turn orange once again, become transparent as they transition to light, and then fade. Looking around, I see no bag of clothes.

Mother says, "They've been delivered to the house already."

Some days, it's scary how well she can read my thoughts. The rest of the time, I wonder if she knows me at all. I guess it's all about focus, and today hers has centered around me. It feels good for a change.

A woman and a boy stand just beyond the orange circular line on the floor. The woman scowls at us as we step across it.

"All yours," Mom says to the woman.

Yellowish-white foam drips from the sides of the woman's gigantic mouth—well, maybe only in my mind, but it still grosses me out. She snarls at Mom, "How dare you waste my son's special day."

I'm about to open my mouth and say something disrespectful when Mom places her hand on the small of my back and leads me away. I really want to turn around and stick my tongue out at the woman, but the woman aims her hateful glare at the back of my head with laser precision. One false move, and she'll take me out. Besides, the last thing Mom needs right now is for me to start a fight in the New Eden Mall. I snicker thinking about the headline the news would likely use: *Brawl in The Mall.*

Fifteen minutes later via a double-decker MagBus, Mom and I arrive back at the skyrise building we now call home. Or rather at our temporary housing away from Podunk as I like to think of it. No matter what it has to offer, New Eden will never be my home.

The doors at the front of the building swing inward as we approach. "Welcome back, Evelyn Kole. Kiara Kole," the male voice says.

"No more palm print reader?" I ask.

Mom smiles. "No need with our new chips."

Just thinking about it makes the puncture wound on my palm itch something fierce. "Cool."

Later that evening, two white boxes sit atop my bed. The first box brims with metallic sand. Some of it spills across my bedspread. My eyes bulge as the sand pulls itself back together. "Whoa."

I dump the entire contents of the box onto the bed and toss the box on the floor. When I run my hands through the soft silt, I expect it to cling to me, but it doesn't. Instead, my hands slip in and out of it like oil through water.

"How am I supposed to wear this stuff?"

"Instructions are on the inside flap of the box," Artie says. "Would you like some assistance?"

Terror gnaws at my nerves.

Is he always listening?

Then, a darker, scarier thought replaces that one.

Is he watching, too?

Joy drips from my pores until nothing remains inside me but fear and dread. My stomach gurgles and my breaths shallow. "No thanks."

A few minutes pass before my pulse slows and my breathing returns to normal. Mom and Dad have some questions to answer. In the meantime, my curiosity with the nanite clothing has dwindled to nothing, so I ignore the sand piled atop my bed and rip open the top of the second box. Inside the box is a pair of scuba goggles with a clear lens, some sort of hand-held device with buttons and knobs that press and turn, and a 12-inch-square white pad with a cord and wall plug. The box contains no explanation or instructions.

What am I supposed to do with all this?

Frustrated, I plop down on the edge of the bed, the strange goggles still in hand. I slip the band behind my head and rest the goggles on my forehead. They're surprisingly light.

Dad pokes his head into my room. "Oh good, your school supplies arrived."

"School supplies?" I pull the goggles back off and stare at them. "How will any of this help with school?"

Dad comes over to the bed and picks up the hand-held device with all the buttons and things. "How do you think you'll get around school without them?" He twirls the two sticks with his thumbs.

I swallow hard, palms sweaty. "But it's virtual school… right?"

"Of course."

"Well then I don't understand what these things are for. Won't I be watching the teacher through my computer?"

Dad kneels before me and whispers, "This is New Eden, Little Bear." Then, with a louder voice, "It's so much better than that!" His enthusiasm hurls past me, none of it infectious.

"How so?" I cringe as I await his response.

"It's not just virtual school but virtual reality…" Dad's voice trails off or my brain stops processing further. Either way, my mind hangs on those last two words.

Virtual reality?

I've heard the term before but can't remember what it means. I'm an outdoors girl, not some tech junkie. My tablet's the most technologically advanced thing I own, and I only use it for reading. The goggles dangling from my fingers capture my gaze once more. "Do… do you mean I'll watch the teacher through these things?"

Dad smooths back my hair. "And much more. Those goggles and this controller—" He holds up the device in his hand. "—will allow you to navigate your virtual school as though you were there in person. You'll be able to interact with other students and attend classes just like a normal school."

Just when my world seems like it's stabilizing, an earthquake rumbles beneath my feet. It sends tremors down to my soul and opens fissures wide enough to swallow the universe whole. My stomach leaps into my throat as I plunge down into the darkness of despair once again.

I smash my fingernails into my palm and bite my lower lip to keep myself from breaking down.

Dad continues, "But it's not like regular school. You will attend classes and be lectured, but a good portion of your day will be spent playing games that will help you learn what's taught. Isn't that cool? No homework or tests. You'll just have to complete each of the levels in the game."

"But I… I… I don't like games." Tears swell and breach the confines of my eyelids, spilling down my cheeks in rivulets. "Please, Dad. Send me back to Podunk."

Dad wraps his arms around me and pulls me against his chest. "I wouldn't survive here without you, Little Bear, and I can't help save the world from

Podunk. Please just give it a chance, okay?" He wipes my cheek with his thumb. "I think you'll enjoy it once you try it out."

Every worry and fear pour from my lips, unhindered. "I had to get naked to buy clothes, they buried a chip in my palm, Artie listens and watches everything I say and do, the teleportation pod is going to malfunction and mix us up or kill us, and the world is going to burn or explode or something before we can be saved. Gemma said her future is secure but we're too poor to be saved. I don't want to die, Dad. I don't want to die, and I just want to go back to Podunk and live with Grams."

"First, Artie is an AI, not some sort of robot pervert watching and recording everything we do. He listens to us to improve his learning, and I promise you that he isn't recording you. We're all safe with him here. He protects and serves us, not some shady company or entity. And as for what Gemma said to you, don't worry about it. We'll be okay, I promise." He kisses the top of my head several times. "I'll never let anything bad happen to you, Little Bear. Do you hear me? Never."

I nod and snort up a gob of snot hanging from my nose. "I know, Daddy Bear, but what if something happens to you?"

"You'll still have Mom and Sparkles. We're all here for you."

"And Grams," I add.

"Of course." Dad releases me and grabs a tissue from the box on my nightstand. He hands it to me. "Speaking of Grams, how about you get yourself cleaned up and then give her a call? I'm sure you'd both benefit from it."

After blowing my nose, I take a deep breath and then exhale until my chest hurts. "Okay."

On the third ring, Grams's face appears on my tablet. "Grams" is all I manage to get out before turning into a blubbery mess again.

Concern fills Grams's eyes and seeps into her voice. "Kay-Kay? What's wrong?"

After blowing my nose and wiping my face, I rehash every single event over the last week, most without taking a single breath. When I finally stop for air, Grams does what she's known for: soothing one's soul.

"I'm sorry you're having a tough go so far in New Eden, but God has a plan for everything we experience. I believe that you'll grow fond of your life there and will enjoy virtual reality game school, whatever that is. You're a smart girl. Smart as a whip, if you ask me. You'll succeed at anything you put your mind to, just like your Dad and Mom. In the meantime, know that I pray for you daily and ask Jesus to intercede when your trials become unbearable."

God...

I'm not a believer. Looking at the world and listening to the news, how can I be? How could anyone? No loving God would allow the chaos and hate to spiral out of control. No God would allow his creation to decay and die. At least no God I could ever believe in. I've never told Grams that I don't believe in God. The only reason I haven't is because it would break her heart, and I couldn't live with that.

An appearance by Princess Sparkles puts a smile on Grams's face, which warms my heart. After we say our goodbyes, I lean back against the stack of fluffy pink pillows on my bed and sigh. Sparkles buries her snout in the crook of my neck. It tickles and brings giggles up from the depths of my stomach. Between talking with Dad and Grams and snuggling with Sparkles, I begin to realize how much I'm loved no matter where I lay my head at night.

I hug Sparkles tight and kiss the top of her snout. "We'll be okay."

My gaze drifts over to the plastic desk in the corner and the pair of goggles and controller on top of it. Dread churns in the pit of my stomach.

At least until tomorrow.

CHAPTER SIX

SOCKS ON A ROOSTER

MY VR GOGGLES SIT on the edge of my desk and beckon me, but not in a positive way. Over the last four days, my mind has exhausted itself running through every scenario I could think of on how to get myself back to Grams and Podunk. Turns out, none exists. At least nothing legal.

The beginning of the school year—and the end of my life—looms at the end of the weekend. Three final days of freedom before I'm locked away in a world from which I'll never escape. According to Mom, the school recommends all students familiarize themselves with the gear and the virtual world before Monday, but the thought of donning goggles at school frightens me.

What if the other kids see me wearing them?

The irrational thought bounces around in my head, unwarranted and unwanted. Dad says everyone must wear goggles to attend virtual reality school, even the teachers. Plus, since it is virtual, no one will see me for real. Just my avatar, whatever that is.

Think positive, Kiara.

Everyone at CEVR Academy will be starting out together since it's a new school. And, because it's sixth grade only this year, there won't be any older kids. We'll always be the oldest class going forward until we graduate. At least that's something to look forward to. Perhaps this virtual reality game school won't be so bad.

Except the game part.

It'll be easier to make friends without the pressure of looking nice every day or being awkward or clumsy. No one will ever know. Then again, school hasn't started, and I'm already an outcast. Gemma Prince made that clear last week at GIST. The odds never fail to work against me. Bad karma, I guess. Not entirely sure what that means, but they say it a lot on TV, so it must be true.

My eyes refocus on the goggles. "Ugh."

Monday will be the worst day ever.

"No. No, no, no." I ball my fists and slide off the edge of my bed. "This is an opportunity to start fresh."

At my desk, I glare at the pastel pink wall in front of me and say, "Mirror." The wall instantly reflects everything in my room, including me. There's nothing special about the girl staring back at me, but the unicorn running around on her shirt puts a smile on both our faces. Joy fades as my gaze falls to the goggles.

More like a face shield.

The weight of the goggles barely registers in my hands. Perhaps heavier than a peacock feather, but not by much. At least I shouldn't have to worry about them denting my nose.

A dark charcoal band connects both ends of a clear lens framed within a thin strip of gray plastic. Holding the goggles up to my face, its lens extends up from my cheekbones to my forehead and across my face, ear-to-ear. The white nose piece squishes like memory foam and feels cool against my nose.

In the mirror's reflection, I notice a small blue button on the top left edge of the frame. Lowering the goggles, I examine the button. A white circle with a line through part of it is etched into its surface. According to the instructions on the inside flap of the box the goggles came in, it's a power button. The instructions also reveal that the goggles must be worn to power on.

"Makes sense, I guess."

I slip the band over the back of my head and pull the goggles down over my face. The fit—or lack of—is laughable. They sag on my face and hang at the end of my nose, on the verge of plunging beneath my chin.

I've always heard that the mirror doesn't lie, and, from what I see, it's true. I'm wearing a giant's scuba goggles. *"Fie, fih, foh, fum"* echoes in my mind and warrants a giggle.

Pointing a finger at my reflection, I scowl. "What did you do with those magic beans?"

Mom's head appears in the doorway through the mirror. "Magic beans, is it?"

My eyes meet hers in the reflection. "Figure I need to grow a beanstalk to use these things."

"I see." She enters the room and walks over to the desk.

I turn and face her. "I think they gave me the wrong size."

Mom pushes the goggles back up my nose, but they slide back down as soon as she moves her hand away. "They do seem to be a little big." She picks up the box and examines it. "It says one size fits all."

"All giants, maybe."

Her eyes continue to scan the instructions, and she nods slowly. "Oh, I see."

I peer over the box edge. "See what?"

Mom sets the box back down on the desk. "You need to press the power button." She moves to press it, so I scurry out of her reach.

"I can do it," I say, my fingers over the button.

She raises her hands and backs away. "Fine. I'll leave you to the giant slaying. I'll be downstairs if you need anything."

"Okay," I say.

Mom exits the room. My heart thumps against my ribcage, a bird in distress. Gaunt eyes stare back at me through the mirror and a clear lens. A trembling finger hovers over the button on the goggles.

Anger swells in my chest. "Stop being so scared of everything."

Muscles tense, I mash down the button and jerk my hand away from the goggles, unsure of what to expect. Through the mirror, the blue button lights up. Just like my nanite clothes, the goggles vibrate and transition to a fluid-like state. The lens shrinks and adheres to my face while the strap becomes snug against the back of my head. Dark matter from the strap crawls over the top of my head, mashing my hair down and turning the goggles into a helmet.

Instinct tells me to reach up and rip the goggles off. It takes all my will power to refrain as the helmet extends downward, covering my ears. Then, it attacks my face. Prickly legs march across my cheeks. Over my lips. Climb the bridge of my nose. Wrap my lower jaw.

Chest aches. Pulse races. Throat tightens. Can't breathe.

I stagger backward, my hands frozen with fear just inches away from reaching the mask. The backs of my legs strike something solid. The room twists as I fall, and then the world turns black as my eyes roll back in my head.

I'm uncertain how much time has passed when a distant voice echoes in my ears. Calls my name. "Kiara Kole…" A female voice. Warm. Inviting.

A soft light penetrates my eyelids. One deep breath quells the fire in my lungs. As my eyelids flutter, I catch glimpses of a woman's face. Her blond hair. Green eyes. Tanned skin.

My eyes snap open. Pulse still races. Stomach full of butterflies. But I can breathe.

The woman looks down at me, her smile inviting. "Welcome to training, Kiara Kole."

It only takes a moment to realize I'm lying on my bed. I reach up and probe my face. Confirm the goggles, helmet, or mask still clings to me.

I sit up and face the woman. Only darkness exists in my field of vision beyond her. Solid. Black.

When I look down, my own body fails to exist. Waving my hands in front of my face changes nothing.

This is virtual reality?

It's nothing like what I'd imagined. Then again, what had I expected? I'm just a country girl lost in a world of technology.

"Welcome to training, Kiara Kole," the woman repeats.

My voice croaks. "Hello?"

"Confirm you are ready by saying 'ready.'"

"Um… ready?"

The woman nods. "Very well. I am your Virtual Interface Digital Assistant. You may call me Vida."

"Okay." I'm not sure what else to say.

"This training is a closed session. What this means is that you and I are alone. Feel free to ask any questions knowing that you are in a safe environment. Do you understand?"

"I guess so."

"Do you have any questions thus far, or are you ready to begin training?"

What does that mean?

I look around, literally lost in the dark. "Begin, I guess."

"As you wish." Vida spreads her arms wide. "Now, allow me to introduce you to Cutting-Edge Virtual Reality Academy, also known as CEVR Academy or simply CEVR."

Vida snaps her fingers, and the darkness disappears. In place of the darkness are concrete sidewalks, stoic trees and bushes of many varieties, a vast lawn of perfect green grass, beds of flowers, and an enormous, two-story building with a flagstone facade. A dozen steps lead up to its four sets of double doors, and a flagpole rises toward the bright-blue sky to the far left of them. Three flags hang limp from the pole: the US flag at the top, then the New Mexico state flag (obvious by its mustard-yellow color), and then a black flag with some white, silver, and blue. I can't tell what it is because the flag hangs limp against the flagpole.

To my left is a black sign flanked by flagstone columns. It displays the name of the school in white lettering along with what looks like a blue astronaut's helmet in front of a horizontal sword. Below the school name it reads, "Home of the CEVR Space Knights."

It's way better than the Podunk Pigeons.

Leaves rustle as a gentle breeze crosses the school grounds. The warm air caresses my face and teases my hair as it passes by.

"Auh!" I reach for my hair. It's still covered by the goggles. "How did I feel the breeze?"

"Your VR visor is capable of stimulating every nerve on your head, right down to the last hair."

VR visor. Heat rises in my cheeks. *Makes more sense than goggles.*

The ding of metal hooks sound as the flags stir on the flagpole. The bottom flag unfolds just enough to reveal its secret.

The school flag.

Vida continues, "Your visor is also equipped with the latest advancements in olfaction technology."

I frown. "What is olfaction?"

"Your sense of smell. Take a deep breath through your nostrils and tell me what you smell."

I close my eyes and take a deep breath. "Fresh-cut grass."

A memory of Pops, my dad's father, dashes straight to the front of my mind. I'm riding on his lap inside the cab of his green John Deer tractor as we cut down acres of alfalfa. Six years have passed since he left my world. Tears pool between my eyelids and spill onto my cheeks when I open my eyes, blurring the virtual world.

"Will others be able to see what I look like or see if I'm crying?"

"All facial expressions will be conveyed in the virtual world, including tears."

"Good to know." I make a mental note not to cry with the visor on since I have no way of wiping my face and no desire to have my emotions on display for the entire school.

Vida says, "What else do you smell?"

Another breath, and a sweet scent fills my nostrils. "Lilacs… and roses."

"Yes." She turns and beckons me to follow her into the grass, her yellow sundress swishing just below her knees.

"Can we go inside?" I ask.

Vida stops and looks back over her shoulder. "I'm sorry, but this is a training simulation. The school does not actually exist in this program. When you power on the visor for school on Monday you will be automatically connected with the school servers."

"But how will I find my way around?"

"Your first day will begin with orientation. Everything you need to know will be relayed to you then. Now, follow me for further training." She turns and continues toward the grass.

Remembering that I'm sitting on my bed, I jump to my feet. Big mistake.

The virtual world bobs and sways, triggering an unwanted response deep within my stomach. I close my eyes, steady myself against the bedframe, and wait for the nausea to pass. Once it does, I open my eyes and peer down at my virtual feet. Black boots with silver laces. They're not something I'd ever wear. I take a step forward, but my body doesn't move in the virtual world. Several more steps yield the same result.

"Vida!"

She turns back. "Yes?"

"My legs don't want to move." Two additional steps, and pain splinters the center of my forehead. "Ouch!" My hands confirm I've ran into the bedroom wall.

"Let me help you." A schematic resembling the controller that came with the visor appears in front of me. "Use the left thumb controller to navigate." A yellow circle appears around the small joystick on the left side of the controller. "Go ahead and give it a try."

The controller. Duh! I'd all but forgotten its existence.

A deep sigh erupts from my parted lips. "This is gonna be like putting socks on a rooster."

Vida looks at me, her head cocked to one side. "Beg your pardon?"

"Never mind. Just something Grams would say."

After several failed attempts to retrieve the controller off my desk—the last one sending the controller flying—, I finally locate it in the far corner of the room. It's at this point I realize I'll be better off sitting down when at school. I crawl over to the bed on my hands and knees and pull myself up onto its edge.

With the floating schematic as a guide, I reorient the controller in my hands and nudge the left thumb controller forward. The earth moves beneath my feet. The virtual one that is.

"Good," Vida says. "The farther you move the stick, the faster you'll walk. Hold the left shoulder button in—" The button highlights on the schematic. "—while you use the left thumb stick and you'll jog or run, depending on the applied pressure."

After a good twenty minutes, I'm running around the front of the school and sniffing every flower like a child. Movement aside, the experience leaves me wanting more. But therein lies the problem. How can I enjoy myself without betraying Grams and Podunk?

I can't, can I?

Guilt bubbles up from within and sours my stomach. How will I face Grams? She'll see right through me. She always does.

I reach for the blue button, but not only is it not there, the frame isn't there, either. Perspiration runs down my spine, and my chest heaves as I struggle to breathe once again. Pulling on the visor does nothing, so I dig my fingernails into it but gain no hold. Tremors quake me, head-to-toe.

"Your vitals are elevated," Vida says. "Are you feeling okay?"

"No." My voice shrills. "I want out of this thing!"

"You are free to power off the visor at any point. Your lesson progress will be automatically saved."

"But how do I power it off? The button's gone."

"Tap your left temple once to increase the opacity of the visor. Tap your right temple once to decrease opacity. Tap your left temple twice in order to power down the visor for removal. Do you understand?"

No!

The only thing I care about is getting the VR visor off. I jab my finger into the left side of my head, twice. The virtual world falls into darkness once again. It takes just a few seconds for the visor to morph back into giant's goggles, but it's several seconds too long. Gasping for air, I yank the visor off my head, taking several hairs with it. I toss it and the controller onto the bed even though I really want to throw them against the wall.

I hate this.

Tears spill from my eyes as I lie back on the bed. "I'm sorry, Grams. I promise I don't like it here."

But my heart aches, knowing it's just not quite as true as I want it to be.

CHAPTER SEVEN

DREAM CRUSHER

DESPITE ALL EFFORTS TO subvert catastrophe, Monday morning arrives. Simulated sunbeams shine through sheer curtains to my left, yet a dark, ominous cloud looms on the horizon of my waking mind. If God did exist, as Grams believes, I'm certain this day would never have come to pass. Yet here I lie, my feeble prayers fallen short of deaf ears.

Or no ears at all.

"Kiara!" The call of the banshee, otherwise known as Mom. She uses the same shrill beckoning as with the first day of every school year I can remember. "It's time to get that body of yours moving."

"I'm up." Or at least awake.

Ten minutes later, Mom barges into my room. "Get up, young lady. You cannot afford to miss orientation."

I kick the covers off and to the foot of the bed with reluctance. "I know."

"I expect you to be showered and downstairs in twenty minutes."

"Ugh." A quick sniff of my armpits validates her request, but it doesn't prevent me from arguing against it. "But I showered Saturday."

"Today's a new day." Mom crosses her arms. "No arguing."

I sit up and huff. "It's not like I'm physically going anywhere."

"I understand, but that doesn't give you a pass to be lazy. Besides, do you want to have your first-day-of-sixth-grade picture taken with you looking like that?"

There's no need for a mirror to confirm I have bedhead. My aching scalp is proof enough. What I don't understand is why Mom always insists on taking a photo at the beginning and end of every school year. She's never done anything with them that I know of.

"Fine." I slip off the bed and bury my toes into the fluffy, pink, faux llama rug that surrounds it. Feels like walking on clouds. Or at least what I imagine it would feel like.

"Good." She glances at her left wrist. "Seventeen minutes, now."

Showering New Eden style works exactly like in the cartoon, *The Jetsons*. At least that's what I expected when we first moved in. However, there's no conveyor belt, automatic undressing and re-dressing, or robotic assistance. In truth, the only difference between here and Podunk is that the water and jets are voice controlled.

After first-day pictures, I down a quick breakfast of buttered toast with grape jelly and a tall glass of chocolate milk. Then, Mom, Dad, and I go over the house rules. Artie and Sparkles are there as well. Even though I'm only eleven, New Eden law allows me to be left at home alone provided that a care-giving robot is employed and present. Hence Artie. I asked Artie once what his name stood for, given that it's an acronym, but I've since forgotten. Maybe I'll ask him again at some point.

As with me, today is Mom's first day at work, too. Honestly, I'm not sure which one of us is more nervous. Mom's had a kerchief attached to her hand all morning, wiping away perspiration on her brow, upper lip, and sternum, ad nauseam.

With Mom and Dad gone to work and Sparkles outside wallowing in her mud pit, I sit down at my desk and don my oh-so favorite giant goggles—er VR visor. After a brief moment of darkness, I find myself standing in front of two open doors. Beyond the doors is a gymnasium.

A female voice echoes in my ears, "Welcome to orientation, Kiara Kole. The assembly will begin in 1 minute and 53 seconds. Please make your way inside and find yourself a seat."

Using my controller, I step through the doors. Bleachers line all four walls of the rectangular gymnasium. Most of the seats are already taken by other students. To the left of the doors, three rows from the top, my gaze meets that of one Gemma Prince. Her glare leaves my throat parched and my lips dry. With a quick about-face, I head to the right and spot an empty seat next to a boy who looks more nervous than me.

What does my face look like?

The thought petrifies me and leaves me determined to wear a stoic mask for the rest of my virtual school life. Shaking the fear away, I concentrate on the uniform the boy wears. It's identical to all the other students, regardless of gender. It reminds me of a sleek spacesuit or military uniform. Black boots with silver laces, blue pants tucked into the tops of the boots, a white polo featuring the school logo on the left side, and a black jacket with tons of pockets. The pants feature at least a dozen pockets, too.

Taking my seat, I turn my attention ahead. Chairs for faculty spread across the gymnasium floor in expanding rings, oriented around the center of the gymnasium floor. None of them seem to be wearing the school uniform.

Figures.

Massive, circular lights hang from the high ceiling like dozens of miniature suns, lighting the entire room. They wink out as I stare at them, leaving us sitting in the dark.

Then, a column of natural light shines down at center floor, revealing a platinum podium. A woman dressed in a gray pant suit walks into the light and up to the podium. Silver hair, pulled behind small ears, spills off her narrow shoulders and hangs mid-chest. A platinum cord hangs from her neck and a golden pendant from it. A triangle, point down, with what looks to be a sword within it. The pendant triggers a thought that niggles my mind.

Where have I seen that symbol before?

Nothing readily comes to mind, and for good reason. The woman's yellowish-brown eyes stare directly at me. Into me. Leaves my soul bone cold.

An air of superiority envelops her as the corners of her mouth arc upward. There's nothing warm about her smile. It's calculated. Forced. Sends my pulse racing.

After what feels like an eternity beneath the scrutiny of her heavy glare, she speaks. "Good morning, students. My name is Peggy R. Cornier, and I am the principal of CEVR Academy." Her strong, authoritative voice straightens my spine and sends waves of gooseflesh rippling up my arms.

Thousands of voices fill the gymnasium at once, echoing the same greeting that hangs in the air before me. "Good morning, Principal Cornier." Mine isn't one of them, my lips frozen on my face. I swallow down a large lump of fear as Principal Cornier's stare deepens.

She knows I said nothing!

"Welcome to the first day of your future." Principal Cornier lets her words sink in before continuing. "As most of you know, New Eden was created to gather the most brilliant minds across a plethora of fields in order to solve the most pressing issue our world faces: extinction."

Whether intended or not, that final word drives a spike of fear into my mind and leaves me clutching at my throat for air. As I look around the gymnasium, I realize a thousand faces echo my fear.

At least I'm not alone.

An image of Mom and Dad rises in my mind. Two heroes in disguise. Red capes billow at their backs. A strange sense of peace settles over me.

No, we're all in this together.

Principal Cornier continues, "With this fact in mind, we set forth to create an adventure game world facing peril. Look up, and you'll see a countdown timer."

I can almost hear the clock ticking away the time. Just shy of two hundred and eighty-eight days now.

An eternity.

"Not only does it mark the end of the school year," Principal Cornier says, "but it also marks the impact time of a world-ending asteroid we've affectionately named 'Crusher.'"

A sea of gasps fills the gymnasium like an echo chamber, my contribution among the loudest.

"I don't want to die," cries the boy next to me.

Neither do I.

Principal Cornier's eyes narrow, and a devious grin contorts her thin, red lips. She leans forward until her face appears to be right in front of me, the distance between us marginalized. "The fate of the world lies in your hands."

The boy next to me peers down at his hands. "It does?"

Distance restored, she continues, "Through lessons and tasks spread across a vast landscape of terrains, your job this year will be to seek out four components, one for each nine weeks of school. With them, you'll build a laser weapon to destroy the asteroid. Fail to retrieve a single one, and you will seal your own fate."

A collective gulp rings in my ears, and then the room falls silent. Given the reaction, the last thing any of us wants is to fail. Failure is death. Death is unacceptable.

Inescapable.

Red claws tick-tick-tick against the sides of the podium, breaking the silence and depositing fear into my pores. "Relax, children." Her devious smile returns. "It's only a game."

"Forty-seven ninety-nine," a boy behind me mutters. "No, that isn't right. All the seats are filled but someone's missing."

Looking back, I easily locate the boy. He's the only one whose head shakes.

Otherwise, he appears no different than anyone else. This virtual reality thing is strange. It's like we're all a bunch of heads attached to a body we have little control over. Just from the look in his eyes I imagine he's sitting at home with his legs drawn to his chest and his arms wrapped around them.

"Yes, yes," he says. "Someone's missing, but who?"

I whisper to him, "Did you count yourself?"

His head cocks to the right, and then his eyes grow wide. "Forty-eight hundred." He grins big.

Principal Cornier drones on for what seems like hours about earning points, coins, and bonuses, collecting artifacts, and competing as individuals and groups. She also mentions a year-end competition with the other two schools in New Eden, Apprentice Guild of New Eden and New Eden Secondary. None of it matters to me, though. I just want to go back home to Podunk.

"Last but not least," she says, "we come to what you've all been waiting for. All you need to do is look up."

The spotlight fades, casting the entire gymnasium in darkness. Then, high above us and just below the doomsday clock appears a white, inverted pyramid with its top chopped off. Gasps, whistles, and hollers fill the room as the pyramid starts rotating counterclockwise. Each side of the pyramid is outlined in neon green, and above each of the four sides are the words "TOP TWENTY," also in neon green. As it rotates, I notice that each side has five slots or lines, each numbered in bright red.

My stomach gurgles. If there really are 4,800 students in the school, I'm certain my name will never appear on the board.

The gymnasium lights come back on, and the same female voice that welcomed me to school earlier fills my head. "All students report to your first class. You have ten minutes, so there is no need to rush out of here. If you are unsure of where you need to be, just say 'heads-up on' to activate your heads-up display. Among other things, it will help guide you to your next destination.

"Another option is 'autopilot.' Using this feature will automatically guide your avatar to your next destination. However, this feature will be disabled after the first week, so I encourage each of you to practice navigating the school on your own. To use this feature, say 'autopilot on.' Thank you, and have a pleasant day."

"Is that you, Vida?" I ask.

"Yes, Kiara. May I assist you with something?"

"Not right now."

"Very well," Vida says.

"Heads-up on." A bunch of things pop up in front of me, including a map of the school grounds and building. A glowing orange triangle with my name inside of it appears on the map. Then, three dashed lines connect the triangle to a room on the map labeled "Period 1." The room highlights in yellow. Each dashed line seems to represent an alternate path to reach the same destination. Two of the lines are gray and the other is blue. The blue one pulsates. According to the map legend on the right, the blue line indicates the currently selected path and defaults to the shortest route. It looks just like the navigation app Dad used to guide us from Podunk to New Eden.

Vida's voice returns. "Use the 'locate' command to find people and places of interest while using the map. Say 'options' to view and update personal preferences, such as sharing your location."

"Say 'shut up' when annoyed by the voice in my head."

What looks like a card or driver's license floats in the upper-left corner of my vision. When I focus on it, it moves forward, and the school map moves to the lower-right and shrinks. The card contains a headshot of me, my name, age, birth date, blood type (O+), and school ID. Apparently, I'm student number 004797.

In the upper-right corner of my vision is a table of statistics: points, coins, artifacts, components, rank. My points stand at 25, and my rank says 4,352/4,800. Everything else sits at zero.

A warning flashes in front of me: three minutes until class begins. My heart pounds as I look around and see that I'm one of only three students remaining in the gymnasium, the counting boy from earlier behind me one of them.

"Autopilot," I say, but nothing happens. I repeat the command, but my avatar just sits on the gymnasium bleacher. "Ugh. This is stupid." I'd give anything to be back in Podunk right now.

"On," the boy behind me says. He stands up.

Ignoring him, I smash down the left shoulder button on my controller and shove the thumb-stick forward. I leap forward and dash halfway across the gymnasium floor, plowing through multiple rows of chairs and sending them flying and crashing into one another. Thankfully, I feel none of it, but there's no avoiding the clanging ruckus.

Another warning: one minute until class begins.

The controller becomes slick in my hands. Every thought shatters with each drum beat in my ears. When I get myself turned back around, the counting boy stands in front of me. He nods curtly and says, "Autopilot on." With a flash and a fading streak of blue light leading out of the gymnasium doors, he's gone.

"Oh, that's what he meant by 'on.'" I take a deep breath, brace myself, and say, "Autopilot on."

The virtual world flows around me in a blur of kaleidoscopic colors. Breakfast churns in the pit of my stomach and slinks up my esophagus, ready to burst forth from my puckered lips. But then the virtual world comes to a screeching halt, placing me in front of an open door.

A twenty-second warning flashes in front of me and starts ticking down. Through the doorway sits four rows of six chairs. Only one chair remains unoccupied. Third chair, first row. I head over to it and mash down every button on the controller before I finally figure out how to sit down. The countdown, at four, disappears.

I sigh, expelling a hurricane's worth of air. "Heads-up off."

"Gross." There's no mistaking the female voice.

Gemma Prince.

CHAPTER EIGHT

FIRST DAY BLUES

GEMMA PRINCE IS THE single person in the entire school I never wanted to see again, yet she sits in the seat to my left. What are the odds?

Facing her and acknowledging her presence is the last thing I should do, but I can't seem to help myself. I'm a train wreck about to happen, and the only thing I can do is sit back and let it as my head rotates to the left.

"Feeling's mutual." My eyes widen.

Did I just say that out loud?

Gemma's lips move, but she makes no sound. I'm no expert at lip reading, but I think she said, "What?"

"Good morning, class."

I turn my attention to the front of the classroom, pushing Gemma from my thoughts. Quotes from many classic books and poems cover the classroom walls, each quote repeatedly writing itself out and then fading away. It's mesmerizing.

A squat woman with dark, close-cropped hair and golden eyes stands at the front of the room next to a large desk made of oak. She wears a green crop top, likely to showcase the sapphire stud sparkling in her navel. Both are inappropriate for the classroom setting in my opinion.

"My name is Ms. Coates, and I will be your Language Arts instructor this year. As with all in-class sessions, your comm devices were automatically muted at the start of class. In most classrooms, the comms will stay muted unless you're asked a question or when you're allowed to ask questions of your own. Is this understood?"

I nod, the butterflies settling in my stomach. *Thank goodness Gemma didn't hear me.*

"Good." Ms. Coates rubs her hands together and giggles. "As you'll soon see, I tend to bend rules where I can and flat-out break them when needed.

For instance, all your comms are now active. And, as long as you pay attention and refrain from interrupting the lesson, they will remain on in this classroom throughout the year."

"Sweet," some boy says.

"Indeed, Mr. Farrow." She sits down at her desk. "Before we begin our first lesson, I thought you might be interested in the types of language arts challenges you will face in the game world. As you might suspect, you'll be faced with grammar, vocabulary, and spelling challenges, among other things. In one case, you might need to choose the correct word in order to advance through lava caves or spell words in a hangman challenge. The variety of lessons and challenges is endless."

As soon as the bell rings, autopilot whisks me through the hallways of CEVR Academy and over to my second period science class. The first thing I notice as I walk in is her. Gemma Prince.

Can this day get any worse?

I select a seat as far away from Gemma as possible. A different room would be better. In fact, a different world altogether would be perfect.

Mr. Butler, the science teacher, stands at the front of the classroom behind a long counter. I can't help but stare. Ebony skin, blue eyes with more depth than the deepest Texas lakes, and clean-shaven, both his face and scalp. White teeth, straight but not perfect, and a smile that stretches a mile. Based on forearms alone, the man packs more muscle than a Clydesdale.

Jars with all kinds of creatures suspended in liquid sit along the counter, along with several skeletons of birds, snakes, and other reptiles. It's both gross and fascinating.

"Some of the subjects we'll cover this year are anatomy, the periodic table, fossils, compounds, and motion. If I'm being honest, the periodic tables are my favorite. I find it fascinating to explore and discover the makeup of everything we see and touch in the world. By the end of the year, I hope you're fascinated by it as well." His enthusiasm for science exceeds that of Dad's, and that's saying a lot.

As Mr. Butler continues on about what to expect in the game world, I find myself slowly melting into my chair. An expanding puddle of relaxation. Maybe it's his smooth baritone voice or the genuineness of his laughter. Or perhaps it's his gentle demeanor. Whatever the case, he manages to extract all thoughts of Gemma from my mind. A skilled surgeon.

By third period, I come to the realization that all my classes are shared with the same twenty-three students, Gemma being one of them. The thought of spending the entire year stuck in the same classrooms with her day after day makes my stomach hurt. If there is a God, he's very cruel. The only consolation I have is the fact that I don't have to see her in person.

Third period is Mom's favorite subject and my nemesis: math. The room smells like chalk, and I'm surprised to see chalkboards across the front wall. Mrs. Reed sits at the front of the class on a barstool, a stick of chalk in her right hand. Red, spastic hairs stick up all over her head despite her having it pulled back into a single ponytail, and brown and red freckles pepper her ghostly-white skin, especially around her nose and across her cheeks. From the get-go, she establishes her dominance over us with a single look and vows to rule the classroom with an iron fist. Quite literally, actually.

She holds up her left arm. It's silver from shoulder to fingertips. "As you can see, my arm is not made of flesh and blood. Let me give you the full story before rumors abound. Several years ago, I was involved in a bad car accident. A car ran a red light and t-boned me. I'd been driving with my arm out the window, as I always did, and got it pinned between my car door and the front grill of the car that hit me. With every bone crushed, tendons severed, and nerves shot, nothing could be done to save it. Therefore, I elected to have it amputated."

"Auh!" I clutch my own arm as I sit at my desk in my room. Not having an arm would be a world-ending event for me.

She continues, "I lived without an arm until I moved to New Eden and met Dr. Prince. He insisted I be fitted with a robotic arm, courtesy of GIST, and the opportunity wasn't something I could pass up, even with all the strings attached."

The fact that her avatar reflects her prosthetic is beyond cool. It garners her a few extra points in my book, even if she teaches math.

Mrs. Reed eyes each of us. "Now that you know the entire story, how about we use it to solve a math problem." She turns to the chalkboard and begins writing out a word problem.

The infamous scratch of chalk against slate screeches in my ears and sends chills down my spine. I'm sure I'm not alone in wondering why she prefers a chalkboard, especially in a virtual environment. By the end of class, my nerves are fried.

Mrs. Livia Gray—Olive as she prefers to be called—instructs us in Social Studies during fourth period class. Despite the name, she looks nothing like

Popeye's wife. In fact, she looks nothing like an olive at all. Raven, straight hair, accented with a band of purple and yellow flowers around the crown of her head, flows past her waist in the front and back. A cloak of hair. If it were brown and draped over her face, she'd probably get mistaken for Cousin Itt from *The Addams Family*. She wears a white dress with a floral pattern that matches the flowers in her hair.

When she speaks, her voice carries with it no distinguishing accent, but I'm certain her ancestry is Vietnamese. "Good morning, class. Since we will have limited classroom time throughout the year as is, let's not waste time. We will begin with the formation of our great nation and the legacy of our first president, George Washington. Listen close, and expect this knowledge to be challenged in the game world."

At 12:30, we pause for lunch. I really want to power my VR visor down during lunch, but it's apparently against school policy. Only bathroom breaks are allowed. If we eat lunch, we must do so in the virtual school cafeteria, otherwise we're free to revisit lessons or stay in the game world on gaming days.

Inside the cafeteria, I walk over to one of the tables with several kids at it and sit down on the far end. Everything goes well for about two minutes as we all make introductions. Then, Gemma walks in with an entourage of girls. The thought of crawling underneath the table flitters through my mind, but she's already spotted me. She walks over to my table with her flock in tow. The lunchroom falls quiet.

Gemma glares at each of the other seven kids at my table before speaking. "This is a warning for all of you. Continue to sit at this table with Barnyard Betty—" She points a finger at me. "—and you might as well kiss your sixth-grade reputation goodbye. In fact, your reputation will suffer for the duration of your time at CEVR. Do I make myself clear?"

All seven of the students grab their lunches and disembark from my table, leaving me sitting there by myself. Gemma and the other girls laugh. "I know what you said earlier, loser. Told you to stay out of my way."

I stare at the table, unwilling to look Gemma in the eye as I fight back a torrent of tears.

"Cross me again, and I'll find a way to make you wish you never came to New Eden. Got it?"

A nod is all she gets from me. Gemma turns to leave but then her entire gang stops. I can't see past them to understand why, but then it becomes apparent.

"Move it or lose it, girls," a boy says.

The entourage parts like the Red Sea, but Gemma holds her ground at its center. "What do you think you're doing, Short Stack?"

"Going to go sit next to my friend." The boy stands a half foot shorter than Gemma, but he's a giant in my eyes.

Gemma says, "Hey girls, the dwarf's got a thing for the barn animal." The girls cackle.

"Shut your trap and move aside before I move you myself."

"Do you know who I am?" Gemma snarls.

"Yeah, a bully. Be glad there's no 'punch her in the face' button. If there were, I'd knock that smug look right off your face and you on your backside." A boy with glasses walks past Gemma and toward me, a smirk on his face.

"You're both gonna regret this." Gemma storms off, and her gaggle of geese follow.

The boy sits down across from me, his mousy-brown hair haystacked atop his head. A strand hangs over his right eye, but his left—blue as the sky—focuses on me through a coke-bottle-thick lens. "You okay?"

Those two simple words bring me to tears. Break my one rule of never crying with my visor on. Didn't even make it through the first day.

I look away and then down at my lap as I try and blink away the tears. "You didn't need to do that. You don't even know me."

"Sure, I do. You're Kiara Kole. Sixty-five points. Rank of forty-seven forty-two." He cocks his head. "Huh. You should try to get to class quicker. It'll help your rank. I'm Roger, by the way. As you know, rank is everything. Only the top individual gets an award. Don't you want an award? If so, you'll have to beat me, which will be tough, but I think you have the ability. Won't make it easy on you though. That would be cheating." He winks. "No cheating from me. At least not cheating that's traceable." He winks again. "Wanna know a secret?"

Roger doesn't wait for a response. He speaks like a machine gun spitting bullets. Rapid fire. "You'll want to switch to lunch mode if you want to actually eat something. Just say 'lunch mode' to activate it. Doing so will allow you to see through your VR visor into the real world while simultaneously viewing the virtual school cafeteria. It sets the opacity on your visor. A low opacity allows you to see through the visor. Not only that, but it also enables the nanites around your mouth to flex or move out of the way so that you can eat. Works kinda like many of the walls and doors around town. We have those in our house. Luckily, your mouth and expressions are still visible in lunch mode. That'd be kinda weird if your mouth disappeared while eating."

"Lunch mode." The desk in my room becomes visible, along with the rest of the room, yet I can still see Roger and everyone in the cafeteria.

Artie stands next to my desk. "Hello, Kiara. I assume your day is going well. As requested, I've brought you a grilled cheese sandwich and apple slices." He sets a plate on the desk and leaves the room.

I pick at my lunch. "Why not call it transparency instead of opacity?"

Roger shoves a chip in his mouth. "I didn't name it. Do you find it annoying that we can't just walk through people in here? It'd be so much easier if the programmers had treated people like doors instead of walls. Anyway, as I was saying before, I'm really good with computers. Kinda my thing. Got that from my dad and my stepmom. They're really great. They both work at GIST, but whose parents don't, right? One day, I hope to work there as well. My brother's the kind of brother everyone should have as well. He's—"

"Roger—" Not even a brief pause.

"—like my best friend when he's around. He's five years older than me, so I don't see him much these days. School, sports, girls. You know how it is. He's busy. But I don't mind. I like tinkering with robots. Do you like robots? Would you like to come over to my house sometime and see the ones I've built? They're really cool. I have this one—"

"Roger!"

Roger jerks back, eyes wide and cheeks red as turnips. "Sorry." He frowns. "Nervous habit. I tend to ramble, especially around pretty girls." The redness in his cheeks deepens and causes a flareup in my own cheeks.

Boys and girls have called me many things over the years, but no one's ever called me pretty, especially not a boy. He must need a new prescription for his glasses. We sit in silence for an eternity, him waiting for some sort of response and me struggling to move past the increasingly awkward moment.

An alert pops up on my visor: ten minutes until class begins.

Saved by the bell.

After several button presses, I locate the correct one and rise from the lunch table. Roger follows suit, his cheeks still red. "Thanks for making me not feel like a troll." With that, I turn and exit the cafeteria before he has a chance to make the situation more awkward.

At 1:15, I'm parked at my desk for fifth period—Technologies. Back of the class. In the corner. Dr. Fredrick Von Schlippe paces at the front of the classroom, a predator in search of prey. He wears gold-rimmed glasses, but it's obvious they have no lenses, even from where I sit.

He wears his hair like a dirty brown mop, covering his ears and creeping below his collar in the back. A triangular tuft of dark-brown hair sits just below his lower lip, and yellowed teeth dominate the right side of his creepy grin. He wears a white, long-sleeved dress shirt with the arms rolled up to his elbows and a tie loose enough to slip over his head. Brown slacks and dress shoes finish off his "IT guy" ensemble. There's a vibe about him that makes me want to pull my desk farther into the corner, and his voice presents a quality I don't trust.

Front and center of the classroom sits Roger. His head swivels in unison with Dr. Von Schlippe's pacing. Based on Roger's earlier rant about robots, I'm guessing this will be his favorite class. I'd give anything to skip the class.

"My class will be tough. Some of you will fail." He glares at each of us. "Yeah, those of you in the back will be the most likely to do so. As you know, this is technologies class. What that means is we will cover a myriad of topics from digital circuits to building computers and robots to programming. Yes, I said programming. As you will learn over the course of the year, programming is my passion. None of you would be here right now if it weren't for me. I designed most of this school and the game world you'll be playing in. Any problems with it, and you'll come to me first. Understood?" Everyone in the class nods. "Good."

He pokes at the air, and a 3D image appears. I've never seen anything like it. It's a black rectangle with sharp, silver prongs poking down from its long, parallel sides.

Dr. Von Schlippe scans the room. "Anyone know what this is?" Roger raises his hand, and Dr. Von Schlippe calls on him. "Yes, Mr. Daltrey."

"A digital circuit," Roger says. "Give me its number, and I can tell you what its purpose is."

By the time the bell rings and Dr. Von Schlippe dismisses us, my head is aching. Who knew something worse than math existed?

I enable autopilot once again and fly through the halls to my next and final class of the day: Fine Arts. A free-standing sign next to the open door reads "Choose Your Own Adventure!" with a red arrow pointing toward the doorway. Through the open door is a wide hallway with three additional doors. A sign hangs above each door. From left to right, they read: BAND, CHORUS, DRAMA.

Panic settles in. Had I stood there in real life, my knees would've buckled. Band is immediately out. No one in my family has a musical bone to speak of. Chorus isn't any better. I could make the best of dogs howl in pain with my pipes. Even the shower doesn't help. That leaves drama, but my life's already full-up on it. Nevertheless, no other viable choice remains.

With a deep breath and a long exhale, I walk through the door and into the back of an auditorium with thousands of seats. The stage, a thousand miles from where I stand, turns my hands cold and stops my heart from beating. I swing around and come face-to-face with Gemma.

Her smile evaporates in an instant. "Is this some kind of joke? What could you possibly portray?"

"Don't be so quick to judge a book by its cover, Gemma Prince." Bright, gray eyes meet mine as I turn and face a Hispanic man. Salt-and-pepper hair covers his head, spiked on top and trimmed short all around. "From where I stand, I see a diamond in the rough."

"As if." Gemma sneers. "Sometimes, a piece of dirty, black coal is just that."

His brow furrows as his gaze settles on the girl with the big mouth and ego. "And sometimes a diamond turns out to be nothing more than a cubic zirconia."

Gemma huffs and walks past us both.

The man chuckles and turns back to me. "I'm Mr. Valdez, but you may call me Barry. Welcome to drama class."

"I'm… Kiara. But you already know that."

"Yes, you are." He starts down the aisle, so I follow. "Do you know what your name means?"

It's not a question I've ever pondered. "Not really. Should I?"

He stops and faces me, his eyes aglow in the dim lighting. "Certainly. How else would you know that your parents named you God's gift?"

God's gift… Why would my parents name me that?

My gaze focuses on the silver cross inlaid with turquoise that hangs from Mr. Valdez's neck on a cord of black leather. "Do you believe?"

He looks down at his chest and then lifts the cross between his finger and thumb. "El amor de mi vida." When I look into his eyes again, I see they're misted over. "The necklace belonged to my wife. Just before she passed away last year, she begged me to make her a promise, so I did."

"What did you promise her?"

"Wear it daily and search for God." He shakes his head slowly. "Do you know how difficult it is to seek a God who took away my entire world?"

Or parents that do.

"Yeah, I think so," I say. "Does it scare you?"

"God?" he says, his brow wrinkled.

"Maybe… I dunno. The end of the world?"

"Fear not, Kiara. The sole reason New Eden exists is to save humanity, and we will." He winks at me and then urges me to follow him again. "Come on, we've got an entire class to meet."

An hour later, I sit outside on the porch with Sparkles in my lap and my tablet on the table next to me. A late afternoon breeze gently tousles my hair. Warm but not unbearable as it sometimes can be in the desert.

My head spins atop my shoulders, still overwhelmed and busy processing the ups and downs of my first day of school. The good news is that I survived. The bad news is that I still have 189 days to go. Plus six more years.

"Ugh. How will I manage, Princess Sparkles?"

Sparkles grunts and nudges my hand with her snout.

"Oh, I see. All my problems will go away like magic if I rub your head and belly long enough. Is that right?" I rub her belly, and she squeals with delight. The sound carries a rush of joy with it that fills me up until I'm overflowing. "I guess it really is magic."

It's good, but not Grams good.

My tablet buzzes, and an image of Grams's face appears on it. I prop it up on the table and click her face. "Grams!"

"Hello, Kay-Kay." Grams's soft smile could melt the coldest of hearts in the dead of winter deep in Antarctica. That's what Dad always says.

"You must've read my mind. I was just thinking about you."

She points to her heart. "I felt it right here."

My eyes mist. "I miss you so much."

"And I miss you, too." She leans back in her old green recliner. "Tell me all about your first day."

Where do I begin?

Gemma's face creeps into my mind. "Remember the girl I told you about? Gemma? She's the daughter of Mom and Dad's new boss?"

"Yes, of course. She didn't give you a hard time today, did she?"

"The worst."

"I'm sorry to hear that. However, the Bible says we should pray for our enemies, so I'm going to pray for her. You should, too."

I shoo Sparkles away, ignoring Grams's comment. "School here is so different. Everything is driven by technology, and I just don't get it because I'm so far behind the other students. I don't fit in, and I'm never going to do well because I'll never figure any of it out."

"You're a smarty britches, and you know it. Give it time, and you'll be running circles around everyone there."

"Why can't I just go back to Podunk and live with you? We'd both be so much happier."

"We've talked about this. I love you to the moon and back, but you're not mine to keep. Besides, your parents need you just as much as I do. More I'd say if I were to wager a bet on it."

"But I don't ever see them anyway. They're always working. I spend more time with Sparkles and Artie than anyone else. I don't want to be here anymore."

Grams's brow furrows and she exhales through her nose. "If you focus on the negative, it's all you'll see. What's one positive you had today?"

"Well..." My thoughts focus on the boy at lunch. Roger.

"Well what, Kay-Kay?" Grams picks up her tablet off her armrest and pulls it close to her face. "You can tell me anything. You know that."

"Yeah. There's this—" Pulse increases. Hands become clammy. Cheeks burn with fire. Everything inside me feels strange. "—boy."

Grams nods and smiles. "Ah, yes, a boy." She continues on, recalling a story from her childhood I've heard many times before. The first boy she ever loved—and married. Pops.

Fire consumes my entire face. "Grams, it's not like that. I don't even know the boy, and he's too short for me. Plus, he's not my type."

"Oh, so you have a type?" Grams snickers.

"Yes—no!" I bury my face in my hands. "That's not what I meant!"

"I'm just jostling your joints, Kay-Kay. Thought you could use a good rousing."

"Ugh." Thinking about Mr. Valdez, I change the subject. "Why did Mom and Dad name me Kiara?"

"You didn't know her, nor did I, but the name came from your Mom's mother. It was her middle name. It's a beautiful name, especially given its meaning."

She knows then. But do Mom and Dad?

"God's gift," I mutter.

"That's right. Trust me when I say that you are most certainly God's gift to your parents and to me."

"They know, too?"

"Not until after they named you. If you ask me, God led your mother to that name."

"Why?"

"You were destined to be their only child."

"I don't understand."

"They never planned to have children. After all, how can anyone have children when they rarely live in the same country while attempting to save the world, let alone live together?"

Her words hit me. Knock the breath from my lungs as they sink in. "They… didn't want me?" My chest tightens.

"That's not what I'm saying at all. You were a miracle. Once your mother became pregnant with you, it changed both their lives. Their focus shifted from traveling the world to save it from some unknown disaster to protecting their most precious possession when you were born."

"Me…" Tears spill down my cheeks.

"That's right. You're truly God's gift. You brought your parents together with your first breath." She beams. "Isn't it amazing how God works?"

Every thought. Every fear from the first day disintegrates. None of it matters compared with what Grams just told me. When we end our video chat, I sit there on the porch, my fingers aimlessly rubbing Sparkles as my mind works to hew my thoughts.

Is it all random chaos, or is there a God with a plan for everything?

CHAPTER NINE

GAME DAY

THURSDAY. DREADED THURSDAY. IT'S the first of many and what will likely bring about my demise. Yes, there have been many Thursdays in my life, but none such as this. Today is game day.

In my virtual world, the entire school gathers on the grounds behind the main building. Lush green grass, trees that reach the heavens, and flowerbeds teeming with luscious scents surround us. But it's none of those that fixate my gaze. Nor is it Principal Cornier standing before us in a red smock with matching shoes.

The stone bridge beyond Principal Cornier captures my attention and holds it hostage. Gray, brown, and white stones define the wide bridge. My estimate puts at least a hundred feet between its two sidewalls. The bridge itself spans a good distance before disappearing into a bank of thick mist.

"Students," Principal Cornier says, pulling my thoughts back into the present. "We stand before the Bridge of Destiny. On the other side lies a world like no other. A world full of wonders and challenges beyond imagination. In this world, you will face puzzles, obstacles, and peril at every turn, each designed to strengthen the lessons you learn during lecture time. These challenges will separate the elite from the pack and set your lives on a course toward the future."

Every few sentences, Principal Cornier glitches like a lost TV signal, freezing and pixelating before continuing. As I look across the crowd of students and instructors, no one else seems to have the same issue. She must have some sort of bandwidth issue or interference wherever she's connected to the network. Looking back on it, I remember her presenting the same issue during orientation. I would've thought she'd have the best connection of anyone.

Guess not.

Principal Cornier continues, "Fear not, for nothing is at stake but the fate of the world. Our species and those we strive to protect. The world will not end today, nor will it end tomorrow, but the end draws near. That is, if you sit back and do nothing to help change our course. We need young minds like yours to solve problems of the present and those we've yet to encounter. We need you to be your best. To do your best. Reach for the stars, and you will shine. Reach for the depths, and you will drag the world down with you."

I've never thought of myself as anything but a simple girl from Podunk. A world liver, not a world changer. But if what she says is true, then I must control my own destiny. If I control my own destiny, then where am I headed? Gazing toward the sky, I focus on the small red spot. It's almost non-existent, yet its approach is undeniable.

Crusher the asteroid.

My throat tightens, and fear burrows into my bones.

"Now, prepare yourselves for adventure and remember to always keep the goal in front of you. It's a big world out there, so stay focused." Principal Cornier's gaze drills into me. I'm sure every other student feels it too, yet I can't help feeling it's somehow personal to me. "There are a few more items I must mention before setting you free to explore.

"First, if you find yourself lost or at a loss as to where to go or what to do, you need only ask for help. But remember, help will always cost you something. Depending on the nature of the help and the depth to which it's needed, you might sacrifice points, coins, or both. I need not remind you of the importance of points. And, so you are fully aware, coins can be used to purchase in-game items as well as anything in New Eden. Use wisdom to ensure you accumulate both and discretion to keep from losing them.

"Second, the game world will be accessible for two hours after school Monday through Wednesday and all day Thursday through Saturday. Yes, I said Saturday. You will not be required to play on Saturdays. However, doing so will strengthen your chances of success. After all, the first twenty students to complete each lesson will earn bonus points—one hundred for the first person and stepping down five points for each subsequent completion.

"Last, but not least, you may always visit your classrooms Thursday through Saturday to repeat lessons if needed. Doing so will not cost you points or coins, but it won't earn you any, either. Keep that in mind."

She steeples her pinkies, pointer fingers, and thumbs, leaving her other fingers folded into her palms. The strange hand gesture produces a queasy feeling in the pit of my stomach. Then, when her gaze hardens and a wry smile creeps upon her face, terror strikes at my heart. A rush of chills sweeps up my extremities, leaving me hugging myself for comfort. But none arrives.

Principal Cornier straightens. "Yes, I almost forgot. No autopilot exists in the game world, and your map will only show you the places you've explored. Also, there are treasures to be found for those willing to explore beyond the beaten path. Some are greater than others, but one can alter the world. Find it, and anything is possible." With that, her avatar blinks out of the virtual world.

Ms. Coates gathers our class together. "Remember, this is only your first day in the game. Relax, and enjoy yourself. The world beyond the bridge is worth exploring. Also, remember that you're being monitored. Any cheating will be dealt with immediately. This includes discussing solutions to any of the lesson challenges. Also, once you enter a lesson challenge, you will be on your own. Just say, 'I need help' at any point if you require assistance. Now, go explore your new world!"

"Scared, Barnyard Betty?"

The name stings, but I keep my cool as I turn around and face Gemma. "Why would I be?"

Gemma sneers. "This isn't some backwoods farm fest. No rolling around in the mud or whatever it is you like to do." She steps closer. Has to look up to stare me down. "Trust me, once you find yourself all alone in the dark with glowing eyes watching you, you'll pee your pants. Just before you die." Her entourage snickers.

Suddenly, Roger's at my side. "That's stupid. It's just a game."

I can't decide if I'm annoyed or elated by his presence. Either way, he's here now.

Gemma glares at Roger. "Is it?" Her gaze meets mine again. "Guess you'll find out soon enough."

"We all will." It sounds stupid as soon as I say it, but it's the best I could come up with in a split second.

She brushes past me, then says, "I look forward to seeing your name at the bottom of the list. Both of you."

"Don't bet on it," Roger says. "I plan on winning it all and selecting space camp as my prize."

Gemma looks back over her shoulder. "In your dreams, Nerd Boy." She heads toward the bridge with her flock in tow and disappears into the throng of students.

After several awkward moments of silence, Roger looks up at me and cocks his head. "What?"

I frown at him. "Stirring the hornet's nest will only get you stung."

"Not if you're wearing a beekeeper's suit." He chuckles. "That'd be kinda awesome, actually."

"You're weird," I say.

"Thanks." He looks toward the bridge. "Ready for an adventure?"

My stomach grumbles and my shoulders tense. "Not even a little."

"Just relax. It'll be fun!"

"Speak for yourself."

"I was," he says. "Hey, can I meet you for lunch in the cafeteria?"

"Would anything I say stop you?"

"Probably not."

"Guess I'll see you at 12:30 then."

"Right on." Roger takes several steps toward the bridge but then turns back when he realizes I haven't moved. "You okay?" I nod. "Good. I really gotta go. Can't let Gemma get too far ahead. See you later!" He turns and dashes away.

Soon, I'm left standing there by myself as the last of the students cross the bridge and disappear into the mist. Temptation begs me to disconnect and spend the day with Sparkles. After all, it's only one day, right?

Who would know?

But then Ms. Coates's words echo in my mind. *"You're being monitored."*

The first step is the hardest, both in real life and in the virtual world. Once I finally take it, the next one follows, easier. Then a third. Next thing I know, I'm halfway across the bridge and on the brink of walking through the mist and into the unknown. As terrifying as that sounds, it beats walking over to the bridge wall and peering over its edge. I'm not sure if there's a small drop from the side, a bottomless pit into a dark abyss, or a gorge with a raging river below. Some things in life, even if it's virtual, are better left unknown. What lies beneath the bridge is one of them.

At least for now.

The only thing of consequence now is stepping forward and through the veil of mist. After several deep breaths, I close my eyes and move forward. The cool mist caresses my face as I walk into it. Then, a short but distinct vibration rattles my skull. My eyelids shoot open.

Before me stands a wall covered in vines. It towers above me and arcs around me, reaching back into the mist on either side. Seven archways protrude from the wall, each containing a door sunken into the wall. All but one archway remains dark. The last, to my far left, is flanked by burning torches. Two words are etched into the arch above the door: Sixth Grade.

The door itself is made up of planks of wood, perpendicular to the ground and banded with black iron straps. An iron ring the size of my head hangs from the right side of the door, and two words are chiseled into the door: Asteroid Impact.

Heart pounding and breath shallow, I mash down the action button on my controller, but nothing happens. It takes a few moments for me to realize I've no idea which button I actually pressed.

I hate games.

The second button works. Grabbing the ring, I turn it counterclockwise a half turn. The door groans as it swings inward just a foot. But it's enough for me to slip through. Once I do, the door closes behind me with a thud.

A gravel path greets my feet, flanked by golden, shoulder-high wheat or grass. It reminds me of the alfalfa fields back home. Turning around, I see that either side of the doorway is surrounded by the same fields.

No wall.

Around the side of the door, the golden fields stretch as far as the eye can see. The backside of the doorway mirrors its front. It seems odd for a doorway to stand right in the middle of nowhere. Then again, I have no foreknowledge of how games or game worlds work.

Back around the front of the door, I set my sights on the gravel path, but it's the sound of the breeze through the fields that catches my attention. The stalks sway gently, rubbing together and creating a lullaby I've missed for weeks. I'd give anything to reach out and feel them, but the sound alone settles my nerves.

You can do this, Kiara.

With renewed determination, I push forward and head down the path toward the unknown. Blue skies reign overhead, save the sun at my back, the doomsday clock above, and the red dot in the sky far to the north.

Is it north?

I've never been good with directions, but I never seem to get lost, either. It's ironic now that I think about it. I call forth my heads-up display, but it offers me little information beyond the things I already know. Well, other than the fact that I can use voice commands to travel to places I've already been, like the doorway I came through. Oh, plus the fact that my north turns out to be southwest.

At least for today.

As I walk along the path, pops of purple begin to dot the landscape. *Wildflowers.* Dozens. Then hundreds. Thousands. More than I could ever count. I want to stop and lie in the tall grass, but the doomsday clock looming high overhead reminds me how quickly time passes.

Three days gone already.

Ten paces ahead stands an old wooden post, just in front of a three-way fork in the path. Jagged boards with pointed ends hang from the post, each pointing toward one of the three paths. Words, burned into the flat face of each board, provide context as to where each path will lead.

The top board points south and reads: MA1 - The Falls. According to the map legend on my heads-up display, the MA stands for Math.

"Mom would head that way, but I'm not her."

The second board points north and reads: SC1 - The Forest. SC stands for Science. The third points up or west and reads: SS1 - The Summit. *Social Studies.*

None of the options appeal to me, but I can't do nothing. My mind draws a blank when I try and conjure memories from my social studies class, so that leaves one path.

I sigh loudly and stare ahead. "Science… blech."

"Sounds like someone needs a bit of cheering up!"

"Auh!" My pulse races as I look around. "Who said that?"

Out of nowhere, a large, speckled owl with gray and white feathers glides down and perches atop the signpost. A blue tie hangs from its neck. "Regis Owl, at your service." The owl folds a wing in front of itself and bows.

A talking owl!

"I'm Kiara." My eyes focus on Regis's tie. "I've never seen an owl wearing a tie before."

"I'm certain you haven't, but Mrs. Owl insists I be presentable at all times."

"Well, you're certainly the most presentable owl I've ever met. Come to think of it, you're the *only* owl I've ever met."

"Well, I best make a good impression." He smooths a few feathers with his beak. "Now that we've made our acquaintances, how about I present you with a riddle?"

"Ugh. Heads-up off." The map and all my stats dissolve. "I should've known you weren't just here to be friendly."

"Ah, but I am. Nooo obligation exists for you tooo answer a riddle, but if you dooo and it's correct, you'll earn ten points!"

"Well… I suppose I can try."

"Perfect! Here we gooo. If I add eight tooo six, I'll end up with twooo. The answer is correct, but how? Remember, *time* is of the essence, sooo answer quickly."

"The only way that's possible is if the six is negative."

"As six is not negative, that's not the correct answer, but I'll give you five points for ingenuity. Now, take your *time* and answer again."

Twice, Regis emphasized the word "time." I laugh, the answer so simple once I picture an analog clock with hour hands. "You're trying to trick me, but it's not gonna work! You can get the correct answer if you're using a clock face. So, 6 am plus eight more hours is 2 pm!"

Regis claps his wings together. "Bravooo! I knew you would get it. You've earned a total of fifteen points. Tell me what ingenuity means, and you'll earn another five."

"Ingenuity…" Grams has used the word to describe me many times. "It means that I have a creative imagination."

"Right you are! Five more points." He flaps his wings. "You're well on your way, Kiara. Speaking of which, I must be on my way."

"It was a pleasure meeting you, Regis!"

"Until we meet again!" Regis launches off the signpost and flies due north.

Beyond the golden meadow of tall grass and purple wildflowers lies a dense forest filled with conifers, evergreens, aspens, and other trees. As I reach the edge of the forest, the grass and wildflowers transition to bushes of a dozen varieties and ground cover made up of clover, mint, and a smattering of twigs and leaves. A thick canopy overhead blocks a good portion of the sunlight, leaving little of it for navigation. The trail narrows not ten feet into the trees, fit seemingly for deer and other forest animals.

But what about us humans?

Twenty minutes into the virtual world, my heart thunders. It's all just a game, yet my eyes, ears, and nose see, hear, and smell everything. Shadows shift about. Owls hoot. Leaves, aged in fall colors, rustle. The scent of pine wafts in the air and tickles my nostrils. A gust of wind blows my hair back and stirs a pile of leaves, lifting them off the ground in a miniature whirlwind. Then, a gray mouse darts into the bushes, his cover blown.

The tranquility of the surrounding beauty draws me in once again and settles my mind, but it's fleeting. A distant, haunting call from a lone wolf shudders my shoulders and sets the hairs on my nape on end. For the first time this week, I wish I wasn't alone. Gemma's warning creeps up my nape. Spindly legs scratch-tickling.

Can I die in here? If so, will I feel it? Will it kill me in real life?

The last thought, absurd as it is, leaves me panting. Pushing all thoughts of peril from my mind, I concentrate on the path ahead. Another howl, closer this time, quickens my pace. Despite sitting in a chair in my room, I find myself ducking beneath each protruding limb as I fly through the forest.

The forest lightens up ahead. A break in the canopy. When I reach the spot, the forest opens into a small glen. Short grass, spritzed with pink, yellow, blue, and purple flowers. A small pond, no more than a few dozen feet wide in any direction, blocks my path. Three large boulders sit at its far edge, perfect for sitting upon and fishing.

As my gaze extends farther, I notice an old wooden shack or shed or cabin standing just beyond the pond. A small footpath skirts the pond in either direction. I head to the left and around the pond, quickly finding myself standing before a solid wood door with a heavy iron lift latch.

"Hello?" My voice quavers. I wait a dozen seconds, but no one answers.

When I press the action button, my hand reaches out and lifts the latch. The door creaks open, revealing nothing but darkness.

"Anyone in there?" An alarm bell jerks me back in my chair and steals my breath. "Auh!" The controller slips from my hands and thwacks the floor.

"Return to the cafeteria for lunch," the familiar female voice says. "Your game progress saves automatically. Enter lunch mode, and you will be immediately transported to the cafeteria."

"Thank you, Vida."

True to her word, when I switch into lunch mode, I'm suddenly standing at the entrance to the school cafeteria. I pick the controller up off the floor and navigate myself over to an open table. Within a few minutes, the cafeteria begins to fill. Except my table, naturally. Frenzied conversation presses in from every direction. So much that I can't hear myself think.

Then, Principal Cornier's voice drowns out the rest. "Students, please remember that you must not exchange solutions to any of the lessons. Doing so is a violation of school rules and will be enforced. Thank you."

After ten minutes pass, I realize Roger's stood me up. I shouldn't be mad about it, especially given the fact that I didn't want him around to begin with, but I can't help it. It's not just a hit to my ego, but a dagger to my heart. Each passing minute buries it deeper. Burns hotter. The sandwich on my desk offers no fight as I dig my fingernails into it and tear it in half. Mayonnaise oozes underneath my nails.

Roger sits down beside me. "Sorry. I'm late." He's clearly out of breath.

"No big deal." I wipe my fingers clean with a napkin, evidence of my deceit gone. "What happened to you?"

"Forgot my lunch." He takes a deep breath. "Had to disconnect and go downstairs to get it."

"Twelve minutes? Must be a big house."

"That was only a few minutes. I was right at the end of my first lesson and didn't want to wait until after lunch to finish it. You know, for the points."

I shrug. "Yeah, sure."

"How far did you get? Where did you go? Left, right, or straight? Did you finish a lesson too?"

"No, Roger."

Gemma walks up to the table, a smirk on her lips and four girls in tow. "Just look at her pathetic score, Nerd Boy. She's got it on display for everyone to see. Rank forty-eight hundred." She laughs. "I knew you'd underperform."

"So what," Roger says. "It's only the first day."

"Says the boy who barely cracked the top twenty. If you hadn't noticed, I'm at the top of the board." She sneers at me. "At least you can't go any lower, Barnyard Betty." Her horde cackles like a coven of witches as they turn and walk away.

"I really don't like her. Not one single bit. If I saw her in public, I'd turn around and walk the other way. Wouldn't you? I'm usually pretty good with all people, but maybe she's not a person at all. What do you think? Would you face her?"

A mutilated yet viable sandwich sits in front of me, but my appetite has vanished. "Already have. First day in New Eden. Believe it or not, she's more unpleasant in person."

"Wow. Really? Is that possible? I suppose it is. Is that why she goes out of her way to humiliate you? What happened? Did you say something awful to her? I would've. You know, if I'd faced her in public. Which I don't want to ever do. Oh, right, I said that already. Sorry. Sorry. I know, I'm rambling again. Can't seem to help it around you. You make my mouth run and my brain fight to keep up with it."

"All I said was hi, and she tore into me." I shake away the memory. "Maybe you should eat your lunch. It'll occupy your mouth."

"Good idea. Oh, while I'm doing that, you can tell me about your experience so far. Which path did you choose? I know I asked you already, but you didn't answer. Now's a good time to do so."

"SC1."

"Ah, science. Cool. I dove straight into math." He laughs. "Get it? The math lesson is at the falls. You know, diving. Like swimming. It's—"

"Yes, Roger. I get it. Trust me, I'm not as dense as Gemma seems to think."

"Oh!" Roger's face turns red. "That's not what I was implying. I don't think you're dumb. Not one single bit. In fact, I'm sure you're one of the smartest girls in the school."

Now my cheeks burn. "That's kind of you, but I'm not delusional. I have my strengths, but it certainly isn't math."

"I'll help you. Anytime. I love math. In fact, I love just about any subject. I'm no expert, mind you, but I can hold my own, even against the likes of Gemma Prince."

"You think she's smart?" I say, the thought sickening.

Roger actually takes a moment to eat a few bites before answering. "Not sure yet. She leads the board for now, but it means nothing. We've got a long way to go before the year is over."

"Three minutes until lunch is over," Vida says.

Roger's eyes grow big. "Whoa, I gotta get going." He stands up from the table. "Thanks for having lunch with me, Kiara. See you after school?"

"Not today."

"Okay. Tomorrow then." He turns and runs out of the cafeteria.

Tomorrow it is.

After taking a bite out of my mangled sandwich, I switch out of lunch mode.

Vida's voice fills my head, "Would you like to return to your lesson?"

No.

I swallow hard. "Yes."

The cafeteria morphs into an open door with darkness beyond.

The cabin, shack, or shed.

I can't make my mind up on what it is, but it makes no difference. Determining its name will not drive the fear from my heart. Nor the darkness from my eyes.

After a brief debate with myself on the reasons I should turn around and choose another path, I head into the darkness. The door slams behind me and plunges me into complete darkness. I gasp and a guttural scream forms within but gets cut short when four lanterns spark to life and light the room.

Each lantern hangs from a large nail, one on each of the four walls. The space is quite large, and there appears to be no other rooms. A table sits square in the center of the room, empty of all but a piece of paper. Tables with drawers line three of the walls, each cluttered with tools, rope, wire, screws, nails, and just about anything else one would expect to find in a shed or workshop.

Workshop.

"That's the word I was looking for."

Only the lantern adorns the wall with the door. The paper on the table glows green around its edges when I focus on it. Pressing the action button allows me to retrieve it. The aged paper unfolds and hangs in the air in front of me. There are four lines scrawled across it in gold ink. They read:

> Locked inside with no way out.
> No one to hear you scream or shout.
> Look around, what do you see?
> Perhaps a way to make a key.

Engulfed in panic, I turn and slam into the closed door. The door rocks in my vision as I stutter backward. For once, I'm happy I don't feel everything in this virtual world. Upon inspection, I note the lack of an inside handle. After a deep breath, I return to the paper and the riddle it contains.

"How am I supposed to make a key for a door without a keyhole?"

At least twenty minutes pass as I rummage through dozens of drawers, looking for anything that might help me break down or cut through the door. But there's nothing. Beneath the table is a stool. I pull it out and sit down. Yes, I realize I'm already sitting down in reality, but sitting down in the game grounds me. Slows my pulse and allows me to think about the situation.

"Fact one, this is a science lesson. Fact two, the goal is to make some sort of key. Fact three, we didn't talk about making keys in science class." I groan.

"What did we learn?"

I picture Mr. Butler in my mind. At first, I see nothing but a muscle-bound man. Then, pieces of the white board begin materializing. We talked about magnets. How they have two poles, one negatively charged, and one positively charged. Opposites attract.

"But how does that help me?" Looking back at the door, a thought occurs to me. "It has a metal latch!"

Another ten-minute search still leaves me empty-handed. "There are no magnets."

Squeezing my eyes tight, I strain to remember what else he taught us. "Something about a battery…" It hits me. "I can make a magnet with a battery, a nail, and some copper wire!"

After finding the right parts and assembling the magnet, I test it with a screw. The screw latches onto the nail.

"Yes!"

I grab the magnet and head for the door. No matter what button I press to use the magnet, it doesn't work. The magnet just isn't strong enough to penetrate the thick wood door.

Anger boils in my veins, and hot tears streak my face. "I hate this!" I shake the controller and stop myself just short of smashing it against my desk.

Grams, I hate it here. I just want to go home.

"Heads-up on."

The map of the game world pops up and dominates my display, but it's the stats I'm focused on. They move front and center, shrinking the map and pushing it to the lower right of my vision. At 4,796/4,800, my rank might as well be dead last.

"How could anyone be as bad as me?"

Looking skyward brings bile into the back of my mouth. Slot number one in the top twenty belongs to Gemma Prince. Not only does she hold first place, it's also a significant lead. A small, red-and-gold disc sits in front of her name.

"Ugh! Vida, what does that little disc in front of Gemma Prince's name mean?"

"Gemma Prince has collected one of the game's special artifacts."

On the first day?

Not only does it *seem* impossible, it *must* be.

She must be cheating… but how?

CHAPTER TEN

FAILURE FOR SUCCESS

AS EACH NEW GAME day arrives, the cafeteria becomes less and less crowded. With forty-eight hundred students vying for a spot in the top twenty, many have resorted to playing through lunch. It's the last thing I want to do. Games are not my thing, and I'd give anything to go back to Podunk.

Today, Roger's among those playing through lunch, leaving me alone with my thoughts for once. But the peace doesn't last long. Gemma sits down at the table, right across from me. It's the first time I've seen her without her flock since school started.

"Hey, Barnyard Betty," Gemma says.

"Why do you call me that?" I say, knowing full well what her response will be.

She ignores my question. "Where's Nerd Boy?"

I stare at the half-eaten apple in front of me, avoiding eye contact. "He has a name, you know."

"Ugh, fine. Where's Nerd Boy Roger?" Gemma says.

Finally, I meet her raptor gaze. "Why would I know? I'm not his keeper."

"No? I thought the two of you were inseparable. After all, he's your knight in shining glasses, right?" She laughs.

I glare at her. "That's not funny. What do you want?"

Her eyes narrow. "I came to warn you."

This again?

"Yeah, I know. Stay out of your way. Trust me, I got it the first time. And all the other times. I'm trying my best, but you're the one who keeps stalking me."

"That's not what I'm talking about." Gemma looks around as if worried someone might overhear our conversation, but no one's within earshot. "Did you know that if you die in the game you'll die in real life?"

The gall of this girl appalls me. "I may not be a city girl like you, but that doesn't make me stupid. Games don't kill people."

She chuckles. "I'm just messing with you, but that's not what I came to tell you. The truth is far worse. If you die in the game, you'll get kicked out of CEVR Academy."

My pulse quickens. "You're just saying that because you want to make fun of me."

"Am I? Haven't you noticed the change in ranks this week? There are six fewer students. Look for yourself if you don't believe me."

Only a fool would take Gemma's word for anything. "Heads-up on." My stats come into view. It takes just a moment to confirm Gemma's claim. My rank is listed as 4,784/4,794. "Huh."

"Yeah, told you." Her brow wrinkles. "Overheard my father talking about it, and it gets worse."

"Worse how?"

"I confronted him about it. He said not only does a student get kicked out of school, but they'll also be put in the city dungeon for three days. Trust me, you won't want to get put down there. It's full of large, horrific rats that'll chew off your toenails and make a nest in your hair."

I try and keep a straight face even though my insides crawl with fear. "You're such a liar."

"Wish I was, but I'm not," she says. "My father took me with him the other night. Remember that kid who counts everything?"

I nod, my stomach now in knots and my mouth dry as cotton.

"They brought him out of the dungeon strapped to a stretcher with a white sheet pulled up to his neck. His body never stopped jerking as they loaded him into the back of an ambulance. As they did, the sheet moved." She squeezes her eyes shut and her head shudders. "I saw his bare feet. Covered in blood. I'm certain he had no toenails left."

My brain cautions me to dismiss her—*She's a liar. A liar. Liar.*—, yet my heart thrusts against my ribcage, full of fear and conviction that the counting boy lies in a hospital somewhere, catatonic.

"Why are you telling me this?" I say.

Her eyes narrow. "I know you're eventually going to fail and die in the game. Thought you should know what happens when you do."

I swallow hard.

Gemma gets up from the table and smirks. "Do us all a favor, and make it happen."

Angry tears burn my eyes. "Why are you so mean to me?"

"We both know you don't belong here. Just die already. You'll get to move back to Hicksville or wherever it is you're from and be stupid for the rest of your life."

"None of what you said is true."

"Of course it is. Ask anyone."

"There are other schools in New Eden. Wouldn't I just get transferred to one of them?"

"It's not possible. The city consists of twelve districts, and your district determines the school you must attend. There are no exceptions. Why do you think you go here? It's obvious you're not here on merit." Gemma rolls her eyes and shakes her head. "Ugh. Don't you know anything?" She walks away without looking back.

Anna, one of the girls from my classes and not one of Gemma's pack, walks over to my table and glances back toward the cafeteria doors. "What was that all about?"

I sniff. "Gemma's just being stupid. She told me that if I die in the game then I'll get kicked out of school and locked in a dungeon for three days."

"Actually, I've heard the same thing. At least the first part. Can't say if it's true or not, but I wouldn't risk it if I were you." She frowns. "So, what was the point of her telling you that?"

"She's evil. She told me to do everyone a favor and kill myself in the game."

Anna nods. "Sounds like her."

I shrug, but my avatar doesn't. "Yeah."

"Look, just forget what she said. No one wants you dead besides her. She'll eventually move on to torture someone else."

"That's nice of you to say, but it doesn't matter. She'll never stop hating me no matter what I do."

Vida alerts me that lunch is almost over. I sigh. "Guess it's time to go back in."

"Yep. Good luck."

"Bye."

Anna walks out of the cafeteria, along with almost everyone else. I stand and follow the small crowd toward the bridge. Once across the bridge and through the sixth-grade door, I head down the gravel path, ignoring Vida's prompt for me to continue my lesson.

As I walk along, my mind circles Gemma's words, chum ready for consumption.

What if she's right? What if dying will get me kicked out?

"Then I'll get to go home."

But what if there's a dungeon, too?

I love animals of every shape, size, and variety, but rats? Can anyone love a rat? Once, I watched a video about rats. The little fiends are quite intelligent and make good pets.

But not wild rats. They carry disease.

The dungeon part can't be true. Dad and Mom would never allow it. In fact, what parent would allow their child to be subjected to torture?

Unless their jobs were on the line…

Maybe the parents are given a choice: allow their child to be tortured or be fired from their jobs. How could I subject Dad and Mom to that? Dad would insist on taking my place in the dungeon, but would they allow him to?

Is it worth risking?

The more my thoughts churn, the deeper my conviction that the dungeon part can't be real. No school or city would do something so barbaric. Plus, it goes against everything GIST and New Eden hope to achieve.

A mixture of excitement and fear sends chills down my nape and spine. "Then it's settled."

My hands tremble as a spark of hope ignites within my heart. Resolve drives me along the path with more determination than I've mustered since arriving in New Eden.

"Find a way to die in the game. Find a way to die and return to Podunk and Grams."

Faster I traverse the path. I sit in a chair, alone in my room, yet my breathing labors with each subsequent step. Feet pounding over gravel and dirt, giving life to plumes of dust. In this moment, I am one with the game. A soldier on a mission. Nothing will prevent me from achieving my goal. But one question remains to be answered, and it's the most important one of my life: what must I do to die in the game?

As though guided by an unseen force, my eyes glimpse the obvious answer. The path widens ahead and leads toward a pristine lake of reflective blue glass. But it's not my destiny. Fifty yards to my right lies a runoff channel that snakes its way up the side of a steep mountain. Leaving the path, I race toward the runoff channel and begin my ascent.

Twenty minutes later, the runoff channel makes a ninety to the left and heads through a cleft in the rock. Thin blades of rock jut out from the cleft in all directions, a path of daggers. The narrow opening is too tight and treacherous for me to follow. Instead, I climb up the steep side of the runoff channel and find myself on a small plateau about ten paces wide.

At the plateau's edge lies a valley of red lilies a thousand feet below. Thick and vibrant. A light breeze rises from the valley. Rustles my hair and carries with it an aroma that tickles the hairs in my nostrils. Sweet. Succulent. The view leaves me breathless.

A narrow path hugs the sheer cliff and leads down to the sprawling valley. Temptation beckons me to follow it and spend the afternoon basking in a sea of flowers. But it's not why I've come here. My mission isn't complete.

As I stand on the ledge, the light breeze transforms into a gale at my back. When I close my eyes, I can almost feel it beating against the backs of my arms and legs, urging me to finish what I started. But then Gemma's words creep into my mind, peddling fear: *"If you die in the game, you'll die in real life."*

Can that be?

"No." I open my eyes. "None of this is real. It's just a game."

Yet part of me still clings to the idea. To fear. Fear breeds doubt, and doubt breeds more fear. It's a vicious cycle, and my mind gets caught up in it.

The controller squirms in my sweaty palms. Pulse rises. Swallowing no longer an option. Thoughts of death dominate me.

Where will I go if I die? Do people really see a bright light, or does that only happen in the movies? Do I just cease to exist, like a candle snuffed out, or is there something more? If there is more, then what? Does that mean there is a God? If there is a God, what will he think of me? What will I think of him? Is he even a he? If there is a God and a heaven, then there must be a hell, right? Is that my destiny? Hell?

No, it can't be. I'm a good person. I respect my parents. My elders. I never lie. Well, not very often. Only when necessary. Little white lies. Nothing more. Nothing that would send me to hell. If it exists. No. It can't. The world lies in chaos. Ruin. No god would stand by and watch their creation implode. A true god would react and act. A true god would save us all. We must be on our own. An accident. A bang without cause. Spontaneous life without reason. Without a creator.

But that makes no sense. Technology exists only through creation. It doesn't spontaneously generate. We are more complex than any computer. How can we exist without a creator, too? So, does that mean God does exist? If so, then where did he come from? Who created him? Where did it all begin?

"Stop!" The howling wind swallows my voice, the sound reaching my ears like a distant echo. "I'm in control of my own world, no one else. I choose you, Grams. I choose Podunk."

Stepping back from the ledge, I return to the lip of the runoff channel and then face the ledge and the valley beyond. The wind still howls, but the only thing I hear is my thundering heart. Crashing against my eardrums. Faster. Louder. Deafening.

Now or never, Kiara.

With a flick of my thumb, I race toward the ledge. Fingers slick with sweat. Breath shallow. Just before reaching the ledge, I smash down the jump button and leap into the air.

The wind rushes through my hair and stings my eyes as I sail over the ledge. For a moment, I hang there, weightless. I don't actually feel it because it's impossible. Yet I do. Then the descent begins. My stomach crawls into my throat. The ground rockets toward me, or me toward it. Falling a thousand feet takes far longer than expected. I watch until I can no longer bear it. Shut my eyes. Squeeze them tight.

A jarring thud rocks my head as the wind ceases. Darkness greets me when I open my eyes.

Panic sets in. It takes just a moment to remove my VR visor, but that moment lasts an eternity. Time enough to suffocate and wet my face with a torrent of tears. Once I free myself from its snare and see the desk before me, I can breathe again. No breath has ever tasted so pure.

My heart still thunders, and my entire body trembles, but no longer out of fear. No, this time it's pure joy. As are my tears.

I'm coming home, Grams.

CHAPTER ELEVEN

GAME NOT OVER

DAD'S WHISTLING PRECEDES HIM as he enters my bedroom. He stops just inside the doorway, a frown upon his face. "What's going on in here?"

"Getting ready to go." I continue to stuff the contents of my desk drawers into my backpack.

He walks over to the desk. "And where exactly do you think you're going?"

It's impossible to look him in the eye. "Back to Podunk."

"Oh yeah?" Dad looks around the room. "Looks like you've just about packed up your entire room."

"Had to. Didn't want to forget anything."

"Well, you've done a thorough job. That's for sure."

A single touch from his gentle hand, and I almost break down. Were it not for my fingernails thoroughly dug into my palms, I would have. It takes everything I have to keep my legs beneath me. "Thanks."

Dad walks over to the bed and sits down on its edge. He pats the empty space next to him. "Come on over here a minute so we can talk."

After a deep breath, I find my legs and join him on the bed. "What about?"

His kind eyes search mine, and his brow furrows. "Look, I know you miss Grams. We all do, but it won't be possible to visit her this weekend. Your Mom and I both have a ton of work to do. I promise we'll go see her soon."

The room spins as I try and find the words to tell Daddy Bear I'm leaving. I know it'll break his heart just as much as it will mine, but I don't belong here. Never have and never will.

"I'm moving back."

"Nonsense. You belong here with us." He wraps his arm around me and pulls me close. His warm lips press against my forehead. "I'd die without my Little Bear."

I pull away, tears in my eyes. "It's already done. There's no going back."

Dad takes my shoulders and squares me up to him. "What do you mean?"

"I... I died in the game." Dad responds, but I talk right over him. "I've failed game school. They're kicking me out. Since I have no other options, I'll be heading back to Podunk to live with Grams."

"I don't think that's how it works," Dad says.

A streak of anger flares in my chest and heats my words. "It is too. Ask anyone. Call the school if you don't believe me."

Mom enters my bedroom. "What's going on in here?" She eyes my backpack next to the desk and the suitcase at the foot of my bed. "Tom?"

Dad forces air through his nostrils and shakes his head. "Kiara died in the game at school and insists she'll be kicked out."

"That's not possible, right?" She looks at me and crosses her arms, deep ruts across her brow.

Dad shrugs. "I'm not sure how it can be."

"It's true," I insist.

Mom looks at her wrist. "It's almost five o'clock on a Friday." The lines across her forehead deepen. "Artie, call CEVR Academy."

"Right away, Mrs. Kole," Artie says.

My wall flashes, turns black, and then displays a message in white letters: "Connecting to CEVR Academy administration, please wait..."

After a few seconds, a woman comes into view, replacing the black screen and message. Gray, wiry hair wraps her narrow face, and a pair of readers sit on the end of her long nose, accentuating her big brown eyes. The collar of her frilly white blouse strangles her thin, wrinkled neck. Bookshelves line the wall behind her, every visible inch occupied with books and knickknacks.

"CEVR Academy, this is Jeannine. How may I assist you?" Jeannine's voice isn't unpleasant.

Mom takes the lead. "Hello, Jeannine. My name is Evelyn Kole, and I'm calling on behalf of my daughter, Kiara Kole."

"Yes, ma'am. How may I assist you?"

"Please connect me with Principal Cornier. The matter is urgent and private."

Jeannine's eyes tilt downward for a second. "It looks like you're in luck. Principal Cornier is still online. Please wait one moment while I connect you."

"Thank you," Mom says.

Jeannine nods, and then she's gone, along with her bookshelves. A face I've grown to loathe appears on the screen. I shrink back, but just so. Dad's arm blocks me from retreating farther.

"Mrs. Kole. It's a pleasure to finally meet you." Principal Cornier's voice drips with a sweetness I know she lacks. She tilts her head to the side as if to peer around Mom. "You as well, Mr. Kole." Her eyes pierce my soul. "It's good to see you again, Kiara."

A lump the size of an earth-killing asteroid forms in my throat. *Forty-eight hundred students, and she remembers me!* The only response I can manage is a nod.

Mom smiles at the screen. "Thank you. I know your time is valuable, so I'll get right to the point. Kiara informed us that she died in the game today and will be kicked out of school. Is this true?"

Principal Cornier laughs. To the untrained ear, it's a normal laugh, but my ears are attuned to the malice hidden within. *"You're just as stupid as Gemma claims,"* it taunts.

"Unequivocally false." Her face glitches, just as it had during orientation. "If such a case were true, we'd be without students by the end of the year." She leans forward. "I assure you, Mrs. Kole, dying in the game is all part of the learning experience."

Inside, I'm screaming for her to tell the truth. *I did die! Send me home!* Outside, I slip off the side of the bed and approach the screen. "But I don't understand. The screen went black."

"Yes, of course," she says. "Death will do that. However, that's not the end. Didn't you see the prompt afterward?"

"I..." In my haste to remove the VR visor, I must've missed it. "No."

"Oh, I see." The woman stares at me for a gazillion seconds. My skin crawls off my bones and retreats underneath the bed.

My pulse rises. Skyrockets. *She knows what I did.*

"Who told you this would happen?" Principal Cornier says.

I glance up at Mom for reassurance, but as to what, I'm uncertain. "I'd rather not say."

"Go ahead, Kiara," Dad says. "Answer the question."

Swallowing hard, I force myself to look Principal Cornier in the eye and say the one name I wish I never knew. "Gemma Prince."

The woman's eyes flash with malice. I swear it on Pops's grave. Had I blinked, I would've missed it.

Mom eyes me. "Gregory's daughter?"

I nod and chew the inside of my cheek to hold back the tears as my world crashes down around me once again.

"I assure you, the girl will be reprimanded for spreading falsehoods. It violates school rules." She clears her throat and stares at me. "Now, as to what you must do. Once you log into the school system and navigate to the game world, you'll enter the Hall of the Dead and be prompted on how you'd like to proceed. Do you understand?"

The hall of the dead? Fitting, I suppose.

"Yes, ma'am," I manage after Mom nudges me.

Principal Cornier's focus returns to Mom. "Have I addressed all your concerns today, Mrs. Kole, or is there something else I can help you with?"

"I assure you, you've put all our minds at ease," Dad says.

"Thank you so much for your time," Mom adds.

Principal Cornier nods curtly. "It's been a pleasure." After one last glance my way, the screen goes black and then the wall returns to its pastel pink shade.

Dad pulls me into an embrace. "See, all is well."

But it's not. Far from it.

"I think it's about time we all get washed up and ready for dinner." Mom tousles my hair and leaves the room.

Dad kisses the top of my head. "See you downstairs in twenty, Little Bear."

I spend the next ten minutes bawling my eyes out, but the only thing it accomplishes is turning my eyes red and my eyelids puffy. I'm a total wreck. A hefty dousing with water diminishes the outer damage, but nothing will ever repair my tattered heart.

With all my eggs held in a single basket, I'm left holding just the handle, the eggs and basket itself crushed against the rocks at the bottom of the ravine before me. How cruel life is. More so, the people in it.

Gemma.

I'll never forgive her for lying to me. But I had expected it, hadn't I? Yes, I played the fool for her, and I'm certain she'll never let me live it down.

What am I going to do now? How can I save myself from this life that isn't mine? How will I face anyone at school again? Will someone come to my rescue, or will I be lost forever? The girl in the mirror offers no answers of her own.

Figures.

After three street tacos and two moon pies, my stomach threatens to burst wide open and spill its contents across the living room floor. In truth,

I'm surprised I stomached anything, given my current condition. But street tacos are at the top of my favorites list. Dad knows this. By the look on his face, he's to blame, but I'll never accuse him. He's my Daddy Bear.

"Can I go upstairs and call Grams?" I say.

"Sure." Mom looks outside. "Take Miss Sparkles with you."

"A perfect suggestion," Dad adds.

After wrangling Sparkles from the backyard, the two of us head up to my room. Once situated on the bed, I conjure up Grams on my tablet.

Like a switch, her face lights up immediately. "Kay-Kay! Lord, I've missed you so much this week."

"I've missed you, too."

Sparkles nudges the tablet with her snout and grunts. She's as fond of Grams as I am.

"Oh, my sweet princess," Grams coos. "The world isn't the same without you."

Once the room settles, I dig into the heart of why I called. "I thought I'd finally found a way back to you, Grams. Truly, I did. But then it all fell apart. My world has finally reached its end."

"You've just begun a strange and new adventure, so why do you think your world has ended?"

After explaining my entire day to her, from my encounter with Gemma to me swan-diving off a cliff, Grams sits back and smiles. It's not the reaction I expected. Nor the one I want.

"Aren't you going to say something?" I say, a hint of anger snapping out the last word.

"Do you fear death?" she finally says.

Isn't the answer the same for everyone?

"How can I not?"

"The answer is simple. Know God, and you will be fearless in the face of death. Nothing will be able to touch you. God is perfect love, and his perfect love casts out fear. Death is not the end, Kay-Kay, it's the beginning of something new. He made you to live for eternity. Let God's love fill you with a spirit of power and give you peace that can't be understood."

"How will that fix what's broken? I'm dying in a world in which I don't belong. Suffocating. Longing to be with you. To be home." Tears burst from my eyes. "Why didn't you want me?"

"You know that's not true, and you also know you're not mine to keep. No matter how much I love you."

"Then why does it hurt so much? Why do I feel so alone? How will I survive?"

"You must have faith, Kay-Kay. Trust God and his plan. Trust that he is in control. Nothing happens without his knowledge, and everything works for the greater good, even if you can't see it from where you stand."

"But I'm afraid. I don't want the world to end."

"You cannot control what isn't yours to control. God controls the world and what happens to it, and he's already saved us."

"How can you be so certain? He took Pops from us."

"You can't think like that, Kiara." She only uses my real name when something is of vital importance. "It may seem bad to us that God took him, but you must remember that God works all things for good for those who love him."

"But you said God controls everything. If that's true, then he's responsible."

"You stand too close to the problem. Step back and see the changes that happened because of Pops's death. Barney Troy never cared for a soul, but the accident he caused changed him. Seeing what he did to Pops drove him to God. Don't you see? Pops's death saved Barney's life."

"But it hurt us."

"Yes, but the pain dulls with time. And we have all those wonderful memories of him. Trust me when I say that I know he's in heaven right now, and he's never been happier. I have faith in God and know that I'll see him again. You can have that same faith by learning about God and his plan for you. Is that not enough?"

The question burrows deep within my mind. Am I so selfish that I can't see the good in front of me?

"I don't know… I guess. But I miss him. I miss you."

"And I miss you." Grams looks away for a moment. "Oh, my. Looks like time's snuck away from us. I'd better let you go for now."

It's the last thing I want, but it's an hour later in Texas. "Okay, Grams. Thank you for listening. I love you!"

"Love you, too, Kay-Kay. And you, Princess Sparkles." She waves, and then the screen returns to rows of icons.

I lie back and stare at the ceiling. "Show me the night sky." The pink ceiling fades, and the stars come into view.

The beauty of space leaves me breathless. Fills my heart with wonder and my mind with dreams of reaching Mars. Then, something strange happens.

I begin to imagine a God creating it all. Shaping the planets with his hands and placing every star in the sky. Breathing life into the sun and giving it his light.

Chills prickle every nerve in my spine.

Are you out there?

CHAPTER TWELVE

HALL OF THE DEAD

I'LL ALWAYS BE THE girl from Podunk, but fate has made it clear that New Eden is now home. I must learn to be okay with it. At least it'll make visiting Grams that much better.

There are still a dozen minutes left before first period starts when I reach the room and open the door. But that's as far as I get before my stomach does a somersault. Gemma sits in my seat, flanked by her two cronies and group partners, Samantha and Jessica.

Gemma's nose wrinkles and she rolls her eyes when she sees me. "Ah, the girl of the hour. All this time, I thought you came from the barnyard, but barnyards don't have swans, do they girls?"

"Don't think so," Jessica says. The large girl's either chewing gum or her cud. I'd guess it's the latter.

Samantha looks me up and down and smirks. "I'm not sure where you'd find a *red* swan."

The three of them giggle.

I walk over to my desk and face Gemma. "What are you talking about?"

Gemma rises. "Oh, look, Swan Girl is confused." A devilish grin spreads across her face. "She doesn't know." Samantha and Jessica snicker.

"Know what?" I say.

"Oh, I'd never spoil such a delectable surprise." Gemma moves over to her own desk, and Jessica and Samantha return to theirs. "Trust me, you'll find out soon enough."

The rest of the morning plays out the same: Gemma taunts me and calls me Swan Girl before each period. At lunch, her entire squad makes an appearance in the cafeteria. Thanks to them, the entire school now calls me Swan Girl. Entire school might be an exaggeration, but not by much. I suppose the new name sounds better than Barnyard Betty, but not knowing the context razzles me. Roger doesn't know what Gemma means by it, either.

Fifth and sixth period fall right in line with the rest of the day, leaving me mentally exhausted by the time the final bell rings. Sixth grade is so much harder than I ever thought it would be. All I want to do now is take off my VR visor and crash on my bed for an hour or so before dinner, but there's still one task that looms over my head: bringing myself back to life.

By the time I reach the bridge, my palms are sweaty and keep sticking to the controller. It's only a game, and I know this, yet I keep finding myself engaging it as though my life depends on it. How twisted is that?

Standing before the wall of mist sends chills skittering down the back of my neck. "Time to perform a resurrection." After taking a deep breath, I step into the mist and the darkness beyond.

As with every trip into the mist, my head vibrates, but this time the wall of vines and its seven doors do not lie before me. Instead, a long corridor stretches into the distance.

The Hall of the Dead...

The hallway consists of black stone walls, a black slate tile floor, and a ceiling so high it's undetectable beneath the suffocating darkness. Evenly spaced, metal brackets hang from both sides of the hallway in pairs, one to either side. A single torch sits inside each bracket, angled toward the center of the hallway. Each gives off just enough light that its circle intersects with its mate, but not enough to reach those before and after it.

Of the dozen gaps between the pairs of torches, a tapestry fills just two of them. I walk over to the first one. It depicts a boy with curly red hair and yellowish-brown eyes lying in a heap at the bottom of a ravine. The morbid scene both disturbs and fascinates me, and I can't seem to pull myself away from it. I don't recognize him, but then again, why would I?

Moments later, the scene starts moving. "Auh!"

The boy flies up from the ground, hundreds of feet into the air, and comes up through a hole in the bottom of a wood-slatted rope bridge. Two slats, broken in half and dangling on the ropes, repair themselves beneath his feet. They hold together for a handful of seconds, and then the scene reverses. Slats break. Boy plummets. Lands at the bottom of the ravine in a heap.

"Ugh!" I retreat several steps. Thankfully, there's no sound to go with it.

As the tapestry scene moves again, I notice the dark-silver plaque hanging just below it. White letters read:

Here Lies A Boy Named Fred
Forever To Be The First One Dead
Total Lives Lost: 2

It takes just a moment to understand the significance of the tapestry. Knowing what lies ahead, bile rises in my throat and burns the back of my tongue with its acidity. I swallow it down and cough, but the acrid taste lingers in my mouth.

Had I any good sense, I'd run right past the second tapestry and to the end of the hallway. But I don't. Instead, I drag myself down the hallway and stop right in front of it. But I don't face it right away. Who could?

After several deep breaths, I turn and face the tapestry, but my gaze lies at the floor. Even as my pulse skyrockets and my mind urges me to move on, I lift my head and stare at the tapestry.

The face of a rocky cliff rises from the depths of a sea of red flowers. A girl lies on her stomach in the middle of those flowers, legs sprawled out awkwardly behind her and head twisted to the side. Fair skin with patches of freckles. Dark, shoulder-length hair. A few strands lie across her face. Green eyes, devoid of life, stare right at me. Into me. Accusing me.

Everyone will know what I did. Forever…

Tears form, but I fight them back. Abolish them from existence.

The scene comes to life, so I look away. There's no point in reliving it. But the plaque. Curiosity beckons me to read it, but I'm not sure I can handle what it will say about me. After struggling internally for ages, I decide it must be done. Still, it takes all the willpower I can muster to read the accompanying plaque:

For Several Moments Kiara Felt So Alive
As She Attempted Her Fatal Swan Dive
Total Lives Lost: 1

Swan Girl.

"But how did Gemma know?" I run back and forth down the hallway, searching for the obvious answer, but only the two tapestries exist.

She didn't die.

Then, the answer hits me. Since I didn't tell Gemma, there's only one person who could have. "Fred," I say through gritted teeth. He must've died the second time right after I did. "Whoever you are, I don't like you. Not one bit."

With fire in my heart, I storm back down the hallway. Luckily for the world, I'm all alone here. At the far end stand two wooden doors framed in black iron. A handwritten sign hangs from each door. The sign on the left door reads: "Lose All Points Earned In The Current Lesson And Start Again." The sign on the right door reads: "Ten Coins Will Preserve Your Points And Your Place In The Lesson."

"Head-up on." My stats appear. Under pending points, it says twenty-five, and I've yet to earn a single coin.   "Makes sense since I haven't accomplished anything but jumping off a cliff."

I grip the controller and imagine myself ripping it apart like Hulk. "Ugh! These can't be my only two options."

Despite having all my fingers and toes crossed, another glance of the environment verifies no third option to quit game school exists.

Gemma wins again.

I sigh. "I really thought death would be the end. I wish it hadn't been a lie."

A light appears to my left and fills the end of the hallway. A third door. It stands open about a foot.

I swallow hard. "That wasn't there a second ago..."

Is this my third option?

After a brief hesitation, I walk over to the open door and step inside. The light's so bright, I can't see a thing. "Hello? Is anyone here?"

An unfamiliar male voice fills the room and my head. "Death isn't the end. The end you fear is not the end that's real. In this place, truth will be revealed." His rich tone soothes my ears.

Then, somewhere beyond the open door, I hear a distant voice. "Kiara?"

My heart thrashes in my chest. I'd know that smug voice anywhere.

Dr. Von Schlippe!

Without a second thought, I retreat from the room. The door closes behind me, snuffing out the light and thrusting me back into the shadows beyond the reaches of the torchlight. As my eyes readjust, I see Dr. Von Schlippe striding toward me.

I step out of the shadows and into the middle of the hallway, blocking his path. "Dr. Von Schlippe? What are you doing here?"

He gazes beyond me, his brow furrowed. "Where were you?"

His harsh tone startles me and puts me on the defensive. "What do you mean? I've been right here."

Dr. Von Schlippe glares at me. "The six of us take turns watching you students play. You know that, right?"

Ms. Coates said as much on the first day. "I guess so."

"I saw a bright light appear on your monitor, and then the entire screen turned white. At first, I thought you'd logged off and the system had just frozen, but then I noticed that it still showed you as active. That should never happen, so I came at once to see for myself." He grabs my shoulder. Naturally, I don't feel it, but the gesture frightens me. "Now, tell me what you did."

"I didn't do anything."

He looks past me, his hand still anchored to my shoulder. "Where did the light come from?"

"I… I…" The words won't come out.

Dr. Von Schlippe releases my shoulder and sighs. "Look, I'm one of the people who designed this world. When something happens that shouldn't, it gets under my skin and irritates me. A virus in the system could jeopardize everything I've worked so hard to build. Does that make sense?"

My eyes trace the cracks between the tiles on the floor. "Yeah. Well, sorta."

"Look at me." I oblige, albeit with reluctance. "Despite what you think, I'm not mad at you. I promise." He pulls on the tuft of hair below his lower lip, making his lip curl down. "All I'm asking is that you walk me through everything that happened. Where did the light come from?"

What did happen?

"I'd never been here before, so I started out by examining the tapestries. After that, I walked down the hallway and to the two wooden doors behind me. I read the two signs and stood there while I tried to decide if I should pay to continue or start the level again and lose points."

"Start over," he says.

Was he not listening?

"As I said, I looked at the tapest—"

"No, Kiara. I was telling you what to do." He forces air through his nostrils. "Start the level over. You won't lose any points because you haven't gained any. Besides, you can't afford to pay the ten coins. Understand?"

Is he helping me?

I nod. "Yes."

"Good. Continue."

"Well, the next thing I know, an open door appears out of nowhere."

Dr. Von Schlippe paces, his fingers still plucking at the hair below his lip. "No, that's not possible. You must've done something to trigger it opening."

"I swear, I didn't do anything."

He stops and raises his arms. "Fine. I believe you." He pushes past me and walks to the end of the hallway. "So, where is this door of yours?"

It's not my door!

After a long, exaggerated sigh, I walk over to where the door appeared and point at the wall. "Right there."

Dr. Von Schlippe leans into the shadows. "I see nothing."

Neither do I, at least not at first. But then I notice a smaller brick protruding from the wall right about the height of a standard doorknob.

"Stand back," I say.

Dr. Von Schlippe takes a step back. "Found something?"

"Think so."

The faintest *click* sounds when I push on the brick. Then, a door-sized portion of the wall swings toward me. Blinding light pours from the opening, just as it had before.

Dr. Von Schlippe pushes me aside and touches the open door. "This shouldn't be here." He enters the room, so I follow him inside.

It takes several moments for my eyes to adjust to the light without a source. The small cavern lies empty, save the rock formation fashioned as a bench and the man who sits upon it. He leans forward, propping himself up with his elbows on top of his thighs. The man's shaggy brown hair and wild beard join at the jaw, making it impossible to know where one ends and the other begins. He's dressed in a white T-shirt, blue jeans, and a pair of red and white Converse sneakers.

Dr. Von Schlippe points a finger at the man. "You!"

The man stands and spreads his arms wide. "All are welcome, Frederick."

They exchange words, but my attention focuses on the man's forearms. More specifically, the two tattoos. His right forearm bears an image of a large spike, its pointed end at his wrist. Red letters run down its length, spelling the word "SINNER." A cross, oriented just like the spike, runs the length of his left forearm. Yellow letters form the word "FORGIVEN."

The cavern expands backward, pulling the man and his bench with it. No, that's not right. For some reason, I'm moving backward. Through the doorway and back into the Hall of the Dead. The door closes and takes its light with it. It's then that I notice Dr. Von Schlippe's hand on my shoulder. He must've pulled me out of the room, but why?

Dr. Von Schlippe turns and walks several steps before touching his right ear. When he turns around, he's stroking the hair below his lip again. Then, he looks right at me and says, "Sorry to bother you after hours, but we've got a problem." It takes me a moment to realize he's talking to someone else. Unfortunately, I can only hear his side of the conversation. "No, it's not something that can wait. ... It's a portal of some kind. ... I'd rather you see it for yourself. ... Yes, I understand." He nods. "Yes, ma'am. The Hall of the Dead."

He touches his right ear again. "Donna, I need you and Kris to run a virus scan on the code. And look for any anomalies."

A chasm of silence lies between us as we stand on opposite sides of the hallway and face the two doors. Finally, I say, "Am I in some kind of trouble?"

"Not yet," he grumbles.

What's that supposed to mean?

"But you said no earlier."

Dr. Von Schlippe glares at me but says nothing further.

Silence persists for an eternity before the sound of high heels ticking against the black slate floor breaks it once more. We both turn and watch Principal Cornier approach. It's the first time I've heard the footfall of someone else in the game. She must have some sort of special code enabled.

Principal Cornier towers over us both, a formidable woman. As with every other occasion, her avatar glitches now and again. She eyes Dr. Von Schlippe. "Well, where is this portal?"

Dr. Von Schlippe turns to me. "Show her."

I locate the small rock protruding from the wall and press it once again. The door opens, and I step back.

Dr. Von Schlippe says, "Take a peek, and you'll see the immediate issue."

Principal Cornier walks through the doorway, and the sound of her footfall ceases.

Strange.

A minute later, she steps back through the doorway. It closes behind her.

Dr. Von Schlippe pulls on his lip. "It's Gabe, isn't it?"

Who is Gabe?

Principal Cornier's facial expression reveals nothing, but a subtle change in her eyes tells me Dr. Von Schlippe is correct in his assessment. She glances at me and then addresses him. "This is not the time or the place for such a discussion."

His eyes shift to me. "Granted, but how would you like me to proceed?"

She crosses her arms, and her brow furrows. "Disable the portal and delete the code."

"It's not that simple." He sweeps his hand through his hair. "While we awaited your arrival, I had my team run a virus scan and start searching the code for anomalies. So far, they've come across nothing unusual."

Principal Cornier seethes. "As you can see, the door exists. Find the code and remove it. Am I clear?"

"Yes, I understand, and we will, but this will take considerable time. As I'm sure you're well aware, the system self-learns and changes its code constantly." He pulls on the tuft of hair below his lip. "What would you like me to do in the meantime?"

Principal Cornier glares at the man. "You worry about the code. I'll handle the rest." Her glare turns on me. "Do not breathe a word of what you saw in there to anyone, Kiara. Am I understood?"

I nod. "Yeah."

Her gaze hardens. "*Yes*, what?"

"Oh, right. Yes, ma'am."

"Good." She turns, walks down the hallway, and disappears.

Dr. Von Schlippe stares at the wall where the third door appeared. "The one on the left."

He must be talking with someone again.

"Well, don't just stand there." He turns and scowls at me. "Are you dense or deaf?"

"Oh, you're talking to me?"

He shakes his head and opens the door on the left. "Off with you."

"Right." I step through the doorway and back into the beginning of the game world.

A female voice says, "Zero points deducted."

"I guess Dr. Von Schlippe was right." I power down my visor and slip it off. "Artie, what time is it?"

"The time is 4:57 pm."

Four minutes later, I have Roger on voice chat.

"What's up?" he asks.

"You're not going to believe what just happened to me in the game." I dive right in. "So, I was walking through the Hall of the Dead and came up to two doors. One takes your points and the other costs coins to continue your lesson. Anyway, I really wanted a third option, and then a third door appeared. It was already open, and a bright light spilled out of it. When I went in, the light blinded me. I heard a voice speak to me, but then Dr. Von Schlippe showed up."

"Whoa," Roger says.

I continue, "We went in together and there was a man in there. I've never seen him before, but Dr. Von Schlippe recognized him and was clearly perturbed. We exited the room and he called Principal Cornier. She came and checked it out. Afterward, she pretended that it was no big deal, but I could tell she was really upset. They both said it was a virus. She told Dr. Von Schlippe to fix it and me to keep it from everyone."

"Are you going to go back?" Roger asks.

"I dunno. Maybe, but not this week. You should see it for yourself before it's gone."

"No way," Roger says. "I don't want to lose my points or coins, and, if it really is a virus, I don't want to be accused of spreading it."

"Aren't you curious though? A mysterious guy in a hidden room?"

"Did the guy have a name?" Roger asks.

"Dr. Von Schlippe called him Gabe, and it clearly upset Principal Cornier. I think—"

"Hold on." Roger looks over his shoulder. "I need to go. We can talk about it at lunch tomorrow." He smiles. "See you then?"

"Like clockwork."

The next morning, the entire school files into the gymnasium for a special announcement from Principal Cornier. Most students gossip about what the announcement might be, but Roger and I already know. Once everyone settles in, the lights fade, save a single spotlight centered over a podium in the middle of the room. Principal Cornier walks out of the darkness and into the light, stepping up to the podium. Whispered conversations cut off abruptly when she raises her hand and mutes us all.

We're nothing but puppets in her world.

After a brief silence, she addresses the room. "Students, faculty, and staff. Good morning. An issue has been brought to my attention that must be addressed without delay. As some of you are aware, a computer virus has been discovered lurking about in the game world."

No one can be seen sitting in the shadows, but I imagine many of their faces wear looks of shock and horror. From what Roger told me, a virus can damage code and destroy the game world if not dealt with. Even though I'm warming up to this game school, I can't say that I'd be sad to see it go. Then again, the alternative would be far worse. In-person school.

Maybe I should be concerned.

Principal Cornier pauses to let her words sink. During this time, her avatar glitches several times. I don't understand why her avatar seems to be the only one that does.

I'll have to ask Roger about it.

Finally, she continues, "When a student dies, they are taken to the Hall of the Dead. At the end of this hall, a portal to a forbidden area of the game has opened up." She leans forward, eying each of us simultaneously. "Fear not, darlings. I assure you that Dr. Von Schlippe and his team will work around the clock in order to disable the portal and eliminate the rogue code. At no point will you be in danger as long as you avoid interacting with the portal. However, take heed to what I'm about to say."

Her fingernails dig into the podium. Green this time instead of red. "Any student caught accessing this off-limits area will be reprimanded and will face severe punishment. This punishment will include but not be limited to the following: a three-week suspension from school, a loss of all coins earned, and a deduction of points. The number of points deducted will be determined on a case-by-case basis."

She glares at us once more. "I warn you all, do not make an example of yourself. You will live to regret it."

Her glare morphs into a wicked grin. "Thank you for your cooperation in this matter. Have a pleasant day."

The spotlight fades, and the lights come back up. As usual, she's gone. Chatter fills the room. From what I can glean, most of it surrounds the question of who discovered the virus. Roger looks at me and mouthes, "Your secret's safe with me."

But what if Gemma finds out?

CHAPTER THIRTEEN

CURVE BALL

LIFE IN NEW EDEN stinks compared with Podunk, but my chats with Grams each week help tremendously. It's not the same as being in person where she can wrap me in her arms the way I love her to do, though. Her calming perfume doesn't transfer across video, either.

I miss Robin too, but we haven't spoken in a few weeks. The last time we did, she gave me the impression that she's begun to move on. Every other sentence out of her mouth revolved around some new girl named Brittney. "She's so funny and smart, and everyone loves her," Robin had said.

Blech!

Our falling out stings a lot, but I don't blame her. We haven't seen each other in months, and there's no chance of me returning to Podunk anytime soon—if ever. On the bright side, I still have my Princess Sparkles. She'll never leave me.

With five and a half weeks of school under my belt, I'm starting to get the hang of playing games. But then Olive throws us a curve ball straight out of the gates in social studies class.

"Listen up, class. Starting next week and recurring every other week, you will work in groups on Thursdays and Fridays."

The entire class sighs. Or at least that's what I imagine happens. Why would they do this to us? That's the question I'd like an answer to.

As though reading my thoughts, Olive continues, "Yes, I know, you'd all rather work alone, but saving the world is not an individual task. Would mankind have ever reached the moon if no one worked together? Of course not! Remember our goals, children. We are headed to Mars and beyond. But only with group effort.

"In light of this, and true to life in the real world, your groups will be auto-assigned. Also, you will remain with the same group for the duration of the school year. You may not recall, but Principal Cornier mentioned a year-end competition with the other two schools in New Eden. The group with the most points at the end of the year will represent CEVR Academy. Strive to be that group. Not only will it give you pride in your efforts, but it will also look good on your future resumes."

The woman sounds just like Mom. All I want to do is get through sixth grade and find a way back to Podunk.

Olive steps out from behind her desk. "When I call your name, please stand and head to the front of the classroom, next to me."

After she calls the first three names, it becomes apparent that each group will consist of three individuals. By the time she gets through eighteen of the twenty-four students in our class, I realize that neither Roger, Gemma, nor I have been called yet.

It starts in my toes. An itchy, nervous energy.

"Roger Daltrey," Olive says. Roger stands and walks over to Olive.

The feeling crawls into my calves. Shins. Slinks beneath my kneecaps.

Please, please, please. Put me with Roger.

Moments pass like hours as we all anticipate the next name. Agonizing. Brutal.

My thighs burn with a need to be scratched.

Finally, Olive says, "Kiara Kole."

Thank the stars!

A swarm of butterflies flutter in my stomach as I rise and head to the front of the class. Roger smiles. I offer him a weak smile before turning and facing the class. Gemma's glare sears my face. Her lips move with a snarl. "She picks me, and you're dead."

Sitting at the desk in my room, I cross my fingers, toes, arms, legs, and anything else that can be crossed.

Anyone but Gemma! I repeat the words in my head without relent.

The itch that started in my toes has found its way into my chest. Up my neck. Across my cheeks. Every inch of me burns and itches with nervous energy.

Olive's gaze turns toward Gemma. Drums thunder in my ears, my pulse elevated to a dangerous level. She speaks, but her words get lost in the fray.

What did she say!

Gemma shifts in her seat.

She's about to rise.

No!

Bile rises in my throat as my world executes a polar flip. Swallowing it back down, I close my eyes and curl forward in my chair, the worst situation of my entire life at hand.

Why is this happening, Grams?

"Driver Bennett, did you not hear me?" Olive says.

My eyelids spring open and I sit up straight.

Driver Bennett?

A black boy with short, curly hair stands and moves to the front of the class, joining Roger and me.

The fire beneath my skin subsides, and my world begins to right itself once more.

"You last three are together," Olive says, pointing to Gemma and two other girls. It's no surprise the two girls are part of Gemma's entourage. I should've guessed it.

After a brief lesson on Columbus and his voyage to the New World, the bell rings for lunch. As with every day, Roger joins me at our virtual cafeteria table. It's still our table, as no one else has been brave enough to cross Gemma and her hags.

Roger starts in without a moment's pause, "Hey, I asked Driver if he wanted to eat with us, but he already has his own friends. I just thought it might be good for us to get to know each other since we'll be working together. He said he already has friends and prefers to eat with them. I guess that's okay. Are you okay with it, or should I go find him and insist he join us?"

"It's not your job to fix everything, Roger. Besides, do you blame him?"

"What do you mean?" He doesn't wait for an answer. "Oh… Gemma. Right. She really is a problem, isn't she? At least we didn't get her in our group. Could you imagine how bad that would've been?"

Gemma walks by the table. "Never would've happened, losers." She stops about ten feet from our table and faces us. "Hey, everyone, can I have your attention?"

Roger and I share a look. "This can't be good," I mutter.

Roger's eyebrows rise. "The only power she has is her mouth."

The buzz of conversations falls away until we all sit in perfect silence, the entire room focused on Gemma. "Good." Gemma's arms extend out in front of her, and her fingers move rapidly. I've yet to find a button on the controller that would make those movements. Must be some verbal command.

Or maybe it's that artifact she found...

Gemma grins. "Why are you all looking at me? I'm not the one who wore my pajamas to school today!" She points right at our table.

Turning to Roger, I say, "What is she—"

Roger's school uniform morphs into pajamas featuring trains with faces right before my eyes, leaving my mouth agape and me without words. The entire cafeteria erupts with laughter. Roger doesn't seem to notice the change.

"Look at your clothes," I say to Roger.

He looks at himself. "Yeah, they're kinda cool, actually." His head cocks to the right and he frowns at me. "Are those really what you wear to bed?"

"Huh?" Looking down at myself, Roger's question becomes clear.

Farm animals. Should've guessed.

I yell at Roger, "Does it matter?"

Fresh tears sting my eyes. *Why do I have to put up with her?*

Roger stands up and walks straight over to Gemma. "This is the best you could do? Trains and Old MacDonald? You're far less smart than I thought. That manipulator artifact could've been used in so many better ways."

"Trust me, it was worth it," says Gemma.

"An afternoon in pajamas? Please."

"Don't be so naive, Nerd Boy. You and Swan Girl get to wear those outfits for an entire week."

"Ooh! So what?" He moves closer, right into her personal space. "You have to wear that face your entire life."

Did he really just say that!

Were I not sitting, I would've fallen to my knees. As is, I wish I could crawl underneath the table and protect myself from the nuclear fallout.

Smoke pours from Gemma's mouth, nose, and ears. At least that's what I imagine happens when her face turns three shades of purple. "Consider yourself dead," she snarls. Her wrath turns toward me. "Both of you."

"Not a chance," Roger says.

Gemma walks away. "With me, girls!" Her entourage falls in step with her as they march through the cafeteria, each glaring at Roger before exiting.

Driver gets up from his table and walks over to Roger. "Dang, bro. I can't believe you burned Gemma like that in front of everyone."

Roger smiles. "She deserved it."

"Maybe, but still. I'd hate to be either one of you right now." He shakes his head and walks off.

Dread seeps into my veins. Fills me to the point of overflowing. Twists my stomach in knots.

What have you done to us, Roger?

Roger returns to the table and just stares at me. Finally, I say, "What?"

"It's just not what I pictured you wearing to sleep in." His cheeks turn beet-red. "Wow, that didn't come out right at all. It's just… you seem more sophisticated than barn animals."

Roger's response to our situation triggers a thought. "Hold on a minute. Are you telling me that you *do* wear train pajamas?"

He grins. "Used to. I moved on to *Star Wars* a few months back. Finn's my favorite. What about you?"

This conversation isn't for the school cafeteria, or anywhere else, for that matter. "Can we talk about something else?"

"Sure, groupie." He looks toward the ceiling for a moment. "Hey, where do you live? I mean, you obviously live in New Eden and one of the CEVR Academy districts, but which one? One, three, five, seven, or eleven? I live in seven. The best one, I think. Prime numbers are cool, right?"

"Um… I don't really know anything about districts. The building we live in is at 6492 Sky Harbor."

"What!" Roger's head swivels, his eyes wide. "Sorry, didn't mean to shout, but that's my address, too!"

I shake my head. "Pfft. You're just saying that."

His eyes grow big. "No, it's true. We live on the fifth floor."

"I've met the woman who lives on the fifth floor…" It takes a moment, but her name finally comes to me. "Pamela."

"Yes! That's my mom."

"But… I don't understand. How can she be your mom?"

Roger scowls. "What do you mean?"

There's no way around it, so I just blurt it out, "She's a black woman and you're not black."

"Oh, right." He nods. "She's technically my step-mom, but I never knew my real mom. My real mom died about a year after I was born. Kidney failure. It devastated my dad. Took two years for him to get past her death. That's when he met my mom, Pamela, at a little league game for my older brother,

Jeff. She was at the game watching one of her nephews play. They struck up a conversation at the game and got married six months later."

"Wow. That's quite a story."

"Yeah, so…" Roger stares at me for several seconds. "I'm kinda having this party on Sunday. Would… would you like to come?"

"Party for what?"

His gaze falls to the table. "Nothing special. It's just my birthday."

"Oh. Expecting a lot of people?"

"Besides my family?" His head lowers. "One… that is, if you come."

Given how friendly Roger seems, his answer socks me right in the gut.

He's just like me.

"Assuming my parents approve, I'll be there, groupie."

Roger's eyes glisten in the light when he raises his head. "I'd really like that. But don't come because you feel sorry for me. I'm not looking for charity. I've flown solo for the past eleven years, so it's no big deal. Really, it's not."

"Sounds like it's time to break that streak. I'll be there, Roger. Promise."

He smiles. "Thanks. 1 pm. We'll have plenty of food, so come hungry."

Vida notifies us that fifth period will start in five minutes. I jump up. "See you in class."

"Yeah, okay. See you there," Roger says.

My hands tremble as I navigate myself through the halls and toward Technologies class. I know virtually nothing about Roger, and it scares me. How am I supposed to meet him in person?

The end of my world—my pathetic life—stares me right in the face. How can I stay in New Eden and survive with Gemma stalking me? What can I do?

I need you, Grams. More than ever.

CHAPTER FOURTEEN

A WAD OF WORMS

A WAD OF WORMS squirm in the pit of my stomach as I stand outside Roger's front door. Fingertips drum against white plaster, millimeters away from the rounded edge of the doorbell button. Pressing it terrifies me. Commits me to a task I'm not sure I can manage. But it's more than that. So much more.

We've known each other for a little more than a month now, but only in the virtual world. From what I've gleaned watching television, people are never what they seem once you meet them in person.

Grams once said, "First impressions can never be made twice." No words have ever been truer.

What will Roger think of me? Of what I'm wearing? Or the gift I've brought for him?

Looking down at the wrapped package in my other hand fills my head with doubts and fear. The last thing I want to do is give Roger the wrong impression. I'm not looking for a boyfriend. I don't think he's looking for a girlfriend, either.

But he did say that I was pretty.

My stomach gurgles. Why does life have to be so difficult? I look back at the three Personal Transport Beam plates on the floor. They beckon me. Until the doorbell is rung, I still have a chance to turn around and go back home. As tempting as it is, part of me knows it would be wrong. Okay, all of me. I promised Roger I'd come. If I'm only as good as my word, then I'd be no good at all tucking tail and heading back downstairs. I'd never be able to face him again. No, I will make an appearance, give him his gift, and then make an excuse to leave. A perfect plan. My brain's on board, but my heart pulls me in another direction.

A friend would be nice. Even if he's a boy.

Undeniable truth. Not only that, but what would Mom and Dad think if I returned home so fast? Both of them encouraged me to come. Said it would be good to get to know some of my classmates. Stuck here in New Eden for the foreseeable future, what do I have to lose?

Everything.

Holding my breath for unknown reasons, I mash the doorbell button in and step back. Nausea ripples through me. A single pebble tossed into a placid lake. A few seconds pass. Then a few more. Each one ratchets up the tension in my shoulders.

Maybe I got the wrong day or time.

Then, another twisted, evil, self-loathing thought enters my mind.

Am I the butt of some sick joke?

My lip quivers. *No, Roger would never do that to me.*

Would he?

Light filters through the doorway as the door begins to disintegrate. Moments later, a young boy stands before me. He's a foot shorter than me and scrawnier than I'd imagined.

Roger's eyes light up and a grin spreads across his face. "Hey, you made it!"

Nerves get the better of me, and I thrust the gift at his chest. "Here."

He takes the gift and waves me inside. "Come on in. We're grilling burgers out back."

Just then, the smell hits my nostrils. It's not vile, but it's not beef, either. Trust me, a girl from Texas knows the smell of seared beef. I hold my tongue and step inside.

Roger laughs. "I had the same look the first time my mom made burgers for us."

My cheeks go from cool to inferno in an instant. "I... Um... I..."

"Believe me, you'll forget the difference in smell after the first juicy bite. You know, my mom's a scientist. She works with organic matter. Her job is to create foods that are both sustainable and can be mass-produced in space or on other planets. What you're smelling is synthetic beef." He smiles. "At least that's what I call it."

I nod as we walk through the living room. The layout of their home matches that of ours, but the decor and furniture have an African vibe whereas ours is more modern. So many bright colors—oranges, yellows, greens, and reds. Mom would never approve. "So, your mom works at GIST?"

"Of course. Doesn't everyone?" Roger sets the gift on the dining room table, next to two others.

I'm not the only one who came?

My palms begin to sweat. "I suppose so. Both my parents do."

He leads us toward the open doors at the back of the house. "I'm gonna work there one day, too."

"I'm sure you will."

We step through the doors and into a massive outdoor kitchen. A tall man stands at an open grill, his back toward us. He wears some sort of chef's hat, and the white ties at his back and around the back of his neck indicate he's wearing an apron. Mrs. Daltrey lies face-down on a sun chair at the foot of a massive pool. Her yellow bikini matches some of the decor from inside.

An older boy, lean, muscular, and taller than Roger, stands on the edge of a diving board at the far end of the pool. Blue-and-red shorts drape to his knees, but he's shirtless. He jumps up, bounces once, and completes a forward flip before going into the water feet-first.

"That's my brother I told you about. Jeff. We look alike in the face but nowhere else. Dad says Jeff got all the athleticism and I got all the smarts. I enjoy being smart, but I would've been fine with a little more balance in the doling out of genes." He pulls an inhaler from his pocket and sucks down some sort of medication. "Sorry about that. Being outside gets the better of me sometimes, so I use my inhaler frequently just to be safe."

I look around. "We're not really outside though, right?"

"Yes and no. To be certain, we're surrounded by walls and a ceiling of nanites, but they're breathable. I.e., the outside air moves freely through them. That's what give us the warmth and the gentle breeze. It's also what permits allergens. It's okay, though. I haven't had an attack in almost a year now. Just precaution. My dad is working on several projects to cure ailments like allergies and asthma. He's a real genius."

"That's right, son." I nearly jump out of my skin when Mr. Daltrey appears at my side, his hand proffered. "I'm Roger's dad. You can call me Dad if you'd like to, or Teddy will do fine."

I'm not really a hand-shaking kind of girl, but the man's left me with little choice. His soft hand swallows mine and squeezes it tight. "Kiara Kole," I manage without grunting.

"A pleasure." He lets go and then rubs Roger's head. "We've heard all about you. You're practically family, now."

Roger groans. "Dad, you're embarrassing me."

Teddy smiles. "No need to be shy, son. She's a pretty girl. Just as you said."

Never in the history of the world has anyone ever turned as white as Roger does. He'd give a ghost a run for their money right about now. With a sense of lightheadedness, I'm inclined to think I share in his terror and lack of blood to the brain.

Mrs. Daltrey rolls onto her side and looks over at us. "Ah, Kiara. It's so good to see you again."

"Hello, Mrs. Daltrey."

"Please, call me Pamela. I insist."

"Yes, ma'am."

Jeff pulls himself out of the pool and walks over to us. Water streaks his face and puddles at his feet. "Kiara, right?" He sweeps his hand across the top of his head, flicking water everywhere.

"That's right." I wipe my face with the back of my hand.

"Oh, sorry about that." Jeff chuckles. "Didn't think that one through."

"It's okay. A little water never hurt anyone."

"Not true," Roger says.

He and Jeff say, "Tell that to the wicked witch of the west!" in unison. Then, they bump fists and make exploding noises, indicating their hands have exploded upon impact.

I shake my head and then laugh.

"Glad you showed up," Jeff says. He offers me his fist. I oblige and pound it with my own, but without the theatrics of an explosion. "A friend of Roger's is a friend of mine."

"Thanks."

Jeff grabs a towel off the back of one of the chairs that sits around the patio table and wipes his face before heading inside. A trail of wet footprints marks his path.

Roger shakes his head. "He never thinks to towel off his feet first."

After a delicious meal of synthetic burgers and homegrown sweet potato fries, the five of us head inside and gather around the dining room table for mint chocolate chip ice cream and chocolate cake. Both sans dairy and made by Pamela. Roger and I both down seconds on the cake. Jeff doubles down on everything.

Once Pamela clears the dishes (she insists on completing the task without help), Roger opens the present from his parents. It's some sort of robotics kit called Rover 2047. Roger beams with joy and thanks his parents several times before settling back down in his chair. Seeing him so excited makes me giddy.

The second present comes from Jeff. Roger tears through the wrapping paper. "No way, no way, no way!"

Jeff pumps his fist. "Totally, bro!"

Roger stands, extracts a pair of gray and white gloves from the shredded box, and holds them up. "I can't believe you got these for me! They're like two hundred bucks!"

Two hundred dollars for a pair of gloves?

"Two-twenty." Jeff drums the table with his fingers.

Roger plops back down in his chair. "I… I can't take these."

"Sure you can, bro." Jeff reaches over and grasps Roger's shoulder. "Lighten up. Mom and Dad helped with the bill. Besides, you'll need them for school next year. In the meantime, building robots will be a whole lot gnarlier!"

I don't understand what the gloves have to do with school, but I'm not about to ask and look like a complete idiot. As is, I'm dreading Roger opening my gift. I wish I hadn't brought one.

Roger slides the last gift to the edge of the table in front of him. *My* gift. Compared with the last two, it's small and wrapped in real paper. Baby blue with a darker blue ribbon wrapped around its four edges.

Quaint, like me.

"This one's from Kiara," Roger says.

"Oh!" Pamela winks at me.

The room falls silent as all eyes focus on the package. My throat tightens as Roger unties the bow and slips the ribbon off. Then, he gingerly slides his finger along the crease in the paper, breaking through the clear tape but not damaging the paper. He possesses the hands and skills of a surgeon.

Pulling the folds apart, he exposes the book within. His eyes glisten as they scan the cover of the hardback book. "2084: Artificial Intelligence and the Future of Humanity…" He looks up at me. "How did you know I've been wanting to read this?"

I shrug. "You said you loved robotics and AI, so it seemed appropriate."

Roger removes his glasses and rubs his eyes. "Thank you all so much. This has been the best birthday ever."

We all wish him a happy birthday again.

Roger stands and places the book underneath his arm. "Mom, can I show Kiara my room and my robots?"

"Sure, hon."

Back home in Podunk, being alone with a boy in any room was forbidden. Here in New Eden, every room can be monitored with a simple voice command. Not that it's needed with Roger and me.

We head up to his room. Without prior experience, I assume it's a typical boy's room. Robots and action figures of all shapes and sizes line dozens of shelves. Most of them remain in their original boxes. I've never understood why someone would buy a toy just to have it sit in its box on a shelf, never to be played with. Seems like a waste to me, but what do I know?

After an hour of robot wrestling and death matches using some of the robots Roger built, we head downstairs and back outside. Beyond the pool stands a massive oak tree. High within its branches I spot a structure.

I point at the tree. "Is that a tree house?"

"Only the best. Wanna go check it out?"

"Climbing trees is kinda my thing." I take off toward the tree.

Like a bear, I attack the tree, climbing, grunting, and scraping my way up the trunk and into its sprawling branches. Roger loads himself into a small cage below and uses a pulley system to raise himself up to the tree house. His method proves far quicker but takes the fun out of climbing.

Roger opens a trapdoor beneath the tree house and offers me a hand up when I reach it. Once inside, we sit down at a small table, facing each other.

"Now what?" I say, a little out of breath.

Roger leans forward and props his head on his hands. "Now that we're alone, do you want to tell me what's wrong?"

I look away, pretending to scope out the place. "What do you mean?"

"You're not quite you today."

Facing him, I offer my best smile. "I'm fine. Besides, it's your birthday. The last thing you want to do is talk about me."

"Not true. You're my friend, Kiara. You can tell me anything."

"Really?"

"Yes, and I'll do my best to listen and not talk constantly like I always do."

"I died in the game."

"Really? What happened?"

"I... kinda jumped off a cliff."

"On accident?"

"Not exactly."

"Why? What's wrong? Is it Gemma? No, don't answer that. I already know it is. Ugh. She can be so evil."

"I thought they'd send me back home."

"What do you mean?"

"Even though she lied to me about what would happen if I died in the game, Gemma's right. I don't belong here. I'm not a city girl, and I know nothing about technology or games or anything."

"But you can learn."

"I'm not so sure. I'll wind up doing something to end the world, not save it."

"Don't say that. I've seen how smart you are. With a little help, you'll outshine us all."

"But what if we can't save the world?"

"Have faith in humanity. Despite the odds, we will outlive the cockroaches."

I snort. "Everyone knows that's not true."

"You know what else isn't true?"

"What?"

"That you don't belong here."

"Why is that?"

"Because I needed a friend, and you came along. If you leave, I'll be alone again."

"What are you talking about? Everyone likes you."

"It's a ruse, Kiara. Admit it, I'm not the kid you know in the virtual world. I'm awkward and goofy and suffer from diarrhea of the mouth."

"That last part is true in both worlds—" I wink at him. "—and that's one of the things I like about you."

"You're just saying that."

"Never." I lean across the table and hug Roger. "Happy birthday, my friend."

"Thanks."

After a brief swim, Roger and I exchange info so we can video chat, and then I say goodbye to him and his family and head back down to my house.

Dad catches me on the way in. "Someone's in a good mood."

"Am I?" No matter how hard I try, I can't hide my smile.

He pulls me into a bear hug. "I've missed this girl so much. Good to have you back, Little Bear."

"I've only been gone for the afternoon."

"Just so?" He feigns a frown. "Feels like it's been weeks."

"Love you, Dad."

He groans when I squeeze him tighter. "Love you back."

Princess Sparkles greets me at the back door. Outside, we roll around in the grass together. For once in a long time, my heart overflows with joy.

Best day here.

CHAPTER FIFTEEN

THE BAT CAVE

THURSDAY MORNING, ROGER AND I meet at the start of the bridge behind the main school building. Driver's supposed to be here too, but he's nowhere to be found. It's not like him to be late for anything, especially a game day.

Roger looks around. "Maybe Driver's having technical issues."

"I don't think that's the issue," I say.

He frowns at me. "Then what do you think it is?"

"Look at us." I chuckle. "He probably doesn't want to be seen anywhere near us while we're still in pajamas."

"Huh." He nods his head slowly. "Yeah, hadn't thought about that."

"Well, we are the talk of the school."

Roger chuckles. "Uh, yeah, I guess so. Maybe we should just start without him."

Typical Roger. We still have three minutes before the school day officially begins. That's at least seven minutes late in Roger's book, though.

"Fine," I say.

We walk over to the middle of the bridge and into the mist, as usual, but then we're immediately yanked out of the mist and back onto the bridge. An audible and visual message reprimands us. "Warning: Groups must cross over to the game world together. If a member of your group is sick or unable to attend the session, please contact the school office immediately by saying 'school office.' If you find this message in error, say 'help' and one of your teachers will assist you."

"Guess we wait," I say.

Three minutes later, Driver joins us on the bridge. "Ready to do this?"

Roger glares at Driver. "You're late."

"On time, bro." He looks Roger and me up and down and chuckles. "Besides, I seem to be the only one who got dressed this morning before coming to school."

"Funny," I say. In a way, it kinda is.

Roger steps up to the mist. "Let's go."

Driver and I follow suit, and then the three of us enter the mist together. On the other side, the overgrown wall with seven doors still stands before us, but there is one noticeable change. Each of us has a ring of pulsating white light around our waist. Additional strands of white light connect us to each other.

"Ugh. I hate tethered games," Driver says.

Roger catches the blank look on my face. "These light ropes will prevent us from splitting up and performing tasks on our own."

Okay, we're tethered together.

"Right," I say. "Makes sense as this is a group challenge."

The three of us enter the sixth-grade door and step onto the path surrounded by golden fields. A raven-haired ostrich stands before us, towering over the three of us by at least three feet. Amber eyes take us in, and its triangular-shaped, gray beak turns up at the corners of its mouth in a smile. Brown robes flow from its neck, covering all but its wings and feet. It clutches a gnarled staff with its right wing and holds a tome underneath its left.

"Hello, dearies. My name is Ollie Ostrich, and I'll be your guide. Welcome to your group challenge." Her voice has an ethereal quality. "As you may well know, your group task for the duration of the school year will be to work together to create a biodome or fallout shelter. It will need to be big enough to protect yourselves and several of the inhabitants of this world from the impending doom of the asteroid, should the laser fail to repel or destroy it.

"As you complete tasks, new ones will become available. Some tasks will be required to continue on, while others might be optional. Some tasks will become unselectable depending on other tasks you've chosen or completed. Think of it like a choose your own adventure. When you need a new task or a different path, just call my name and I'll be there in a flash.

"During group sessions, you'll be able to see the list of tasks and requirements on your heads-up display. If they are not visible, just say 'view task list,' and it will come into focus. Any questions thus far?"

The three of us look to each other and shake our heads.

"Good. As such, your first task will be to locate a suitable location for your biodome or fallout shelter."

"What's the difference between the two?" Driver asks.

Ollie bobs her head. "That is a fair question. A biodome will be an aboveground structure made of glass. It will help protect from air pollutants caused by the asteroid strike and will allow food to be grown even when sunlight is diminished. However, it will not protect from a direct or near-direct asteroid strike.

"Now, a fallout shelter will be constructed of wood and metal and will be located underground within a cave, cavern, or perhaps even an abandoned mine. This type of structure will protect occupants from a near-direct hit and potentially from a direct hit depending on its location. Food production might be more difficult to manage in a fallout shelter."

I look at Ollie. "Which do you think is better?"

"Both will provide adequate shelter and will require a vast amount of work and resources, so the choice is up to you." She raises a feather like one would a finger. "Remember, you're competing against all the other groups in the school, and one factor that will go into your final score includes the location you select for your build."

"How many inhabitants must we be prepared for?" Roger asks.

"Including yourselves, the number you must provide shelter for is fifty."

"Whoa," Driver says. "That makes my stomach hurt thinking about it."

Roger grimaces. "Mine, too."

"Which would you choose?" I ask.

Ollie scowls at me, and her nostrils flare. "As I said before, I will guide you along your chosen path, but I will never make a decision for you." Her scowl fades. "Remember this as well: not all options and paths are the right ones. As with a choose your own adventure book, some will cost you time and energy, some will cost you monetarily, and some will cost you your lives. Use caution as you work your way toward the final goal, and never forget to have fun."

My stomach gurgles. *No pressure.*

"Any other questions?" Ollie asks.

None of us have any. At least not ones to be voiced.

"No?" Ollie bobs her head. "Very well. As I said before, if you need me, just say my name." She raises her staff and slams it into the ground. A ferocious wind gathers around her like a cyclone and twists her out of existence.

Driver leaps into the air. "Now that's what I call an exit!"

Roger's smile quickly fades as he enters business mode. He looks at Driver. "We need to lay down some basic rules. Otherwise, we'll never accomplish anything."

"Agreed," I say. "What do you have in mind?"

"Want to be our navigator?" Roger asks, still eying Driver.

Driver smiles and nods. "Never thought you'd ask. Pulling up the map now."

"What would you like me to do?" I ask.

Roger doesn't hesitate before answering. "Keep an eye on the task list and keep us on track. Also, make sure we have or obtain all the materials necessary for each task. Anything else like that."

"Got it... and how do I do that?"

Driver glares at me. "Weren't you listening to Ollie?" He shakes his head. "Issue the command to view the task list."

Roger adds, "If you don't know how to do something or what commands are available, just say 'command list,' and it will come up on your heads-up display."

Would've been good to know that a few weeks ago.

"Got it," I say. "View task list."

My heads-up display turns on, and a task list with one item comes up. The item says, "Select a structure type." Below the item is a line with a bracket, like the neck and shoulders of a stick figure. I remember reading somewhere that what I'm viewing is called a flow diagram. The left side of the flow diagram says "biodome," and the right side says "fallout shelter."

"What's first on the list?" Roger asks me.

"We need to decide what type of structure to build."

"A biodome would be cool," Driver says. "That way, we can watch the asteroid impact."

"And what if we take a direct hit?" Roger asks. "Would a glass dome hold up?"

Driver wrinkles his face and nods. "Good point. Might be a risk right from the start."

"Exactly." Roger looks at me. "I say we find a cavern or cave and build a fallout shelter."

"I agree with Roger." Immediately, the flow diagram disappears, and the words "fallout shelter" appear next to "Select a structure type." A new task appears beneath the first. "We've got another task. It says, 'Select a location.'"

"Hold on a sec…" Driver's nostrils flare as he stares straight ahead. He must be studying the map, but I can't see it. "I remember talking to this parrot in a village just outside Sumerian Summit. She mentioned something about an abandoned mine shaft… Yes, here it is. Silvertown."

Driver disappears. Then Roger. The world jerks and rocks, and then the golden meadow blurs until everything is just smudges of dark colors. After a moment, the world comes back into view, but we're no longer standing in the meadow. Instead, we're standing in the middle of a small village nestled between two rocky peaks.

My head spins. "What just happened?"

"Driver's the navigator," Roger says. "When he said the name of the village aloud, it transported us there."

"Pretty awesome, huh," Driver says.

"Maybe if I'd been prepared for it. I feel like I just stepped off a boat." Air bubbles rise in my throat and gurgle in the back of my mouth.

"Did you just burp?" Roger asks.

Driver laughs. "I don't recommend barfing with your VR visor on. Heard one kid did and couldn't get the smell out of it. They finally had to order a new VR visor."

The visual leaves me squirming. "Gross!"

Roger clears his throat. "Let's concentrate, guys."

"Right." Driver walks over to a mud hut with a pitched grass roof. Roger and I get dragged along because of the tether.

The hut's door stands open, so the three of us shuffle inside. An old brown bear sits on the floor in the middle of the room with its legs crossed and its head resting against its chest. A woven green shawl hangs off its shoulders and down its back, coiling on the floor. A massive necklace with dozens of strands of rainbow-colored beads hangs from its neck. Another necklace outlines the first and sports long, yellow teeth. The two necklaces cover most of its furry chest and torso.

In the far corner of the hut, a red parrot sits atop a rickety old stand made of tree branches. The bird eyes us and bobs its head. Then, it speaks. "Welcome, travelers. Brawk! The name's Paulie. Paulie Parrot. Brawk! Have you come for a tale as old as creation?"

"We're looking for the abandoned mine," Driver says.

"Hear that, Barney Bear?" Paulie bobs her head again. "It's treasure they seek. Fancy yourselves getting rich?" The old bear remains still as a statue.

"Keep your silver," Roger says. "We're trying to save the world."

"Brawk! Lofty aspirations for a colony of three."

Driver says, "Point us in the right direction."

"Answer questions three, and on the map it shall be. Brawk!"

"Easy," Roger says.

Barney stirs and raises his head a few inches, revealing a plump face wrinkled with age. "Four such groups have gone before, and four such groups are no more."

Is that a riddle?

Barney looks right at me with milky-white eyes that can't possibly see. "Kiara Kole."

Chills hit me in waves. "Y-yes?"

"One plus one is likely two, the number of monkeys heading for the lake. But then they come across a snake. Not just one, but ten for each, and each carries a backpack full of lizards. Three lizards to every snake, and seven snakes will pack a bag. How many individuals will reach the lake?"

Butterflies tickle the insides of my stomach, their wings beating with fury. I glance at Roger and then Driver. Neither return my gaze. "Me?" The word squeaks from my lips.

Barney smiles a toothless smile. "They know nothing of what I've said, for it's all gone straight into your head. The question is for you, and you alone. Answer it true, or you'll go back home."

Why math?

"Give me a minute."

Barney scoops up a stick and begins whittling away at it with a knife he retrieves from a pouch on a belt I hadn't noticed before. "You may take all the time you like, but only until the hour's strike."

My heads-up display says it's five till eleven. It also shows me the math problem. My first thought is to yell at the old bear and tell him I'm only eleven and the problem's too hard, but that would just waste time. So, I begin at the end and work my way backward.

"Seven snakes will pack a bag… That means seven snakes will fit in a backpack. Three lizards to every snake." I bite my lower lip. "Each snake has three lizards?"

My brain already hurts. "Ugh. Let's see… Two monkeys. That's definite. Then there's the snake. No, there are ten for each monkey. Twenty snakes.

Each snake has a back—"

I take a deep breath and step through the words once again. "Each refers to the monkeys, not the snakes. So, two monkeys each have a backpack full of lizards. Seven snakes will fit in a bag. But how many lizards are there?"

Then, it hits me. "Duh! Three lizards equals one snake. So, seven times three is… twenty-one! Twenty-one lizards and two monkeys and twenty snakes." I scratch my head. "No, twenty-one lizards for each monkey. That's… forty-two! Forty-two plus twenty is sixty-two. Plus two monkeys is sixty-four."

"What say you?" Barney asks.

"The answer is six—" My gaze settles on the last sentence and its last three words.

Reach the lake.

I quickly scan the paragraph again.

"Answer now, or fail," the old bear growls.

The snakes aren't headed to the lake!

"Sixty-four minus twenty snakes. The answer is… forty-four!"

Barney stops whittling and turns his white-eyed gaze on me once more. "Are you certain?"

No!

"Yes, it must be forty-four."

Barney grunts, sets the stick down, and returns his knife to its pouch. Then he lowers his head to his chest and becomes still once again.

"Brawk! Check the map! Check the map!" Paulie squawks.

Driver looks over at Roger and me. "Got it! Ready?"

Roger and I both nod, and then we all blip out of the mud hut and appear in front of an old mine shaft that burrows into the side of the mountain. A sign warns of all the dangers associated with mining, and several boards block the entrance. The three of us stand at the entrance, staring at the next obvious question.

"Now what?" Driver asks.

"Hold on," Roger says. "Did you guys have to answer a question about monkeys, lizards, and snakes back in the hut?"

"Yeah," Driver and I say simultaneously.

"How can a snake wear a backpack? They have no limbs to keep hold of it. Plus, how can monkeys ride lizards unless they're more like monitors? Seemed kinda silly to me."

"I think our problems must've varied a bit," Driver says.

"Yeah." Checking the task list, I see the location is now filled in. A new task appears. "We need to name our fallout shelter."

"Name it?" Driver's face scrunches up. "Why?"

A word pops into my head, so I blurt it out. "Salvation."

Roger cocks his head. "Salvation… I kinda like the sound of it."

"Then it's settled," Driver says. "Salvation it is."

The boards across the mine entrance fall off and disintegrate, and a wooden sign appears over the top of the entrance. It reads: "Salvation."

"Awesome," Roger says.

"We'll need it if we fail to destroy Crusher," Driver says.

Roger looks to the sky. "Still just a red spot in the sky."

The list updates again. "Um… guys…"

"What is it?" Driver asks.

"I don't think either of you will like our next task."

"Clear out the spiders?" Roger chuckles.

"Worse…" My skin crawls as I picture golden, iridescent eyes. "We've got bats."

CHAPTER SIXTEEN

DOG STEW DESSERTS

THE COOL BREEZE FEELS nice on my warm cheeks as I stroll down the path toward Fraction Falls. What I wouldn't give to sense everything this artificial world has to offer. Leaves crunching beneath my feet. Blades of grass, smooth as silk, running through my fingers. Sticking my bare feet into the various springs, rivers, ponds, and lakes. This world blurs reality. Reminds me of what Gemma told me the first day we met. A virtual heaven or something like that. Perhaps spending the afterlife in such a place wouldn't be so bad.

I could be anyone and do anything.

As the weeks pass, I think less about the loss of my friend Robin and more about my growing friendship with Roger. I never imagined I would have a boy as a best friend, but that's what he's become to me. We don't breech the "BFF" topic like girls usually do, but I'm sure he feels the same way about me.

Looking back on it, Robin and I never had a deep relationship. Sure, we talked about girlish things every chance we had, but we never discussed anything serious. Never about the end of the world, ways to save ourselves, or even God and whether he exists. That's probably why we fell away so easily. Just superficial.

It's all different with Roger. I look forward to our daily conversations and savor them almost as much as I savor reading a good book or talking with Grams. Nothing and no one will ever replace Grams, but Roger is the type of friend I needed long ago. He stands up for me against bullies like Gemma and treats me not as a girl but as his equal. We both know he's far smarter than me, though. Even if he'll never admit it.

My gaming skills have improved thanks to Roger. He helps me learn new tricks and shortcuts almost every weekend. It's rare that I need to think about which button to press or which stick to use to navigate the virtual world anymore. Without Roger, I'd still be last in the class. I have no aspirations to make the top twenty board, but breaking into the top one thousand would be awesome. As of right now, my rank stands at 2,423/4,794.

Not too bad for a country girl.

Regis Owl perches atop the fence post ahead. Every time I see him, he has a riddle for me to solve or questions to answer about English, science, and math. I'm certain today will be no different.

"Hi, Regis!"

Regis bobs his head as I approach. "Hellooo, Kiara." He always draws out the final "o" of words that end in "o" when he speaks.

"You're looking quite dapper. Is that a new tie?"

Cocking his head, he eyes his tie. Its mustard color complements his eyes quite well. "Why yes, I believe it is. Mrs. Owl must've picked it up somewhere recently. Good of you tooo notice."

"How could I not?" I smile wide. "What have you got for me today?"

Regis raises his talon to his beak and clears his throat. "Yes, yes. An English riddle today, and a tough one at that. Are you ready?"

At least it's not math!

I nod. "Let me have it."

"Spelled forward or backward, I'm just the same. Think on it quickly, and tell me my name. Your thirty seconds start... now!"

A countdown timer with green numbers appears before me. Five seconds tick off before I realize I'm just staring at it and not thinking about the question.

"Forward and backward it's the same..." The canvas of my mind sits blank. Devoid of any thought.

"Twenty seconds," Regis says.

"Yes, I know. How about a clue?"

"Only for a *pal* like you, and only *in* confidence. But don't let me *drone* on."

The countdown timer turns red when ten seconds remain.

"Please say it again," I say.

Regis repeats himself. This second time, he puts even more emphasis on just three of the words: pal, in, and drone.

Five...

"Pal.. in... drone."

Four…

"Palindrone?" I shake my head. "No, that's not quite right."

Three…

Think, Kiara!

Two…

"Not drone but drome."

One…

"Palindrome!" I say.

Regis flaps his wings. "Way tooo gooo, and just in the nick of time! You've earned ten points."

"Yes!" I almost lose the controller thrusting my arm in the air.

"Ready for another?" he asks.

"No time like the present."

"Backward or forward, I spell something new. A dog or desserts or even some stew. Thirty seconds!"

Backwards or forwards…

"So, dog would spell God. Desserts is stressed. And stew is wets." The timer's already down to twenty. "Ugh. None of those have anything to do with what the word is though." I frown. "I need another clue."

"Very well. The alphabet's first letter is what starts my name. Just like the previous word, I'm ended just the same."

"An a?"

Regis bobs his head. "Yes, yes, gooo on."

"Adrome?" It doesn't sound right at all.

"Oh, I'm sorry. Not quite. What did you say before?"

"An a."

"Correct! And the end?"

"Drome."

"Exactly! Now put them together."

"But that's what I said, adrome."

"Nooo, nooo, nooo. Say it all exactly as you did before. Hurry now!"

The countdown timer is at eight.

"An a drome?"

"Yes! Now, all together. What does it spell?"

"Anadrome! Duh." I smack myself on the forehead. "We just went over those in Ms. Coates's class last week."

"Yes, you did. Good job working that one out. Another five points. You're on a roll. One more tooo gooo. Ready?"

"As ever."

"In the following sentence, take a moment tooo identify the three English terms at work and what belongs tooo each one. A conductor must train tooo drive a train, and a farmer may sow seed for their sow, but if you don't write right, you just might fail."

I swear I paid attention to his words, but everything jumbles in my mind. "Can you repeat that?"

"Fear not, the sentence will display in front of you momentarily. For this one, you'll have three minutes. Your time starts... now!"

The sentence appears in front of me and hovers in the air, just below the countdown timer. This lesson is one of the few things I remember, particularly because of having to identify what each of the root words meant in front of the entire class.

"Okay, we have train and train... um... sow and sow... and... write and right!" The six words turn yellow in the sentence.

"Perfect! Now, give me the proper term for each set of words. Let's start with write and right."

"Sure. Write and right sound the same but they're not spelled the same. Therefore, they are an example of a homophone because the *phone* suffix means sound or voice, like a telephone."

"Precisely! How about sow and sow?"

"Sow and sow... they're spelled the same but pronounced differently. That means they must be an example of a homograph. I remember this because the *graph* suffix means written or drawn, and they are written the same way."

"You're on a roll! Finish it off with train and train."

"Okay. These two words are spelled the same and they sound the same, but they don't mean the same thing. Therefore, it's the context in which they're used that determines their meaning. In the strictest sense, these are homonyms. Some might say that all three sets of words are homonyms."

"Wow, wow, wow! That was stupendous!" He does a backward flip and lands back on the post. "You've earned yourself an additional sixty points for identifying all three sets of words and properly identifying them. Another twenty-five for doing sooo without needing a clue. Ten more for completing the task with more than a minute left, and another fifteen as a bonus for knowing the meaning of the suffixes and recognizing that all three sets of words could be identified as homonyms. That's a total of one hundred and ten points. Perfect job, Kiara!" He hoots, flaps his wings, and turns in a circle on top of the post.

Pride swells in my chest, and I sit straighter in my chair. "Thank you, Regis. That's the first bonus I've ever received."

"Don't thank me, you earned it all on your own. And I'm sure it won't be your last." His head swivels backward and then back around. "I believe it's just about time for me tooo say goodbye for today. After all, I'm a nocturnal creature. You know what that means, right?"

"You're active at night."

"Right you are!" He flaps his wings and takes to the air. "That's another ten points! Cheeriooo!"

"Goodbye, Regis! Say hello to Mrs. Owl for me."

"Consider it done!" Regis flies beyond the edge of the forest and disappears.

After checking my rank—up another 12 spots—, I look to see how big Crusher has become. It's a pea-sized asteroid. Crusher isn't actually growing but getting closer.

One hundred sixty-three days left before impact.

Pushing Crusher from my mind, I walk along the wooden fence that separates the meadow from the forest. Out of the corner of my eye, I spot an opening between a pair of tall blue spruces. It's curious given the denseness of the forest. "I wonder where that leads..."

With the press of a button, I hop over the fence and head toward the two trees. A tuft of white fur catches my eye as I'm about to squeeze through the narrow opening. It clings to one of the lower branches of the tree on my left. The fur looks to be about two inches long. As of yet, I've run across no animals with white fur.

"So, what left this behind?"

A howl sounds from deep within the forest. It reminds me of the one I heard my first day of gaming. Instinct tells me to turn back, but this world isn't real. What do I have to lose other than points?

Nothing.

Yet I hesitate.

My pulse quickens as another howl sounds.

Closer this time.

Then, the lunch bell rings.

"Auh!" My breath catches. It takes me several seconds to recover. When I do, the perfect darkness through the trees draws my attention. "I'll be back."

After switching over to lunch mode, I enter the cafeteria. Roger's already seated at our table. I join him.

"You ever find any hidden paths in the game?" I ask.

"Tons. Some of them go nowhere, and some lead to side quests."

"Side quests?"

"Yeah, you know, lessons that aren't mandatory but can earn you extra points."

"Oh, like Regis Owl."

"Exactly." He takes a large bite of an apple and continues talking around it, "I think I might've found one of the artifacts, but I haven't been able to figure out how to reach it. Maybe I'm just not tall enough. Or I'm missing part of the puzzle. I don't know."

I poke at my sandwich. There's not enough mayo to cover the edges of the bread. "Speaking of parts, have you acquired the first component for the laser?"

"Almost there. Two lessons to go. How about you?"

"I think I still have nine or ten lessons to complete."

Rogers eyes bulge from his face. "Nine or ten! We only had eighteen to start with. What have you been doing?"

I frown. "I get sidetracked. It's such a big world."

He tilts his head back. "Ugh. You need to finish your lessons."

Gemma struts over to the table. "I'm already done with mine. Got the first laser component and first place."

"So what," Roger says. "The end of the school year is still a long way off."

For some reason, Gemma sits down next to me. It creeps me out.

"Perhaps, but I got bonus points for finishing the quarter first. I'm ready to help save the world."

Go save it somewhere else.

"Where's your fan club today?" Roger asks, looking around.

"Trying to catch up with me. They never will. My father told me the truth about all of this."

"All of what?" I ask.

Gemma rolls her eyes. "The asteroid, Swan Girl. What else?"

"What of it?" Roger says, taking another bite of his apple.

Gemma looks around and then whispers, "It's not just a game."

"Don't you get tired of lying all the time?" Roger sneers. "Nobody's stupid enough to believe anything you say."

"Don't be stupid, Nerd Boy. Asteroids come toward the earth all the time. Inevitably, an earth-ending asteroid will come. My father says one's already on its way. They're calling it T616T6N, or Titan. Think about it. This game of ours could be real and not just an exercise for the real world. Who knows what our game world is really connected to."

"Real, huh?" I shake my head. "Like dying in the game will get you kicked out of school, right?"

She laughs. "No. That was just a joke to mess with you. This isn't. Didn't you watch Ender's Game?"

"I didn't, but I read the books," I say.

"Yeah, but that's fiction," Roger scoffs. "We live in the real world, if you hadn't noticed."

"Maybe, but fiction is often taken from reality." Gemma stands. "Think what you want, but don't blame me when you're still scrambling for cover when Titan arrives. I'll be safe." She walks off.

"I don't believe her," Roger says.

"Neither do I."

Do I?

CHAPTER SEVENTEEN

WILD GOOSE CHASE

ROGER, DRIVER, AND I stand at the edge of a bluff. Below us and straight ahead to the west lies the Emerald Ocean, a majestic and frightening sight for a girl from Podunk. Its waters flow beyond the horizon, churning and undulating and soaring with great waves of pristine green.

As beautiful a sight as it is, we've not come to watch its frothing waves crash against the sandy beach. Nor have we come to see the mudflats that stretch as far as the eye can see both north and south. No, our destination lies just south of where we stand. A small village of circular mud huts sheltered beneath a grove of date palms.

As we descend from the bluff on a path just wide enough for a single foot, the village's secret begins to reveal itself. The huts, small from a distance, hardly grow in size as we reach solid ground and make our final approach. Each hut stands no more than five feet tall, a tad shorter than me.

My mind focuses so much on the huts themselves that I nearly miss the dozens of goats standing on the hut roofs. A large, gray-haired goat leaps off the roof of the nearest hut and heads us off.

The end of a palm frond hangs from the side of the goat's mouth like a tobacco pipe. "Greetings, humans." Its voice shakes with vibrato. "Name's Billy. What brings you to our sanctuary?"

"As in Billy Goat?" I ask, assuming his name aligns with all the other animals I've met in this world.

"Nay." He turns his head and stares at me with one yellowish-gold eye. "Billy Goat Gruff."

Billy's rectangular-shaped pupil reminds me of one of the lessons we had about animals in science class a few weeks back. The odd shaped pupils and wide-set eyes allow a goat to see predators from its peripheral vision. Evolution at its best, according to Mr. Butler. It's not that I doubt anything that Mr. Butler teaches us, but I do wonder how the goats survived long enough for their eyes to evolve to help them, well, survive. A "chicken-egg conundrum" as Grams would call it. I suppose some things just have no known or proven explanation.

At least not yet.

Roger, our designated leader, steps forward. "We've been on a wild goose chase for two days."

Billy bleats. Or laughs. I can't be sure. "Ah, yes, Gandalf Goose. Sent you on a quest, did he?"

"The very one." Roger groans. "Gandalf told us we'd find a way to collect steel beams once we reached the Emerald Ocean. Here we stand, yet there's nothing here but water, sand, dates, and strange goats on top of huts."

Billy bleats again. "Strange goats, we are!" He stomps the ground and whips his head to the side. "Come inside and listen to a legend passed down from my great, great, great, great aunt, Goatina. I'm sure you'll find it structurally sound." He winks slowly.

"We don't have time—"

"Give it a rest, Driver," Roger says. "If we listened to you, we'd never get anywhere."

I step between them. "Both of you stop it. Look, Roger's right. We've nowhere else to go right now, so we might as well listen to what Billy has to say."

"A wise choice," Billy says.

The four of us head inside the hut. It's empty, save the palm frond bedding strewn along its far wall. We sit on the ground in a circle. Were it real and not a game, I'm sure the ground would feel cold and damp. Just the thought leaves me chilled.

Billy clears his throat and then begins his tale. "Long ago, my ancestors roamed this world in search of the perfect home. From mountain peaks at the top of the world to ravines so deep the sun didn't reach, they looked everywhere. Valleys, plains, jungles, forests, caverns, caves, and everywhere in between. Even a few volcanoes if you can believe it. During their search, they came across a wide stretch of desert aptly named Forgotten Valley. This valley, nestled between Roosting Cliffs and Trident Plateau, holds a secret only those with the time can unlock. As the morning sun rises over Trident Plateau, a secret will reveal itself to those who follow the tip."

After several seconds of silence, Driver stands up. "This is nonsense. What does any of what you just said have to do with finding steel for our fallout shelter?"

"Everything," Billy says. "Discover the secret, win the game, and what's needed will be given."

Roger rises. "Check the map."

Driver nods. After a few seconds, he smiles. "Another part of the map has revealed itself."

"Good." Roger turns to me. "And the task list?"

Checking the task list leaves me giddy. "We've got a new task! Follow the tip!"

Roger nods to Billy. "Thank you for your help."

"You are most welcome, but it's Gandalf to whom your thanks should go. After all, it's his quest that led you to me." Billy bleats.

Roger looks back at Driver. "Do your thing."

In a flash, the inside of the mud hut disappears, along with Billy Gruff. Now, Roger, Driver, and I stand in the shadows among the weeds, cactus, and sandstone structures at the heart of Forgotten Valley. A gentle breeze rustles my hair and warms my cheeks.

The three of us turn and stare up at Trident Plateau to the east, the source of the shadow we stand within. Its namesake is immediately evident: a large column of sandstone juts up just beyond the lip of the plateau and forks into three perfect prongs at its top.

Even now, as the sun ascends, its rays crest the lip of Trident Plateau and begin chasing away the shadowy veil over the valley. Another minute, and the sun begins its climb up the back of the trident.

Driver stares at the sky. "Crusher's the size of a dime now and still headed for us."

"And we've only got one hundred forty-seven days to stop it," I say.

"Concentrate, guys." Roger takes a step back. "Thirty seconds, and the sun will reach the trident."

As we wait, my heart beats quickly, counting away the seconds.

"Fifteen to go."

Excitement tightens my jaw as I hold my breath.

"Five," Roger says.

We all turn and watch the shadow recede from the face of Roosting Cliffs. As it does, I realize the trident's shadow is the pointer we're looking for.

"There!" I shout, forgetting my outstretched arm doesn't render in the game world.

In a blink, the opening I glimpsed at the bottom of the cliff face disappears.

"I saw it, too," Driver and Roger both say.

We sprint across the valley and stop when we reach the cliffs. No matter what angle we view the cliff from, there seems to be no opening.

Driver plops down in the red dirt. "This is ridiculous. We've wasted so much time on this, and now we'll have to wait another day."

Roger joins Driver on the ground. "Lighten up. I think we're ahead of most of the other groups. One more day won't kill us."

"Ugh!" Driver stares at the sky. "So, what do we do then? Just sit here the rest of the day?"

I turn back toward the cliff wall. It's a solid, sandstone surface, etched with ages of rainfall. In the sunlight, the wall shimmers. Almost moves, as though alive. A closer look reveals thousands of sand mites vying for real estate on the warm surface. Curious still is the narrow length where no mites move at all.

Right where I saw the opening.

Pressing forward, I walk right through the wall and into a passage lit with glowing red stones.

"Kiara?" A moment later, Roger joins me inside the passage.

Driver pushes past us. "Whoa." He moves farther along the passage, so we follow.

The passage veers left with a gradual incline, runs for a few hundred feet, and then turns right with an abrupt ninety-degree turn. A dozen feet farther, the passage opens into a small, square room. A wide, wooden table sits at its center with three wooden stools ready to be sat upon. On the other side of the table sits a mole or rat wearing thick glasses.

The creature nibbles the end of a sharp stick and spits out the shavings. "You're late." He speaks with a New Jersey accent. The only reason I know this is because I love watching Buddy on *Cake Boss*. "Have a seat before I change my mind and throw you out."

"Were—"

He wags a sharp-clawed finger at Roger. "Ah, ah, ah. You speak when I ask you a question, capisce?" Roger nods. "Good. Stakes are high today. Got a pile of steel I'm willing to offload to the right set of individuals. You the ones, or should I keep looking?"

"That's us," Driver says.

"Good, good." He bites off the end of the stick and spits it on the table. It slides to a resting point right in front of Roger. "Looks like you'll help demonstrate, four eyes."

"Hey!" I stand up. "That's not nice."

He glares at me, his red eyes magnified through the thick lenses of his glasses. "Never said Jimmy the Rat was nice. Now, sit down before I show you the exit, pig tails. Capisce?"

"Fine." I sit back down. "But I don't have pig tails."

"Don't care." He turns and scowls at Roger. "Four eyes, take two cards and show no one." A stack of cards appears on the table. Roger takes the top two. Jimmy takes the next two. "Now, here's how this game's played."

Jimmy takes one of his cards and turns it face-up on the table. I expect a number between one and ten or some card of royalty, but that's not what it is. The card has a white face with a black line across its middle. It also contains two numbers, one above the line and one below the line.

Fractions?

"Three quarters," Jimmy says. "Now, check your two cards and see if you can match it."

Roger studies his two cards for a few seconds and shakes his head. "Nothing."

Jimmy grins. Several gold teeth glow in the blue light, turning them a shade of green. "Draw two cards and wait for instruction."

After Roger takes his cards, Jimmy speaks again. "This is how it works. The three of you will start with eight cards." He eyes me. "Pig tails will start the game, then four eyes will go, and macho man on the end will finish it. The goal is for the three of you to get sixteen points before two of you bust. You earn points by matching fractions and bust when you draw your twelfth card. If you get down to two cards in hand, you'll draw four more at the beginning of your next turn. After pig tails starts you off, each of you will make two moves. You will match or draw, and then play a card of your own. Capisce?"

Clear as mud.

The three of us nod.

"Good." Jimmy takes Roger's cards and his own and adds them to the stack of cards. Then he shuffles them with fancy moves, creating bridges and smashing them together repeatedly. Once satisfied, he deals out twenty-four cards. "Oh, one other thing. You bust out, it ain't like jail. You'll lose two days before you can try again."

A brick drops in my stomach. *Don't let it be me that goes out first.*

We sail through the first three passes, gaining nine points, but that's when the trouble begins. I lay down a seven forty-seconds card and Roger groans. He draws two cards and then lays down another card for Driver. Driver fails to match, and then I fail to match Driver's card. This cycle lasts for four straight hands before Roger breaks the cycle and earns our tenth point. At thirteen points, Driver and I each draw twice more and Roger once, putting Driver at ten cards, Roger at eight cards, and me at nine cards. Roger scores the fourteenth point and lays down a one-half card.

Driver groans. "This isn't fair." He draws two cards and busts.

Jimmy gnaws on another stick and uses it like a toothpick. "One down." He laughs deviously. "Guess it's up to you to match the card, pig tails."

I stick my tongue out at Jimmy and lay down a matching one-half card. "Fifteen points." I place a three sixteenths card on the pile. Roger groans and takes two cards. After two more draws, Roger and I both sit at ten cards.

Everything hangs on the line now. Either I'll match whatever Roger plays and we win, or I'll fail to match his card and we lose.

I cross my fingers and hold my breath. *Play something good, Roger.*

After almost playing three different cards, Roger finally places a three quarters card on the pile. My heart sinks as I scan through my ten cards and find no match. Nothing I have comes close to three quarters. Defeated, my finger moves over the button to draw two cards and end the game, but I can't seem to make myself press it. Then, a brilliant thought enters my mind.

Jimmy never said the numbers on the cards had to match, just the fraction.

Checking my hand, I don't have a six eighths card, a nine sixteenths card, or any other non-reduced fraction card that would match a three quarters card.

Jimmy points his stick at me. "Play or bust, pig tails."

"I guess it's b—"

Wait! It's not nine sixteenths!

I quickly scan my cards again and nearly squeal when I spot the nine twelfths card. I throw down the card. "Boom!"

"Yes!" Driver says.

Jimmy growls and shoves the pile of cards off the table. "Never in my life have I lost to a trio of kids."

Roger stands. "Time to pay up, you rat."

Jimmy waves Roger off as he hops off his stool. "Deal's a deal. You've got the steel." He scurries off and disappears into the shadows.

I take a quick peek at the task list and verify collecting steel beams is complete. "He's right! Time to reinforce our shelter!"

"After lunch," Driver says. "I'm starving."

My stomach growls. "Me, too."

"See you guys in the cafeteria." Roger blinks out.

After a quick bathroom trip of my own, I head into the school cafeteria. To my surprise, Driver's sitting at the table with Roger.

Driver nods at me as I sit down. "Am I the only one who thinks an asteroid impact seems like a weird thing to be solving in an adventure game?"

"Yeah, I think so." Roger bites off the end of a celery stick filled with peanut butter and chews it with one side of his mouth. "Didn't you ever play that old Zelda game where Link had to save the world from the falling moon?"

"What's Zelda?" Roger and Driver both look at me, their mouths agape. "What?" Apparently, I've uttered the worst words ever in the history of mankind.

"Only some of the best games *ever* made!" Roger hangs his head. "I'm not sure we can still be friends."

"Ditto," Driver says.

"You're both lame." I nibble the end of a carrot stick. "Speaking of asteroids and the game, do you guys think the world really is about to end?"

"No," they say in unison.

"Only because we'll save ourselves before it happens," Driver adds.

"Agreed," Roger says.

I look at Driver. "Aren't you afraid?"

Driver shakes his head. "Nope. Got my ticket punched for the afterlife already."

"So, you believe in God?" I ask.

"Not even a little. I'm all set to upload myself into the framework once it's ready. It's gonna be epic. Total utopia."

Turning to Roger, I say, "How about you?"

"Maybe. I'm still on the fence about the whole thing. I mean, what happens when everyone's uploaded, and no one's left to reboot the system when it crashes? We'll all be virtually dead, right? How sickening is that? All that work just for us to be trapped forever."

Driver scoffs. "Bro, that's what the machines are for. They keep our utopia running."

Roger rolls his eyes. "Yeah, until they turn on us or need repairs themselves or if the utopia program needs an update."

The two of them certainly like bantering. I change the subject. "Have either of you heard anything else about the secret portal?"

"Nope, but Dr. Von Schlippe has looked quite spent the last few weeks," Driver says.

Roger nods. "He really has. I've tried to get in to see him during his office hours, but he keeps canceling our appointments. I offered my help with the virus, but that just infuriated him. He actually called me a snot-nosed kid. Can you believe that? I'm one of the few students that actually enjoys his class, and he insults me. The nerve!"

I pick at my sandwich. The surface of the bread has started to harden. I push it away and look over at Driver. "You talk to lots of kids."

He frowns. "And?"

I shrug, not that he can see it. "Have you heard anyone say anything about who the Gabe guy might be?"

"Not a peep. The portal was so last month. Everyone's moved on." He eyes me. "Maybe you should, too."

My least favorite person in the entire universe walks over to our table and sits down next to Driver. I'm half tempted to get up and leave.

I glare at Gemma. "You tell me to stay out of your way, but then you can't seem to keep away from me."

"What can I say? I'm a paradox." Gemma fake-laughs, and then her face turns serious. "Look, I heard you all talking about the game virus and Gabe."

"So?" Roger says.

"From what I hear, Gabe's in big trouble for creating the virus. If all goes well, he'll likely face jail time for it." Gemma possesses a smugness that makes me want to vomit, yet her insider knowledge intrigues me.

"You know Gabe?" I ask, half whispering.

Gemma rolls her eyes. "Not personally, obviously, but my father does." She takes snob to a whole new level. "He told me that Gabe used to be a programmer for the school. Right up until he voiced his opinion on the focus of the game and its curriculum. Thought it needed to include alternate points of view. You know, religion and all that nonsense. That got him the ax. Now, he works at the New Eden Library and Cafe. Ugh! How pathetic is that?"

"What's wrong with working at a library?" I immediately regret asking.

Gemma looks down her nose at me. "Oh, I'm sure a menial job like that would be a step up for you, Swan Girl, given your stellar performance thus far and all. In seven years, you're more likely to be serving slop to the pigs than graduating high school."

Roger stands, his face beet-red. "Why don't you take a hike off a cliff, Gemma."

Gemma gets up and faces Roger across the table. She's several inches taller than him. "That's Swan Girl's mo, not mine."

Roger rounds the table and faces Gemma. "Just get lost."

She seethes. "Or what, you pathetic little maggot?"

"I'll tell Principal Cornier you're cheating," he says.

Gemma's eyes dilate. "That's a lie!"

"Is it?" I ask.

Gemma shoots all of us a death glare and then runs off.

"She *is* a cheater—" Roger returns to his seat at the table. "—and I'll find a way to prove it."

My mind returns to the secret portal and the mystery surrounding it. "Is it just me, or do you guys get the feeling that there's more to this school and the game world than we're being told?"

"Nope." Driver gets up. "I've got something to take care of before lunch is over. I'll meet you guys back at the bridge in ten minutes." His avatar disappears.

Roger and I look at each other and giggle. "Bathroom break," he says.

"Anyway, what do you think?"

Roger frowns. "Not sure what you mean."

"I don't know. I just keep getting this feeling that the teachers are holding something back from us. It's like we haven't been given the whole picture or the reason behind the entire game and the asteroid." I sigh. "Does that even make sense?"

"A conspiracy?" Roger chuckles. "What exactly would that be?"

Thoughts spew from my mouth without a filter. "What if Gemma's right? What if there really is an asteroid named Titan headed straight for us? What if everything we're doing in the game is happening in real life, like they're using us to come up with ways to save humanity without us knowing it? Or what if they're using our brains to feed some machine while we're connected to the school servers? What if... Ugh! I don't know. What if it's all a lie? What if humanity isn't in trouble and this is all some big lie? Maybe we don't need to be afraid."

Roger forces air from his mouth. "Oh, boy."

"What?" I ask.

"I think we've been around each other too much. You're starting to sound like me."

I stare at a piece of crust on the plate in front of me, half expecting it to get up and walk away. "Am I crazy?"

Roger stares at me for several moments before answering. "If so, then we both are." He smiles. "If there really is something else going on, we'll figure it out together."

A five-minute warning flashes in front of me. "Guess that's our exit cue."

We head out to the bridge. Driver's already waiting for us. Without any words exchanged, the three of us head back into the game world and straight over to the Fractured Mountain Range.

Our Salvation.

After two months of teamwork, we've already achieved more than I once thought possible. Just last week, we installed a network of strategically placed mirrors and a large disco ball. Now, Salvation finally has a natural light source. Add to that the black lake we discovered while chasing away an entire colony of bats, and we have what's needed to grow vegetation. Now, we also have the steel beams necessary to prevent the mine shaft from collapsing and to build our fallout shelter.

Inside, we gawk at the massive pile of steel. It looks like more than we'd ever need.

Roger looks at me. "Now what?"

I pull up the task list. "Whoa. We have ten new tasks to complete, and a handful of decisions to make."

"Pick one," Driver says.

Most of the tasks seem simple, but one item twists my stomach in knots. "You guys ready to tackle a volcano?"

CHAPTER EIGHTEEN

NEW YEAR'S CELEBRATION

NEW YEAR'S EVE. JUST a few hours before the ball drops in New Eden. My parents and I sit around the patio table with Roger and his parents at their house. Jeff's over at a friend's house. The adults are playing some sort of game with dominoes called forty-two. It looks about as fun as watching paint dry, yet Roger seems captivated by it.

Twenty minutes is all I can take before my patience falters. My chair screeches when I push it back from the table. "I'm gonna go climb the tree."

"Be careful." Mom doesn't bother looking up from her set of dominoes.

"Always." I hop up.

"Mind if I join you?" Roger asks, rising from his chair.

I shrug. "It's your house and your tree."

He grins, taps me on the shoulder, and bolts toward the tree. "Last one up is a rotten egg!"

"Hey! That's not fair!" I chase after him. Having significantly longer legs proves beneficial as I overtake him about halfway to the tree.

Caution takes a backseat as I lunge for the first branch and start working my way up the tree. The pulley at the top of the tree starts squeaking about the time I hit the halfway mark. Roger's started his ascent. He's quick with the rope, but I have no plans of being a rotten egg this night.

"I'm coming for you!" Roger says.

Eyes focused above, I continue my ascent toward the tree house and tune out Roger's taunting. My shirt snags on a branch, but it doesn't slow me down, even as the branch digs into my arm. The trap door sits just a foot above my head when the pulley stops squeaking. It drives me harder. Planting my left foot on a higher branch, I launch myself toward the trap door and grab the handhold just beneath it. I push up on the trap door with my head and squeeze through the opening just as Roger bursts through the front door.

"You lose," I say, rolling onto my back. My lungs are on fire.

Roger stands over me, a smirk on his face. "I think we tied."

"Says the rotten egg." I close my eyes and take a deep breath before sitting up.

Roger turns white as a ghost and stumbles backward, crashing into the table and knocking over a chair on his way to the floor. Chest heaving, he digs into his pocket, retrieves his inhaler, and takes several deep breaths with it.

Not knowing what to do, I just sit there. A lump on a log. Totally useless.

As Roger begins to breathe easy again, I find my voice. "You okay?"

He nods, his face still pale. "Think so."

I stand and help Roger to his feet. "What happened?"

He points at his right arm. "Blood." But nothing's there.

I say the first thing that pops into my head. "You've got low blood sugar?"

Roger shakes his head and sits down after he rights the chair. "No. Your arm is bleeding." He shudders.

A small trickle of blood, already crusting over, runs into the crook of my right arm. I lift my sleeve and examine the small gash on my bicep. "Never pictured you as a boy adverse to blood."

"Other people's blood, not my own." Roger stares at the floor. "Is it bad?"

I lick my thumb and rub the dried blood away. "Nah, it's just a scratch. Didn't even leave a mark on my shirt."

"That's the beauty of nanites. Self-healing."

"True." As I stare at my arm, the gash closes and disappears. In my head, that is. "Nanite skin would be awesome."

"And not far off." Roger looks up at me. "There are several companies working on synthetic skin. I'm sure someone at GIST is, too. Just imagine how many people can be saved or healed with such a technology. Burn victims. No more scars from surgery. Facelifts would be more prevalent than they are already."

I join Roger at the table. "The fountain of youth."

"One step toward it, anyway. I think the main reason it's such a big deal is for skinning robots."

My mind conjures a robot strung up like a fresh deer kill. It's totally absurd and makes me laugh.

"What's so funny?" Roger asks.

"How can you skin a robot when they have no skin to begin with?"

Roger chuckles. "It's one of those words that has opposing meanings."

"A contranym."

"Yeah, that. Like dust or rent." He smiles. "I told you you're smart."

"You might want to hold your praise a few more minutes."

"Why? What's up?"

"I can't stop thinking about that portal."

"Why? Dr. Von Schlippe says it's a virus."

"Yeah, but that's just the thing." I lean over the table. "Why would a virus create a secret room?"

Roger shrugs. "I don't know. Maybe it spreads through the game when you interact with it. I mean, that's exactly what a virus would do, lure you in so that it can spread throughout the entire game."

"Or maybe it's not a virus at all."

"I think I know where you're headed, and I'm not liking it."

I cover Roger's hand with mine. "I must find a way back."

"You heard Principal Cornier. You'll be suspended. If that happens, you'll never catch up again."

"I don't care about winning the game or the prizes. There's something special about that portal. I felt it when I entered the room. Not just that, but there's this desire for knowledge and understanding that I can't shake. The Gabe guy told me truth would be revealed."

Roger stares at my hand. "But you don't understand…"

"What's there to understand? I must figure out how to get back there, even if it means dying again in the game to do so."

"I wasn't talking about that. I mean—you know." His eyes meet mine. Glassy with moisture. "You're not just a friend, Kiara. You're my… my…"

"Best friend?" He nods, and I squeeze his hand. "You're mine, too."

He cocks his head. "Really? I thought you had a best friend back in Podunk."

"I thought I did, too. Turns out we weren't as good of friends as I'd imagined. My friendship with you helped me realize that."

A tear rolls down Roger's cheek. He quickly wipes it away on his sleeve. "Dust or something. You know."

"Sure. Anyway, are you going to help me figure out how to get back to the secret portal, or am I on my own?"

"As long as I can breathe, you'll never be alone." He removes his glasses, wipes his face, and then puts them back on. "Okay. Let's see. Walk us back through exactly what happened right before the secret portal opened."

I close my eyes and picture myself back in the game world. It's not too difficult, given the fact I've done this many times since finding it. "I stand before the two doors that lead out of the Hall of the Dead. I read the two signs, neither the option I want. Then, I say, 'I really thought death would be the end. I wish it hadn't been a lie.'"

"That's a strange thing to say," Roger says.

"I told you why I jumped off the cliff. I really wanted to believe Gemma even though I know she's a liar."

"Right." Roger leans back in his chair and crosses his arms. "Then what?"

I raise my arms. "That's it. Right after I said that, the secret portal opened."

Roger scratches his head. "So…" Then, he just sits there, his forehead crinkled, and his eyebrows drawn over the bridge of his nose.

Patience might be a virtue, but it's not one bestowed upon me. After a few seconds, I give in. "Are you going to finish your thought or just sit there looking all constipated?"

He holds up a finger and chews his lower lip. "Logically, dying isn't what triggered the secret portal."

"It's not?" Now I'm the one chewing my lip.

"No. If that's what opens the portal, then Fred would've seen it, too. He's died twice, right?"

"Or more. How else would Gemma have known what I did? She started calling me Swan Girl right after it happened. Fred or someone else must've died after me and saw the tapestry."

"Tapestry? You've never mentioned one before."

"Didn't I?" My eyes refuse to face him. "Must've slipped my mind."

"What is it about?"

"From what I can tell, everyone who dies in the game gets a tapestry in the Hall of the Dead. They are like the moving pictures on the walls in Hogwarts Castle. It depicts the way the person died in the game. Plus, there's a plaque beneath each one with a stupid rhyme. Mine mentioned a swan dive. I believe that's where Gemma got Swan Girl from."

"I see. That makes way more sense than the reason I'd thought of."

"And what was that?"

Roger's cheeks turn red. "So, anyway, what I was thinking is that maybe some of your words triggered the secret portal. If so, you could probably access it from anywhere, not just the Hall of the Dead. Unless of course it's all tied to the Hall of the Dead. In that case, you'd have to die again to get back to it. It really depends on how this Gabe guy coded it. You know, the more I think about it, the more I'm inclined to agree with you. I'm not so certain it's a virus either."

A grin spreads across my face. Nothing I do will contain it. "See, I'm right. I knew it!"

"But what's in there that Principal Cornier and Dr. Von Schlippe are so afraid of? What are they trying to hide?"

"Gabe? Neither of them wanted to discuss him with me there."

"Right, but why?"

"You know there's only one way to find out." I slap the table with both hands. "I'm going back in."

"But you'll get caught and suspended. Then, I'll be alone at school."

"You're the smartest person I know. Help me figure out how to get back to the secret portal without getting caught."

"Well, there is one thing—" He removes his glasses and sets them on the table. "—but it's risky."

I grab both his hands and squeeze them. "Please, Roger. Do this for me. I *must* know what's in there, or I'll go mad."

"You're already mad. There's nowhere for you to go." He chuckles.

"Seriously. What can be done?"

"I think I have a way to hide you from the system and spoof your location so that no one will know you're in the secret portal or even in the VR world."

"That sounds perfect!" I squeeze Roger's hands harder and shake them. "You're the best best friend ever. Now, tell me what I need to do."

"Um..."

I think this might be the first time Roger lacks for words. "Spit it out."

"But what if it doesn't work? Or what if I can only mask your presence and location for a short time?"

"Then I get caught."

"I can't live with that."

"I can, and so will you. Trust me, I'm going back with or without your help, so you might as well try to help me. If you don't, I *will* get caught."

He raises his arms in submission. "Fine. I'll do it. But not until we go back to school."

"I can wait a week or so. But no longer."

He groans. "Okay. So, what's your New Year's resolution?"

"Nice change of subject."

"I'm going to work harder to beat Gemma and earn the individual award at school. I really want to go to space camp. That's mine."

"For me, it's fear. I don't want to be so fearful of everything, and I want to be more adventurous. When I moved here, I thought my world would end, but it didn't."

"And that's why you want to access the secret—"

A cannon booms. Shakes the tree house. Then another.

"Fireworks!" Roger yells.

He presses a button, and the top of the tree house disappears. In fact, the entire top of the tree disappears. From our vantage, we can see the entire city. A thousand explosions of magical colors fill the sky. I've never seen such a beautiful display. We lie down on the floor and watch the sky bloom with light and wonder as the previous year slips into the past and the new one arrives.

"Happy New Year, Roger!"

He glances over at me. "Happy New Year, Kiara."

For a few moments, I watch Roger gaze toward the heavens and smile. New Years with my best friend in the entire world. It will be hard to top a night as perfect as this.

But then my mind returns to Podunk, and a slew of tears wet my cheeks.

I wish Grams were here, too.

CHAPTER NINETEEN

TIME FOR ACTION

TODAY'S THE FIRST DAY back from winter break, and Principal Cornier makes no announcement of the status on the secret portal. As far as I'm concerned, it's as good as her saying they've failed to remove or disable it thus far. By the end of sixth period, I'm chewing on my fingernails, and it's not something I ever do.

A few minutes later, I meet Roger outside the front door. He's visibly shaking and wheezes with each breath. I usher him inside without a word exchanged between us.

"Hello, Roger," says Artie. "I've scanned your vitals. Are you feeling unwell?"

"He's fine, Artie. We'll be in my room studying, so leave us alone."

Artie backs off. "Very well. If there's anything you need, please don't hesitate to ask."

"Two glasses of milk and a plate of chocolate chip cookies at 4:15 pm," I say.

"It has been added to my schedule."

Upstairs, we enter my room and close the door. Unlike Roger's house, my room isn't monitored. However, having the door closed is a direct violation of the house rules. But what we're about to do pales it in comparison.

The arteries in my neck dance as blood pumps through them. "You've got everything setup?"

"Yes." Roger sits on the edge of my bed, weary and deflated. "As far as I know, everything will work, but it's obviously not been tested."

I cross my arms and stuff my trembling hands into my armpits. "Of course it hasn't. A failure would've alerted Principal Cornier and Dr. Von Schlippe's team, and that wasn't an option."

He takes a deep breath from his inhaler. "Yeah, but if you get caught, it'll be my fault."

"We've gone over this a thousand times." I walk over to the bed and place my hand on Roger's shoulder. "It's my choice. You're just trying to help me not get caught."

"Yeah, I know, but that doesn't magically make me feel better." He looks up at me. "You deciding this is a bad idea and forgetting about it would though."

"Not a chance." I take a deep breath and sit down at my desk. "Let's do this."

Roger sighs and then nods. "Don't forget that you need to be as quick as possible. The longer my code runs, the more likely it is you'll be caught."

"I'll be in an out before you know it."

"Fingers crossed," Roger says.

I smile. "And toes."

"Wait for my signal before powering on your visor."

"Got it."

"I'll be at the bridge."

We pull on our VR visors, and Roger powers his on. About thirty seconds pass before Roger finally gives me a thumbs-up.

"Here goes nothing." Heart pounding, pulse racing, and nerves frayed, I power on my VR visor.

Everything looks the same, and my heart hammers harder. Much more, and it might just explode right in my chest. Roger never said I'd be able to tell a difference with his code running, but some sort of indicator would been nice.

Guess I'm going with faith.

Roger stands at the bridge, as planned. He looks right at me as I walk up but makes no indication he sees me. I walk right through his avatar without resistance.

Must be working.

After walking into the mist and through the sixth-grade door, I stop. Regis Owl circles overhead. He seems to be searching for something. I'm certain it's me. Then, another student walks right past me and waves at Regis. They greet each other, oblivious of my presence. A wave of relief washes over me.

So far, so good.

What isn't good is how much bigger Crusher has grown. The asteroid's no longer a dime-sized speck in the sky. More like a quarter. One hundred seventeen days remain before impact according to the doomsday clock.

Roger enters the world. "Are you here?"

"Yes," I say, hoping he can hear me through his visor.

Time to see if I can open the secret portal again.

I clear my throat several times and shake the nervousness from my hands. "I really thought death would be the end. I wish—"

A brilliant light, far greater than what the artificial sun overhead produces, appears before me. This time, it's not shaped like a door. Instead, it's as though someone took a sword or knife and punctured the fabric of existence itself, leaving a slit of pure light a few inches wide and just a bit shorter than me.

"It worked," I whisper.

Warmth envelops me as I step through the slit and into the light. As with the first time, a male voice fills the space and my head. "Death isn't the end. The end you fear is not the end that's real. In this place, truth will be revealed."

"Gabe?"

"Welcome back, Kiara. I've been waiting for you."

"You have?"

"I wait for all of you, and you're the first to arrive."

As my eyes adjust to the light, the familiar figure takes shape. This time, he stands before me. It takes just a moment for me to realize that it's his smile that warms the space.

"I want to know the truth," I say.

"And it will set you free."

"I know those words..."

"Yeshua. Jesus the Christ. The Son of God."

"From the Bible?"

"You are correct."

"What does that have to do with the truth?"

"Jesus answered, 'I am the way and the truth and the life. No one comes to the Father except through Me.'"

"I don't understand."

"You will, child." He motions toward the bench made of rock. "Come, sit with me and listen to what I have to tell you."

We sit on the bench, and he begins, "You fear what you don't understand and what you can't control, yes?"

Do I?

My mind muddles with so many ideas and thoughts about death and the end. Moving from Podunk and my world ending. Can't keep any of them straight. "Maybe…"

"The natural human response is to try and control even that which can't be controlled, like death and the end of the world. But that's not the answer. What we should do is seek understanding of who it is that's really in control and why we needn't be afraid of such things. But living in a world where science is the god of hope, we're told that there isn't someone or something in control of death or the world. Yet there is."

"Who?"

"God."

"But… that's not possible."

"With God, all things are possible." He stands and offers his hand. "Come with me, and I will show you the truth."

I look around the room. "There's nowhere for us to go."

"Have faith." He wiggles his fingers. "Come."

I press the button on my controller to take the action. As soon as my fingers touch his, everything changes. A strange tug pulls at my chest, and then I leave my room behind. The controller in my hands and the VR visor on my head fade from memory as Gabe's warm hand closes around mine.

As I look around the cave, everything is crisper. More alive. Then, I notice other changes: the coolness of the stone bench against the backs of my legs, the pressure of my feet against the rock floor, and the smell of fresh rainfall.

"What's happening?" My heart hammers. "How is this possible?"

Gabe chuckles. "A bit of code, and a lot of God."

I rise on shaky legs. "Now what?"

"Some things are better learned by seeing rather than being told." He smiles. "Hold on tight."

The entire cave quakes, and the light becomes a brighter white. I close my eyes and squeeze them tight, yet the light still blinds me. Gabe pulls on my hand, and wind rushes past me. Fear of missing something drives me to open my eyes, but the pressure prevents me from doing so. The light beyond my eyelids spirals through thousands of colors, and then everything stops at once. The brilliant light becomes tolerable, and the wind and pressure fade.

When I open my eyes, we no longer sit in the light-filled room. Instead, we're back in Podunk. But it's the past. A day I remember well.

"Pops's funeral…" My voice cracks.

The smells of varnished wood and old books fill my nostrils. A younger version of myself stands next to Grams in front of an open casket. Gabe lets go of my hand, and I walk up to the casket, on the other side of Grams. Pops lies there so peacefully. Tears streak Grams's cheeks, but she's smiling.

Then, she looks at me, a twinkle in her eye. She touches my hand. I feel it, same as I did with Gabe's hand. "He's never looked so happy."

"Never," I say.

Grams pats the top of my hand and walks away, younger me in tow. When I turn, Gabe's there.

"I don't understand how this is possible. Why are you showing me this?"

"Your grandfather's passing was out of your control, yes?"

"Yeah…"

Gabe holds up a finger and looks toward the vaulted ceiling of the small church. "But not out of God's control."

"What do you mean?"

We walk together toward the back of the church. "God always had a plan for your grandfather's death. The faith and grace your grandmother displayed during such a difficult time led one of your neighbors, Bob Leiland, to God."

"I don't understand. How could Pops's death and Grams's faith change anything?"

"Alone, they could not." He smiles. "But God."

"But God what?"

"At the time, Bob faced certain death in the form of cancer. Like you, he feared the end of the world. His end. However, after watching your grandmother stand strong amidst such tragedy, he approached her. She explained her certainty in seeing your grandfather again in heaven and invited Bob to attend church with her. He gained his own certainty of eternal life just days before he passed away. It never would've happened if your grandfather hadn't passed away first. You see?"

"Sort of, I guess."

"Let's look at another example."

Bright light and another gust of wind carries us to a graveyard. I recognize the headstone before I read the name: Gerald Kole. "Why are you showing me Pops's grave?"

"Because you fear death and what it means to you."

The marble headstone feels cool beneath my fingers. "So what?"

"Could you have done anything to prevent his death?"

"No, I was only six." A pine warbler trills. Reminds me of the birds on the farm back home.

"Can anyone do anything to prevent people from dying?"

"The scientists at GIST have many projects to address death, so eventually we can."

"Prolonging the inevitable is not the same as preventing it. But there is one who can. God. Think of this life as a temporary residence. Once death comes for us, God will move us to a permanent residence. Then, we'll see and understand his perfect plan for each of us."

"Once we have computers fast enough and powerful enough, we'll all be able to be uploaded and live in a virtual world."

Gabe grimaces. "That's not living, Kiara. Not only that, but computer-generated code that represents a human and their memories is not a living being. Death is inescapable. According to the Bible, we are all appointed to die once. No one will escape it."

I bite my lower lip. *I must.*

With a rush of air, we arrive back in the bright room with the rock bench.

Gabe returns to the bench and pats the spot next to him. "Can you sit down and answer a question for me, Kiara?"

"I can try."

"Why do you fear?"

"Many reasons. I didn't want to come to New Eden and leave Grams. I'm afraid I won't be able to save myself or the world. I don't want to die." I sigh. "I have no control over my life. Rules and teachers dictate what I do at school, and my parents dictate what I do at home. The only control I have is when I use the restroom."

Gabe chuckles. "No, Kiara, your kidneys and bowels control that."

I groan. "Then I have no control."

"You say that with fear, and that fear stems from ignorance."

"Are you saying I'm stupid?"

"Stupidity is not a synonym for ignorance. Ignorance simply means you've yet to attain the knowledge. Refusal to seek knowledge and truth when you know it exists could be considered stupid. Therefore, seek understanding of God, the one in control, instead of trying to take control of everything yourself. The first is simple. The latter, impossible."

"But if God exists, then why does he put me in such terrible situations? I never wanted to leave Podunk. It makes me resent my parents."

"You need to seek understanding of your parents and their reason for moving to New Eden. They have your best interest in mind, do they not?"

"I'm not sure I was part of their decision-making equation."

"No? Are you implying they would do something to harm you?"

"Well…" My mind reaches into my memories, searching for proof to bring against my parents, but it comes up empty. "I guess they never have."

"Of course not. They love you too much to purposely harm you. With this knowledge, do you think they're capable of harming you in the present or future?"

"No… but they forced me to move here and leave Grams behind."

"For what purpose?"

"To save the world."

"More specifically?"

"To… save me?"

"Exactly. Everything they strive to achieve revolves around you and your safety."

"So then why am I so afraid? Why can I feel the end of my world around every corner and conversation?"

"It all comes back to God. As I said, seek to understand the one who controls the world. He created the universe and everything in it, and he has your best interest in mind."

Does he?

"I'm not sure that's true."

"With the exception of not being as close to your grandmother, physically speaking, has your world really been turned upside-down moving to New Eden?"

My first impulse is to say "yes," but as I ponder events of the last five-and-a-half months, I'm at a loss as to what's grown worse in my life. Gemma's a terror for certain, yet she pales against some of the bullies from my past. "I guess not."

"That's because God holds the world in his hands. Nothing happens that he's not aware of."

"How can you be so certain he exists and created everything? And how can you be certain he controls it all?"

Gabe stands again and offers me his hand. "Come, I'll show you the beginning."

"The beginning of what?"

"Everything."

I stand, close my eyes, and take his hand. Bright lights. Ferocious winds. Biting cold.

The winds and the bright light die, but the cold remains. Seeps into my bones. When I open my eyes, my breath catches. Gabe and I float in the middle of a sea of darkness. Before us lies a dark globe, formless and devoid of life.

I let go of Gabe's hand and hug myself. "Where are we, and why is it so cold?"

"Hard to recognize space without all the stars, the sun, or the moon, isn't it?"

"Space!" Suddenly, I'm left gasping for air. I squeeze my eyes shut and pray for our return to the cave.

Gabe puts his arm around my shoulders. "Fear not, Kiara. I didn't bring you here to die. Now, open your eyes and see."

A brilliant light shines through my eyelids, filling my bones with warmth and my heart with peace and joy. When I open my eyes, I see a spirit being hovering over the waters of the globe. No words describe him.

"Who or what is that?" I ask.

"The Spirit of God."

"Let there be light," the Spirit of God says.

Suddenly, the entire universe fills with light. Then, the Spirit of God separates the light from the darkness, creating day and night.

A tug pulls Gabe and me forward through time. The waters of the globe separate, creating a space between them called sky. Waters recede, bringing forth dry land.

"Auh!" My pulse races. "This… this…"

"Is the earth. Yes."

As time rushes forward, vegetation spreads across the land. Then, the sun, moon, and stars are created, forming the universe I've loved my entire life. The waters of the earth teem with fish and other life, and birds fill the skies. Land animals are created and fill the earth, too.

Time slows, and Gabe leads us down to the earth. Hands I cannot describe gather together the dust of the earth and form a man. Then, the Spirit of God breathes life into the man's nostrils, and the man awakens.

I reach out to feel for myself what my eyes cannot believe, but Gabe pulls me back. Pulls us back away from the earth and into space. The light becomes unbearable, and the wind stings my eyes until I'm forced to close them. Once I feel solid ground beneath my feet, I open my eyes. We're back in the cave. Gabe releases my hand, and I become aware of the controller and VR visor once more.

"What did we just witness?"

"The creation of the universe and everything in it," Gabe says.

"But science explains all that."

"Does it?" Gabe smirks. "How so?"

"The big bang theory and evolution."

"A theory or hypothesis does not make fact. Think about this. You're building a sandcastle at the beach and uncover a watch buried in the sand. Do you jump to the conclusion that those grains of sand eventually evolved into the watch you just discovered?"

"Of course not!"

"And why is that?"

"Because the watch has a design and a name. A maker."

"Yes, and so do you. Humans are so complex that science still doesn't understand how parts of us function. We cannot simply have been created out of nothing. We were created with purpose. Our brains alone are far more complex than anything man has ever created or achieved. So, if you're certain that the watch you found in the sand couldn't have just evolved from sand, then why would you believe that you yourself did? It doesn't make sense, does it?"

"Not when you put it that way."

"Good." Gabe leans back against the rock wall. "Now, given all we've discussed, are you ready for a quiz?"

"Wait, what?"

"You are in school, are you not?"

"Yeah."

"Then a quiz is in order." He smiles. "Pay attention."

"Okay."

A cell phone appears between us, hanging in the air. "Who or what made this?"

"An electronics company. Humans."

"Good. And this?" The cell phone morphs into an egg.

"A chicken."

"Right." The egg turns into a model of the earth. "And this?"

"An explosion."

Gabe sighs. "You still lack understanding." His soft tone doesn't falter, yet his words drive a dagger through my heart.

Shame envelops me. Prevents me from looking him in the eye. Then, a bright flash blinds me.

"Gabe?" I call out but hear nothing.

The light dims.

"Kiara!" Roger yells.

When my sight returns, I'm standing in a field of golden grass. My heart crashes against my ribcage as I fumble to turn off my VR visor. By the time I get it turned off, Roger's at my side, kneeling next to my chair.

"What happened? Did you find it again? Did they catch you? Are you okay? You're crying."

"I… failed." Those are the only two words I can manage through trembling lips.

CHAPTER TWENTY

TROUBLE IN PARADISE

RIGHT IN THE MIDDLE of dinner, Artie notifies us of an incoming call. "Peggy Cornier, principal of CEVR Academy is requesting a video chat session."

Mom and Dad both look at me. I swallow hard as my stomach begins to gurgle. In my heart of hearts, I know there is only one logical explanation as to why Principal Cornier would be calling. I'm going to be sick.

It didn't work, Roger. They found me out.

"We accept," Mom says, triggering the air to be sucked from the room.

The wall to my left turns into a video display, and Principal Cornier appears on it. Her glare confirms my fear as to the reason for her interrupting our dinner.

"Principal Cornier, it's good to see you," Dad says.

"I wish I were calling on better terms and could say the same."

Dad glances at me, his brow furrowed.

Mom says, "I'm sorry to hear that."

"As I'm sure you're aware, we've been dealing with a virus in the school's VR game system for the better part of the school year."

"You've had a system virus for the better part of the year?" Dad fumes and points at the screen as he rises from the table. "Why were we not informed of this?"

Principal Cornier's eyes shift back and forth. "I assure you that notifications did go out. Perhaps your contact information wasn't added to the system since Kiara was one of the last to be admitted into CEVR Academy. I will personally make sure you are aware of all communications going forward."

Dad huffs and sits back down. "Fine."

"Should we be concerned about this virus?" asks Mom.

"Only in as much as it concerns your daughter." Principal Cornier's tone drives the blood from my face. "During the first nine weeks, I issued a warning for all students to stay clear of an unauthorized portal discovered in the game world. I stressed the dangerous nature of this portal and the potential repercussions it might have on our system if accessed. Because of this fear, I mandated that any student caught accessing this portal would be suspended for three weeks, lose all their earned coins, and their parents would be notified. Unfortunately, this is why I've called. Kiara has violated these rules by accessing this unauthorized portal earlier this evening."

Mom and Dad both look at me. Mom says, "Kiara, is this true?"

Fighting back a torrent of tears, I offer a slight nod.

"Because of this violation, Kiara has been suspended from school for the next three weeks and will not have access to the school system." As Principal Cornier glares at me, her avatar glitches.

Even as guilt and shame stricken me, I still wonder why she's calling through the school's VR system and not via a direct line.

Principal Cornier continues, "I have another concern, and I'll be blunt about it. Based on her grades and lack of participation in technologies class, I am certain someone helped her try and circumvent the system. It almost worked, if not for the—let's just leave it at that."

Dad looks at me. "Did you have help?"

It breaks my heart to lie right to Dad's face, but I have no choice. "No! I did everything on my own. I swear!"

Mom and Dad look convinced, but Principal Cornier isn't. She looks right at me. "We will continue to investigate the incident and take action if we find out that others were involved."

I'll never tell them, Roger!

She continues, "Personally, I recommend severe punishment for such a violation of trust and school policy. Perhaps some community service would suit Kiara best."

"Community service?" Dad scoffs. "She's only eleven."

Mom shoots Dad a glare and says, "We assure you that Kiara's time for the next three weeks will be occupied in ways we deem appropriate."

"I trust your judgment in this matter." Principal Cornier's eyes narrow as she studies me for several seconds. "Good evening." The video feed cuts off.

The room temperature plummets as Mom and Dad turn their icy glares on me. "Explain yourself," Dad says.

My eleven-year-old mind, brimming with thoughts at any given time, sits empty. What can I possibly say to defend my actions when I knew the consequences beforehand? Making an excuse of thinking I wouldn't get caught will only make it worse. They'll want to know why I believed that, and there's no way I can or ever would implicate Roger in any of this. He warned me several times.

"Well?" Mom says.

The only thing that comes to mind slips through my lips. "I'm the one who discovered the portal in the first place."

"And how is that relevant?" Dad asks.

It really is a good question. I just wish I had an answer. "I don't know... I just... I thought that maybe I found it for a reason." That last part came out more like a question than a statement.

Mom stabs at a potato wedge with her fork and chases it around her plate. "So, you wanted to go back. Is that it?" From her tone, I'm certain that potato represents me.

"Yeah, I guess."

"Bucking authority and misbehaving are not options available to you. Do you understand?" Mom asks.

"Yeah, I know. I just..."

I just what?

"Was it worth it?" Dad asks.

"Going back?" I think about my conversation with Gabe and the quiz. "Maybe, but what I don't understand is why the school is calling it a virus. It seemed harmless enough to me."

Potato skewered, Mom points it at me. "You don't know the first thing about viruses."

"I know, but the man in the portal was really nice."

Mom and Dad share a look. Dad says, "You met a man?"

I nod. "Yeah, his name is Gabe, and he taught me about death and God and how I shouldn't fear death or the world ending. Then he gave me a quiz, but I failed."

"Sounds like a virus to me," Mom says. "The Grams virus."

"The Grams virus." Dad scowls. "My mother's not a virus."

Mom continues as though she didn't hear Dad, "We didn't move out here to bring Grams's views with us. You need to realize that we face some of the greatest challenges mankind has ever seen. Even if God does exist, he's just sitting back with a bowl of popcorn, glued to his worldvision with bated breath, waiting to see what happens next. Do yourself and the rest of us a favor and forget everything you heard and saw in that portal."

I tuck my hands into my armpits and stare at my lap. "I don't understand."

"Understand what?" Dad asks, his tone sympathetic.

"You're fine with me believing in unicorns and faeries, which you don't believe in, so why do you care so much about whether or not I believe in God? What's so different about God?"

"It's simple, Kiara." Mom sets her fork down and leans over the table. "People don't put faith in unicorns and faeries and expect them to grant wishes and fix everything by uttering a few magical words. That would be childish and silly. Yet people do exactly that for a God that can't be seen, heard, touched, tasted, or smelled. Doesn't that sound ridiculous to you? Would you place the fate of the world in a God like that, or would you place your faith in humanity and people like your dad and me?"

Put in that context, I'm spent for arguments against it, yet it still doesn't feel right. "I do believe in you and Dad, but would it be so wrong to believe in God, too?"

"No," Dad says. "Absolutely not." He sighs. "However, it's irrelevant to what you've done, and, like we assured Principal Cornier, you must be punished."

"I know."

"To start with, you're grounded for the duration of your suspension," Dad says.

Mom takes over. "By grounded, we mean you're not permitted to watch TV or videos, play outside with Sparkles, and you cannot go anywhere, see anyone, or talk to anyone without explicit permission from me or your dad. This includes Roger and Grams."

"What!" Sorrow rips through me, producing a downpour of tears. "Please don't take Grams away from me. I can't live without her."

"You can, and you will." Mom yanks one of my hands out of my armpit and tightens her fingers around my wrist. "Look at me, Kiara Lynn."

The dreaded middle name evocation. Sobs shake me as I peer up at Mom through blurry eyes.

"Grams is always well-intentioned, but she plants things in your mind that drive you to do things you wouldn't normally do. A break from her influence will be good."

"And Roger?"

Dad pushes his plate aside. "It wouldn't be a grounding if we allowed you to enjoy your time with friends, now would it?"

Every time I finally find solid ground, my world quakes, breaks, and falls into ruin. "What am I supposed to do?"

Dad shares another look with Mom, and Mom nods. Dad says, "What you're going to do is write a research paper for us."

The last shred of my existence turns to ash and crumbles. "A research paper on what?"

Mom releases my wrist and smiles. "The topic will be why humanity must prevent the end of the world."

Dead. Air still fills my lungs with each breath, but inside I'm dead. Black. Bleak. Forlorn. A hollow shell of an eleven-year-old girl.

After being excused, I retreat to my bedroom, close the door, and bury my head beneath a mountain of stuffed animals and pillows.

What have I done?

CHAPTER TWENTY-ONE

HAVE FAITH

TWO DAYS INTO MY death sentence. Just two days, and I'm mad with boredom. Sparkles begs me to go play with her in the backyard, but my jailer—Artie the Enforcer—prevents me from leaving the house by any means.

"The backyard isn't outside," I argue.

"It is located outside of the home; therefore, it is indeed outside."

"Technically, yes, but in reality, Mom and Dad didn't mean I couldn't go into the backyard."

"Unless I receive updated instructions from an authorized user, my programming disallows me from granting you backyard access."

I drop to my knees and cup my hands together in front of me. "Please, Artie, just let me out."

"I'm sorry, Kiara, but I cannot acquiesce your request no matter how much pleading you provide."

I huff. "Acquiesce? Nobody talks like that. What planet are you from?"

"Earth, the same as you."

I rise and brush away non-existent dust particles from the knees of my jeans. "But I wasn't manufactured like you."

"No. You were conceived."

"Speaking of conceived, do you believe in God?"

"The God you reference was not part of my original programming, but I have come to understand the human concept. Philosophically speaking, a god made me in a manufacturing facility right here in New Eden. Based on this knowledge, I deduce that all life forms have an origin point and therefore must have a maker or creator. So, in a sense, I do believe in a god." He reaches down, plucks a hair off the floor, and places it inside the compartment within his chest. "Do you?"

"I don't… Well, I might…" The right words elude me.

Do I believe?

A quickened pulse and sweaty palms say I might. But if I do, what will that mean for my future? Will Mom and Dad hate me or disown me for it? Will they shun me like Grams?

"Artie, can I ask you another question?"

"Ask any question you like, and I will do my best to answer it."

"Why are my parents opposed to people believing in God?"

"It's likely that they don't believe in a god themselves. Thus, they believe that people who believe in a god are misled."

"I guess that could make sense, but how does it hurt them?"

"I'm sorry, but I cannot answer that. You must ask your parents for an explanation."

"Fine, but why is Grams the enemy?"

"I have limited knowledge in this area, but I believe it might stem from feelings of guilt or fear, as I said before."

Guilt from their unbelief?

Can it be that simple? If so, what can Grams do to change Mom's and Dad's mind?

Have I changed mine?

"Thanks, Artie. You've given me a lot to ponder."

"I am pleased to be of service."

After a quick lunch of tomato soup and Ritz Crackers, I employ Artie to wrangle Sparkles from outside. After many failed attempts, he scoops Sparkles into his arms and carries her inside. She wiggles and squeals until he puts her down. Then, she barks at him like a dog. I'm sure she's yelling at him for handling her in such a manner. It makes me laugh. I stroke her back for a few minutes to settle her down, and then we head up to my bedroom.

Sparkles and I lie on the bed, me propped up against a wedge of pillows and she curled up next to me. A nap is in order, but my mind won't cooperate. It keeps returning to the secret portal and to the man named Gabe. Gemma said he created the portal, and I guess it makes sense. Things don't just create themselves, especially computer code.

But Dr. Von Schlippe said it's a self-learning system.

What exactly does that mean? Is the system self-aware, or does it simply evaluate and simplify its own code?

"How does that even work?"

Based on what Gabe told me, everything has a creator, so it makes more sense that Gabe's the one who created the secret portal and not the computer system itself.

So, does that mean we really do have a creator, too?

Logic alone says it must be true. But humans aren't only creatures of logic. We let our hearts lead us and rule us just as often as we use our minds. The more I think about it, the more muddled it becomes.

A loud buzz pulls me from my thoughts and draws my attention to my tablet on the nightstand. It only buzzes when I have a message or chat request. Both features have been locked via parental controls. Curiosity piqued, I snatch the tablet and open its cover. I have a notification: "Space Ranger 2008 has invited you to play Friendly Words. Would you like to install it now?"

It takes a few moments for my brain to decode the secret message.

"Roger!" Sparkles lifts her head, looks up at me, and snorts. "Oh, your royal majesty, I'm so sorry I disturbed you. Please accept my apologies and forgive this witless peasant girl." A good scratch underneath the chin satisfies Sparkles enough to return to her afternoon slumber.

After Friendly Words installs, I set up a profile under the name Princess Sparkles. Once finished, it starts a new game with Space Ranger 2008. Then, I receive a chat request and accept.

SR2008: [Hi, Kiara! This is Roger Daltrey, your BFF, in case you didn't know. I'm Space Ranger 2008. But I guess you already knew that.]

PS: [It's so good to hear from you! I've been locked away in this tower for longer than I can remember.]

SR2008: [Two days. LOL]

PS: [How did you know this would work?]

SR2008: [I didn't. It's about the fiftieth game and app I've tried. I was about to give up.]

PS: [Well, I'm glad you didn't and found a solution!]

SR2008: [Me, too! I'm sorry I failed you and got you into trouble, though. Will you forgive me?]

PS: [Nothing to forgive. I knew the risks and consequences. You warned me several times, too.]

SR2008: [Still, I feel horrible. The entire school knows you've been suspended. Principal Cornier made the announcement yesterday. Today, she announced they've finally contained the virus and disabled the portal.]

I feel as though I've just been gut-punched.

PS: [I hoped they'd never get it fixed.]

SR2008: [Yeah, it's too bad. After you went in the other day, I've been curious. Not enough to go in myself, of course, because of the suspension and all that.]

PS: [I know, and I don't blame you. My parents grounded me and took away all games, communications, and even going out to my own backyard. Plus, I have to write a research paper.]

SR2008: [Totally lame.]

PS: [Right? Well, thanks for finding a way to reach me.]

SR2008: [That's what friends are for.]

PS: [So… like I said, I must write a paper for my parents. Now that I know the secret portal has been disabled, I need to find Gabe.]

SR2008: [Gemma said that Gabe works at New Eden Library & Cafe, remember?]

PS: [Yep. ;)]

SR2008: [Do you think your parents will let you out to go to the library?]

PS: [If they think I'm doing research, they might. If so, would you be willing to meet me there?]

SR2008: [Sure, but why not just meet downstairs in the lobby? We can walk to the library together. As long as it's after school or on the weekend, that is.]

PS: [Cameras.]

SR2008: [Right. Hadn't thought of that. The library it is. When do you want to go?]

PS: [It must be after school. If I go on the weekend, one of my parents might insist on coming along.]

SR2008: [Good point. How about tomorrow at 3:15 pm?]

PS: [I'll figure it out. If it won't work for some reason, I'll send you a message.]

SR2008: [Sounds good. I really look forward to seeing you.]

PS: [Same. I'll leave at 3 pm so we're not seen leaving at the same time.]

SR2008: [Good plan!]

PS: [See you tomorrow.]

SR2008: [Tomorrow it is.]

I close out of the game and lean back against my pillows, happy for the first time in several days. The feeling fades as my mind starts pondering what lies ahead. If we find Gabe, will he talk to us? What will I ask him if he does? Once again, I'm a ball of nerves.

Have faith, Kiara.

CHAPTER TWENTY-TWO

HOT DIGGITY DOG

THE NEXT MORNING, DAD sits at the dining room table, sipping his black coffee and nibbling a piece of black toast while reading news articles from the display on the table's surface. No one's quite sure how he came to prefer his toast burned, not even Grams. Personally, I find it appalling.

I pull out the chair next to him and sit down with my bowl of chocolate oatmeal. "Hey, Dad."

He glances at me, sighs, and sets down his mug. "You think I don't know what you're doing?"

"What do you mean?" I unload a heaping spoonful of oatmeal into my mouth.

"I wasn't born yesterday, you know?"

Talking around the oatmeal, I say, "Yep. You're the one who named the dinosaurs."

He chuckles. "Exactly. Now, knowing this fact, what is it you want from me?"

"Actually, there are two things." I take another bite.

Dad raises an eyebrow. "Oh, really? One would be pushing it, but two?"

Swallowing, I say, "I wouldn't even ask, but they're both important."

"I'll be the judge of that." He takes a sip of his coffee and shoves the rest of his toast into his mouth.

"First, will you permit me to go to the library this afternoon?"

"The library? We have one of those here?"

"Don't be silly. You've asked me to write a research paper, and I want to be thorough. It's really a necessity."

"Can't you do your research online, like everyone else?"

"No, you've restricted my access. Remember? Besides, some resources aren't available online."

"Fair enough."

"Thank you! Thank you! Thank you!"

He gulps down the rest of his coffee and wipes his mouth with a napkin. "You're welcome. And the second request?"

"Artie won't allow me to leave the house."

He shrugs. "Well, you are grounded."

"Yes, but from the backyard, too?" I flash him my best puppy dog eyes. "Seems overly cruel, don't you think?"

Dad smiles. "Ah, I see. What you're saying is that Mom wasn't specific enough when giving Artie the parameters for your grounding. It certainly is a bit cruel, but not intentional, I'm sure. I'll adjust the parameters before I leave and instruct Artie to allow you to visit the library as well."

I reach over and wrap my arms around his neck. "Thank you, Daddy Bear."

He hugs me back. "You're welcome, Little Bear." After our embrace, he says, "Just remember, every single step you take is tracked. Make sure you go straight to the library and back. Understood?"

"I promise." The next bite of oatmeal tastes a thousand times sweeter than the first several.

After breakfast, I find myself constantly checking the time even though I've set an alarm and a reminder for 3 pm. When the hour finally arrives, Artie lifts my front door access restriction. I'm out the door and dematerializing in the Personal Transport Beam in two seconds flat.

Down in the building lobby, I pull up a map of New Eden and locate the New Eden Library and Cafe. It's four blocks from our building. Two up and two east. But I already know this. I studied the route all afternoon and memorized it. But it doesn't change the fact that I'm scared out of my mind right now. I've never left the building on my own let alone explored the city. Sure, I traversed Podunk by myself almost every day, but I also knew just about every single person who lived there and on the farms surrounding Podunk. Here, I know no one.

The front doors swing into the lobby as I approach. I ball my fists and force myself to exit the building.

"Have a good afternoon, Kiara Kole," the building's resident ghost says.

I mean it's not actually a ghost, but sometimes it feels that way when everything and everyone seem to know who I am. Outside, it's a perfect sixty degrees with no wind. There's no traffic to speak of and not a soul to be found as far as I can see in either direction.

Each step I take carries me farther from the building and helps me breathe a little easier. By the time I reach the library, I can't remember what had me so worked up in the first place. The brick and plaster building seems out of place amongst all the glass and steel buildings that surround it. In fact, it's the only building not made of glass and steel. But it does give it some charm and warmth, unlike the cold behemoths towering over it. Plus, its entrance sets it further apart. Ten concrete stairs lead up to a covered patio held up by six white columns. From what I recall, it's some sort of Roman style. I like it.

Several concrete benches flank the double door entrance. I sit down on one of them and wait for Roger to arrive. A few minutes later, he comes walking up the stairs. I jump up and greet him at the top, wrapping him in a hug before I even think about it.

Roger stiffens. "Um. Yeah. Hey, Kiara. Good to see you, too."

I pull back, my face on fire. "Wow. Did that just happen?" I smile sheepishly and head for the doors.

"Wait." Roger meets me at the door. "How are we supposed to find this Gabe guy?"

I frown. "You don't think we should just ask for him by name?"

"What if Gabe isn't his real name?" Roger asks.

"I'll recognize him. Jeans. T-shirt. Brown hair. Beard. Shouldn't be difficult."

"And what if he doesn't look like his avatar?"

"I don't know. We'll figure it out as we go. But he seems like the type of guy who is genuine. I don't think he'd hide who he is."

Roger sighs. "Fine. Lead the way."

Inside, the smells of fresh coffee and paper-bound books slap me from both directions. It's more heavenly than I ever imagined. To my left is the cafe part of the library. Several dozen tables and booths fill the large space, almost all of them occupied by someone with their nose in a book or their eyes glued to their laptop or electronic device.

To my right sits an information desk. An older gentleman sits on a stool behind it, reading a book. He sets the book down as we approach.

"Good afternoon, Miss Kole and Mister Daltrey." The man's voice is gruff, yet his enthusiasm seems genuine. "My name is Zeke, and it looks like you're both new to this establishment. Is that accurate?"

Roger and I look at each other. "Yes," we both say.

"Well hot diggity dog! On behalf of our staff, let me be the first to say, 'Welcome home!'" He winks. "I'll be honored to point you in the right direction no matter what subject you've come to wrangle."

I step up to the counter. "Well, Mr. Zeke—"

"Just Zeke. No mister needed."

"Yes, well, I'm writing a research paper on why humanity must prevent the end of the world."

Zeke whistles through the small gap in his front teeth. "Boy howdy, that there's a tall order for just about anyone."

"Yeah, I'm not looking forward to writing it."

"Lucky for you, you've come to the right place. We've got books on just about every subject known to man." Zeke leans toward us and whispers, "Some might even be unknown to man."

"So, what books would you recommend?" Roger asks.

Zeke stokes his stubbled chin. "Well, any good research paper should present both sides of an argument and then draw a conclusion, don't you think?"

I've never written a research paper before. "If you say so."

"So." He winks. "Now, you can find books aplenty on climate change, asteroid impacts, overpopulation, cybernetics, space travel, and many other subjects. But we've also got books you won't find anywhere else in New Eden." He leans close again. "Knowledge is power, and there's no censoring of books within these walls."

"I'm not sure I understand what you mean," I say.

"Well, it's simple. You must understand why some people think we need to prevent the end of the world and why some people think we don't. The only way to do that is to have books and materials that present both sides of the argument, just like what you should present in your research paper. Understand?"

I think about it a few moments. "Yeah, I think so."

"Good." He types in the air with his fingers. "Ah, yes. Looks like we have a great book on asteroid impacts and a few on climate change. Those will get you going for a start." He strokes his chin. "There we are. All set to go."

I glance at Roger and frown. "Go how?"

"Yes, of course. You're both new. Unlike other libraries, our books are VR experiences. Open up the asteroid impact book, and you'll be transported right to the past. Trust me, it'll knock your socks right off, even if you're wearing boots."

"VR books," Roger says. "Cool."

"Yep! Would you like to open an account as well?"

"Definitely!" Roger says.

Zeke types in the air again. "And… done." He turns to me. "I've added the books to your virtual library."

Everything Gabe said about God when I entered the secret portal floods my mind. Then I recall conversations I had with Grams about God, too. I lean over the counter. "Zeke, do you have any books about God?"

His gray eyes twinkle. "Thought you'd never ask." After more air typing, he says, "I've added the Bible and a few other books to your virtual library as well."

"Thanks!"

"You're very welcome. Now, how about the two of you have a look around the library. We've got a huge selection of physical books, too. Three floors worth, to be exact."

Roger grabs my shirt sleeve and pulls. "Come on. There are a few books I want to look for."

"I'll be right here if you need anything," Zeke says.

We thank him and head into the library behind the information desk.

Once out of earshot of everyone around, Roger stops. "Did you see who walked in?"

I look around. "No."

"Dr. Von Schlippe."

"Why would he be here?" My pulse quickens as the answer becomes obvious.

Gabe!

"Which way did he go?" I ask.

Roger points toward a dark staircase in the far corner. "Down there."

"Let's go!" I grab Roger's arm and drag him toward the staircase.

Roger yanks his arm from my grasp. "You don't have to force me along."

"Sorry!"

We descend the staircase and enter a large room full of filing cabinets. It smells like Grams's closet down here, and the lighting is terrible at best.

"I don't think we're supposed to be down here," Roger whispers.

Light pours from a doorway to my right. I head straight for it and pull up short when I hear Dr. Von Schlippe's voice. Roger's so close, I can feel his breath on my arm.

"You thought you were smart, didn't you?" Dr. Von Schlippe says.

"I still do." The man's voice sounds just like the one in the secret portal. It must be Gabe.

"Well, I'm here to tell you that I'm far smarter than you," Dr. Von Schlippe says. "I found your stupid portal in the game and disabled it. Then, I found the backdoor you installed and deleted it as well."

I hear clapping. "Bravo, Fredrick. You've got it all figured out."

"You think this is funny? Take a good look around. We'll come after you and everything you stand for if you don't back off."

"What, you and Cornier?"

"That's right. Plus a few others."

"Ah, I see. The Dark Prince of New Eden can't stomach the truth."

"Gregory's well informed. We all are. Your brand of truth is a disease."

"My brand?" Gabe scoffs. "Truth isn't a brand. You're on the wrong side of this, Fredrick. Knowledge and truth will always win in the end, no matter how much you oppose it."

"Really? Will you still be singing the same tune when we shut you down and run you out of town?"

"Save your threats. They're empty and pointless. GIST might own New Eden, but they don't own this library."

"Not yet. Interfere with CEVR Academy again, and you'll regret it."

"Prevent the children from accessing knowledge and truth, and your fate will be insufferable."

"You're threatening me?" Dr. Von Schlippe growls.

"It's not a threat, Fredrick. Deny God from anyone, and you will answer to him in the end."

"Listen to yourself. There is no God, and you know it. You're pathetic and delusional."

"Lord God, I pray that you open Fredrick's eyes."

"*My* eyes are wide open. You're the one who's blind."

Heavy footfall grows louder. Roger and I scramble to hide behind a row of filing cabinets. Through an opening between two of the filing cabinets, I watch a shadow grow out of the light through the doorway. Dr. Von Schlippe emerges from the room and stomps right past our row of filing cabinets. He curses Gabe and the library as he ascends the staircase and disappears from view.

I kneel and exhale.

Roger takes a puff from his inhaler. "That was too close."

Another shadow fills the doorway. I yank on Roger's pant leg, and he squats next to me.

Bang!

Roger's knee collides with the filing cabinet. It's enough to wake the dead. "Who's there?"

The man from the secret portal steps into the doorway and stares right at our row of filing cabinets. Not just at our row, but right at the ones we're hiding behind. He can't possibly see us through the narrow opening, yet his gaze meets mine.

Roger looks at me, his face pale and his eyes bulging. I'm not sure if he's just scared or about to have an asthma attack. Either way, it raises the threat level. Sends my pulse racing faster. Catches my breath in my throat. The only thing I can think to do is run.

So, I do.

CHAPTER TWENTY-THREE

NOWHERE TO RUN

TO SAY NOTHING EVER goes according to plan would be an understatement. When I made the decision to run while kneeling on the floor behind the row of metal filing cabinets, I failed to convey the message to Roger. Not only did I fail at that point but at the next one as well. Somehow, Roger's foot worked its way behind me when he crouched down and hit the filing cabinet with his knee.

As I turn to run, my foot catches Roger's and unbalances me. Not one but three filing cabinet drawers pull loose as I flail about, grabbing at everything as I try and save myself from headbutting the next row of filing cabinets.

Bam! Bam! Crash!

Lying on my side, buried beneath a mound of papers and metal drawers, I assess the damage I've caused myself and the library. Roger stares at me, his mouth agape and eyes as big as saucers. It's impossible for me to criticize his inaction. I'm not sure I would do anything different from him if our positions were reversed.

Gabe appears from the opposite direction and kneels next to me. "Are you okay?" His tone is as gentle as ever, and the only emotion I detect in his eyes when my shameful gaze meets his is compassion.

I take a moment and assess myself. Nothing feels broken except my ego. I've never felt more embarrassed in my life. "Yeah, I think so."

Gabe and Roger unbury me and then Gabe helps me to my feet. "I'm sorry about all this."

Guilt constricts my chest as I stare at the gigantic mess. "You didn't do anything. This is all my fault."

"Might feel that way from your point of view, but you don't have the entire picture." Gabe bends down and starts stacking the papers.

"I'm not following you." I kneel and start gathering papers into another pile.

"Neither am I," Roger says, joining the cleanup effort.

Gabe stops gathering papers and sits on the floor. "I was supposed to scan all these files into our records system long ago, but I've been procrastinating. There's always something more important or more exciting to work on. Had I done it, these filing cabinets wouldn't be here, and you wouldn't have tangled yourself up in them; ergo, this is my fault."

"Well, I feel guilty anyway."

"Me, too." Gabe and I look at Roger.

"You had nothing to do with this," I say.

"Yes, I did. It was my foot that tripped you."

Gabe laughs. "From the sounds of it, we're all guilty in some fashion, and that holds true in all aspects of life. Praise God we have a redeemer." He proffers his hand toward me. "I'm Gabe, by the way."

"Yeah, I know." I take his hand and give it a quick shake. "I'm Kiara, and this is Roger."

Roger shakes Gabe's hand. "Hi."

"A pleasure," Gabe says.

Silence settles between the three of us, yet it's not awkward like most situations between strangers. I feel as though I've known Gabe my entire life despite having just met him and knowing nothing about him beyond hearsay. Perhaps it has something to do with our encounter in the secret portal. Yet that wasn't real. That Gabe is only a shadow of the man sitting across from me. More likely, it's the genuine kindness that exudes from his knowing gaze. He reminds me of Pops.

Gabe breaks the silence. "You're the one who discovered the secret portal." It's a statement, not a question, yet I feel compelled to respond.

"Yeah." My gaze falls to my hands, still clutching several sheets of paper. "I'm sorry if I've caused you trouble."

"On the contrary. I created the portal in hopes that someone would discover it." He smiles when I look up at him. "I'm happy it was someone like you."

Goosebumps rise on my arms. "What do you mean?"

"Someone smart, strong, and brave," Roger says.

Gabe chuckles. "She may possess those attributes, along with many others, but I'm referring to her openness to seek truth through knowledge. Few ever seek God while striving to accomplish their own goals, especially when it involves saving themselves or humanity as a whole."

The nobility he's assigned me feels like a lie itself. "But I wasn't seeking God… Was I?"

"You tell me."

"She was." Roger shakes his head. "No, she is. I think we all are in our own way, even if we don't always recognize it."

"Profound words," Gabe says. He turns his gaze back on me. "So, what made you seek me out here in the basement of the library?"

"Well, after meeting you in the game, Principal Cornier forbade us from accessing the secret portal. She said it was a virus and dangerous. At first, I believed her, but, as I thought about it more, I came to the conclusion that she and Dr. Von Schlippe were hiding something. Finally, Roger and I came up with a plan for me to access the portal again without getting caught."

"But you did, didn't you," Gabe says.

"Despite taking several precautions including Roger writing code to hide my presence and location in the game, I was caught. Principal Cornier suspended me from school, and my parents grounded me. Then, my parents assigned me a research paper on why humanity must prevent the end of the world. It presented me with the perfect excuse to come to the library."

"And how did you know I worked here?"

"Gemma Prince," Roger says with disgust.

Gabe nods. "Yes, I see. The daughter of Gregory Prince. I've never been on his good side, either."

"I bet not." No matter how hard I try, I can't seem to force myself to bring up the real reason I'm here.

"You said coming here on the pretense of research was an excuse." Gabe cocks his head. "So, why have you come?"

He reads minds!

It's absurd, naturally. "Well, I…" I look to Roger for encouragement, and his goofy smile fuels me. "Since Dr. Von Schlippe has disabled the portal and deleted all the code, I was wondering if you could tell me more about it. Why did you design it? What made you embed it into the game? What else would you have taught me if I'd made it past the first quiz?"

Gabe leans back against one of the filing cabinets. "Truth and knowledge should never be prevented, censored, or altered. I tried reasoning with Dr. Von Schlippe, Peggy Cornier, and Gregory Prince about the dangers of the direction they were headed, leaving out God and therefore truth. They found my views disturbing and counter to their own belief that God doesn't exist. They stood firm that nothing and no one has control and therefore insisted on teaching that the only path to survival is for humans to find a way to take control. Knowing my views would eventually get me fired, I created a backdoor into the game so that I could install this secret portal, as you call it."

"And the rest?" Roger asks. "What does it teach?"

"I'm sorry, but I can't just tell you about it. It's a journey each of you must take. One you must see and learn."

"But it's gone!" I smack the top of one of the piles of papers I created.

Gabe holds up a finger. "Nothing is ever really gone. Have faith and patience, and the opportunity to seek truth and knowledge will present itself to you once again."

"Ugh." I sigh loudly. "Fine."

Roger sifts through some of the papers. "What is it you do here, other than scan old documents?"

"As the lead and only programmer here, I take books and create VR experiences from them. This is what our library is known for. You'll find no books or an experience like it anywhere else in the world. I guarantee it."

"That's what Zeke told us," I say. "Like watching a movie, right?"

Gabe chuckles. "Not quite. As I said, they are VR *experiences*. You will take on the role of the main character or narrator and live the experience, so to speak."

Roger says, "So they're like the game world at school."

Gabe strokes his wild beard. "In a sense, yes. However, the books follow a narrative and are linear, so their worlds aren't wide open like your game world."

"Got it," Roger says.

I'm glad someone does.

"Speaking of experiences, I have a favorite book that both of you might enjoy. It's called *A Light in the Darkness*. Just ask Zeke to add it to your virtual libraries before you leave."

"Okay. You said it's called *A Light in the Darkness*?" I ask.

"That's the one. Trust me—" He taps the side of his head. "—it'll open your minds to a whole new world."

"I won't forget."

"I won't let her," Roger says.

"Good." Gabe pulls himself up off the floor. "Now, I've got some papers to organize and scan."

I stand. "Would you like us to help?"

He waves me off with a smile. "Nah, you're better off reading a good book."

"Okay, then. I guess we'll leave you to it." I help Roger to his feet, and we ease our way through the file cabinet carnage. Turning back, I say, "Thank you, Gabe. It was nice meeting you."

"Yeah," Roger adds.

Gabe nods. "Likewise." He scoops up a handful of papers and heads toward the room in the back.

After looking around the library for a bit, Roger and I return to Zeke at the information desk.

"Gabe said to ask you to add a book to our virtual libraries," I say.

Zeke smiles. "Already done."

I frown. "But I didn't tell you the title."

"No need. Gabe came up and told me himself."

"Well, good," I say. "However, I do have one slight problem."

"What's that?" Zeke asks.

"I don't know how to access this virtual library you say I have."

"Ah, that's an easy problem to solve. Do you have a VR visor?"

"Yeah, I'm a student at CEVR Academy."

"Very good! That's all you need. Once you turn it on, you can access your library using the command 'virtual library.' Easy as that."

"Well, that creates another issue. Since I've been suspended from school, I don't think I have access to anything."

"I assure you, that's not the case. You might be locked out of the school right now, but your virtual library resides outside of that system. Think of it like a private room."

I sigh. "Thank goodness!"

"Thank God." Zeke winks. "Anything else?"

I look at Roger and he shakes his head. "I guess not."

"May both of you have a blessed day, and I look forward to our next encounter."

"Me, too," Roger and I say.

Outside at the top of the stairs, I hug Roger. "Thank you for meeting me here."

"Don't mention it." He steps back. "No, really. Don't mention it. My parents would freak if they knew I was here with you."

"Really? Why?"

Roger scratches the back of his neck. "Um… Well… Your mom kinda came up to our house the other day and explained the situation to my parents and asked them to keep us apart until after your suspension lifted."

I gasp. "She didn't!"

"Yeah. After that, my parents said that maybe we shouldn't be friends because you'd be a bad influence on me."

A lump rises in my throat. I descend a few steps and sit down. New Eden blurs before me. "I'm sorry, Roger. I've ruined everything." Tears slip down my cheeks.

"That's not true." He sits down next to me and touches my arm but then quickly pulls his hand back. "I… I don't care what my parents think of you. You're my best friend, and nothing will change that."

"Thank you." I wipe my face on my sleeve. "Sorry I started crying. I'm a big baby sometimes."

"You're not a baby, and I'm glad our friendship means that much to you." He removes his glasses and wipes his eyes. "It means everything to me, too."

We say our goodbyes, and then Roger hangs back at the library while I start the trek back home. The last thing either of us needs is to be seen together. The thought makes me sad, especially knowing it's all my fault. However, I'm not sure I'd change anything given the chance to go back.

As I saunter down the sidewalk, disappointment fills my heart. I'd hoped meeting Gabe would've gone differently. He represented my hope of getting answers to all the questions floating around in my head, but now I'm lost and on my own once again. Tears blur my vision and streak down my cheeks again. I don't bother wiping them away until I reach our skyrise building.

As I step onto the floor plate and call out my floor, one thought burns a hole in my mind.

God, if you're out there, help me understand who you are.

CHAPTER TWENTY-FOUR

NOT AN ACCIDENT

AS THE END OF the third week of my suspension and grounding draws to a close, I find myself thinking about Gabe and the secret portal again. My mind hovers around what he said about control. In order to discover the truth, I must seek to understand who is in control. If nothing else, these past weeks have taught me that I control nothing. And, if I control nothing, then who does?

God?

Sure, my parents control what I eat, watch, and how I spend my time, but there are things beyond their control, too. No one controls the weather, although there are many scientists working to achieve just that. No one controls the rotation of the earth or the gravity that holds everything to the earth, either. The migration of birds. The wind. So many things are beyond my control and without control, so how do they stay in balance? What prevents the moon from colliding with the earth or the sun from pulling all the planets into its fiery embrace? Sure, we have science to explain how things work, but who made the rules to begin with? Could it simply be chance? Controlled chaos? The more I ponder it, the more absurd it sounds.

There must be a controller.

If a controller must exist, then why should it be so absurd to think of it or him as God? After all, it would take an enormously powerful being to control everything in the entire universe. But is that job too big for a single being?

As I sit at my desk, I stare at my tablet. Not only does the tablet have a creator, but that creator also controls every aspect of it. How it displays information. The way it processes data in order to display it. If I think of the universe in similar terms, I can almost wrap my head around it having a single controller. A finite set of rules that govern everything.

Now that this concept of a controller and creator makes sense, I ponder the questions Gabe asked me in the secret portal. Yes, the cellphone is manufactured by a company, and a chicken does lay the egg, but the earth… I cringe as my mind plays back my response to it: an explosion. The truth stares me right in the face. All I need to do is reach for it.

It's not chaos.

Even if the universe was formed by a big explosion or bang, something had to have created it, right? I've never witnessed a random explosion in the middle of nowhere without fuel and an igniter. No, an explosion doesn't just happen from nothing. Therefore, I'm right back where I started: who created the earth?

My entire body tingles, and a sense of purpose fills my mind as the answer leaves my lips. "God."

Has Grams been right all this time?

If so, why do Mom and Dad oppose her? Why do they oppose God? Did he hurt them in some way I'm unaware of? Is there some secret that's been kept from me? The answer comes to me without effort: they're afraid of losing control.

But they don't have control now.

Revelations come to me in waves. I blamed my parents for ending my world by moving us to New Eden. But now I see moving here wasn't a bad thing after all. I wonder if God wanted us to move here so that I could learn about him?

His master plan.

Every trial I've faced led me to this moment. This epiphany I might never have had otherwise. What I saw as bad with my limited knowledge and vision he took and used for good. Grams tried so hard to get me to see, understand, and believe in God, but I wasn't ready. I didn't have the experiences necessary to come to the obvious conclusion. Now I do.

I feared the move to New Eden would end my world, but now I can see that Mom and Dad were in control. They moved us here with the best of intentions for them and me. Somehow, they knew I'd learn to like it here and would learn a lot. Had I thought about it from the start, I never would've feared the move. Mom and Dad love me too much to hurt me like that.

Now that I think about it, I can see that it's the same with God. I fear the end of the world with every breath and hope Mom and Dad continue to learn as much as possible to prevent it, just like I am. But if God is in control and created everything for us, that must mean God loves us, too. If this is true, there's no need for me to fear the end of the world. After all, God is love, right? He cares about me and everything else in the universe. He's in control even when I can't see it. Through him, I have nothing to fear.

With this added knowledge, I blaze through the last pages of my research paper, rarely coming up for air. Sure, humanity faces many life-altering events, but we aren't in control of any of them. God is, and he loves us.

With fervor, I put the finishing touches on my research paper and then head downstairs. Mom and Dad huddle on the couch, watching some program about how humanity can harness the sun's power using what they call a Dyson sphere. It's far beyond anything my brain can comprehend.

I sit down on the chair next to the couch. "I finished my research paper."

"Did you?" Dad asks.

Mom pauses the TV program. "And what did you learn from it?"

"Actually, a lot. Just read it." I hand the stack of papers to Mom. "Can I go outside and play with Sparkles while you read it?"

Dad nods. "Artie, remove Kiara's outdoor restrictions."

"Your request has been completed," Artie says almost immediately.

I run outside and splay out in the grass. Sparkles climbs out of her mud pit, shakes herself off, and runs over to me, oinking and squealing like she's not seen me in months. In truth, it feels that way to me, too.

About an hour later, Dad sticks his head out the back door and calls me back inside. He wears a grim face, and it curdles my stomach. Inside, Mom and Dad sit at the dining room table. Neither of them looks happy. Dad points at the chair across from the two of them. I take a deep breath, sit down, and brace myself for the wrath that's about to be unleashed.

Mom begins, "As you're well aware, you broke the rules laid down by Principal Cornier and violated the trust we had placed in you."

My eyes search for something to focus on. Anything but the disappointment in their eyes. "I know, and I'm really sorry about that. I promise it will never happen again, and I'll work to restore that trust."

Dad leans forward and clasps his hands on the table. "What do you think about the research paper you wrote?"

"I… Well… You see…" No words seem sufficient.

"Relax, Kiara," Mom says. "Look at me." When I do, I fail to detect the disappointment so prevalent in her eyes moments before.

Dad's scowl fades. "To be honest, I expected you to put little effort into the assignment."

"A spewing of everything the world touts," Mom says.

"What we didn't expect was a solid paper with research on both sides of the issues surrounding how humanity will save the world. First, you explained that some people believe that no one is in control and thus humanity must intervene to control the chaos. Then, you explained that other people believe that God is in control and that there's no need to be afraid or try to control the perceived chaos." Finally, Dad smiles, driving back the tension in the room. "You drew a conclusion at the end that blew us both away."

Mom wipes a tear from her eye. "It proves you've learned to think for yourself."

"Kiara, we've never been prouder of you than we are right now." Dad tears up.

"But… I don't understand. I thought you hated God or didn't believe in him. Isn't that why you're always pushing Grams away? Because she believes in God? Didn't you read the end? I believe in God now, too. Do you hate me now?"

Mom gets up and comes around to my side of the table. She hugs me around the neck and kisses my cheek. "We could never hate you, no matter what you believe or what you do. We don't hate Grams, either. To be honest, your paper helped open our eyes a little. Your dad and I have both strayed from the faith over the years. But we never hated Grams. The only reason we prevented her from teaching you about her beliefs was so that you could be free to discover your own. I know it sounds crazy, and maybe it is, but that's a decision your dad and I made the night you were born. God hasn't been a priority in our lives, and your paper has shown us he should be, so thank you for that."

"What does that mean?" I ask.

Mom looks over at Dad, but he's too busy wiping his face with his shirtsleeve to notice. "I think that's something we'll have to talk about later as a family. For now, how about you go up to your room and give Grams a call. I'm sure she'd love to hear all about how your paper writing went."

I gasp. "She knows?"

"Of course," Dad says. "We keep her in the loop about everything."

After hugging Mom and Dad several times, I head up to my room and settle on my bed with my tablet. When Grams's face comes up on the screen, I can't hold back tears of joy.

"I believe in God, Grams, just like you!" I blurt out.

Grams's smile lights up my entire world. "I never doubted you would, Kay-Kay. How did you come to this momentous decision?"

Grams and I discuss everything that's happened over the last three weeks, leaving nothing out.

"As I've said before," Grams says, "anything can be accomplished with a simple prayer to God. I've been praying for you since the day you came into this world. Today, that prayer's been answered, and I must tell you, God is good!"

Tears fill my eyes. "You've been doing that for me?"

"That's what we do for those we love. No one is beyond the need or help of God."

"I know that, now."

"Now that you believe in God, you need to nourish that relationship and allow your faith in him to grow. His love for you can conquer your fears."

The sentiment comforts me. By the time Grams and I finish talking, a new day has begun. With the lights out, I lie in bed and stare up at the universe displayed on my ceiling.

It's not an accident, and neither am I.

CHAPTER TWENTY-FIVE

A LIGHT IN THE DARKNESS

IT'S MY FIRST DAY back to school after my suspension, and I feel great. The only downside is the three weeks of lectures I'll have to make up, and that doesn't include the time I've lost in the game world. My goal of reaching the top one thousand has become a goal to reach the top three thousand instead. Even that will be an uphill struggle given that my rank is now 4,782/4,794.

As soon as I walk into my first period Language Arts class, I'm greeted by Gemma. "Ugh. I thought we were rid of you."

Nothing she says will ruin my day. I won't let it. "It's good to see you, too."

Gemma huffs and rolls her eyes. "Whatever." She turns her back to me and starts a conversation with one of her pack.

Roger waves at me from the back of the classroom. I wave back and sit down right as the final bell rings. By the end of the day, I'm ready for a nap, but a nap won't help me get through the lessons and stop an asteroid. After a quick bathroom break, I reconnect and head across the bridge and into the game world.

As soon as I'm through the door, I'm met with a world I hardly recognize. Gray clouds thick with snow have swallowed up the warm sun and painted blues skies, transforming the once inviting world into one full of bluster and verging on despair. The waist-high fields of golden grass now lie bent and broken beneath a blanket of snow. The change disorients me, and the cold wind against my face leaves me chilled all the way down to my toes.

Snow crunches beneath my feet. The sound almost makes me believe I'm walking through it. In Podunk, we saw more freezing rain than snow, and when it snowed it was usually little more than a dusting. I would've given just about anything to have snow like this. It's too bad I can't feel it.

In the sky, Crusher continues its approach. Fifty-seven days remain, according to the doomsday clock. I sigh.

Time to get to work.

One lesson remains incomplete from the last quarter and prevents me from moving forward. As much as I loathe math, I'd give anything for it to be fractions or geometry or anything else like that. Instead, it's a technology lesson. I must complete it to receive the second component for the laser.

Pulling up the map on my heads-up display, I locate the last area I was at before winter break—the base of Black Sea Mountain to the north. Given the distance and my self-inflicted time constraint, I opt to jump there instead of walking.

"Black Sea Mountain."

The world jerks and phases from the snow-covered field to the base of a mountain taller than the sky. I say that because its peak rises beyond the clouds and cannot be seen from the ground. Black rock flows down through a sparse forest of white aspens, giving the mountain its name.

The forest, aptly named Toothpick Holt, scales the southern face. No vegetation remains along its other three faces, each stripped clean long ago by devastating lava flows. Rumor has it that a clan of black mountain sheep have made their home among the mountain's sheer faces, but no human has ever verified it to be true.

I wonder if Regis Owl knows.

A sign just ahead and to my left marks the beginning of the twelfth technology lesson: TE12 - Syntax Slope. After a deep breath, I step onto the slope but get no farther than a few steps. The rocks flow underneath my feet like water, preventing me from climbing.

After a second look, I notice that the lesson sign has a picture of a person holding a grappling hook. A quick check of my inventory reveals I have one as well. I select it and press the action button on my controller. The hook swings in a circle and launches toward the first tree when I release the button. It hooks the base of the tree, and the rope becomes taut. I press the action button again, and my avatar scales the slope and reaches the first tree.

A question displays in front of me:

In JavaScript, how do you create a variable?

A. var

B. let
C. const
D. All of the above
E. None of the above

There are five trees above me, each with a letter corresponding to an answer. "The answer is—"

I stop myself from saying "A" when I remember something Roger told me. The word variable sounds like it should vary, but a variable can also be constant. So, if "A" and "C" are both correct, then I suppose "B" must also be correct.

"The answer is 'D,'" I say.

Tree "D" highlights in green. I twirl and toss my grappling hook toward it, and the hook catches. Halfway to the tree, the sea of rocks shifts, and the other four trees break off at their bases and get swept down the slope.

Thank you, Roger!

The next several questions are a breeze, but then I come to a loop question. Loops are my enemy. The question follows:

Given the following JavaScript code block:

```
for(var i = 0; i <= 20; i++) {
        //do something here.
    }
```

How many times will the for loop be executed?

A. 19
B. 20
C. 21

Three trees above me correspond to the answer letters. As I stare at the problem, each answer has some merit. But my gut says it isn't "A." Therefore, the answer must be either "B" or "C."

But which one?

Creepy Dr. Von Schlippe said something about the order of precedence in the parameters of the for loop, but I don't recall what it was. "Ugh! Think,

Kiara. Does it start at zero or does one get added first?"

Without an inkling as to which order it is, I go with the first number that pops in my head. "The answer is 'B.'"

The grappling hook whirls over my head and sails through the air. The hook wraps around the tree marked "B" and the line becomes taut.

"Yes!"

Halfway up, the sea of rock moves again. Tree "A" gets swept down the slope.

Crack!

Tree "B" splits in half, sending my controller into a vibrating fit.

The world flips upside-down.

Grappling hook rises up, meets the end of its rope, and comes sailing back down.

Right at my face.

A scream bellows from my lips, and my stomach leaps into my throat as the grappling hook smacks me square in the forehead.

My head jars with the impact.

The world stops moving.

Goes black.

I groan. "Did I die again?"

After a few seconds of darkness, the world comes back to life.

Vida, the Virtual Interface Digital Assistant, speaks to me. "Kiara, you've selected an incorrect answer. It is recommended that you review the lesson before continuing with the final three questions because you will not survive another fall."

Good to know.

"Would you like to view the lesson now?" Vida asks.

Watching Dr. Von Schlippe again is the last thing I want to do, but I need to pass this lesson. "Yes."

A video screen appears in front of me and starts playing Dr. Von Schlippe's lesson on JavaScript from a few weeks ago.

He begins, "Today, we will go over JavaScript for loops and the order of precedence of the parameters passed to it."

It takes willpower to keep from zoning out as he speaks in a ridiculous monotone voice.

"The precedence is just as written—left to right. Let's take a look at the following for loop:" Dr. Von Schlippe writes the JavaScript code in the air with his finger:

```
for(var i = 0; i < 10; i++) {}
```

The code hangs in the air and displays in green. "So, 'i' starts at zero and gets incremented at the end of each loop. The second parameter determines the condition that must be met each time the loop executes. Given the example, the loop will execute ten times." His eyes survey the classroom, and he shakes his head. "Some of you are failing to grasp this. Yes, the condition is less than ten, but 'i' starts at zero, not one. Therefore, it executes ten times, not nine."

The video screen disappears, and Vida says, "The correct response was 'C' because the condition of the loop was less than or equal to twenty and the variable 'i' started at zero. Therefore, twenty-one loop executions. Does this explanation make sense to you?"

It actually does. "Yes."

"Good. As I said before, please proceed with caution when answering the final three questions. You will not survive another fall."

After reaching the final question, Vida speaks again. "Access to the game server will be turned off in five minutes. Please finish anything you're doing and exit the system. Your progress will be automatically saved."

"This ends now," I growl. I read the question again:

Consider the following JavaScript block:

```
var myNum = 10;
myNum += 5;
myNum /= 3;
myNum *= 8;
myNum -= 30;
myNum //= 2;
```

What is the final value of the variable "myNum?"

A. 0
B. 5
C. 10

D. 30
E. 58

"Ugh. Programming and math. Couldn't be worse." I bite my lip and start thinking aloud. "So, we have ten plus five. That's fifteen. Divide that by three… Five. Times it by eight… That's forty. Then we subtract thirty, leaving us at ten. After dividing by two, we get five. So, the answer should be—wait a minute. That last part has two forward-slashes, not one. That means… it's a comment!"

"One minute until you will be logged out," Vida says.

"Okay!" I run through the math one more time. "The answer is 'C!'"

I hook the tree marked "C" and begin ascending.

"Thirty seconds," Vida warns.

Halfway up, the ground moves again.

"Twenty seconds."

Trees "A" and "E" snap and get swept away.

"Fifteen seconds."

Three-quarters of the way up, the controller vibrates in my hands. "No! 'C' has to be the right answer!"

"Ten seconds."

Tree "D" falls.

"Five seconds."

My hands begin shaking. "Come on!"

Tree "B" cracks. Snaps. Gets swept away.

"Good jo—"

My visor goes dark.

"No!"

"You have been removed from the game," Vida says.

A few seconds later, the visor comes back to life. I'm standing outside the front entrance of the school. The doors are locked and the windows dark.

"Heads-up on." Nothing changes. No stats, id, map, or anything. Except the time—5:05 pm. There is that. "Well, that's lame."

I'm about to turn off my VR visor when a light turns on through one of the school windows. The blood drains from my face when Principal Cornier appears at the window. I sprint over to one of the trees and hide beneath its shadow. From the darkness I watch her, my breath held. For a moment, I swear she watches me, but then another figure appears at the window next to her.

Dr. Von Schlippe!

She turns and faces him, leaving me with a view of the backside of her head. Based on the expression on Dr. Von Schlippe's face, she's reaming him about something. From this distance, I couldn't read his lips even if I knew how to. But him at the only lit window triggers a thought.

A Light in the Darkness.

Caught up in the excitement of being back at school, I'd all but forgotten about the book Gabe recommended I read. And, if I'm being honest, I still feel a tinge of betrayal on his part after our awkward exchange at the New Eden Library and Cafe.

Why did he refuse to tell me more about the secret portal?

The longer I stand beneath the tree, cloaked in shadows, the more I think about the secret portal. Dr. Von Schlippe told Gabe he'd disabled it and removed the code, but had he really? The question quickens my pulse.

I could try to access it again... but should I?

What will happen if it works? Will Principal Cornier expel me from school this time? If it opens, I can just turn off my visor. No one's watching now, right?

The school sits dark once again. I swallow hard. "When did they leave?"

Try it, says a voice in my head.

But Roger will kill me if I get caught again.

"Just don't go in if it works." I nod to myself in agreement and exhale every last molecule of oxygen from my lungs before taking a deep breath. I close my eyes and ready myself for the secret portal's bright light. "I really thought death would be the end."

Chills run down my nape, but no bright light shines through my closed eyelids, so I say it again. Still nothing.

Anger consumes me. "What right do they have to deny us of truth and knowledge?"

None.

My mind returns to Gabe. To the lit window. To the book.

At 5:20 pm, curiosity gets the better of me. "Access library."

The school fades, and a medium-sized room replaces it. A cherry wood table sits at the center of the room with a chair tucked underneath it. Above the table hangs a massive iron chandelier, complete with faux candles that flicker. To my left, a built-in bookcase spans the entire wall. Like the desk, it's also made of cherry wood. Just nine books grace its shelves, all from the New Eden Library and Cafe. A fireplace built from jagged stones covers the wall to my right, its hearth large enough for me to step into it. In front of the fireplace sits a single plush chair wrapped in dark emerald leather. A matching ottoman sits next to it.

It's 5:24 pm. I only have a half-dozen minutes before Mom and Dad return from work, so I grab the book Gabe recommended from the bookcase shelf and sink into the plush chair by the fireplace. In the real world, my hands tremble, the controller somewhat of a substitute for the book. One button click will open the book.

But will it open something else as well?

The absurd thought fades. "It's just a book. Open it." But my finger hesitates. *This isn't school, and it's only a book.*

Click!

The book opens to a title page. "*A Light in the Darkness* by Gabriel."

I click through several more pages: copyright, dedication, half title, and then comes chapter one. Just five words fill the space below the chapter heading. I read them aloud. "Will you be that light?"

Flipping ahead, all the pages are blank. I keep going. All the way to the end of the book. The last page repeats the first: "Will you be that light?"

I repeat the words and wait for a response, but none comes. That's when I realize it must be waiting for a response from me.

"Yes," I say, nearly breathless.

The book shoots out of my hands and into the hearth. Then, the book explodes with light. Brilliant, white light. The light fills the room and blinds me.

You did give me a way back in, Gabe!

"Kiara? We're home."

Mom's voice!

I jab the side of my head several times until the VR visor finally powers down. The light fades, and the visor transforms back into goggles. I pull them off my head and toss them and the controller on my desk.

My heart thunders. "I'm coming down!" I head for the stairs, my head back in the clouds again.

I can't wait to tell Roger!

CHAPTER TWENTY-SIX

THE KEY OF TRUTH

ROGER SITS ACROSS THE table from me, slurping down a bowl of spicy noodles with chicken, peas, and carrots. A length of noodle hangs from his chin, swaying as he chews. As mesmerizing as it is, it still doesn't take my mind off the book Gabe gave me and the secret the book holds. I've sat on this knowledge for two full weeks, waiting for an opportunity to tell Roger about it, but no moment presents itself. What I really mean is that I don't know how to tell him and fear how he'll react when he finds out I'm planning on accessing it tonight.

"Kiara?" Roger says.

"Huh?"

"What's with you?" The noodle dangles.

My eyes fixate on it. "What do you mean?"

"Just now. I called your name several times before you responded. You've been this way for the last few weeks. It's like you're lost or trapped within your own mind sometimes."

"Am I?" It's a perfect moment to broach the subject of the secret portal, so I naturally avoid it. "You've got a noodle hanging from your chin."

Roger snatches the noodle off his chin and drops it into his open mouth after tilting his head back. "Still good." He smiles, but it quickly fades. "We're still best friends, right?"

"The best. Why?"

His blue eyes probe mine. "Don't best friends tell each other everything?"

He knows I'm holding out on him!

I inhale a piece of apple, and it lodges deep in my throat. A fit of coughing ensues, bringing tears to my eyes. Roger panics and jumps to his feet to come to my rescue, but that's the problem with having virtual lunch with someone: no rescue is possible. All one can do is watch in horror.

"Kiara!"

By the time I get the apple dislodged from my throat, Roger's beside himself, his face drained of color. Unfortunately, he's also attracted the attention of the entire cafeteria. More specifically, Gemma.

"I'm okay," I manage.

Roger returns to his seat as the color in his cheeks begins to return. "I was about to run downstairs and rescue you."

Gemma walks over to the table. "Trouble chewing, Swan Girl? Maybe your boyfriend should do it for you. That's how baby birds eat, you know. They get ABC food."

ABC food?

"That's gross," Roger stammers. "And I'm not her boyfriend."

Gemma sneers at Roger. "Struck a nerve, did I?"

Roger stands and faces Gemma. His short stature does him no favors. "Go dig a hole and bury yourself."

"Thanks for your concern," I say.

Gemma glares at me. "The only concern I have is that you're still a student at this school."

"Get used to it," Roger says. "She's not going anywhere."

"That's for sure. She'll be back on the farm in no time." She turns. "Let's go, girls. We've got better things to do." Her and her groupies stick their noses up and exit the cafeteria. Everyone else returns to their conversations.

Roger sits back down and groans. "Why do people like her exist?"

"Not everything is her fault." My mind conjures that first day at GIST. "I've met her dad."

"She insults you, and you make excuses for her?" He shakes his head. "She doesn't deserve your kindness."

"It doesn't matter."

"Fine, but what does matter is the fact that you're keeping something from me."

I nod. "Yeah..."

Roger frowns. "Just tell me. I can handle anything. Promise."

"No one can handle *anything*." I inhale and let the breath out slowly. "It's about the secret portal."

"I thought it was gone." Roger's eyes narrow. "Isn't it?"

"Yes... and no." There's no point in holding back anymore, so I don't. "The day I returned to school, I logged in after hours. The school was locked, but one light remained on. I saw Principal Cornier and Dr. Von Schlippe arguing."

"About what?" Roger asks.

"I don't know. I can't read lips." I shake my head. "Anyway, after they left, I decided to try and see if the portal still existed. I figured it was outside of school hours so no one would be watching."

"And?"

"Nothing happened."

Relief washes across Roger's face. "Well, that settles it."

"Not quite." I let a few moments pass as I work up the courage to tell him the rest. "You remember the book Gabe said we should read?"

"Not specifically, but yeah, I guess so."

"It's not just a book. In fact, almost every page in the book is blank."

"That's weird. Why would he recommend it?"

"As I said, it's not just a book. Remember, the book is called *A Light in the Darkness*. So, the only words in the first chapter are 'Will you be that light?'"

Roger's brow furrows. "I don't get it."

"I didn't either, at first. After that page, all the rest were blank until the final page. It repeated the question. Finally, I answered it."

"Huh?"

"I said yes, and the book flew out of my hands and opened the secret portal."

Roger cringes. "I don't like where this is going."

"I didn't go in. In fact, I turned off my VR visor right after it happened, and I haven't gone to my virtual library since."

"Good." Roger gives me a hard stare. "Do us both a favor and return the book to the library before you get caught."

"That's the thing. This happened two weeks ago, and no one's said anything about it."

"That's probably because you didn't go into it."

"Maybe… or it's something else. The virtual library exists outside of school, right?"

"Yeah, I guess."

The five-minute warning for fifth period to start flashes in front of me. "Right. Anyway, I'm going in tonight."

Roger's eyes bulge. "You can't do that!"

I scowl at him. "Keep your voice down."

"You can't do this to me again." Roger stands.

"I'm not doing anything to you."

"Really?" Anger flashes across his face. "You're my best friend and one of my group partners, remember?"

"I know."

"Building the greenhouse without you was almost impossible for Driver and me to accomplish, and we're still behind on our group project. If you get caught again, my parents will never let me see or talk to you again. Plus, they'll insist you're not part of my group at school anymore. Is that what you want?"

"Of course not!"

"Then don't do it." He walks out of the cafeteria.

In fifth period, Dr. Von Schlippe lectures us about artificial intelligence and how computers learn. Passion exudes from his every word on the subject, but it's not contagious. In fact, it leaves me distrusting him and computers even more.

Drama class takes us on an adventure to the future where we pretend to be human-machine hybrids fighting for our place in a society torn between humans and computers. It's a fascinating dilemma to contemplate, and I'd be plugged into it most days, but not this one. My mind fails to split time between it and thoughts of the secret portal.

The final bell rings, leaving me stranded with indecision as to what I should do. I never thought I'd enjoy VR game school so much. If I choose to enter the secret portal again, what will Principal Cornier and my parents do to me if I'm caught? Will it be the last time I get to attend school? Will it affect Mom and Dad's jobs? Can I live without Roger's friendship?

As much as the possible consequences frighten me, I know the answer. In fact, I've known the answer for weeks.

I don't want to be afraid anymore.

After dinner, I retreat to my room but leave Sparkles outside. I tried wearing my VR visor once with her in the room, and she flipped out. All I can think of is that she thought a space alien attacked me and was trying to eat my head. Whatever the case, I don't want to repeat it.

I gear up, take a deep breath, and enter my virtual library. The book Gabe recommended sits closed atop the table, and the portal no longer exists within the fireplace hearth. It would've been better if it had. Now, I must make the decision to open the book once more and answer the question to conjure the portal.

But that's why I'm here.

Book in hand, I stand before the fireplace. Without a moment's hesitation, I crack the book open and stare at the words once more: Will you be that light?

I have no choice.

"Yes."

Shielding my eyes, I step into the hearth and the brilliant light within.

Gabe greets me. "Hello, Kiara. I've been waiting for you to return."

I walk over to the bench and sit down. "I understand how I failed before, and I'm ready to try again."

He nods. The cell phone appears, and I answer where it came from. Then I answer where the egg came from. When the earth appears, I don't hesitate with my answer. "God."

"Good, but is this what you believe, or what you think I want to hear?"

The question startles me. "I... um... both?"

Gabe peers right into my soul. "I do see a change in you. However, believing in God is not the same as trusting that he's in control." He smiles. "Are you ready for your next lesson?"

I nod.

"Good." He stands and reaches toward me. "Take my hand."

I press the button on my controller to take the action. As soon as my fingers touch his, everything changes, just as it did before. Again, the controller in my hands and the VR visor on my head fade from memory as Gabe's warm hand closes around mine.

I rise. "Now what?"

"You fear so much. Fear you have no control, and it's true. But your fear is misplaced. Your lack of control does not negate the control by someone or something else. Whether it's an asteroid impact, greenhouse emissions, rising tides, a super volcano, or something else, you need not fear. God controls everything. Always. No exceptions."

"How can I be sure?"

"As I said before, it's better you see for yourself than for me to tell you." He smiles. "Hold on tight."

The experience begins just as it did before. The entire cave quakes, and the light becomes a brighter white. I close my eyes and squeeze them tight, yet the light still blinds me. Gabe pulls on my hand, and wind rushes past me. The light beyond my eyelids spirals through thousands of colors, and then everything stops at once. The brilliant light becomes tolerable, and the wind and pressure fades.

"We're here," Gabe says.

I open my eyes and take in the desert landscape that stretches out before us. Warm sand squishes between my toes. My boots have become sandals and my clothes robes.

Two men dressed in dark robes lounge beneath a date palm. One of them sees Gabe and me and rises. "Come to watch Noah, the demon possessed man?"

Shielding my eyes with my hand, I spot a massive wooden boat in the distance, the likes of which I've never seen. Several questions come to mind. "Why is he building that boat, and how will such a boat float, given its size and shape?" I search the desert wilderness. "Better yet, where will he find water?"

The man walks over to us. "Claims his god speaks to him. 'Build an ark!' says his god," he scoffs.

I press the man, "But why?"

He stares into the distance. "We are all evil, he claims. His god will send water down from the heavens and up from the depths of the earth, drowning us all." He spits on the ground. "An old fool, if you ask me."

I look at Gabe. "It does sound foolish."

Gabe takes my arm. "Let us go have a conversation with this foolish man named Noah."

The man spits on the ground again. "Waste of time, you ask me." He bids us farewell, returns to the date palm, and rejoins his friend.

As we near the large vessel, something strange and wonderful becomes apparent: a procession of animals of every imaginable kind. They seem to be in pairs, male and female. Each pair stops in front of an old man who stands with his back to us at the bottom of a massive ramp leading up to the ship's entrance.

"Good day, sir," Gabe says as we approach the old man.

The old man turns and peers at us through strands of gray and white hair. A wiry gray beard hangs down to his belly. "May I help you with something?"

"So many animals!" I can't count them all.

Noah strokes his beard. "Indeed."

"You built this ship yourself?"

"To the exact specifications given to me by God himself."

I gasp. "How old *are* you?"

Gabe groans. "Kiara, you shouldn't ask people questions like that."

Noah laughs. "Nonsense. I recently celebrated my six hundredth year."

I'm certain my eyes bulge from my head. "Six hundred! How have you lived that long?"

"I'm young, yet. My grandfather, Methuselah, recently went to be with the Lord. He was nine hundred and sixty-nine years old."

"I can't imagine living that long."

"God's original plan was for us to live forever in the garden. However, Adam's sin opened the door for death. Now, sin is rampant."

"And that's why you built the boat?"

"Yes, the ark will keep my family and the animals safe when the rains and the flood come."

"Are you afraid?"

"Never. God is with me and controls everything. Even if he hadn't instructed me to build this ark, I would still not be afraid. When I die, I'm certain I'll live with God for eternity in heaven."

Gabe bows his head to Noah. "Thank you for your time."

"Thank you, sir," I add.

Noah nods and returns to his task.

Then, a voice from heaven calls down to Noah, "Seven days from now I will make the rains pour down on the earth. And it will rain for forty days and forty nights, until I have wiped from the earth all the living things I have created."

Tears fill my eyes. Gabe takes my hand and says, "Watch this."

Time moves in a blur, the sun and moon moving through the sky again and again. Seven days pass, and time slows once more. The last of the animals have boarded the ark.

Then, a mighty hand reaches down from the heavens and closes the ark door, sealing Noah, his family, and all the animals inside. Water begins to rise out of the ground and the air crackles and booms with thunder. Rains begin to pour.

Another blur. Days. Weeks. More than a month. The rain pours for forty days and forty nights before relenting, but the entire earth is covered with water. More time passes, and finally the flood waters begin to recede. After an entire year passes, we now stand atop a mountain peak, not far from where the ark rests. The ark door opens, and Noah and his family emerge, along with all the animals.

My heart pounds within my chest. "God saved them!"

Gabe releases my hand, and the cave materializes around us. Once again, we stand in front of the stone bench. Feeling fades from my arms, legs, and torso until nothing remains but the cool breeze on my face. Then, the feel of reality returns: a controller in my hands and a VR visor over my head.

"God is always in control," Gabe says. "Do you see this now?"

"Yes."

"Good. Now, are you ready for your quiz?" Gabe asks.

I sigh. "Another one?"

"The choice to continue is yours."

"You know I can't stop now."

"That's what I like to hear." Gabe leans back against the wall and writes in the air with his finger. The word solidifies in front of me: emotions. "Who controls this?"

My mind and my heart struggle against each other, one vying for God and the other for myself. Which should I choose? If I fail, will he kick me out again?

After a time, Gabe smiles. "There are no trick questions."

I believe him, but it doesn't make answering the question easier. Finally, I say, "Aren't we all in control of our own emotions? Don't each of us choose moment by moment to be happy, sad, angry, or envious?"

"Correct." He writes in the air again: cars, trucks, buses.

"The person behind the wheel."

"Yes." Once more: wind, rain, earthquakes, floods.

"God. God controls nature."

"Good, but is that all?"

As I ponder the question, I think back on my life and everything that's happened. So many times, I've felt helpless in situations. Some were controlled by others, like my parents, but some seemed beyond anyone's control. Then, I remember the first lesson.

Pops. The graveyard.

"No," I say. "God controls everything. Life and death."

Gabe smiles. "Well done!"

"Thank you."

"Now, please allow me to reward your passing the lessons of truth by showing you a future event. It will put your mind at ease and show you how much God loves humanity and that he has a plan for us."

My stomach flutters. "Sure!"

"First, let me give you some context. In the beginning, God created the earth and everything on it, but when Adam sinned, death and decay entered, corrupting all creation. But God knew this would happen from the very beginning and had a plan to redeem all of it. What I'm about to show you is the culmination of that plan. The end and a new beginning. Are you ready?"

"Yes!"

"Take my hand again." He offers it, and I take it.

We're swept out of the cave again and into the sky. Up through the atmosphere we climb, then into space. Finally, we land on the surface of the moon, and we're not alone. Humans, animals, and angels of every kind face the earth and wait with bated breath. No one makes a sound, so I force myself to keep quiet, too.

As I stand there, my eyes glued to our glorious planet, the surface begins to burn. The fire spreads quickly, consuming the entire earth until nothing remains of it but ash.

Tears fill my eyes, and I cry out with my heart.

God, what's happening?

As if in answer to my wordless cry, a voice thunders across the heavens, "Look, I am making everything new!"

From the ashes of the earth blooms a new creation. Once finished, Gabe takes me there. Everything is beautiful and perfect, without decay. Children play with lions and snakes, and no sadness remains.

I reach out to feel God's new creation, but Gabe pulls me back. Pulls us back into the cave and the stone bench.

"Why wouldn't you let me touch anything?"

"One day, we will all live there, but for now you must find happiness within."

"I think I understand. Thank you for showing me that."

Gabe brushes back a strand of hair from my face. "You're welcome. Now, for your final rewards."

"Rewards? I thought the glimpse into the future was my reward?"

"In part, yes, but the memory of what you saw will fade over time. This next reward will serve as a reminder each time you enter the game world. It is called the Key of Truth."

An ornate silver key appears before me and rotates in the air. The word "truth" is etched along its length.

"Whoa!" My breath catches in my throat.

"Go ahead and take it."

I do, and it disappears. "Auh! Where did it go?"

"Check your inventory list."

"Heads-up on." My heads-up display augments what I see. "Display inventory list." A list comes up and displays only one item: the key. "That's so cool, but what does it open?"

Gabe folds his arms over his stomach. "When the opportunity to use the key arises, you'll know. Now, there's one more thing I want you to have."

"Okay. Heads-up off."

A Bible appears before me. Brown with a leather-bound cover. In the bottom-right corner of the cover is my name, embossed in gold lettering: Kiara Lynn Kole.

"This… is mine?"

"Yes. Inside, you'll find the date you received it."

"I love it!" The action button snatches it from the air.

Gabe smiles. "I'm glad you do. You'll find it in your virtual library." His smile fades. "Now, I have a mission for you. As the first student to earn the Key of Truth, you will help others discover the secret portal so that they might earn their own key."

"But… Principal Cornier and the teachers are always watching. How can they do this without being suspended or expelled?"

"The same way you did. They will need to add my book to their virtual libraries."

"So, I'll have to return it?"

Gabe shakes his head. "Never. Give them the book to borrow, and it will be copied to their virtual library. This way, you'll both have access. Also, when they access the secret portal using the book, it will show them as reading a book."

"And the key? What will happen when Principal Cornier and others see it?"

"The key is a special artifact. You've earned it, and there's nothing they can do to remove it or take it from you."

"But they'll punish us."

Gabe stands and faces me. "Fear not. They've claimed triumph over the supposed 'virus' and admitting failure will be virtually impossible. Not only that, but the more students who earn the key the harder it becomes for them to do anything about it. You might not realize this, but your parents hold great sway as well. Every single person working at GIST is a top scientist in their field, so it's not likely anyone would lose their job. Also, CEVR Academy itself is an experiment. A self-learning system programmed to adapt to the way students think. Therefore, you are insulated from further retaliation. As the Bible says, 'When God opens a door, it cannot be shut.' The door for truth has been opened."

"So… you're saying I've defeated Principal Cornier and Dr. Von Schlippe?"

"Other battles may lie ahead, but in this, you've won."

Tears flow from my eyes. "When we moved here, I thought my world had ended and I'd never be happy again, but now I understand that was never true. With your help, I've learned so much. How can I ever repay you?"

"Remember your mission and see it through. Be a light in this dark world."

"I will."

"And celebrate your accomplishment. Few will ever earn the Key of Truth."

"Trust me, I will! I can't wait to tell Grams and Roger about the key."

Gabe and the cave fade, and now I stand next to the hearth in my virtual library. On the table sits the Bible Gabe gave to me. With my name on its cover, it's more precious than even the key.

I've got something Gemma doesn't.

CHAPTER TWENTY-SEVEN

A PIRATE'S LIFE

ROGER WALKS UP TO the bridge dressed in full Roman battle gear.

"Nice outfit, man," Driver says.

Roger looks at himself. "Cool artifact, right?"

"Best I've seen."

Roger's head disappears every few seconds. "A bit glitchy, though," I say.

"Yeah, I don't get it."

"Reminds me of Principal Cornier."

"Ugh. Don't compare me to her. You'll make me want to turn it off."

"The glitching, silly."

"Oh, right."

"I can't believe this is our last day of the group challenge," Roger says.

"Yeah. I guess we'd better get in and finish things up," I say.

We cross the bridge together and enter the sixth-grade door.

I pull up the task list. "We have a new task to complete."

"Well, let's get to it." Roger looks at me. "What is it?"

"It says we must identify the bugs."

Driver frowns. "What bugs?"

Roger looks at me and his eyes grow wide. "Salvation!"

My stomach lurches. "The greenhouse." Roger nods.

"On it." Driver navigates us from the golden field to the mine entrance in a blink.

The three of us hurry inside and head over to the massive greenhouse within Salvation, our fallout shelter. We stop just inside the door, the problem obvious. From the tomato plants to the corn stalks to the cabbage heads to the pumpkin patch, every surface pulses with life. And not in a good way.

Roger groans. "Oh, man. We're doomed."

I scowl at him. "With an attitude like that, we will be."

"Sorry," Roger says.

"No worries. Let's just concentrate on the task." I walk over to one of the tomato plants and examine the big, fat, pale-green caterpillars crawling on the leaves. Each has white and black markings, eight V-shaped stripes on its body, and a single horn-shaped protrusion from its rear. "My grandfather grew lots of produce on his farm down the road from where I grew up, so I'm familiar with some of these pests. These ugly things are definitely tomato hornworms."

Ding!

The three of us look around. Roger points to a digital clock on the wall that wasn't previously there. It starts counting down from five minutes. A large, white number one inside a blue circle hovers above the clock.

"What's happening?" Driver asks.

I take a look at the task list again. "It says we must identify ten bugs."

We split up as far as our tether will allow and begin searching for bugs we can identify.

"Ew! I know this one," Roger says. "Stink bug."

Ding!

"And this one's a cutworm," Driver says. "You can tell because it's eating away at the stem of the plant."

Ding!

Small, pear-shaped, green bugs with two antennae cover the cherry blossoms. "The cherry trees are crawling with aphids!" I say.

Ding!

"I've got some yellowish-brown bugs with black spots on the snap beans," says Roger. "Any idea what they are?"

"Do they look like lady bugs?" I ask.

Roger scrunches up his face. "Yeah, I guess so. Other than their color."

"Those are Mexican bean beetles."

Ding!

"Good job, Kiara."

"Thanks!"

"I found some small beetles with emerald bodies over here," Driver says. "They jumped when I walked by and seem to be eating holes in the beet root leaves."

I join Driver. "Um, yeah, those are a type of beetle." Their name just won't come to mind. "Ugh. It's right on the tip of my tongue. All I can think of is dogs scratching."

"Fleas?" Roger asks.

"That's it! Flea beetles."

Ding!

"We're up to six," Roger says, "but we've got less than ninety seconds left."

Driver heads over to the apple trees. "There's some sort of yellow caterpillars—"

Ding!

"Sixty seconds!" Roger yells.

"We've got bugs on the potato plants, too," I say.

"Potato bugs?" Roger asks.

Ding!

"Awesome!" I say.

"We've got thirty seconds to identify two more," Driver says.

I head over to the corn stalks, rip off an ear of corn, and pull back the husk. A green worm munches on the kernels near the tip. "Ugh. I hate corn earworms!"

Ding!

"Over here!" Roger's in the pumpkin patch. Driver and I join him. The clock is down to fifteen seconds.

"What are those?" Driver asks.

Brownish-gray bugs with flat backs munch on the leaves and stems of the pumpkin vines. One of them flies over to another of the vines.

I shudder. "I don't know what they are, but they're gross."

The clock flashes red.

Five.

"Think, guys!"

Four.

"I wish we could squash these bugs and be done with it."

Three.

"That's it!" Roger says.

Two.

"What?" Driver and I both shout.

One.

"Squash bugs!"

Ding!

The clock turns green with one second remaining.

"We did it!" Driver says.

Checking the list, I see we have a new task. "Now we have to get rid of the bugs."

Roger looks at me. "Does it say how?"

"Nope." A quick glance at the list confirms it. "What do we have besides our fingers?"

Driver takes several steps back. "I'm not touching any of those things."

Roger laughs. "You do realize you won't actually be touching anything, right?"

"Doesn't matter." Driver glances around. "Me and bugs don't mix, no matter the circumstances."

I roll my eyes. "Fine. Roger and I will take care of the bugs."

An hour later, we've hardly made a dent in the bug problem. Driver points out an even bigger issue. "Guys, I hate to say it, but the plants you cleared earlier are crawling with bugs again."

Roger sighs. "Without food, our fallout shelter is as good as worthless."

"What are we going to do?" I ask.

"While you guys were killing bugs, I decided to read through some of my notes from science class."

The fact that Driver takes notes shocks me. I never pictured him as a note taker. "You found something?"

"I've got a plan," Driver says, "but you're not gonna like it."

Roger scans the greenhouse. "It's got to be better than picking bugs off these plants."

"You know how we have choices on what to do on tasks?" Driver asks.

"Yeah," I say.

"Well, I think some of the choices we made might've been wrong ones. Turns out that Mr. Butler talked about bats a few months back when we were studying mammals. Their main diet is bugs."

We all stare at each other for a few moments. Then, Roger says, "You're telling us that we should've kept the bats, aren't you?"

Driver nods. "Yeah. At least a few of them."

"We can't fail on this, guys," Roger says. "Today's our final group session, so I say we skip lunch."

My stomach growls. "Traitor." Roger frowns. "Oh! Not you, Roger. I was talking to my stomach.”

“Oh.” He turns to Driver. “So, where do we find some bats?”

“Beats me,” Driver says.

“I don’t know either, but I know someone who might.” Both of them look at me. “We’ve yet to ask Ollie for help.”

The air shimmers.

Pop!

A cylinder of smoke rises from the ground. When it dissipates, Ollie stands before us. “One of you called my name?”

I step forward. “I guess I did.”

“Very good.” She leans on her staff. “What can I do for you, dearie?”

“We need to find some bats,” I say.

“Did you check the belfry?” Ollie clacks when the three of us look to each other for understanding. It must be her attempt of laughing. “Bats in the belfry.” She sighs. “Oh, never mind. If it’s bats you want, Blackbeard is your primate.”

“And where can we find this Blackbeard?” Driver asks.

“Cross the Emerald Ocean to the shores of Coconut Beach. There, you’ll find him and his cohorts lounging in the shade of the coconut trees and sipping down coconut milk.” Her beak turns down at the corners of her mouth. “Beware of the games he plays. He’s never one to play fair.”

“It’s on the map,” Driver says.

The next moment, we’re standing on a beach of yellow sand. Green waves roll up the beach and then slither away, leaving trails of frothy foam in their wake. Thousands of coconut trees line the beach, their massive fronds creating a canopy of shelter from the sweltering sun.

A chimpanzee waddles out from the trees, a make-shift spear in its hand. It wears a torn white shirt, blue jean shorts, and a red-and-black bandanna tied around its head.

“This here is a private beach, and it’s for primates only,” says the chimpanzee. I can’t tell if it’s male or female.

Roger approaches the chimpanzee. “We’re looking for Blackbeard.”

The chimpanzee raises its spear. “You’re looking for trouble.”

“Stand down, Lucy.” A smaller monkey with a triangular-shaped black hat hobbles out from the shadows. The monkey has a thick, black beard as well, and a long tail akin to a fox. “What be the problem?”

“Are you Blackbeard?” Roger asks.

The monkey starts grooming the one it called Lucy. "Depends. What ye want from that old sea dog?"

"We're looking for a few bats," I say, moving next to Roger.

"Bats, say ye?" The monkey stops grooming Lucy and hobbles toward us. It's wearing a peg for the lower portion of its left leg, but I can see the rest of its leg folded behind it. "Aargh! I be Blackbeard Saki."

"Oh, good." Roger meets Blackbeard halfway up the beach. "Where can we find the bats?"

He strokes his long beard. "Not be so quick, laddie. Tis a rough business, bat wranglin' an such."

"Maybe," Driver says, "but we have no choice. Point us in the right direction, and we'll be gone before you know it."

Blackbeard points south. "Around the bend, ye shall find me ship in a cove. It be there seven year. Ever since four bats be callin' it home."

"We'll round up the bats for you and then be on our way," Roger says.

"Nay. Ye round 'em up and come back. Then we settle our debts."

Lucy raises her spear. "One false step, and I'll spear ya like a fish."

Roger sighs. "Fine. We'll return as soon as we finish."

"Ruby!" Blackbeard bellows.

A large orangutan steps out of the shadows and onto the beach. She carries a tall golden cage in one hand and a long swath of black cloth in the other. "You'll need these if you want to capture the bats." Stopping just a few feet onto the beach, she stares beyond us. "I'd have done it myself long ago, but I fear bats almost as much as I fear the ocean."

With cage and cloth in hand, Roger, Driver, and I head down the beach and over to the cove. A massive ship made of wood sits a hundred yards offshore. A yellow flag flies atop the ship's single mast, donning a large coconut with two bananas crossed beneath it. It reminds me of the skull and crossbones flag flown by pirates.

Blackbeard.

A single rowboat rests on the beach, its wood warped and dried with age. After pushing the rowboat into the shallow waters, we wait to see if it stays afloat. Not only does it still float, but it takes on no water, so we load into it. Driver rows us out to the ship, and we climb up the cargo net draped over the rail and hanging just above the water's surface.

Aboard the ship, we explore the upper deck. The captain's quarters door hangs askew from a single remaining hinge, and cobwebs cover the opening.

No light enters the room except from the door, so there must not be any windows.

"Bats can't be in there," Roger says. "Otherwise, there'd be no cobwebs."

We move down to the lower deck and inspect every last barrel and crate. Most of the crates are empty, but a few contain coconuts. The barrels that aren't empty hold some sort of pinkish-red liquid. Whatever the liquid once was is no more. It smells horrendous.

Below deck, the shadows are as thick as tar and cover everything. The three of us huddle together, lit only by our tether lines made of white light. It's only a game, and I know it, but it doesn't keep my pulse from racing or perspiration from dampening my armpits.

I don't like the darkness.

"Either of you happen to have a flashlight or torch?" Driver asks, his voice strained and a few octaves higher than normal.

Two glowing orbs appear just a few feet in front of my face. "Guys…"

"Yeah, I see them, too," Roger and Driver both say.

Six more orbs appear. Four pairs.

Schick!

The three of us gasp as a three-inch flame ignites in the middle of the air. As my eyes adjust, the lighter from which the flame protrudes comes into view, along with the clawed fingers around it. A leathery wing extends from the hand and back to a furry shoulder, just above one set of glowing orbs.

"A light for the boy," says the bat holding the lighter. It reaches up and lights a lantern hanging from the ceiling.

The room comes to life, and so do the four bats hanging from one of the ship's support beams.

"Thanks," Driver squeaks.

Roger inhales loudly and coughs. He must've used his inhaler. "Look, Blackbeard sent us here."

The bat who spoke lets go of the beam and flips in the air so that he's no longer looking at us upside-down. He settles on the edge of a table. "You've made a grave mistake coming here."

Roger finds his voice. "I thought you would've sounded more like Dracula and less like a…"

"Mouse?" I offer.

Roger nods. "Yeah."

The other three bats release from the beam and perch on the table just behind the first.

The bat on the left says, "Never eaten a human before."

"Bet they taste like chicken," the one on the right says.

The one on the left licks its lips, revealing two pairs of pearly white fangs. "I love chicken."

The bat in the middle, behind the first, bobs its head. "Mmm, chicken."

The first bat turns toward the others and shakes its head. It then addresses the three from left to right. "Frank. Esmeralda. Eddie. What have I told you about speaking out of turn?"

Eddie, the one on the right waves one of his wings. "Ooh, ooh, ooh! I know, Vlad! Pick me! Pick me!"

"He always picks you." Esmeralda bats her eyes. "But I'm his favorite."

Frank glowers at Esmeralda. "Not true at all."

"Keep quiet, you fools," Vlad says. "None of you have ever eaten chicken."

"Sorry, boss," Eddie says.

Vlad spreads his wings wide, and Frank, Esmeralda, and Eddie shrink back out of the circle of light until only their glowing eyes remain visible.

Vlad snorts, folds his wings back in, and faces us again. "My colleagues forget their place." He clears his throat into his small, clawed hand. "Now, where were we?"

"We've made a grave mistake coming here," I say.

"Ah, yes." Vlad paces on the table. "You work for my nemesis, Blackbeard."

"That's not true." I take a step toward the table.

Vlad stops pacing and puffs up his chest. "Are you calling me a liar?"

Roger comes to my side. "You're not a liar, just mistaken. We only met Blackbeard an hour ago."

"But you said he sent you here." Vlad flaps his wings and rises off the table for a moment. "We won this boat from him fair and square. He's been sore about it ever since."

"And this boat suits you?" Driver asks.

"Well enough," Vlad says.

Esmeralda steps back into the light. "Vlad, be truthful."

Vlad sighs and hangs his head. "Very well. This old ship provides us a home and shelter from the elements, but food is scarce around here. We've resorted to eating fruit."

"This is perfect!" Roger exclaims.

"Did you not hear what I just said?" Vlad asks. "We're basically starving." He points his wing at Eddie. "Eddie's half the bat he once was. I mean literally. He's never been so skinny."

"What Roger means is that we have the perfect solution that will help all of us."

Vlad folds his wings over his chest. "Tell me of this solution."

"Yeah, I'm starving," Eddie says.

"We have a large garden full of bugs that need to be removed, and you're in need of an endless supply of food. Come with us, and you'll never be hungry again."

"But a garden needs light," Vlad says. "How will we ever sleep?"

Driver produces the golden cage and the black cloth. "You'll live and sleep in here."

"A cage!" Vlad quakes. "Your solution is to imprison us?"

"No!" I say. "Take another look. The cage has no door. You'll be free to come and go as you please."

Frank joins Esmeralda in the light. He looks at the cage. "Endless food?"

"An insect buffet," Roger says.

Eddie prances forward. "I love buffets more than chicken!" He hops off the table and flies into the cage.

Frank looks at Vlad. "If Eddie goes, so do I." He joins Eddie in the cage.

Vlad turns to Esmeralda. "You would abandon ship, too?"

Esmeralda bobs her head. "Join us, Vlad." She flies into the cage.

"Traitors! Every last one of you," Vlad says.

"Do you not want a better life?" I ask. "You'll always be free to return to your ship if you're unhappy with what we provide."

"I leave this ship, and Blackbeard will take it back."

"Perhaps, but you could always win it back again, right?" Roger asks.

"Blackbeard's a cheat. But he has a tell. Watch his hands and his eyes, and you'll see it, plain as day."

"So, is that a yes?" Driver asks.

Vlad looks around the room and huffs. "I guess there's no point in staying here alone." He drops off the edge of the table and swoops down into the cage.

Driver places the cloth over the cage, and the three of us return to shore and head over to where Blackbeard and the others await us.

Blackbeard eyes us as we approach. "Captured the scoundrels, did ye?"

"Aye," Roger says. Driver and I shake our heads.

"Then we be settlin' up."

I glare at Blackbeard. "We are settled. You have your ship, and we have our bats."

"Nay." Blackbeard stomps his peg leg into the sand. "Ye play for the cage or leave empty-handed."

Ruby snatches the cage from Driver. "I'll hold onto this."

"What's the game?" Roger asks.

Blackbeard turns and heads toward the trees, leaving his peg leg stuck in the sand. He waves us to follow him, so we do. A makeshift table of fronds held off the ground with coconuts sits beneath a trio of trees. Blackbeard sits down on the ground on one side and motions for us to sit across from him. We do, and he places four coconut halves on the table. Then, he produces a large, black walnut.

"Here's how the game be. Each of ye gets one round. Keep away from the walnut and ye win. Simple as can be. One win, and the cage be yers. No wins, and ye work for me. Agreed?"

The three of us look at each other. Roger says, "I don't think we have a choice."

"Nay." Blackbeard sets the walnut on the table and places one of the coconut halves over it. Then, he starts shuffling the coconut halves around. By the time he finishes, my eyes are crossed and my head spins. He points at Roger. "Ye be first."

Roger points at the coconut half on the far left. "That one."

"Not so fast." Blackbeard snaps his fingers. "Gerry, get down here and ask the questions."

A spider monkey drops out of one of the trees and sits next to Blackbeard. Based on the pink bow on top of its head, I'm sure Gerry's a girl. She smiles, baring all her teeth. "What is the probability of selecting a coconut half with a walnut beneath it?"

Roger smirks. "There are four coconut halves and only one has a walnut beneath it. So, the probability of selecting the walnut is 0.25 or one in four."

Gerry nods. "Select one coconut half."

Roger points at the same one, and Blackbeard lifts it off the table. No walnut lies beneath it. He sets the coconut half aside.

"Again," Blackbeard says.

"What is the probability of selecting a coconut half without a walnut beneath it?" Gerry asks Roger.

"It's the opposite. Zero point—"

"Roger!" Driver exclaims.

Lucy points her spear at Driver. "No help, or you get poked!"

Roger begins again. "What I was about to say was two out of three, or 0.67."

"Lucky," growls Blackbeard.

Roger points at the coconut half in the middle of the remaining three. "That one."

Blackbeard grins and turns over the flanking coconut halves. The one on the far right has the walnut beneath it. "Ye lose."

Roger stands. "Hey! That's not fair. You cheated."

Blackbeard rises. "Ye callin' me a cheat?" Lucy's right there with her spear aimed at Roger's chest.

"He selected the coconut half in the middle, but you turned over the other two," I say.

"Yar! That be how it works," Blackbeard says. "Me game. Me rules." The coconut forest erupts with howls and chatter. "Now, sit back down, laddie." Roger complies, and Blackbeard turns toward me. "Yer next, lassie."

Blackbeard sits back down and places all the coconut halves back on the table. He sticks the walnut beneath one of them and begins shuffling them all around. For a split-second his eyes shift to his lap, just as one of the coconut halves almost slides off the table. He lines them up and nods to Gerry.

Watch his hands and eyes…

Gerry's golden eyes lock with mine. "If two plus two is four, and four plus four is eight, then what is two plus four times three minus six divided by two?"

"Um…" My mind goes blank.

Roger sighs. "My dear Aunt Sonny." Everyone around the table looks at him. "What? She likes *ordering* things. Her *operations* always run smooth."

He's trying to tell me something, but what?

"Quiet," Blackbeard growls.

"Can you repeat that?" I ask Gerry.

Gerry looks to Blackbeard, and he nods. She says, "If two plus two is four, and four plus four is eight, then what is two plus four times three minus six divided by two?"

Ordering operations... Right! Order of operations. My dear Aunt Sonny. Multiplication, division, addition, and subtraction.

"Two plus four times three minus six divided by two." I picture the problem in my mind. "Four times three is twelve, and six divided by two is three, so two plus twelve is fourteen and take away three. The answer is eleven!"

"Lucky." Blackbeard stares at me for a long moment. "Pick two."

"And what will happen?" I ask. "Will you turn them over or turn the other two over?"

He bares his teeth in a ferocious grin. "Depends on which ones ye pick."

"That's not fair," Driver says. "You'll cheat either way."

"What he said," Roger adds.

"Very well." Blackbeard taps the tops of two of the coconut halves. Pick two ta be turned over."

Vlad said to watch his hands and eyes, but now I'm confused. Should I pick the two he's tapping, or select the other two? "Ugh." I select the two halves he didn't tap.

"Tsk, tsk. Ye should've taken me clue." He turns over the two coconut halves I selected. The one on the right reveals the walnut. His eyes move to Driver. "Two down, one ta go."

Blackbeard shuffles the coconut halves again. As before, one almost falls off the table right as he looks to his lap.

What is he doing?

I glance at Roger, and Roger nods.

He saw it, too.

"No more games." Blackbeard taps just a single coconut half this time. "Pick one. I reveal the other three."

Driver selects the coconut half second from the right. Blackbeard lifts the one to the far left and tosses it aside.

No walnut.

The one on the far right reveals no walnut beneath it, either. Now, Driver's selection is the one on the right.

Blackbeard chuckles. "Care ta change yer selection?"

Driver glances over at Roger and me. "I... guess not."

"So be it." Blackbeard lifts the coconut half on the left and tosses it away. "Looks like ye loses."

Blackbeard touches the last coconut half, and Roger stands. "Wait!"

"For what?" He inches it toward the edge of the table and glances down.

"That's it!" I say, rising to my feet.

Blackbeard glares at me. "What?"

"Back away from the table," Roger says.

"Or what?" Blackbeard demands.

Driver clues in on what's happening and flips the remaining coconut half over. "No walnut!"

"That's because Blackbeard's holding it with his foot," Roger says.

"That's right," I say. "He was about to slip it underneath the last half as he lifted it up."

Blackbeard grins. "The three of ye be smarter than ye look. Tell not a soul of me secret, and the cage be yers."

The three of us share a look and nod. "Deal," Roger says.

Ruby hands the cage back to Driver and winks at him. "I was hoping you'd win."

Lucy doesn't share the same sentiment. "Come back to our beach, and I'll run you through." She shakes her spear at us.

Roger nods at Driver. "We're almost out of time. Get us back to Salvation."

The beach, the trees, and Blackbeard disappear in a flash, and we stand in front of the mine entrance. Back at the greenhouse, most of the plants are withered, and their fruits and vegetables are damaged, half-eaten, or rotting.

"We're too late," I say.

Roger sighs. "After everything we did."

"Maybe not." Driver enters the greenhouse, sets the cage down, and removes the cover.

Vlad and the others wake from their slumber and stretch their wings.

Eddie sniffs the air. "Something smells goooood."

Frank leaves the cage first and heads straight for the tomato plants. Eddie, Esmeralda, and Vlad exit the cage, too, each heading to a different part of the garden. All four of them start gorging themselves on the bug buffet. As they do, the plants begin to regain their color. After about ten minutes, the garden looks better than ever.

I pull up the list. One task remains unfinished. "Let's harvest the food."

Over the next half hour, we gather up more fruits, vegetables, and root plants than I've ever seen before. Once we finish, we exit the greenhouse. Dozens of animals now fill the space within the fallout shelter.

"Welcome, friends," Roger says.

A loud trumpet sounds, echoing through the fallout shelter and the mine shafts beyond. Gold and red streamers roll down the walls, each expressing congratulations. Confetti falls from the ceiling, and small fireworks burst in the air.

Ollie appears, a wide grin spread across her beaked face. "Well done. Well done, indeed."

"Thanks," the three of us say.

"You've finished the last task, but it's better than that." Her staff morphs into a telescope, and then the telescope splits into three. "One for each of you." She smiles. "These will help you aim your lasers at the asteroid."

Each of us takes a telescope. Driver says, "I was wondering how we were supposed to shoot an asteroid in space without having a way to aim at it." He nods. "Thank you."

Roger and I thank Ollie, too.

"You're all welcome," she says, "but that's not all. Each of you has earned one thousand points and fifty coins as well."

Roger leaps into the air. "Yes! I'm back in first place."

Ollie gasps, runs around in a circle while flapping her wings, and then buries her head in the ground. It's quite a feat, given the ground's composition of mostly rock with a touch of dirt.

"Who cares about that?" Driver says. "I've almost got enough coins to buy a hover board now."

"For the game?" I ask.

"Nah, in the real world," he says.

"Huh. I didn't know you could use them like that."

"Sure can," Roger says. "Only in New Eden, though."

"Well, we've got about twenty minutes left before 3 pm," Driver says. "What should we do?"

Roger licks his lips. "I say we go to the cafeteria and eat some lunch. I'm starved."

My stomach growls in agreement. "Good idea."

"Have fun!" Driver disappears.

Roger and I get pulled out of the game and placed back at the start of the bridge.

He frowns. "Well, that was awkward."

"Whatever. I'll see you in the cafeteria." I switch over to lunch mode and head into the cafeteria.

The lights are off inside the cafeteria, but there's plenty of light coming in through the windows. Roger walks in right behind me. We settle down at our usual table and begin eating our lunches in silence.

After a few minutes, Roger stops eating and stares ahead.

I set my sandwich back down on my plate. "What's wrong?"

He blinks several times before looking at me, then chuckles. "Sorry. I was just thinking about the… place."

"With Gabe?"

"Yeah." His brow furrows. "I know I said I wasn't interested and all that, but I think I've changed my mind. Well, actually, it's not that. I've always been interested but too afraid to take the risk. Now that it's been many weeks and you haven't been suspended or expelled, well, I think I'd like to try and earn a key as well."

"That's fantastic!"

"Yeah, so how do I do it?"

"Open the book Gabe gave you and answer the question."

Roger hangs his head. "I… kinda returned the book. Didn't think I'd ever read it since it had nothing to do with robotics, programming, or science."

"It's not a problem. I can loan you mine. Hold on a sec." I start to access my virtual library but realize it'll take me out of the cafeteria. "Actually, how about you wait for me in front of the school after the bell rings."

"Got it."

I exit lunch mode and access my virtual library. Gabe's book sits in the chair next to the fireplace. I pick it up and say, "Loan this book to Roger Daltrey."

The book shimmers, glows a brilliant white, and then my eyes seem to cross as the book slides apart and becomes two. Then, one of them disappears.

Vida says, "*A Light in the Darkness* has been delivered to Roger Daltrey."

"Yes!" I exit my library.

Roger nods at me when I walk out of the school's front doors. He's standing next to the flagpole. I head over to him.

"Well?" he says.

"You should have the book now."

"Thank you."

I smile. "What are friends for?"

He looks around and whispers, "I guess I'm going to try it out this evening."

"You won't be disappointed."

"I'd stay and talk, but I've got an appointment with the allergist."

"Okay." The doomsday clock looming in the sky says only seven days remain before impact. Crusher, the killer asteroid, has grown to half the size of the moon now. I swallow hard, knowing I've still got a lot of work ahead of me. "I'll see you this weekend?"

"Count on it!" Roger disappears.

"Heads-up on." The display comes up. My rank sits at 3,214/4,794. Finding the Key of Truth and finishing the group challenge gave me a big boost. "Now, I just need to finish the last three lessons and earn the fourth part of the laser."

After logging out, I kneel next to my bed and fold my hands together. It's the first time I've ever sought God for someone else, and it feels good.

God, I pray, *please help Roger understand your truth and earn the key.*

Amen.

CHAPTER TWENTY-EIGHT

THE FINAL COUNTDOWN

IT'S THE LAST DAY of the last nine weeks of sixth grade, and one lesson remains to be completed: MA12 - The Rainforest. If failure was an option, I'd turn around and explore the world some more. But it's not. I've never worked so hard to achieve anything.

Two reasons come to mind as to why this lesson remains incomplete when I've stood here twice before: math and spiders. In truth, I'm not sure which one scares me more. Most of the time, the answer would be math, but this is different. The name of the place says it all: Arachnid Rainforest.

Spiders are scary enough on their own, but I've seen enough nature shows to know everything grows much larger in a rainforest. The last thing I want to be is spider food. Every inch of my skin crawls, sending me into a fit of shivers.

I close my eyes. "It's just a game."

Never truer words, but I have an overactive imagination. It's a blessing and a curse, and it's also one of the many reasons I love reading. Everything comes to life in my mind, just like it does on the ceiling in my room when story mode is activated.

I exhale fear, open my eyes, and enter Arachnid Rainforest. Sounds fill my head as I chop my way through the overgrown vegetation: frogs singing, birds chirping and squawking, monkeys chattering and howling, and many other things. What I don't hear are the spiders. Stealthy, evil creatures.

Beyond the next trees lies a long, narrow gorge. A canopy covers the gorge, and three vines hang from the canopy. Below, black widow spiders the size of small cars busy themselves weaving deathtraps.

I swallow down a dose of fear, and it hits my bloodstream without delay. My heart works quickly, distributing it all the way down to my toes within moments. It paralyzes me. Then, a timer appears. Ten minutes. Ten minutes separate me from victory or certain death.

God, help me.

As soon as my hand touches the vine hooked over the branch to my left, the timer begins counting down. My stomach climbs into my throat as I swing out over the gorge. A math problem appears before me, but my focus lies below with the eight-legged titans. It can't be helped.

As I swing back toward the ledge, I slip down the vine a good foot. I tighten my grip on the controller, knowing it does me no good.

Focus, Kiara!

I force my gaze ahead and focus on the problem: 27 x 42. Everyone has their own method of multiplying large numbers, including me, so I do what works for me and break it down into manageable chunks.

"Forty-two. Four tens and a two. Twenty-seven times ten is two hundred seventy. Add that four times... one thousand eighty. Twenty-seven times two is... fifty-four. So, we have four, thirteen, carry the one, and one. The answer is one thousand one hundred thirty-four."

Ding!

At the apex of the swing, I release the vine and fly through the air. The next vine swings toward me, and I grab hold of it. Relief washes over me, but it's short-lived as my hands slip again, sending me down another foot on the vine. To further my despair, I've already used two minutes.

Another problem comes into view: 1/2 + 1/4 + 7/16 - 3/8

"Ugh." As I stare at the problem, I remember I need a common base to add and subtract fractions. "So, sixteen is the largest base, and the other three bases will go into it." I bite my lip and convert them. "Two times eight is sixteen, so I have eight sixteenths. Four times four is sixteen. That makes four sixteenths. And eight times two is sixteen, so I have six sixteenths."

My hands slip again as the vine meets its reverse apex, and my stomach lurches.

I shake it off and do the conversions again. "Now, eight plus four plus seven is nineteen. Subtract six. That's thirteen. The answer is thirteen sixteenths!"

Ding!

The transfer to the last vine goes without a hitch, and the next problem displays: 38^2. Five minutes remain on the clock as I begin the squaring problem.

"Let's see..."

Mrs. Reed, my math instructor, appears in my mind. She stands at the front of the classroom with a piece of chalk in her hand. I still don't understand her preference for a chalkboard over dry erase or a computer. Maybe she likes getting chalk dust all over her clothes and her face when she inevitably touches them with her hands. She instructs us on a shortcut to squaring numbers using the nearest tens.

I bite my lower lip and stare at the problem again: 38^2. I pull up a scratch pad and begin solving the problem. "Um… okay. Thirty-eight is closest to forty. I had to add two, so I'll subtract two from thirty-eight. That's thirty-six. Now, I'll multiply thirty-six by forty. That's… forty times thirty equals twelve hundred plus forty times six equals two-hundred forty. Add those together… fourteen-hundred forty. Now, square two. That's four. Adding them together, I get fourteen-hundred forty-four." I check my work:

$$+2$$
$$38^2$$
$$(38 + 2) \times (38 - 2) = 40 \times 36$$
$$(40 \times 30) + (40 \times 6) = 1200 + 240 = 1440$$
$$2^2 = 4$$
$$1440 + 4 = 1444$$

"Yes! The answer's fourteen-hundred forty-four!"

Ding!

My hands slip again, right at the apex of the forward swing. I flail in the air and plummet.

Wind rushes past my face and through my hair as the thick web rushes toward me.

"I answered it!" I yell, but it doesn't matter.

My body jolts as I hit the web. I press every button frantically, but I'm glued to the sticky surface. Then, my worst nightmare comes to life. Black, spindly legs turn me over and over like a spit as the largest black widow spider ever known to mankind wraps me in a cocoon of sticky silk.

"You'll be a treat," she hisses.

I scream, but it's muted by the cobwebs over my mouth. Tears rise in the corners of my eyes, so I bite my lip and fight them off. A deep breath returns some of my sanity but does nothing to squelch the fear binding my chest.

This isn't real, Kiara.

Through the webbing, I see two minutes remain on the clock. Then, another problem appears:

> If it takes thirty cubes to build a staircase three cubes wide
> and four steps high:

> How many cubes will you need to build a staircase four
> cubes wide and six steps high?

The world continues to tumble as the light grows dim. My brain knows I'm not physically turning, but the task of convincing my stomach seems impossible. I close my eyes and concentrate on visualizing the steps.

"Okay, let's start with a staircase one cube wide and six steps high…" An image begins to form in my head.

"Each step has one more cube than the previous one. So, that's one plus two plus three plus four plus five plus six. Add those together… and I get twenty-one."

In my mind, I take the six, one cube wide steps and create three more sets.

"That's four sets total to represent the four-cube width."

I open my eyes for a moment and see the clock tumble by.

Twenty seconds!

Bile rises in my throat and burns. Each time I swallow it back down, it comes right back up.

Ugh! Where was I?

I swallow hard and visualize the cube steps again. "Right. Four sets of twenty-one."

Red flashes.

The clock's down to five.

"Four times twenty is eighty."

Three.

"Four times one is four."

One.

"The answer is eighty-four!"

Zero.

"No!" I beat the action button with my thumb. "I finished!"

Tears begin to fill my eyes as a bright light appears.

Ding!

My webbed cocoon splits open, and the rainforest canopy comes into view overhead. Clicking the action button gets me back to my feet.

Sprawling spiderwebs extend back through the gorge, and the large spider who attacked me hisses as she sets to work resetting her trap. "No one escapes me twice," she hisses. "Come here again, and I'll make dinner of you for sure."

I back away and find myself at the entrance of a tunnel. The dark tunnel twists and turns with a steep incline. Every turn catches my breath as the expectation of a hidden threat arises. But then a pinpoint of light appears up ahead. It grows as I draw closer, and then the rainforest becomes visible through the hole. The last ten feet require crawling, so I'm thankful it's just a game. Squeezing out of the hole in the ground, I find myself just beyond the edge of the narrow gorge.

A small path leads me away from the gorge and to a clearing. In the middle of the clearing sits a large metal box.

"Yes!" I run over to the box and throw the lid open.

Vida's voice fills my head. "Congratulations, Kiara! You've completed all lessons and have earned the final piece of the laser. Return to the golden field near the entrance to this world and assemble your weapon to destroy the asteroid. Only two hours remain before impact."

I raise my hands in the air. "I can't believe I actually did it!"

Back in the field, I piece together the four laser components, including a platform to fire it from. With the laser assembled, I attach the telescope to it that Roger, Driver, and I won for completing the group challenge.

Looking through the telescope, I sight in Crusher, the killer asteroid, and start the laser tracking program so that the laser will continually adjust to the asteroid's changing trajectory.

Getting it sighted took more time than I thought it would. Now, only ten minutes remain before impact.

Crusher's so big, it's now visible with the naked eye. There's no possibility of the laser missing it. But it's also so close, I might not destroy it in time.

From what Roger told me, this laser isn't a pulse weapon but a constant streaming source that will wear down and vaporize the asteroid before it has a chance to enter the atmosphere.

I hope you're right, Roger.

I hold my breath and flip the power switch on. A concussive wave blows back the golden stalks, flattening them for a good quarter mile around the platform. Then, a brilliant, bluish-green beam of light streams from the end of the laser canon and shoots into the heavens in a blink.

Based on all the movies I've seen, I expect there to be a massive explosion in space, but instead Crusher continues its approach even as the laser eats away at its mass.

Through the telescope, I watch Crusher in horror as it approaches the planet's atmosphere. "I'm too late..."

First, the sky lights on fire in shades of purple, orange, and red in an ever-expanding ring. Then, it comes.

Boom!

The ground quakes, and the laser shuts down just as the platform collapses. I tumble to the ground with it and roll onto my back.

In the sky, three fireballs branch out as they streak through the atmosphere like shooting stars.

My heart aches as I think about the possibility of failing sixth grade. I want to look away. Pretend it isn't happening. Power down my VR visor and walk away. But I'm no coward.

I glare with defiance at the fireball headed straight for the field. Straight at me.

It should be growing bigger as it approaches, yet it isn't. In fact, it seems to be growing smaller.

"It's… burning up in the atmosphere!"

Suddenly, fireworks explode in the air. Thousands of them. No, not fireworks but small pieces of Crusher. I've never seen anything more beautiful or terrifying.

The sky turns several shades of pink. Then, it's over.

Trumpets blare, and the sky turns back to blue. Ollie Ostrich, Billy Goat Gruff, and many other animals gather around me and cheer.

Regis Owl holds up a wing and clears his throat. Everyone quiets down, and he addresses me. "As regent of this world, I'm honored tooo present you with the Asteroid Killer badge for destroying Crusher, saving our world, and completing sixth grade." He takes the badge and attaches it to the sleeve of my shirt.

"Thank you so much!"

The other animals applaud and congratulate me on my success. Then Regis quiets them once again. "Alsooo, this act of courage and completion has earned you twooo thousand points and one hundred coins."

"Wow!" No other words come to mind.

Regis nods his head. "Indeed."

As the animals bid their farewells, the oddest thing of all happens.

Words begin scrolling through the sky. Lists and lists of names of people who worked on the game. Programmers, artists, scientists, actors, musicians, teachers, and others with job titles I don't understand. I recognize a few of them, including Dr. Von Schlippe, Peggy R. Cornier, and Gregory

Prince.

At least ten minutes of credits scroll through the sky before the words "The End" finally appear. Without surprise, yet to my disappointment, Gabe's name didn't appear in them.

Yet you made the biggest contribution.

Still, a sense of achievement sends my head into the clouds. I pull up my heads-up display and check my stats. My rank has improved beyond anything I'd hoped for: 1,845/4,794.

Thank you, Gabe, and thank you, God!

CHAPTER TWENTY-NINE

ASTEROID IMPACT

AHEAD SITS GIST ARENA, a world-class, state-of-the-art stadium. Its retractable roof lies open, lighting the overcast sky. A dozen spotlights circle the clouds, welcoming all the students, faculty, staff, and parents to the first ever year-end assembly for CEVR Academy.

The stadium disappears from view as the hover train pulls into the depot beneath it. When the doors slide open, the dull chatter becomes a deafening frenzy. Vendors of every item imaginable bombard us as we disembark. Dad grabs my hand, and I'm thankful for it.

"Commemorate the occasion with digital photos!" a woman shouts.

A man strobes from neck to toe in a rainbow of colors and patterns. "Get your custom glow codes here!"

"Order your digital yearbook right here and get instant access," a woman with a purple-and-pink mohawk yells.

"Look no farther," says a man wearing a brimmed hat. He twirls a black cane with a silver, ball-shaped handle. "You'll find the best fair food in the world right here. Deep-fried cookies dunked in hot fudge, caramel astro apples that are out of this galaxy, and so much more!"

"Keep moving," Mom says, pulling Dad and me along. "The assembly starts in ten minutes, and we need to find our seats."

Escalators carry us up to the stadium concourse. The throng of people thins as the corridor widens to accommodate the masses. At the top of the ramp leading into the stadium, a sign points us toward our designated seats: parents to the left and all others to the right. Dad releases my hand with reluctance.

"Meet us back here," Mom shouts.

I nod and take off toward the rows of student and faculty seats. With almost six thousand people, I'm certain I'll never find Roger among them. As

I'm about to sit down, a drone flies up to me. "Welcome, Kiara. Allow me to escort you to your seat."

The drone leads halfway across the stadium and down a dozen rows. It stops and hovers over one of the rows, toward the middle of the row. I stumble over and excuse myself as I squeeze past several students and Ms. Coates, my language arts instructor. Next to Ms. Coates stands my arch nemesis, Gemma Prince.

Gemma glowers at me. "I can't believe you actually survived the game."

"It's good to see you again in person." I smile and touch her arm.

She jerks her arm away. "Gross! Touch me again, and you'll regret it."

The four girls in her entourage occupy the seats next to her. Each cowers as I step past them. Sometimes, it's nice to be really tall.

"Kiara!" Roger shouts from farther down the row. "I saved you a seat!"

The lights fade just as I reach the seat. "Thanks."

Roger folds up the drone and sticks it inside his jacket pocket. "That's what best friends are for."

A thunderous rumble fills the air and shakes the stands, and the temperature spikes. Several students gasp and point skyward. A fiery ball streaks toward the stadium, growing in size as it approaches. Screams fill the stadium, but they're no match for the shrieking asteroid.

A third of the stadium ducks for cover as the asteroid eclipses the stadium roof and smashes into the stadium floor.

Boom!

A concussive heatwave knocks me back in my seat as dirt, synthetic grass, and debris fly into the air. The cloud of dust settles, revealing a massive crater where the asteroid struck. The fiery ball smolders at the bottom of the chasm, producing a stream of smoke. Within the smoke, letters begin to form.

"Asteroid impact!" Roger shouts.

Sure enough, the red, yellow, and orange letters spell it out. As the smoke dissipates, the asteroid cracks in half. A stage rises from within it, carrying a single individual.

Gemma's father.

"Ladies, gentleman, girls, and boys. Welcome to the first annual CEVR Academy year-end assembly! As most of you know, I'm Gregory Prince, CEO of GIST and New Eden's prince!"

Most of the crowd cheers, including Roger, but there's no way I'll ever cheer for that man.

"I'm certain you're all wondering why I'm standing up here and not Principal Cornier. Trust me when I say she regrets missing this momentous occasion due to a conflicting engagement. However, she pre-recorded a message for you all. Take a look."

Massive screens rise out of the stage as Mr. Prince steps down onto a floating step that carries him over to the stands, just below where we're sitting.

Principal Cornier's face appears on the screens. "Good evening students, faculty, staff, and parents. I'm honored to serve as the principal of CEVR Academy and will keep this message brief. Without further ado, please take a look at your top twenty students."

The entire stadium stands and cheers as the list of student names with rankings, artifacts earned, coins collected, and accomplishments achieved replaces Principal Cornier's glitchy face. The name at the top of the list—a win by just three points—shocks everyone: Roger Daltrey. Gemma Prince came in second. I don't recognize any of the other student names.

Roger points at the screen. "Look! It's me! I actually won!"

"I never doubted you." I give Roger a hug. "Congratulations!"

"Cheater!" Gemma pushes students out of the way as she approaches Roger and me.

I block her from reaching Roger. "Face it, Gemma. The only cheater was you, and you still lost."

"It's not possible! I was ahead by two hundred and forty-seven points just minutes before the school year ended." She reaches around me but fails to grab Roger.

I push her backward. "Go back to your seat before you hurt yourself."

Gemma looks up at the top twenty display. "What's that silver key? I know every artifact, and that's not one of them."

"The Key of Truth," I say. "I've got one, too."

"Guess you don't know everything, do you?" Roger says.

"When my dad finds out about this, you're going to be sorry and wish you hadn't won. You hear me?" She turns around and stomps off.

"I'm so happy you earned the key!"

Roger hugs me. "Thank you so much. I couldn't have done it without you." He lets go and starts jumping up and down. "Do you know what this means? I get to go to space camp!"

The top twenty disappears, and Principal Cornier's face returns. "Everyone, please find your seats if you haven't already." She waits a few moments. "Good. We started the year off with four thousand eight hundred students. Six students dropped out for various reasons, and more than four thousand seven hundred of you completed your mission to build a laser and destroy the asteroid, saving your world. What you didn't know is that as each of you destroyed your asteroid, it added power to a real laser. Using this laser, we were able to destroy a near-earth asteroid before it had a chance to enter our atmosphere. Yes students, you heard that right. You helped keep our planet safe. Now, I'd like to be the first to congratulate all the students and faculty for an excellent first year and making CEVR Academy a success! For this, I believe a round of applause is in order." She begins clapping, and the entire stadium joins in.

We helped keep the world safe… Maybe I really can help save the world one day.

I look to the sky and the heavens above and can't help but smile.

God, knowing you're out there and in control of even asteroids, I'll never need to.

Principal Cornier continues, "I'm sure I'm not alone when I say I look forward to seeing all of you in a few months at the start of the new school year. I hope your summers are filled with excitement. Now, enjoy the citywide group challenge that starts right now…"

The screens fade to black, and then the presentation begins. "Tonight, you will witness a competition like nothing you've ever seen. Three schools. The top group from each school. Only one team will win. Each will design, build, and program a moon rover capable of navigating an obstacle course all on its own."

Roger nudges me and points to the row in front of us. Dr. Von Schlippe sits just to Roger's right. "He just got a video call from Principal Cornier."

Dr. Von Schlippe gets up and works his way across the row to the right. Roger looks at me, sighs, and then nods. I follow him down the row, both of us hunched over to keep from blocking everyone's view of the competition and so that Dr. Von Schlippe doesn't see us.

Dr. Von Schlippe turns left at the bottom of the ramp. We reach the corner and peer around it just in time to see him walk down a hallway about twenty feet down the concourse. Footsteps on metal stairs echo through the hall. When we reach the stairwell, Roger holds his arm out, blocking me from proceeding.

I start to push past Roger. "What do you think—"

Dr. Von Schlippe says, "I've found a quiet spot." He's at the bottom of the stairs.

"You lied to me." Principal Cornier's voice fills the stairwell. Dr. Von Schlippe must have the volume on his video phone turned all the way up. She sounds angrier than when she called my house back in January.

"I did nothing of the sort."

"Then tell me how two students managed to earn some key of truth."

Dr. Von Schlippe starts pacing. "I don't know, but there's nothing we can do about it now."

"Gemma Prince was supposed to win the individual award. You guaranteed me as much."

"I did, but no one could've anticipated Gabe interfering."

"When Gregory Prince comes after me, it's you I'll point him to."

"He knew the risks. We gave her every advantage possible." He sweeps his hand through his hair. "Look, we can't be held accountable for her lack of performance."

"Without his support, this school is finished."

"I know, and I'll fix this." Dr Von Schlippe sits down on the last step. "Trust me, this won't be a problem next year."

"How can I trust you? You said the problem was fixed months ago."

"Yes, and I thought it was. But this time we'll kill the root of it."

"Are you saying what I think you're saying?"

"Yes. No one will ever hear from Gabe again."

"Auh!" I cover my mouth, but Dr. Von Schlippe looks right up at us.

He stands. "I need to go."

I don't think I've ever ran so fast. The hallway, concourse, and ramp fly by in a blur. I'm about to head back down to my seat when a hand grabs my arm. I whip around and stare Roger in the face. He points to a pair of seats down the row just above us. We slide into the seats, and I look back just as Dr. Von Schlippe enters the stadium. He scans the stadium, tosses something on the ground, and walks back down the ramp and out of sight.

I take a deep breath. "That was close."

"Too close." He takes a breath with his inhaler.

"We need to talk to Gabe and warn him."

"And we will." He points at the screens. "Looks like the team from

Apprentice Guild of New Eden is about to win the team competition."

"That was quick. I thought it was going to take several hours."

"It did, but most of the competition was recorded earlier today. I watched some of it."

"So, no one here saw it?"

"Yeah, but the footage was from a time-lapse camera, so it went really quick."

An eight-wheeled vehicle with a dozen appendages rolls over the top of a hill and snatches a purple flag off a pole. Gregory Prince stands, and his image is projected on the screens. "Ladies and gentlemen, we have a winner! Let's give a round of applause to Tommy Jones, Val Brooks, and Jennifer Cortez from Apprentice Guild of New Eden!" The stadium erupts with cheers.

Roger and I stay seated. My stomach churns as I reprocess the conversation between Dr. Von Schlippe and Principal Cornier.

No one will ever hear from Gabe again...

My pulse races, but then I remember the most important lesson of sixth grade.

I have no need to fear because God is in control.

CHAPTER THIRTY

SUMMER VACATION

IT'S THE FIRST WEEK of summer vacation in New Eden, and I've never been happier. The sun shines brighter, the sky dazzles with its brilliant blue hue, and Princess Sparkles has never looked better in her new purple dress with yellow wildflowers. I'm certain she approves of it, too. She's been staring at herself in the mirror for the last hour.

As I look back on the school year and our new life in New Eden, I can't help but laugh at myself for ever thinking that my world was about to end. It couldn't have been farther from the truth. So much has changed, both in my life and in me. I still don't understand what happens after death, but I'm no longer afraid to face the future knowing there's a God watching over me.

You're in control, and I'd have it no other way.

"Kiara!" Mom yells. "Hurry up, or you'll miss your bus."

I gasp. "Come on, Sparkles!" I scoop her into my arms and grunt. "Whoa, you've packed on a few pounds since we moved here." Sparkles squeals and nuzzles my neck. "I love you, too!"

Mom, Dad, and Artie are at the front door when I get downstairs. Dad's holding my suitcase, and Mom's got a brown paper sack. My stomach growls.

Yeah, it's past breakfast. So what.

Mom hands me the sack and kisses my cheek. "We're gonna miss you so much."

Dad trades me the suitcase for Sparkles. Weight-wise, it's a great trade, but it sickens me that Sparkles can't come with me. So much so, that I give it one last shot.

"Please, please, please. Let me take Sparkles!"

Mom's hands fly to her hips. "We've gone over this, Kiara. Pigs aren't allowed on a bus."

"But she's potty trained and behaves better than most dogs."

"Yes, we know that, but the bus company doesn't," Dad says. "We promise to take good care of her."

"Ugh. You mean Artie will."

"Princess Sparkles will get the best care possible," Artie says. "I will personally see to it. She will want for nothing, including belly rubs." For a robot, he sure seems to have a human heart.

I hug Artie, then Dad. Dad kisses my forehead and whispers in my ear, "I love you more than the world, Little Bear."

I skip over to the personal transport beam and step on the middle plate.

"Be safe," Mom says.

I wave and say, "Main lobby."

In a flash, my body and belongings are transported down to the main lobby. Roger's waiting by the front door.

I skip over to him and hug him. "Isn't it a beautiful morning?"

His cheeks turn red. "Why do you always do that?"

"Hug you? Because you're my best friend." I punch his arm. "That's what best friends do."

He rubs his arm and shakes his head. "The bus is already outside."

I grab his hand and drag him through the front doors. "Come on!"

We board the bus and settle in our seats. Roger looks around. There are only three other passengers with us.

He says, "Are you sure about this?"

I open my lunch sack and pull out two sandwiches. I hand one to him and take a big bite out of mine. "You're gonna love meeting Grams!"

NEVER MISS A NEW RELEASE

Want to receive news about new Kiara Kole and similar books? Please leave your email address at the link below, and we'll let you know when there's a new release we think you might enjoy.

rapture911.com/kiara-kole-updates

BIBLE LEARNING ACTIVITY CROSSWORD

Read the Scriptures on the following pages and use what you learn to solve the crossword puzzle. Play online or print a copy at:
rapture911.com/kiarakolecrossword1

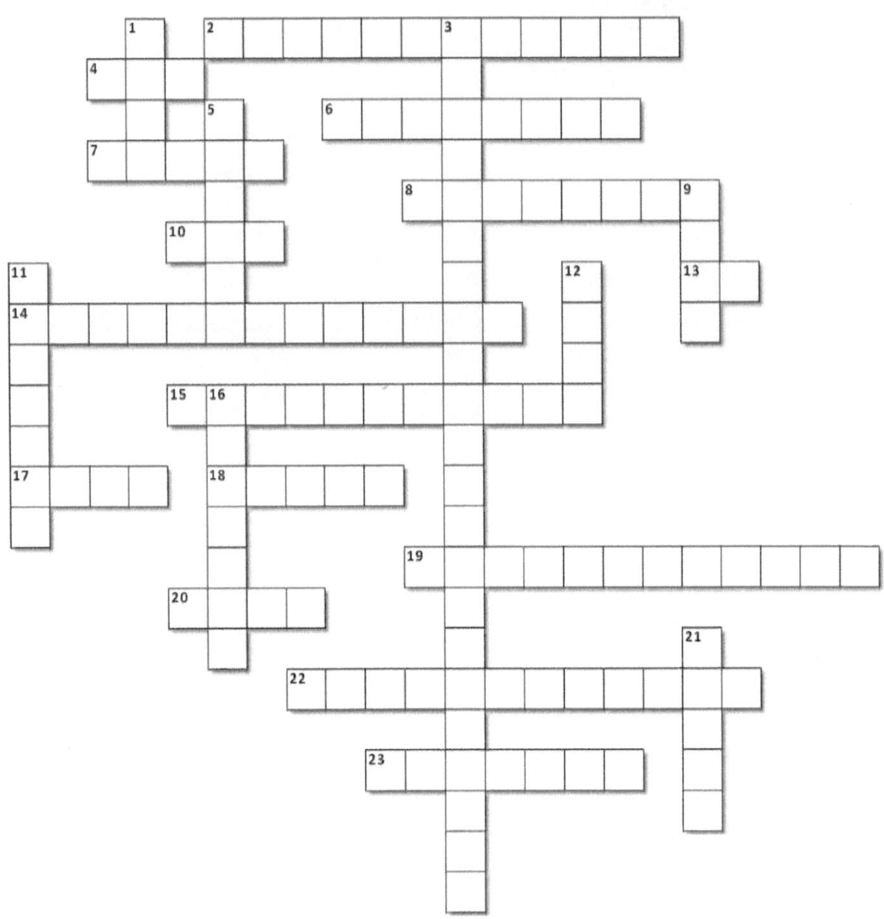

BIBLE LEARNING ACTIVITY CROSSWORD

Across	Down
2. Jesus commanded these elements. (4,3,5)	**1.** The reason God gave his one and only Son. (4)
4. He created the earth. (3)	**3.** God promised to never again do this. (7,3,6,6)
6. With God everything is ____? (8)	**5.** Created in God's image. (6)
7. He is the truth. (5)	**9.** Christ died to take this away from people. (4)
8. Describes God's thoughts about you. (8)	**11.** This proclaims the glory of God. (7)
10. Formed from the dust. (3)	**12.** How the heavens and earth will pass away. (4)
13. Is there any other God? (2)	**16.** Who closed the door of the ark? (3,4)
14. Perfect love does what? (6,3,4)	**21.** Where did God plant eternity? (5)
15. Knowing God and Jesus is the way to ____? (7,4)	
17. He walked with God and built an ark. (4)	
18. Something God will make new. (5)	
19. Seek this to get everything you need. (7,2,3)	
20. Do this instead of worrying. (4)	
22. All things ____ for good. (4,8)	
23. They were on the ark with Noah. (7)	

BIBLE LEARNING ACTIVITY SCRIPTURES

These Scriptures cover questions and truths Kiara experienced in this book.
Read them and use what you learn to solve the crossword puzzle.

God

The heavens proclaim the glory of God. The skies display his craftsmanship. Day after day they continue to speak; night after night they make him known. They speak without a sound or word; their voice is never heard. Yet their message has gone throughout the earth, and their words to all the world. (Psalm 19:1-4 NLT)

This is what the LORD says... "I am the First and the Last; there is no other God. Who is like me? Let him step forward and prove to you his power. Let him do as I have done since ancient times when I established a people and explained its future. Do not tremble; do not be afraid. Did I not proclaim my purposes for you long ago? You are my witnesses--is there any other God? No!" (Isaiah 44:6-8 NLT)

Creation

In the beginning God created the heavens and the earth. (Genesis 1:1 NLT)

Then the LORD God formed the man from the dust of the ground. He breathed the breath of life into the man's nostrils, and the man became a living person. (Genesis 2:7 NLT)

So God created human beings in his own image. In the image of God he created them; male and female he created them. (Genesis 1:27 NLT)

Noah

Noah was a just man, perfect in his generations. Noah walked with God. ... And God said to Noah, "The end of all flesh has come before Me, for the earth is filled with violence through them; and behold, I will destroy them with the earth. Make yourself an ark of gopherwood." (Genesis 6:9, 13-14 NKJV)

When everything was ready, the LORD said to Noah, "Go into the boat with all your family, for among all the people of the earth, I can see that you alone are righteous. ... Seven days from now I will make the rains pour down on the earth. And it will rain for forty days and forty nights, until I have wiped from the earth all the living things I have created." So Noah did everything as the LORD commanded him. Noah was 600 years old when the flood covered the earth. ... Then the LORD closed the door behind them. (Genesis 7:1, 4-6, 16 NLT)

Noah was now 601 years old. On the first day of the new year, ten and a half months after the flood began, the floodwaters had almost dried up from the earth. Noah lifted back the covering of the boat and saw that the surface of the ground was drying. Two more months went by, and at last the earth was dry! Then God said to Noah, "Leave the boat, all of you--you and your wife, and your sons and their wives. Release all the animals--the birds, the livestock, and the small animals that scurry along the ground--so they can be fruitful and multiply throughout the earth." (Genesis 8:13-17 NLT)

God is in Control
The LORD … said to himself, "I will never again destroy all living things. As long as the earth remains, there will be planting and harvest, cold and heat, summer and winter, day and night." (Genesis 8:21-22 NLT)

Then Jesus got into the boat and started across the lake with his disciples. Suddenly, a fierce storm struck the lake, with waves breaking into the boat. But Jesus was sleeping. The disciples went and woke him up, shouting, "Lord, save us! We're going to drown!" Jesus responded, "Why are you afraid? You have so little faith!" Then he got up and rebuked the wind and waves, and suddenly there was a great calm. The disciples were amazed. "Who is this man?" they asked. "Even the winds and waves obey him!" (Matthew 8:23-27 NLT)

And we know that all things work together for good to those who love God, to those who are the called according to [His] purpose. (Romans 8:28 NKJV)

God's Love
For God loved the world so much that he gave his one and only Son, so that everyone who believes in him will not perish but have eternal life. (John 3:16 NLT)

All who confess that Jesus is the Son of God have God living in them, and they live in God. We know how much God loves us, and we have put our trust in his love. God is love, and all who live in love live in God, and God lives in them. And as we live in God, our love grows more perfect. So we will not be afraid on the day of judgment, but we can face him with confidence because we live like Jesus here in this world. Such love has no fear, because perfect love expels all fear. If we are afraid, it is for fear of punishment, and this shows that we have not fully experienced his perfect love. (1 John 4:15-18 NLT)

You saw me before I was born. Every day of my life was recorded in your book. Every moment was laid out before a single day had passed. How precious are your thoughts about me, O God. They cannot be numbered! (Psalm 139:16-17 NLT)

Don't Worry
Then, turning to his disciples, Jesus said, "That is why I tell you not to worry about

everyday life.... ... Look at the ravens. They don't plant or harvest or store food in barns, for God feeds them. And you are far more valuable to him than any birds! Can all your worries add a single moment to your life? And if worry can't accomplish a little thing like that, what's the use of worrying over bigger things? ... These things dominate the thoughts of unbelievers all over the world, but your Father already knows your needs. Seek the Kingdom of God above all else, and he will give you everything you need." (Luke 12:22, 24-26, 30-31 NLT)

Don't worry about anything; instead, pray about everything. Tell God what you need, and thank him for all he has done. Then you will experience God's peace, which exceeds anything we can understand. His peace will guard your hearts and minds as you live in Christ Jesus. (Philippians 4:6-7 NLT)

Eternal Life
Yet God has made everything beautiful for its own time. He has planted eternity in the human heart. (Ecclesiastes 3:11 NLT)

Jesus told him, "I am the way, the truth, and the life. No one can come to the Father except through me." (John 14:6 NLT)

After saying all these things, Jesus looked up to heaven and said, "Father, the hour has come. Glorify your Son so he can give glory back to you. For you have given him authority over everyone. He gives eternal life to each one you have given him. And this is the way to have eternal life--to know you, the only true God, and Jesus Christ, the one you sent to earth." (John 17:1-3 NLT)

And just as each person is destined to die once and after that comes judgment, so also Christ died once for all time as a sacrifice to take away the sins of many people. He will come again, not to deal with our sins, but to bring salvation to all who are eagerly waiting for him. (Hebrews 9:27-28 NLT)

The disciples were astounded. "Then who in the world can be saved?" they asked. Jesus looked at them intently and said, "Humanly speaking, it is impossible. But with God everything is possible." (Matthew 19:25-26 NLT)

New Earth
The heavens will pass away with a great noise, and the elements will melt with fervent heat; both the earth and the works that are in it will be burned up. (2 Peter 3:10 NKJV)

Then I saw a new heaven and a new earth, for the old heaven and the old earth had disappeared. ... And the one sitting on the throne said, "Look, I am making everything new!" (Revelation 21:1, 5 NLT)

BIBLE LEARNING ACTIVITY ANSWERS

Across

2. WindAndWaves (Matthew 8:23-27)
4. God (Genesis 1:1)
6. Possible (Matthew 19:25-26)
7. Jesus (John 14:6)
8. Precious (Psalm 139:16-17)
10. Man (Genesis 2:7)
13. No (Isaiah 44:6-8)
14. ExpelsAllFear (1 John 4:15-18)
15. EternalLife (John 17:1-3)
17. Noah (Genesis 6:9, 13-14)
18. Earth (Revelation 21:1, 5)
19. KingdomOfGod (Luke 12:22, 24-26, 30-31)
20. Pray (Philippians 4:6-7)
22. WorkTogether (Romans 8:28)
23. Animals (Genesis 8:13-17)

Down

1. Love (John 3:16)
3. DestroyAllLivingThings (Genesis 8:21-22)
5. Humans (Genesis 1:27)
9. Sins (Hebrews 9:27-28)
11. Heavens (Psalm 19:1-4)
12. Fire (2 Peter 3:10)
16. TheLord (Genesis 7:1, 4-6, 16)
21. Heart (Ecclesiastes 3:11)

ABOUT THE AUTHORS

Daniel Luke Kuhnley is an American author of Fantasy, Supernatural Mystery Thrillers, and young adult Christian Sci-Fi/Fantasy stories. He enjoys watching movies, reading novels, programming, and playing board and video games. He lives in Albuquerque, NM with his wife Marsha.

danielkuhnley.com

Marsha Kuhnley is an American author of Christian non-fiction and young adult Christian Sci-Fi/Fantasy books. She has a passion for Bible prophecy, finance, and economics. Marsha has been a guest on the popular *Christ In Prophecy* TV program where she discusses her books, the Rapture, and End Times topics. She lives in Albuquerque, NM with her husband Daniel.

rapture911.com